# To Love A Grimm

## Fairy Tale Hearts

Everbound
Press

A FAIRY TALE HEARTS NOVEL

THE PRINCE OF MY HEART, THE HUNTER OF MY SOUL

# TO LOVE A GRIMM

## CHRISTINA FARLEY

Published by Everbound Press

Copyright © 2025 by Christina Farley

Library of Congress Control Number: 2025920819

www.ChristinaFarley.com

Paperback Cover, Dustcover, and Interior Artwork: Trif Book Designs

Special Edition Hardcover: Yosbe Design

Character Artwork: Lulybot

Page Edge Design: Painted Wings Publishing

ASIN: B0FPRBRXK7

ISBN (hardcover): 979-8-9985737-2-9

ISBN (paperback): 979-8-9985737-1-2

# ALSO BY CHRISTINA FARLEY

**The Immortal Bound Series**

The Immortal Legend (Novella)

The Immortal Secret

The Immortal Heart

The Immortal Warrior

The Immortal Crown

**The Gilded Series**

Gilded

Silvern

Brazen

**The Dreamscape Series**

The Dream Heist

The Dream Hunt

**Choose Your Happily Ever After**

Fairy Tale Road

**Fairy Tale Hearts**

To Love a Grimm

To Love a Siren

*For
Amy Christine Parker
for being the best friend I could ever dream of.*

"In the fairy tales, a world of magic is opened up before us, one which still exists among us in secret forests, in underground caves, and in the deepest sea."
- Jacob Grimm

# PROLOGUE
## JACOB

*Landgraviate of Hesse-Kassel*

Death hovers at our door, fingers clawing at the edges, rattling the doorknob. It's only a matter of hours before the end swoops in, and yet I refuse to believe it—refuse to leave my brother's side.

I need a miracle.

I want the impossible.

"When I go," Wilhelm says between gasping breaths, "take care of Mother."

"No." I grind my teeth in frustration and press a hand on his shoulder. "You must take care of her. You're so much better at that sort of thing."

"Hardly." Wilhelm tries to smile, but a cough wracks his frail body.

How did this happen? Yesterday, he was reciting Shakespeare with me. I can't lose him. When Father died, that had been hard, life-changing even. But to lose Wilhelm? Unimaginable. He's one of the few truly good people in this world. People like him are supposed to live and make a difference.

"Where is the doctor?" I growl, abandoning the bed for the door. "I sent for him hours ago."

Impatient, I step outside, searching the silent cobblestone street. Mist curls around the lampposts like a dragon's tail, dimming their light into pale yellows and corrupting the shadows.

Snowflakes flutter onto my lashes, cold and fragile. I frown. Snow this time of year? I must be imagining things, or maybe it's a sign of Death's arrival, hungrily waiting for my brother's soul. Shivering, I stride back inside only to freeze.

A woman stands at my brother's bedside.

No. More than a woman. Her presence fills the shadows and dusty cracks with a radiance that only a rainbow after a storm can bring. Slowly, this creature—for she can't possibly belong to this world—drags her eyes from Wilhelm's face to mine. She smiles, thick red lips curving seductively. Her eyes gleam bright as stars, and her long white hair cascades over thin shoulders in tight, glistening curls.

"Hello, Jacob Grimm." She glides to the foot of the bed. Her dress sparkles with gems, and the chiffon floats lighter than summer clouds. Her radiance practically blinds me.

"Who are you?" I demand. "How do you know my name?"

"I'm here to save your brother, for he will die soon." She purses her lips as if deep in thought. "Quite soon."

Her words rattle me. Too close to my greatest fear. "Except, you aren't a doctor, are you?" I give a pointed look at her shimmering gown. "I'll wait for his diagnosis."

"It hardly takes talent to see your brother is using his last breaths. Besides, Death has been here, and his poison has seeped into Wilhelm's soul."

"You will leave right now," I grind out.

"Feisty, aren't you? I like that in a man. Take a moment and hear what I have to offer."

"There's nothing you could possibly offer me." I wave her away as a cough shudders through Wilhelm. I move to his side. His eyes are closed, face pale. "Leave us. I want to spend these last minutes with my brother in peace."

"What if I were to tell you I could heal him?" She steps closer to me. The scent of lilies wafts across my face.

My heart stutters. "What do you mean?"

"Work for me and I will heal him."

"You speak like a witch."

She tosses her head back and laughs, full and rich.

"Hardly," she says, and her tone switches like she tasted something sour. "My powers surpass those of a petty witch. Those meaningless wenches thought they were so powerful, but who holds their names between her fingertips now?"

I groan. This woman isn't dangerous—she's completely mad. I need to get her out of the room and focus on finding a real doctor.

A flash of light cuts through the darkness, and an ancient scroll appears in her palm. I gasp. Wilhelm makes a croaking sound, opening his eyes. The woman flicks her other hand, and slowly the scroll unravels, trailing across the ground like a runner unleashed before a king at his coronation. Words glisten on the page.

"What is this?" I demand.

"You are scholars, are you not?" She doesn't bother waiting for a response. "I've searched a great deal for talent like you two possess. You both work hard and excel in your studies. How would you like to help me with a little project?"

"A project. My brother is dying, and you want to talk about a project?" I shoot her a glare, then dip a cloth into a bowl of water and gently dab Wilhelm's forehead with it.

"This is a list of people who are lost and must be found. I'm looking to acquire hunters to find them."

"Hunters? You must have confused us with someone else. We aren't hunters, we're law students."

She pushes her scroll into my hands. "These people who belong in my world are forbidden to be in this one. They must be returned to their own land, or the consequences to your world will be disastrous."

"My world?" I ask, my eyes narrowing. "You act like you aren't from this place."

"But of course not!" She snorts. "The Forbidden's presence has caused problems, including one named Death that has made your brother sick. As long as these creatures remain in this realm, their power will increase and poison your people."

"A creature from your realm did this to my brother?"

"Think of it like a plague. If you want your brother and others in your world to live, listen carefully. You have the power to change everything by becoming my hunter and seeking out these Forbidden. All you must do is write their story into little books like this one. It's so simple, really."

A whoosh of cool air flushes across the room, and a leather-bound book thuds onto the table.

"Let me understand." I rise from the bed and study it. "You want us to find all the people on that list and write their life stories?"

"Exactly." She beams. "I knew you were perfect for the task."

"This list is long. It will take a lifetime."

"Would you rather a lifetime alone, visiting your brother's grave year after year? Or one with the two of you writing as a team, bonded together in a common goal?"

"You do have a way of persuasion." I study Wilhelm, frail and coughing. Dying. My heart feels like it's ripping in half. I can't stand life without him. If there's a way to save him, how can I say no? "Fine. I'll do this task of yours *if* you save my brother. Once he has been given the medicine, and we know it works, then I'll begin on your collection of stories."

The scroll tucks back into a neat roll, landing in my hand with a snap. Her eyes light up, and she withdraws a quill with a tip sharp as an icicle.

"What's this? Some kind of magic?"

"Call it whatever you like." She shrugs as another piece of paper flutters to the table. Paragraphs of text fill the page, but the words are foreign to me despite being fluent in numerous languages. "Our contract. The three of us will sign our names in blood to bind the agreement."

"I can't read it." I toss the pen onto the table. "Get it translated before I'm signing anything."

Wilhelm coughs blood onto his pillow. I storm to his side.

"Wilhelm," I say, leaning down. "Fight a little longer."

"Don't do this," Wilhelm pleads in a wheezing whisper. "My time has ended. Let me go in peace."

"No!" Fear thickens my blood. "I won't. I can't."

"Too late." The woman clucks her tongue. "Better say your farewells."

Will I be able to live with myself knowing I could've saved him but chose not to? I'd curse every day I took a breath. Gritting my teeth, I march to the parchment and pick up the slender quill. It tingles between my fingers as if whispering deadly secrets.

"Where is the ink to sign?" I demand.

"Hold out your hand." Her voice is heavy as darkness. "You shall provide the ink."

I obey. She cuts a tiny slice along its center with her razor-sharp nail. Fresh blood gushes out, dripping to the floor. I dip the pen's tip into it.

And sign my name.

The woman flicks her hand, and an hourglass appears on the table. It consists of a pair of glass bulbs joined together by a narrow, twisted neck. Three gnarled iron trees hold up the protective frame. She lifts the top off and taps the tip of my pen against the edge of the top bulb. My blood plops inside.

The room spins. Everything blurs before my eyes. Something is wrong. My body trembles. She picks up Wilhelm's hand next.

"No," I say. "Not him. Just me."

"Too late," she says brightly.

I try to stop her, but my knees buckle and I drop to the ground. She holds his limp hand, using his blood to scrawl out a signature, the pen's tip scraping like a knife. She taps the liquid into the hourglass and adds a prick of her own blood. It all swirls, mixing together.

*What did I do?*

Pain ripples through my muscles like they're being coated in iron. Fire burns my blood, and stabbing knives prick my skin. I scream in agony, my back arching like an unseen hand has picked me off the floor.

Finally, my body collapses to the ground. I lay still, heaving and sweating.

The room rights itself sharply and everything focuses. The objects in the room appear brighter, the shadows sharper, and sounds I've never noticed before reach my ears. The creak of the floorboards. The skitter of a rat behind the walls. The plod of horse hooves clomping down a distant street.

The woman's lips quirk and her icy blue eyes flash victoriously as I stagger to my feet.

"What did you do to us?" I growl.

"I just saved your brother's life. You're welcome." She rolls her eyes like I'm an idiot. "To keep you on task, I created this lovely hourglass. A Forbidden's name will appear at the top when they are near you. You have until the hourglass runs out to complete that Forbidden's story."

Fear chills my bones. "What happens if we don't write the story in time?"

"Your brother will die. Then after that, the deaths will continue for everyone in your bloodline. Jacob, I suggest you stay on task."

She sets the hourglass on the table and signs her name.

*Enchantress of the Candora Realm*

She sighs. "It is done and it's beautiful."

Fury takes over all rational thought, and I lunge for her. But then my brother sits up in bed and my steps falter.

"Wilhelm!" I rush to his side. His cheeks are back to their normal color, and his eyes are bright. He looks great. In fact, better than I've ever seen him. "You're healed."

"What have you done?" Wilhelm asks sharply. "You just made a deal with the Devil."

My heart sinks. I turn to face the Enchantress.

But she's vanished with the winds of snow, leaving behind her tome, pen, and an hourglass trickling its deadly descent.

# CHAPTER 1

## ELLA

### KINGDOM OF WÜRTTEMBERG

"Don't leave," I beg Claire for the third time this afternoon. She's been a trusted housemaid for my family since I was a child. What will I do without her?

"Ella, I have to go." She gives me a pleading look. "I'm sorry, but I've got to feed my family. I've waited two months for your father to return and pay me. Two months of nothing doesn't feed little ones. Besides, Dr. Wissen said he's hiring."

"Dr. Wissen?" My mouth falls open. "Not that vile man."

She scrunches her nose. "I have to take my chances."

"But you've been with our family forever."

"I'm sorry, you know I am. Your mother was a wonderful mistress—even if she was from the Southlands—but she's gone, bless her soul, and who knows where your father is."

My heart pangs at the mention of my mother, but I shove down those emotions. "He'll return. I'm sure of it."

"I hope he does for your sake, but I can't wait any longer. And Dr. Wissen pays."

I grimace, unable to deny her words. Instead, I wish her luck and walk her to the front door of the manor. My heart sags as she hurries away, and I clutch the bluebird pendant my mother gave me like a talisman. She isn't the only servant who has left, and I'm tired of it. Tired of keeping this manor running. Tired of managing a household without the funds to do so.

Tears threaten to escape, but there isn't time for tears. If anyone needs to be strong, it's me. It's been nearly a year since Father and I buried Mother, and three months since he up and left without so much as a goodbye. It's taken every ounce of willpower to get out of bed each morning, eat my meals, take care of the animals, and try to keep the manor running.

"Any day he'll arrive," I'd tell Gertude, our housekeeper. Or when I spotted Herman, our steward, fretting over the crops, I assured him with, "Father said not to worry over the harvest. It won't be long before he returns."

But deep down, I know Father never got over Mother's death. He loved her too much. He hasn't been the same since her passing. Maybe I haven't either.

But the immediate issue is that the servants and field-hands are leaving. Soon I'll be rattling alone in this massive house with fields of ripe crops that can't be harvested. I clench my fists. Father may have abandoned us, but I refuse to give up. This is my home. My mother's home. Someday he'll return, and when he does, he'll see my success and be proud I kept our family name from ruin.

With renewed determination, I stalk down the time-worn wooden hallway to Father's office. Oddly, the door is cracked open. Voices drift out to where I hover at the edge of the door—Herman and an unfamiliar male voice.

Who could that be? And why didn't anyone tell me we had a visitor?

I smooth down my black muslin dress, straighten my back, and step into the office. The visitor whose back is to me is tall, with brown hair and wearing an expensive jacket with long tails.

"Hello," I say.

Herman stiffens. A horrified expression washes over his usually bored features. Probably because I entered without introductions. Not that he should be surprised. I tend to toss protocol to the winds.

But when the visitor turns, my heart sinks. Unfortunately, I know him all too well.

Dr. Wissen.

He's almost unrecognizable in all his finery and—I hate to admit—looking quite handsome. Once he was a lowly local carpenter. He decided to change his profession and somehow amassed more power and wealth than a man could possibly gain without foul play.

Rumor has it he sold his cart and oxen for fine clothes and a medical ABC book. Then he nailed a sign on his door, offering doctoring services. It sounds ridiculous. Probably because it is.

"Good morning, Ella." The doctor bows smoothly, blue eyes twinkling in delight. "Word in the village is you're in a bit of trouble. A full harvest without the funds to pay workers to reap it does put you in a difficult situation."

My eyes narrow. "Our estate is none of your concern, Dr. Wissen."

"I came as soon as I heard about your trials. I'd love to offer my assistance."

I frown as I take in the scar running along his cheek, the only blemish on his perfectly chiseled features. "I can hardly think why you'd come to help me."

"I'll harvest the crops and sell them for you. We'll split the profits. Seems fair enough to me."

"That's hardly fair," I cross my arms, "and you know it."

"Come now." He steps closer. "I know your father abandoned you. Let me help. Otherwise, you're going to lose everything, and then you'll be forced to sell the property to me anyway, but for a lower price."

"I'm afraid whatever rumors you've heard are simply... rumors," I counter loftily. "We're not in need of your help, but thank you kindly. You may leave at once."

"Ella," Hermon whispers, stepping forward. "Please reconsider."

"Leave at once?" Wissen's forehead wrinkles. His eyebrows lift, taking on a hurt expression. "My dear Ella, you must let me help. I insist. Allow me to finish my conversation with your steward, and then we'll have coffee and cake to celebrate."

I'd rather sleep with the vermin than let him rule my house.

"If I'm going to have coffee and cake, it won't be with you," I say.

"If you'll excuse us for a moment, Dr. Wissen," Herman says. He scrambles to my side and draws me into the hall.

"Ella, what are you doing?"

"You brought that crook into my house?" I seethe.

"You don't understand." Herman mops the sweat from his brow with his handkerchief. "I checked your father's records and the coffers to pay the servants. There's no money. Your father took everything when he left. Five servants left just today when I told them I can't pay them until the master returns. The crops are ready to be harvested, but we don't have enough servants to collect them. We need Dr. Wissen's help. With that money, we can survive through the winter."

"Through the winter?" I scoff. "Dr. Wissen is getting the upper hand here. What will Father think when he returns?"

Herman's face falls. He withdraws a parchment from his breast pocket, opening it. "A letter from your father arrived last week. He's not returning for some time."

"What?" I snatch the paper. Scanning it, I discover he's right. Father has no plans to return anytime soon. This is a disaster. "Why didn't you show me this letter?"

"Ella, you're twenty years old, no longer a young lady. Right now, you need to put your focus on searching for a husband. All could be righted instantly with a wealthy match." His voice switches to a whisper. "And I think he's interested in your hand."

"Why didn't I think of that? I'll just stroll through our village's streets, announcing I'm ready to wed but only to a man with a heavy purse." I choke out a laugh. "Herman, it doesn't work that way. Besides, we don't have time for me to enter society or money for dresses so I can attend the latest balls. We need answers now. Father said I should run this estate, and I will."

"I don't know why you hate Dr. Wissen, but he's a good man. He's saved the village time and again from the wolf pack. I advise you to consider his offer."

"I'd rather be devoured by wolves than marry Dr. Wissen."

Herman's face falls. But he also has a point. I've spent every hour since Father left moping about, ignoring the problems around me, and accomplishing nothing other than stitching some horrible needlework. What else can he expect?

"Tell the servants I'll pay them tonight after I return from the village," I say, undaunted. "Also, tell them that anyone who helps harvest the crops will receive a payment reward for their efforts."

"How can you promise the impossible?" Herman sputters.

A crawling sensation skitters over my skin. I look back at Father's office to find the doctor practically hugging the doorway.

"Eavesdropping, Dr. Wissen?" I lift my eyebrows. "I'd think that was beneath a man of your caliber."

"I couldn't help overhearing your situation. I didn't realize it was so bad."

Wretched man. "Thank you kindly for your offer. Herman will escort you to the door. Good day."

"Of course. But if you change your mind, send a courier to my home right away. I'll be happy to oblige." He smiles, one that would make most women's hearts melt. "But do remember, Ella. I always get what I want."

# CHAPTER 2

# JACOB

## THE BLACK FOREST

"Faster!" I urge Storm, flicking his reins and hunkering lower in the saddle as we canter across the meadow.

Tall grass whips against my riding boots and sweat drips from my brow even though it's autumn. The hoofbeats create their own rhythm, and I allow my body to sink into the hunt. Not far ahead, I spot the balding head of a small man, ducking in and out of the bramble of the hazel trees before he darts into the forest.

Bleeding skies. The last place I want to enter is the forest. Locals warned me it's haunted, grounds inhabited by witches and prowling with wolves hungry for a midnight snack. Outsiders likely scoff at those tales, chuckling over the stories while enjoying a brew at the tavern.

But I believe every word.

My life's a cursed existence. I suppose it's only fitting I haunt these lands, rather than settle with a family. I certainly deserve it. As I draw up to the forest edge, Storm skitters alongside the brush and snarling tree boughs.

"Don't worry, old boy." I slip to the ground, patting his

lathered side. "Stay here and munch on this juicy grass while I dare the unthinkable. Again."

That last word is more of a grumble as I tie him to an oak, giving him a wide berth to graze. From my pouch, I withdraw the hourglass, heavy as stone, and assess how much time I have left. The crimson liquid nearly fills the entire bottom bulb. Panic rises inside me, threatening to choke all reason. This is the closest we've come to not completing a story.

I left Wilhelm sitting in our new bookshop, hunched over and ashen. Every minute of my delay means his time is ticking. Before I left, he smiled, promising he'd unpack the rest of our belongings.

I grind my teeth. I need to find a way to free us of this madness. Until then, I'll finish this story. Even if it kills me.

A chill spiders over my skin as I creep into the forest. The trees fold around me, the sharp tang of magic clinging to the air. Footprints imprinted into the soft earth create a trail, which I follow. Whispers shudder around me. The wind wails, rattling the tree boughs. I spin in a circle, trying to pinpoint where the voices are coming from.

"This way."

"Jaaaaccoooobb."

"Come, come, come."

I hunker to the forest floor and press my palm to the dirt. Closing my eyes, I listen. My professor used to tell me I was a poor listener, but that was only because I found he had little worth listening to. This forest, on the other hand, overflows with stories. They call to me, itching at my skin, whispering in my ears, tingling my nerves.

A smile curves my lips. I'm close.

I take off until I find the hovel tucked in the hillside. Thorny brambles and moss offer protection from the careless eye. Probably fooled travelers or hunters. But I'm not your average hunter. Lightly, I inch closer, sword ready. There isn't much to the place other than a tiny window, hardly bigger than my torso, and a wooden door fit for a child.

I rap my fist on the door. Might as well be civilized, right?

"Go away!" a voice squawks from inside.

"You and I are due for a long chat."

"Never!"

"Over a nice drink perhaps?"

"Over my dead body!"

I lean against the door and sigh, twirling my sword in my palm. Truth is, being civilized is never effective.

"Fine," I say. "Have it your way then. I know how you tried to steal that child. Because of that your time here is finished."

Not to mention his name is on the hourglass. I try the door. Locked. Gritting my teeth, I step back, and with a running start, crash my body into the wooden frame. The wood buckles, and a piece even splinters, but the bolt on the other side holds fast. I stalk to the window and peer inside.

The room is simply outfitted with a table, single chair, bed made of straw, and large pile of additional straw with a golden sheen in the corner. But it's the spinning wheel glistening like honey that makes my eyes narrow. No sign of the little man. Then I spot his bottom, sticking out of the fireplace as he ducks inside to climb the chimney.

I glower, hating when the scoundrels make me work for it. Sheathing my sword, I abandon the hut and scurry to the edge of the hillside where his hut is built. I reach the chimney just as the man's head pops out.

I grab him by the cuff of his shirt, but he wiggles and squirms free like a slippery trout. Thin golden threads shoot out from his palms. They twist through the air and wrap around my wrists, cinching so tight the strands cut deep into my skin.

Blood spurts from my wrists, causing my temples to throb.

Ashes and bone, I hate these Forbidden. The sooner we get rid of them from our world, the better. The man spins around, studying me with large eyes that drink in the whole world with one glance. He breaks into a cackling laugh that makes his pointed white beard jiggle. More of his gold threads snake across the ground toward me, folding around my legs as if to mummify me.

"Release me this instant!" I demand, struggling.

"You think you're so smart," he taunts, hopping on one foot like this is a Summerfest game. "No one visits me without consequences. You'll bleed to death just like the others. But unlike those before you, I'll laugh and dance over your dead body."

"And here I was merely hoping we could have a nice chat."

The trees blur as my blood seeps out of me, dripping from my fingertips, splattering over my boots. My palms are so slick, it takes every ounce of mental energy to lift my sword and slice the golden threads binding me. In seconds, I close the space and press the tip of my steel to his neck.

He stills. "How did you do that?"

"Run away and I'll slice off your head," I say in a half-growl. "I'm in no mood to go gallivanting through the forest and ruining my new cloak, so if you must be killed, so be it."

"Who are you and what do you want?"

"Jacob Grimm, and I merely wish to hear your life story. Is that too much to ask?"

"Probably."

"So much bitterness for a Monday. The week has hardly begun."

I check his neck for the mark just to be sure. It's there. Whirls like the golden straw he spins. Every Forbidden's mark is different, and from what I can tell, each signifies an element of that Forbidden's magic. Satisfied, I haul him down the incline and through the forest, where I hope Storm is happily munching on grass.

"Listen," the man says. "How about we trade? I'll give you whatever you wish if you just let me free."

"You speak as if you have great power."

"A beautiful woman to keep you warm at night?"

"I've no time for love or warmth."

"Then gold. Infinite riches. Yes, that's what you wish, isn't it? I can spin gold for you. Heaps of it! Just take me back to my home."

"The only thing I wish for is something no king, witch, or even the Devil himself can offer." Then I mutter, "That said, a decent necktie which doesn't get bloody every time I go on a hunt might be nice."

"I have the power of a king," the man presses. "Merely guess my name and your wish will be granted."

This conversation teeters on territory I avoid at all costs.

"Power? Granting wishes?" I chuckle mirthlessly as I clean myself off in a stream. "I learned that lesson the hard way."

"Your wounds." His eyes widen as he points to my now clean, smooth wrists. "They're healed. Not a single mark from my threads. How is that possible?"

"I'd rather not discuss private matters."

Why do the Forbidden always ask so many maddening questions? I need Wilhelm to make up a list of excuses I can use. I march the man out of the forest and into the open field. Thankfully, Storm is still where I left him. In one piece to boot. Sure, he's a bit frantic, pacing about, but he's alive.

"Fine," I say, tying Baldy up so he's attached to me. "Might as well play his game to pass the time. "How many guesses do I get?"

"How many?" He scratches the top of his head as if the question bothers him greatly. "No one has asked that of me before."

"How about three?" I offer as I untie my horse, who's pawing at the earth. "I guess your name, you tell me your story. I don't, you trot along free as a weasel."

I hold out my hand to shake on it. He spits on his palm and then slaps the slimy gooeyness into the handshake.

"Lovely." I grimace and try to wipe my hand free. "Is your name Conrad?"

The man stands taller, adjusting his brown tunic and belt. "Nope."

"Harry."

"Not even close." He eyes the forest with a smile.

"Perhaps it's Rumpelstiltskin?" I finish with a wicked grin.

His face falls. He studies me in a mix of surprise and horror. I sigh, deciding there's actually no joy in playing this ridiculous game of mouse trap. It's been years of misery, hunting for stories. I'm supposed to be full-time at the university, but instead, here I am, traipsing about the country-side like a lunatic.

Curse the Enchantress and her Forbidden minions.

"You are evil! The Devil himself!" Rumpelstiltskin cries. "Nasty man. You knew who I was even before you laid eyes on me."

"So much sour just makes Mondays dull." I pat the saddle of my horse. "Come along and I'll give you a ride back—"

Dark forms slip out of the forest, padding with calculating sureness over the soft earth. Their fur juts up at the ends like blades, and their size is triple to my own. Wolves, a whole pack of them. Strange red eyes focus on me, sharp teeth glinting in the sunlight.

I mount my horse in one swift move, dragging the man up behind me. The wolves launch out of the shadows. The horse rears up on its hind legs. It takes all my strength to keep both of us on the horse.

"Ride!" I order, and we take off, streaking across the plain like a bolt of lightning on a summer's night.

But the wolves are clever. Too clever. They flank themselves out to keep us from heading back to the road, instead forcing us toward a manor rising up in the distance.

"I thought you said you wouldn't kill me if I told you my story!" Rumpelstiltskin says.

Ahead, a wooden fence stretches out, running along the full expanse of the field. Oxen and cows graze in a pasture while another field is golden with wheat ready to be harvested. I flick the reins, urging my horse faster. He leaps over the low stone wall. I glance back. Oddly, the wolves halt at the barrier, even though they easily could have bounded over the wall. They pace along the edge, whining as if wishing to cross.

"Well, look who's swifter now?" Rumpelstiltskin laughs.

My muscles relax, and I allow our pace to slow.

"We got away from them too easily," I mutter. "Something isn't right."

As if in answer, dark forms swoop down from the sky. Ravens—seven in fact—along with a flock of crows squawking as if crying out a battle charge, start flying our way. Experience warns me they could be trouble.

"That doesn't look promising," Rumpelstiltskin says. "I'm fairly certain that staying at your side guarantees death."

"So it would seem."

I calculate the distance to the manor, but gauging the swiftness of the birds, there's no way we can make it there in time. The only thing close is a large hazel tree stretched out in the center of the field. It will at least keep them from attacking us mid-air. I urge Storm faster.

The ravens swoop down, veering straight for us like birds of prey.

And attack.

Beaks peck at my hair. Claws rip into my flesh. Sharp feathers slice my skin. It won't be long before they devour us, piece by piece.

I really hate my job.

# CHAPTER 3

## ELLA

### MAIER MANOR

A cold shiver curls down my spine as Dr. Wissen saunters out the front door like he already owns the place. His words felt like threats. Jesse, my personal maid, rushes into the room, panting, eyes wild.

"Ella!" she exclaims. "There's a problem."

"What now?" I rub my forehead.

"There are men in the fields. The birds are attacking them."

I sigh. The birds on the estate have been known to be vicious. "I'll take care of them."

In the kitchen, I grab my basket of day-old bread. As I march outside, I wonder what else could possibly go wrong. The wind snaps at my long golden hair and whips my skirts against my legs. Shouts and cawing fill the air. Wings and claws, black feathers of the darkest night circle Mother's tree.

I hurry, clutching my basket tighter.

The whirlwind of black-feathered ravens with dagger-like beaks dive at the men. One hunkers beneath his cloak at the tree's base while the other fights back, slashing at his attackers with a silver blade. Each move is fluid and precise like he battles monsters in his sleep.

"Need a hand?" I call out.

The man with the sword startles, eyes flicking to me. They're stormy blue like an approaching thunderhead on the horizon. "Unless you can cast a spell on these demons, I'm a bit occupied."

"Afraid I can't help there. But I have breadcrumbs."

I toss a handful to the ground. Instantly, the birds abandon their prey, scrambling to peck at the snack happily. The man lowers his weapon and tilts his head with a look of disbelief.

"If I didn't know better," he says, "I'd think this death flock were your pets."

Dark hair clings to his forehead in damp waves, tight breeches are tucked into spurred boots, and his tunic is torn across one shoulder, exposing a line of muscle I try not to look at.

*Try* being the key word.

"Sometimes food speaks louder than the sword." I throw him a smirk and toss another handful of crumbs to the ground.

His lips curve. "In the future, I must remember to travel with snacks."

"Do you always trespass when traveling?"

"We were being chased by wolves." He sheaths his sword and steps closer. "I thought it was odd they didn't follow us onto your property. Now, I see why."

"Chased by wolves?" I scan the perimeter to spot dark forms melding into the forest. I shove down my fear. They're venturing into these parts of the forest now. "Seems as if you like to cause trouble everywhere you go."

"So it appears." There's a glint of playfulness in his eyes.

"Speak for yourself," the smaller man mutters, finally

daring to emerge from beneath his cloak. A long, shaggy white beard hangs from his chin, and wrinkles fill every inch of his face. A few tufts of hair poke out of his balding head. "*I* was minding my own business."

"We are terribly sorry to disrupt your—" The larger man waves at the birds now perched in the trees as if he's trying to think of a name for them.

"Pets," the smaller man supplies with a grin, displaying numerous missing teeth. He glances worriedly above his head where the seven ravens now perch, eyeing him with disapproving looks. "Such sweet little birds."

"They're not my pets, nor particularly sweet," I say. "But they do well to protect our lands from intruders. And you are?"

"Jacob Grimm," he says with a bow, "and this here is um... Otto, at your service."

Blood drips from Jacob's neck and ears. Guilt spears me. The birds were more vicious than usual.

"I see." I nod politely, flinching as Jacob wipes blood from his earlobe with his handkerchief. "I insist my servants bring you water to freshen up before you continue your journey."

"We're actually on our way to the village of Honau, where my brother is setting up a new bookshop as we speak," Jacob explains, checking something in his bag. "Just show us the road to the village, and we'll be out of your way."

"I'm headed there myself." I bite my lip, guilt tugging at me. Both travelers are bleeding from my birds just a hand's throw from my mother's grave. She'd be horrified if I turned them away without offering help. "Please, I insist on getting you some bandages. Then you can follow me to town."

The two bow again and head to where the servants are prepping my carriage. The ravens squawk from above as I start off. Spinning around, I fist my hands on my hips.

"You could've seriously hurt them," I lecture the creatures

as if they can understand me. "What if they'd been killed? I have enough problems to deal with. Father's never coming back, the servants are leaving, and I have a full crop with no one to harvest. An impossible job, and yet somehow, I must perform a miracle."

The ravens cock their heads to the side, staring blandly at me, while a bluebird bursts into song. Rolling my eyes, I chuckle only to spot a handkerchief on the grass. I pick it up to find a G sewn onto it. G for Grimm.

"Do those birds truly understand you, Ella?" Jesse calls out from where she's waiting just ahead. She, along with the entire staff, refuses to come close to the tree.

"Good heavens, no. But it would be grand, wouldn't it? Mother used to talk to them. I suppose I picked up the habit."

I glance over my shoulder as the ravens take flight across the fields. Jesse has a point. They do have a knowing look in their eyes. Or maybe it's me wishing someone understood the pain that still knifes at my soul ever since Mother left, even if they're just birds.

# CHAPTER 4

# JACOB

### MAIER MANOR

A servant hands us clean towels, bandages, and a bowl of water. I barely thank her before she scurries off.

"Can't say I trust these people," Rumpelstiltskin mutters. "Keeping ravens and crows as pets. No good can come of that."

"You're one to talk." I scrub away the dried blood.

The memory of the woman striding across the field, black skirts kicking up in the wind, golden curls whipping about her, while the ravens soared above as if flying under her command. She's altogether terrifying, clever, and stunning mixed into one.

Unlike anyone I've ever seen.

But the wolf attack is alarming. Strange creatures. Too large and vicious to be typical gray wolves. And far too clever.

"I'm a fool." I smack the towel against my thigh. "I forgot to ask her name."

"How unfortunate for you." Rumpelstiltskin grimaces as he pats his ear. "I, on the other hand, know it. Lucky me."

"I wouldn't bother wiping down that ear. Might be a waste of time should I decide to kill you."

"I'm surprised you haven't yet."

"Stay on good behavior and you'll live. The moment you try anything, our deal is done. Got it?"

He glares at me. "Her name is Ella von Maier, daughter of an unrenowned noble on the brink of ruin." His eyes perk up as Ella exits the manor, escorted by her chaperone. "Ah, and here she is now."

"You know a lot for a man who lives under a hill."

"That's my business. Know everything and everyone. Especially their weaknesses." The old man winks and turns to Ella as she walks to her carriage. "Good day, miss."

"Otto." She pauses. "You're still bleeding. Let me give you a ride. I'd like to look at your head wound. I won't have you dying under my watch."

"Don't mind if I do!" Otto soaks up her kind smile like a gremlin sneaking cookies from the pantry and shoots me a triumphant look. "Now who's wishing he didn't heal so quickly, eh?"

I scowl as he hurries into the carriage. Now I'll have to follow them the whole way to make sure the fiend doesn't escape. The footman opens the door, but Ella waves me over, holding out a piece of material.

"Your handkerchief, Jacob Grimm," she says, climbing into the carriage.

I come to her side and stare up at her. Thick lashes frame eyes so blue they must have been stolen from the summer sky —bright, endless, and far too dangerous. My heart does this strange flip like it's forgotten how to beat properly.

"You keep it." I push it back, trying to ignore the scent of lilacs drifting off her skin. "A small token of gratitude."

"If I were you," Otto interrupts us, "I'd burn that. Nasty."

I expect her to toss it back at me, but she tucks it into the folds of her gown. "Then I will keep it." A mischievous smile curls on her pink lips. "Nasty kerchief and all."

"As you wish." I bow.

The footman closes the door, and I retreat to my horse. I flick my reins and ride alongside the carriage, needing to keep a close eye on Otto. He spots me watching Ella bandage him up and grins a toothless smile. Sending this Forbidden back to his realm can't come soon enough.

I peek at the hourglass again. Even as it lies on its side, the liquid flows. I have two hours, three tops, before Wilhelm dies. I suck in deep breaths, reminding myself that Wilhelm has most of the story already written. We only need a few final touches for it to be complete, which Rumpelstiltskin will provide. As long as I don't lose him between here and the bookshop.

Feeling eyes on me, I look over and find Ella studying me through the open window. Quickly, I close my sack.

"So you're setting up a bookshop?" she asks. "You won't get much business, I'm afraid. Not much happens in our little village."

"I've heard the king has finished his new castle. That might change things."

She frowns. "Perhaps, but I doubt King Frederick cares about our success. Many people are angry he hasn't dealt with the wolf attacks."

I wish I could tell her Wilhelm and I are the help sent by the king, but that's another secret added to the mounting pile I'm bound to never share.

"When we get to the village, you should report your wolf sighting," I offer. "That will get people's attention."

"So confident for a stranger. I think you'll find the villagers aren't that welcoming to foreigners, nor quick to help a lord's daughter."

"Fear makes people do strange things."

Shadows worry her face. "We've had too much loss and sorrow to find room for generosity."

I grip my reins tighter. Loss, sorrow, suffering. Those have been my language and life ever since I signed the Enchantress's contract.

"My brother and I are hunters," I find myself saying. "I'll do what I can to get rid of these wolves."

The wind tugs the curls beneath her brimmed hat. "You would do this sort of thing for me? Why?"

"You rescued me from certain death. It's the least I can do."

"Considering my birds could've skinned you, I'm not sure you're worthy of the task."

I scowl, ready to defend myself, only to find those large eyes twinkling. Curse it all, this woman might be trouble for me. "I suppose I must prove myself then."

"I look forward to it." And with a knowing grin, she leans back against her seat.

We're coming up on the first thatched roofs, white walls laced with dark wooden beams, and I remind myself that I can't afford distractions. Especially ones that make the day seem brighter.

Honau is a small village, alive with children racing across the dirt road, playing tag while a woman scolds them from her flower-boxed window. We clatter past the mill and then the blacksmith until we reach the village center, cluttered with shops and houses and a tiny white-steepled church tucked in its center.

"What do you think of our little village?" Ella interrupts my thoughts. "Not as fancy as you're used to?"

"It reminds me of better days." My mind clings to memories running through the streets of Steinau with Wilhelm, where sticks were swords and our greatest enemies were our shadows.

"And there's the castle." She points to the hill.

Above, clinging atop the rocky cliffs, sits Lichtenstein

Castle, one of King Frederick's many homes, outlined against the cobalt sky. Misty clouds shroud its white tower, transforming it into a relic of haunting beauty.

I press my lips together, hating the reminder of our true purpose for imposing on this quaint village. In Wilhelm's and my recent travels, we heard rumors about strange occurrences coming from the area surrounding the Black Forest. Needing an excuse to investigate the region, Wilhelm concocted a plan to send a letter offering our hunting services to King Frederick, which he promptly replied to with a yes and a bag of coins. So here we are, already chasing a story before we've time to gather our wits about us.

The carriage halts at the village square, where a market is set up. On the church steps, a mob gathers, yelling as a man hammers a piece of paper on one of the double wooden doors already cluttered with other notices. A sketch of a young man and the word MISSING is scrawled on top of the parchment.

"It was the beast!" the man hammering tries to explain to the angry group. "Someone needs to go out and take care of it."

Gasps mixed with laughter erupt. The moment I hear the word beast, I halt my horse.

"It's not a beast," someone calls out. "Just some pesky wolf."

"Pesky wolves?"

"You're a fool. You know nothing!"

"Don't be lying to us." A burly man steps up, wagging a finger in the hammer man's face. "That idiot son of yours ran off to join the Southlands' army. You just don't want to admit it."

"Take those words back!"

The tense mob transforms into a brawl. Once this all clears up, I'm going to have to look at those notices on the door. Ella's carriage parks a safe distance away, and I dismount, ready to grab Baldy should he try to escape.

When she steps onto the cobblestone street, she assesses the mob. "Appears things have gotten worse."

Ella's chaperone gives me a pointed look as if warning me to keep my distance.

"What do you mean?" I ask and then clap Rumpelstiltskin on the shoulder. He futilely wiggles against my iron grip.

"In the last month, many of our villagers have gone missing," she explains. "Some people think it's the wolves. Others claim it's a beast. Then last week, the baker's wife said the sound of a flute woke her. According to her, she looked out her window to find a bunch of townsfolk walking down the street. They disappeared into the forest. No one has seen them since."

"What do you think?"

"I think people make up all sorts of stories to explain things they don't understand."

I'm inclined to believe the baker's wife.

"I'm indebted to your kindness." I bow. "If you ever need anything, stop by our bookshop."

"Such a gentleman," Rumpelstiltskin mutters, rolling his eyes.

"I appreciate that." She adjusts her silk gloves. "But what I need right now is a miracle. Don't imagine you have any of those up your sleeve?"

"He can only promise pain and death." Rumpelstiltskin steps in front of me, flourishing a bow. "I, on the other hand, can be trusted. Should you wish for a miracle? I'll provide it for you. Money? Power? Love?"

"What a funny man you are." Ella chuckles and taps her chin, a smile tipping her lips. "Let's see—"

"Don't listen to him," I interrupt, pushing Baldy aside,

heart pounding. The last thing I need is for her to become indebted to him. "He's a liar and a thief."

Rumpelstiltskin shrugs. "It's why Grimm has been debating whether he should slice my head off now and later."

"How barbaric!" Ella exclaims in mock humor.

"Indeed." It's best not to tell her the old villain is telling the truth.

"If you'll excuse me," she says. "I must go make a trade of goods. Good day."

I bow as she leaves, while her chaperone continues glaring at me as she trails behind Ella.

I grab Rumpelstiltskin by the arm and start hauling him down the street with one hand while leading my horse with the other. I've not gotten three feet when a stately carriage led by six horses thunders into the village, blocking my path.

The carriage bears the crest of a black lion and golden deer on either side of the shield of Swabia. King Frederick's coat of arms. *Strange.* I didn't expect the king until winter. It also means I need to get involved. I suppose if there was ever a good time, it's now.

"Lucky for you," I tell Baldy. "Your head gets to stay on your neck for another few minutes."

"How fortuitous." He spits on the ground.

Dust billows around the carriage as a footman opens the door and out steps a man about my age with reddish curly hair and a thick beard. He's wearing a striking blue tunic with lace billowing around his neck. Bright green eyes assess the village square as he brushes off the road dust from his fine clothes.

This isn't the king—it's his son, Prince William.

The mob surveys him, oddly quiet.

"Your Highness," the hammer man calls out, nose bleeding. "What's to be done with the beast?"

"Beast?" The prince pinches the bridge of his nose,

muttering to his head guard, "I don't have time to deal with these villagers' superstitions."

"Six young men missing in the past week," a woman adds. "That makes fifteen in all!"

"When will the king realize his people need him?" another asks.

The crowd advances on the prince. Quickly, the guards surround him.

"I believe you're looking for me," I announce, striding forward, dragging Rumpelstiltskin behind me.

The prince raises his eyebrows while the group turns to me in surprise.

"The king cares very much about his subjects," I continue, though I doubt it's true. "He has sent my brother and me to scout the land and take note of any unusual activity. If you have any interesting stories to share with us, we're eager to hear them. You can find us in our new bookshop."

"Stories? Foreigners prowling about our lands?" The accusations boom from a man standing on top of the village well. He's wearing a patterned cravat and a double-breasted brown coat with a dark fur collar. His hair is perfectly groomed beneath his hat. He waves a cane to get our attention. "This is how the king deals with our problems. Now I understand how little King Frederick cares for us. How do we not know that you aren't responsible?"

The mob cries out with approval. My mouth dries up. He's right.

"Dr. Wissen, maybe you can help," the hammer man says. "My son went missing last night. I've scoured the countryside for him."

"Come to the town hall tomorrow night for a meeting," Dr. Wissen announces. "We'll find a way to save our village. Everyone is invited. Even you, Your Royal Highness."

"How considerate." Prince William looks anything but pleased.

There's some rumbling from the group, villagers eyeing Rumpelstiltskin and me, but they finally back off. Of course, it doesn't hurt when the prince orders his guards to assist.

"Your Royal Highness." I bow. "Jacob Grimm, at your service."

"Your service was appreciated," Prince William says, taking in the scene as he rips off his jacket and frilly collar. He tosses the clothing at his footman, who desperately tries to catch them. "It appears next time I enter the village, I'll need a disguise. A good way to learn about your kingdom is when no one knows who you are, right? You wouldn't happen to know of an inferior tailor who'll do a fine job of ruining my ensemble or perhaps pants and a shirt like a commoner such as yourself?"

I stiffen in annoyance. My family is hardly wealthy. I've always believed our station in life doesn't represent who we are, but rather our work ethic and contributions to society. I point to the shop Ella entered. "Perhaps that place might be able to help you."

Without thanks, the prince heads off. Fine by me. Time is flying, and the hourglass waits for no one. Not even a prince.

## CHAPTER 5

## ELLA

### HONAU

"They're worth far more than you're offering," I argue with Harriett, the shopkeeper.

My mother's jewels glisten on the counter. I hate how they sparkle as if begging me to keep them. Letting them go is like allowing another part of my mother to slip away.

"Sorry, sweets." She waves her hand, showing off finger-nails caked with dirt. Her straw-colored hair looks desperate to escape its bun, and her brown eyes stare dully at me like I'm wasting her time. "I don't even know who'd buy such finery. Not a soul in these parts has time for such frivolity. The only reason I'm even offering thirty thalers is I heard about your father abandoning you. I'm sure it's not your fault. Likely, he couldn't get over your mother's death. Sad news, for sure. Is it true your mother never got a proper church burial?"

My chaperone, Madame Wagner, clears her throat in obvious annoyance from where she stands by the window.

I clasp my gloved hands and hold back a cutting remark. What did I expect? Everyone around here knows everyone's business. A part of me begs to run out of the shop right now, but the other part keeps my feet rooted to the floor. I refuse to let pride stand in the way of keeping my household running.

"Thirty thalers isn't even close to what these are worth," I finally say.

"Excuse me," a male's voice says from behind me.

I turn to discover a handsome man with mesmerizing emerald eyes and auburn curls, dressed in a white tunic of fine linen and tan breeches. Definitely not from these parts. I know everyone here.

"Such lovely pieces," he says, stepping up to the counter beside me. He smells of expensive cologne.

"Thank you." My cheeks burn in embarrassment. A lady isn't supposed to be in town hawking off family heirlooms. Then again, he doesn't have to know who I am.

"My stepmother is out of sorts of late." He touches one of the bracelets with hands that have clearly never seen hard labor. "Perhaps I could purchase them for a good price. You *are* selling them, yes?"

I lift my eyebrows. Is he serious? If so, he might pay more.

"Hey, there," Harriett interjects sourly. "I don't know who you are, coming to my shop, trying to take over. Once Ella and I finish our exchange, then you can speak to me. That's the way of it."

My mouth drops open. The dirty little trickster was only seconds ago trying to undersell me, and now this? Well.

"Actually, I *am* selling them," I tell him firmly.

"Excellent." The man's green eyes twinkle, and he shoots the shopkeeper a look that's a mix of mirth and utter contempt.

"You're selling them to *me*," Harriett emphasizes. "This is my shop."

I ignore her and focus on the man. "I haven't finalized my

deal with Harriett because we couldn't reach an acceptable arrangement. Perhaps you'd like to make an offer?"

"You're trusting this stranger over me?" Harriett huffs. "He could be the one kidnapping the villagers!"

He chuckles like he's thoroughly enjoying this game. "I'm a traveling merchant. This one might be my favorite."

He lifts my mother's intricate ruby-studded necklace. It glitters in the dim shop light. My heart pangs, remembering the last time she wore it. Christmas dinner. We had just sat down to a table of roasted duck, red cabbage, and potato dumplings when a scream vibrated from the kitchen. A goose had gotten loose in the house, flapping down the hall, honking frantically.

It knocked over our Christmas tree. Furious, Father tackled it. As he wrestled the animal, Mother started laughing, and the anger in Father's face vanished. We called it our Goose Christmas. It's my favorite holiday memory.

"It was my mother's." I swallow the lump forming in my throat. "I'm sure it will look stunning on your stepmother."

"I must have it," the man decides. "How much?"

I toss out a higher number than the shopkeeper offered, but a fair price, too.

"I will have it, along with three more pieces." He withdraws a purse and passes it to me. It's heavy. A peek inside tells me he'd been generous.

"Thank you," I say, even though I feel a tinge of sadness from losing the jewels.

"Perhaps you'd like to join—"

The merchant's words are interrupted by a scream, followed by wailing. Shivers race down my arms.

"Is there always so much drama in this town?" the man asks, peeking out the window.

I rush outside and find the baker's daughter, Scarlet,

sobbing by a cart. But before I have the chance to ask her what's wrong, my steps falter and I gasp in horror.

A body is sprawled inside the cart, mangled beyond recognition. Broken legs lie unnaturally twisted. The left side of the face looks as if some monster raked its claws across it. I press my hands over my mouth, trying to hold back the vomit threatening to spew out of me.

A man is trying to console her, saying, "We found your mother in the forest. Brought her back as quickly as we could, but she didn't survive."

A crowd forms around the cart. I don't know Scarlet well, but we used to chat whenever Mother and I came into town for shopping. Murmurs break through the crowd.

"A wolf attack."

"Out in the woods."

"Should've been in her bakery working," Madame Ketting says in her typical condescending tone. "Not running about in the woods, that's what."

"Who did this?" I clench Scarlet's arm.

She turns to stare bloodshot eyes at me. "Monsters," she whispers.

Monsters? Surely, she must be mistaken. I stand numb as Dr. Wissen marches onto the scene.

"Do not fret!" he calls out to the crowd. "I will investigate the situation and send out my men. We'll find whoever did this and bring justice to our village."

The crowd calms, and people slowly drift away. Two men carry off the body while some ladies lead Scarlet away, arms wrapped around her. My heart clatters against my ribcage. I barely notice Madame Wagner coming to my side, pleading for me to return to my carriage. Emotions roll through me like a summer storm. Something is desperately wrong with our village. First missing people and now this. If only I knew a way to fix it.

# CHAPTER 6

# JACOB

## HONAU

I scan the houses, complete with slanted roofs, balconies, and paned-glass windows, trying to remember where our shop was. We visit so many villages, they're all starting to blur together.

"Where are you taking me?" Rumpelstiltskin asks. "If you're going to murder me, why bother waiting?"

As we turn the corner, I spot Wilhelm leaning against a shop door, a crate at his feet. My heart sinks. He's been working rather than resting.

"Wilhelm!" I hurry to his side, dragging a complaining Baldy along. "Let me help. You go find a chair."

Wearily, Wilhelm cracks his lips, attempting a smile. "You've found our friend."

"Friend?" Rumpelstiltskin harrumphs. "Hardly. What's wrong with your brother?"

"Nothing you can't fix."

"Why don't I like the sound of that?" Rumpelstiltskin narrows his beady eyes.

"Get inside." When he hesitates, I warn him, "Don't try me."

He sighs dramatically but enters the shop. I throw Wilhelm's arm over my shoulder, helping him through the door and into a chair beside the large wooden table in the center of the room. I dig through one of the crates he's already brought inside until I find a blanket and wrap it over him.

"That's not necessary." He tries to wave me off. "I can take care of myself."

"Of course you can," I say as I survey the room. Opened crates are scattered about, and two of the bookshelves are already stuffed with books. Wilhelm's been busy. "Where's the equipment?"

"There." My brother points to a smaller wooden box sitting on the end of the table.

"Nice place you've got here," Rumpelstiltskin says and starts digging through the hay of one of the crates.

"Don't touch anything," I order.

I unpack the Enchantress's pen, book, clock, and inkwell she so kindly gave us, setting them methodically on the table.

Wilhelm leans forward. "I didn't realize he was just an old man," he says in a whisper. "Shouldn't we let him live out his last days in peace?"

"You aren't insinuating we don't finish the story, are you? Wilhelm, you know we must." I pull out the hourglass from my pack. There's just a trickle of blood left in the upper globe. Less than an hour. "Now sit back down and let me finish this cursed story."

"I can't keep doing this." Wilhelm rubs his knuckles across his forehead. "Is my life really worth all these other lives? What if the Enchantress is lying? Have you ever thought about that? We could be taking away this old man's last days."

"He looks to be two centuries old. He's lived a good life. And from what I've been gathering, better than he deserves."

Not to mention those gold strands. How many people have bled to death from those? "Besides, we don't have any proof that the Enchantress is lying. Now sit down before you collapse."

"I don't like it."

Anger roars up within me. "And I do?"

"I started another story. We can use that one instead."

"No, we can't." I slam myself into the chair opposite Rumpelstiltskin, ready to get the dreadful deed over with.

And yet for all of Baldy's annoyances, the Enchantress's book feels heavy as stone.

"There must be something I can offer you?" Rumpelstiltskin turns to Wilhelm, realizing my younger brother is his ticket to freedom. "A healing spell? I've got plenty. Or a nice plump woman to warm you up?"

Wilhelm glares at me and shuffles outside. I should yell at him to get back here, but I don't have the seconds to spare. The book cracks as I open it, smelling of fresh ink.

Nearly all of Rumpelstiltskin's story is finished. I dip the quill into the ink. A trickle of magic spills from the tip, dripping golden dust along the table. "Now, Rumpelstiltskin, let's start at the beginning for a quick review of the facts. You're a spinner, yes? Did you trick the—"

"Stop." Wilhelm stumbles back inside, wheezing. He's holding a bulging sack.

"What are you doing?" I ask.

"Rumpelstiltskin," he continues, "if we give you more time, will you serve us as need be?"

"Serve you?" The old man spits on the floor. "I serve no one."

"Serve or be banished from this world!" Wilhelm's voice rings oddly strong, considering he looks as pale as death.

"There can't be choices," I snap. "He's leaving, and that's final."

"This is my life, so I'm choosing the story." Wilhelm drops the bag on the ground. A goose tumbles out. It squawks and begins peeking at the floor.

"Wilhelm!" I leap to my feet. "What are you doing?"

"Let me guess." Rumpelstiltskin chuckles. "You didn't read the terms and conditions of your contract with this enchantress, did you?"

I'm too busy staring at the hourglass in horror to bother with the trickster.

*Drip, drip, drip.*

My hands shake. "I can't let you die." I sit back down and start writing, but Wilhelm snatches the pen from me. Wheezing, he pulls out a second book. I pause. "What are you doing?"

He ignores me and flips through the pages to the end. Grimacing, he scratches out words. The goose starts chewing on the buttons of my jacket.

"It won't work," I remind him, pushing the animal away. "Rumpelstiltskin's name is on the hourglass. She won't accept it."

"If we're going to talk about names," Baldy interjects, "I'd prefer you keep mine a secret between us."

"Then I die," Wilhelm says without looking up from the page. Beads of sweat drip off his forehead and splatter on the page.

"Wait." Baldy joins us. "You'd die for *me*?"

"I can't let you do this!" I slam my fist on the table.

"Can't let me?" Wilhelm snorts. "You chose for me to live this cursed life. You don't get to make my choices anymore. From now on, I have a say. Understand?"

His words crash against my chest. He's right. This is all my fault. My hesitation allows him to scrawl out what must be the final words because suddenly, like magic of its own, the words, *The End*, appear at the bottom.

I freeze. Terrified of what may happen next.

The words on the page rise into the air just like every other story we've written. I hold my breath, begging for it to work. Ink whizzes and rushes around the goose, faster and faster, until it's caught in a funnel.

The goose honks and flaps its wings but remains firmly in place. I rise to my feet, hope and fear rumbling through me.

"What's happening?" Rumpelstiltskin asks. "This is wizardry!"

A golden egg pops out of the goose, shiny and bright. The goose is sucked into the inky funnel. With a swoosh, the ink returns to the pages, solidifying and drying. Wilhelm slams the book closed. His hands are paper-thin. A shimmering gold title appears across the front and spine: *The Golden Goose*.

"The goose..." Rumpelstiltskin stammers, "disappeared... into the book."

Wilhelm and I share a look, but neither of us dares speak. I swallow my fear and unravel the scroll with the list of names. My finger shakes as I run it down the list until I find the title *The Golden Goose*. I strike a line through it. The whole process is always terrifying, but today is far worse.

We both rise to our feet. I pick up *The Golden Goose* while Wilhelm turns the hands of the clock to point to twelve.

Meanwhile, Rumpelstiltskin inches toward the door.

"I wouldn't leave if I were you," I warn him. "Unless you want the same fate as the goose."

"I wouldn't dream of leaving," he says and plops into a chair, fear finally filling those dark eyes of his. "I'll just sit my tush right here."

Wilhelm and I wait. I study the walls, wondering which one the clock will open in this location. A groan yanks our attention to the wall on our right. It slides inward, and mist curls into the room.

"It always works." Wilhelm's voice quivers. "No matter where we are."

"I'll do it." Clenching the book, I step through the doorway and into the Enchantress's tower.

My skin tingles, and a slight dizziness washes over me just like it does every time I enter her world. I stride across the worn bridge of a round room that rises up to a domed roof. Every wall is lined with ornate bookshelves, most empty. Brass sconces burn, lighting the tower in an amber hue.

The end of the bridge leads me to an empty bookshelf, as it always does. I slide the newest story vertically onto the ledge. The words *The Golden Goose* sparkle on the spine in the murky light.

"Another name, another story." I run my thumb over the words.

My heart tightens. No matter how many times I tell myself I'm doing the right thing, I still question it. What if Wilhelm is right and we're actually locking people into these pages? Even if they are evil, who are we to make this judgment?

Once I step out of the Enchantress's tower and into our new bookshop, the secret door slides shut, sealing off her realm from ours. I rush to the hourglass, gripping the cold metal trees protecting the glass. Rumpelstiltskin's name has vanished from the top while our blood slowly starts to return to the upper globe through the twisted center. Color returns to Wilhelm's face, and his shoulders lift.

"It worked." Wilhelm releases a long breath. "Somehow it worked."

Which is unsettling in itself. But time is back on our side. At least for today.

# CHAPTER 7

# ELLA

## HONAU

The hood of my cloak conceals my face in shadows as I tuck myself into the back of the packed town hall. The last thing I need is to be discovered. It's hardly a place for an unescorted lady, and I don't need more reasons for people to talk about my family.

When I heard Dr. Wissen called a town meeting about the wolves, I made sure to show up. I cast my eyes about the room to see if anyone might recognize me and spot Jacob Grimm leaning against the left wall. His sharp blue eyes survey the room with an attitude that only an outsider could have. As if he sees our little village in a way we never could. My heart skips as I take in his lean, agile body, but I shut down those thoughts immediately. We're not even in the same social circles to have a conversation. He's a hunter, while I'm a nobleman's daughter.

A commotion at the front of the hall drags my eyes away from Jacob.

My stomach instantly sours as Dr. Wissen strides up to the platform, bright-eyed and flashing that gorgeous smile

46

half the town swoons under. He's wearing his usual black coat and hat.

Dr. Wissen's right-hand man claps, calling out, "Attention! Attention please. Dr. Wissen will speak."

Everyone settles onto the benches, and the rowdy crowd hushes.

"My esteemed neighbors and fellow citizens," Dr. Wissen begins. "We face difficult times in our land. Our people are suffering. As you may have heard, my late wife was killed by one of those creatures prowling about in our woods. God rest her soul."

He bows his head. The room remains silent. He clears his throat and continues, "It is with great sorrow that today one of our own died from one of these vicious creatures. And yet, our king does nothing. Nor does he care about us."

A murmur of agreement spreads through the crowd. I suck in a breath, shocked at his words against King Frederick. Some might even call it treason.

"But do not fear!" Dr. Wissen continues. "I personally will do everything in my power and use all my resources to make sure our lands remain safe. The king may fail in keeping the peace, but we'll show him we can take care of our own."

He gives a slight bow, and the crowd bursts into cheers, rising from the benches and clapping. I can't deny that I'm hoping he's being truthful. Sure, Dr. Wissen makes my skin itch like poison ivy, but if he can keep our land safe from these wolves, who am I to stop him?

Dr. Wissen's right-hand man starts explaining the plan of action.

"We'll be visiting every household," the man says, "to assess any potential threats and needs you may have. Before you leave tonight, it's important to let us know the name and age of each individual in your household. We'll have men at the doors gathering information."

I frown. The last thing I want is Dr. Wissen or his men skulking about my home. I should leave before anyone notices me. Tucking my hood further over my face, I dart into the hallway to find two large men standing by the front door, checking villagers' names before they leave. I freeze.

If I remember correctly, there's a door in the back of the hall. I turn and duck down the darkened corridor only to collide with a hard chest. Fear clenches me in a vice grip. I open my mouth in a scream, but a hand closes over my lips.

"It's me. Jacob Grimm." His voice is low and velvety smooth against the shell of my ear.

My heart thumps even faster, and my head spins. I've never been this close to a man before. It's altogether improper, and yet, all I can think about is how he smells of ink and pine.

And I like it.

"I'm going to trust that you're not going to scream." His eyes glitter in the shadows as he eases his hand away.

"I didn't take you for one to lurk in hallways to attack ladies."

"Then you don't know me that well."

I step backward, but for some reason, I don't leave. Pure stupidity, likely. "What do you want?"

"I thought I'd spied you across the room. I was surprised to find you here." He searches my face. "You know something about these wolves, don't you?"

"I need to leave." I pull away, but he moves his hand lightly to my elbow. I slip my hand into the pocket of my skirt where I hid a knife for moments like this.

"I must speak with you, but not here. It's not safe."

"And you're safe?" I sputter.

"That's a valid point. I promise not to hurt you."

Against my better judgment, I follow him down the

hallway into a small nook. Whispers of moonlight trickle through the tiny window beside him, outlining his figure.

"What do you want?" I ask again.

"This Dr. Wissen. What do you know about him? Trustworthy?"

"Hardly," I scoff. "He came by our house after he heard we were desperate. He was trying to make money off our situation. It wouldn't be the first I've heard of him doing this."

He nods and rubs the slight scruff on his chin, considering my words. "The villagers seem quite enamored by him."

"He has given many people jobs." I sigh, trying not to think about how many of my staff have left to work for him. "He has this inherent knack to know everything that goes on in this village. Why are you so curious about the doctor?"

I study Jacob carefully. That nose, so sharp and proud. The way his jaw tightens with worry. The way he's focused on me, as if every word I say has purpose. His presence consumes the air around me, dangerously drawing me closer to him.

"You heard him back there. His words are borderline treasonous to the crown, and as one who works for the king, it concerns me."

"Yet Dr. Wissen speaks the truth, doesn't he?" I press. "What has the king done to protect us? Or are you his solution?"

Jacob's eyes flash, silvery in the moonlight. He leans closer, his breath skimming across my skin. "Wolves are prowling your lands. It won't be long before they come to your doorstep."

"What are you saying?" Anxiety nips at my mind. "You think the wolves are purposely hunting people?"

"I'm saying no one is safe as long as the wolves are alive. Do I have your permission to hunt them on your land?"

I bite my lip. So, this is the real reason he wished to speak to me. Not to ask my opinion, but to ask a favor. I stand taller, lifting my chin. "You may hunt on my lands, but it will cost you. You'll pay my steward before entering, and I want a full report on anything you find."

"That sounds reasonable."

Once we agree on the price, he shakes my hand. But as I duck out the back door, a sinking dread pools in my stomach like I just made a dangerous deal I didn't completely understand.

# CHAPTER 8

## JACOB

### THE BLACK FOREST

As children, Wilhelm and I loved running about in the fruit trees, playing tag, and recreating stories Gretchen, our nanny, would tell us. Some were quite terrifying, which of course made our prayers all the more earnest. Now, as I tromp through the Black Forest, my muscles taut as a bowstring, it's almost like I've stepped into the world of the wallpaper in my home in Steinau. Its pattern of earthy browns and forest greens showed off huntsmen adventuring over snow-frosted forests, their swords and bows ever ready.

I pause, taking in the view. My breath curls tentacles of white mist into the cool autumn afternoon. The Swabian Alps spike above the evergreens, vibrant in crimsons and dripping in honey golds. They circle the valley where the tiny village of Honau is nestled. At first glance, this place is paradise, except I know what really lurks within this valley.

I stride to the edge of a pond, sparkling as if it captured the sun's light, thinking about the other night's town meeting. The moment I arrived, every villager gave me a suspicious look. It was then I knew there'd be no help among the locals.

Except for one.

Eyes as bright as the stars, even the shadow of her hood couldn't conceal them from me. When I spotted Ella tucked into the back corner, it was impossible to focus on anything or anyone else in the room but her. I found myself following her. I told myself I was just asking for permission to hunt her grounds, but the truth is, it took everything in me not to lean closer and trace my fingers across those plump lips.

I groan and shove all thoughts of Ella von Maier out of my head. They'll just lead to impossible ideas, thanks to this curse I'm bound to.

Wilhelm stayed home today, taking notes on what we've observed in the village, while keeping an eye out for the next name that would appear on the hourglass. Meanwhile, I've been tracking these mysterious wolves. Unfortunately, I lost their trail on the outer rim of the Maiers' lands.

I fill my canteen with fresh water and settle onto a log near an old, abandoned mill. A little rest won't hurt, I decide, and pull out my sketchbook and charcoal and start sketching the landscape before me. Drawing always helps me think and process the world. The pond comes to life in my sketch, and I soak in the melody of the birds and the wind rushing through the trees.

As I study the pond, a ripple pushes from its center and sends a gentle tumble of waves against the bank. I frown, searching for the source, but nothing is there. Must have been a fish.

Singing breaks the silence. It's a beautiful voice that joins in with the chirping of the birds. I look around until I spot the woman.

Ella von Maier.

My heart stumbles as if it isn't sure how to beat. She hasn't seen me yet. Too busy balancing on a log, arms stretched out with a basket dangling at her elbow.

Her black mourning gown is replaced with a pale green dress. Mud lines the hem, hugging her ankles, and she's wearing sturdy boots, perfect for hiking. Her golden hair is twisted into two braids that trail down her back, but some strands have fallen loose and now dangle over pink cheeks.

If fairies truly existed, Ella would very well be one of them. She plucks herbs and flowers as she wanders through the forest, tucking them into her basket. I'm mesmerized, just watching her.

"Hello, there," I call out from my log before she thinks I'm spying on her.

She startles, dropping her basket. A knife flies into her hand from stars know where.

"You," she says, still not dropping the knife even as I lift my hands and smile. "What are you doing here?"

"If you remember correctly, you gave me permission to hunt on your land. Don't worry, I paid your steward before entering." I rise from my log and gather her herbs and heliotrope flowers as she continues pointing her knife at me. "You shouldn't be walking through the forest alone, especially after what happened to the baker's wife."

"I know." She lifts her chin. "Two of our cows have taken ill. I needed some herbs for a healing remedy. I guess I got a little carried away. It's a beautiful day."

"You know, you can put that weapon away. I'm not going to hurt you."

"I suppose that's true." She lowers the knife. "You do seem like a gentleman."

"My mother can be blamed for that. She made sure all of us children were well-trained."

"Did she now?" She tilts her head to the side, assessing me. "And how did she do that?"

"Do dance lessons at age five count? Or being tutored in Greek and Latin?"

"Only Greek and Latin?" A smile creeps on her lips.

"It was quite a sacrifice, especially when our friends were out running wild, building forts and snowmen."

"Hmm." She taps her mouth. "You say you're hunting, but it appears as if you're drawing."

She marches to the log I was sitting on and snatches up my sketchbook before I can stop her. I reach for it, but she side-steps, holding it away from me.

"Perhaps this will tell me the secrets you keep," she says, those mischievous eyes taunting me.

"That's personal."

"And a lady being alone deep in the forest with a man isn't?"

"Fine. Look at the sketches if you must."

She sets down her basket and, with careful fingers, begins flipping through the pages. Her brow puckers, making the tiny scar on her forehead more prominent. Slowly, she eases onto the log. Unease shifts through me as she scrutinizes my art. I've never shown my sketches to anyone.

"They're nothing but scribblings of a novice." I try to take the book from her again, but she twists out of my reach.

"These are good. Quite good, actually. You have an eye for detail. The bark on this oak looks like I could touch it. And the way you drew the neck of this swan is lovely. Interesting name. Mute Swan."

"My brother and I are working on a story relating to swans." My gaze strays to her lips.

"It's beautiful." She traces its lines. "So you're a hunter, drawer, dancer, and writer? What can't you do?"

"You give me too much credit. Let's see, I despise school."

"Now you sound pretentious."

"My brother would agree." I chuckle. "I was always bored in school. Felt like a waste of time, I guess. My teacher, Master Zinckham, was mean as typhoid and would give us beatings for no reason. What else? I'm highly opin-ionated, and I don't like large crowds. Have I scared you yet?"

She shakes her head and laughs. "I still don't know what to think about you."

We talk for too long, and yet not long enough. She explains the different healing properties of the herbs, and I sketch them into my notebook for reference. She's telling me her plans for her estate when my attention is pulled to a thin trail of water snaking across the ground, heading directly toward us.

"We need to move," I say, leaping to my feet.

I push Ella behind me, but the liquid is too quick. It coils around her ankle and rises up her leg.

"What's happening!" she asks, fear rattling her voice.

Whatever it is, it can't be good. "Run, Ella!"

She screams and reaches for me, fighting against the cord of water. I grab her hand, but her grip slips from mine as the water yanks her to the ground and drags her body into the pond. She vanishes into its murky depths before I can even blink.

Horrified, I race for the shore, but as I splash into the pond, water rises and forms a wall.

"Ella!" I throw myself into it, but it only pushes me back-ward. "Let me through! She doesn't belong to you."

As if hearing me, the wall pulls back to form an archway. In the center stands a woman with flowing ebony hair and stone-white skin. Iridescent sea-green eyes study me. Her white lips turn up in a hungry smile, and a forked tongue flicks out, licking her lips.

*A nixie.*

"What brings you, Hunter, to my pond?" Her voice rises and falls like rushing water. It's the most beautiful voice I've heard. One that lures victims to their death.

"What did you do with her?" I growl, pulling out my sword. "Give her back or I'll slice you to ribbons."

"She's a sweet thing, but does she know of your violent nature? I think she might not ask to be your friend if she knew what you really are."

My pulse rams against my temples. I don't have time to chat with this creature. I splash through the pond searching for Ella. How much longer can she stay underwater before she drowns?

"She's not very exciting," the nixie says. "But you, you're a prize. Let's make an exchange. Your life for hers. I could make you happy in my little abode."

It takes all my willpower to resist the pull of her voice. With a cry, I run at the nixie, ready to plunge my sword into her heart, but she disappears into the water. Panic seizes me. Ella is going to drown if I don't find her soon.

I dive under the pond's surface, searching for her, but it's too murky and dark to see anything. Desperately, I come up for air and then go back under. Again and again.

I refuse to let her suffer because of me. I live in a world haunted by nightmares. I knew better than to let Ella get close to me, but I didn't listen to that warning.

Now she's paying the price.

# CHAPTER 9

# ELLA

## THE BLACK FOREST

T scream Jacob's name as water floods my lungs. My body sinks beneath the pond's surface. I flail my arms. I punch and kick with all my might, but my skirts tangle in my legs, and vines slither around my wrists. Panic fills my burning lungs. What's happening?

I need to keep my wits about me if I have any hope of surviving. I search for a way to untangle myself. My heart drops. Bones litter the pond's floor. I'm floating over a rotting spinning wheel and a ditch piled with combs.

*What is this place?*

Fear spikes through me. I kick even harder.

A woman floats toward me. Her hair splays out around her like spilled ink. A crown studded with gems circles her head, and she's wearing a sheer, misty gown that looks as if it's made from sand. My lungs are burning, but I try to swim to her. Maybe she can help me. But then she smiles, revealing razor-sharp teeth that gleam like they're waiting to sink into my skin. Dread fills my chest. Her crown isn't created from gems, but eyeballs blinking at me as if warning me to flee.

*A water spirit.*

I backpedal, swimming against the vines. She reaches out a skinless hand, bony fingers beckoning. I shake my head. My lungs burn.

*I need air!*

Cold bones wrap around my wrist. There's a pull on my chest like she's digging inside me, trying to yank out my soul. Fire bursts from my lungs. It shivers through my entire body, tingling from my fingertips to toes. My vision blurs, but the fire brings oxygen and energy to fight back. I bat her away, scratching her with my nails. Except my fingers aren't fingers. They're talons, sharp and deadly as the steel tip of an arrow.

Confusion swirls through me.

The water spirit cries out. Her voice trembles through the water like endless ripples. She releases me, and I float away. I need air. I need to swim. But I'm too weak. My arms hang at my sides. My body sinks.

The world goes dark.

Hands wrap around me, arms locking around my trembling body. Then something is pushing hard on my chest.

*Pain. Fire.*

I choke. Then I'm gasping, drinking in sweet, glorious pine air.

Blinking against the blurred world, I stare up into stormy gray eyes.

"Jacob," I whisper.

Dark hair hangs in strands over his face, worry stretching that perfect mouth into a frown. He's kneeling at my side, cradling me against his warm body. His hand tenderly brushes my wet hair away from my face.

"Almost couldn't find you," he murmurs, more to himself, I think. "Thought she took you."

I sink against his firm chest. "You saved me."

"Of course." He offers a half-smile, but his jaw is tight. "Couldn't just watch you drown."

I close my eyes as he sets me on the soft grass, but the image of the woman floating in the water, dancing like mist in a lost sky, reappears. A nightmare I'm not sure I'll ever shake.

"There was a woman." I try to sit up, but I'm shivering too hard.

"Here, take this." He strips off his shirt in one smooth motion, and I can't help but notice the way his muscles flex and ripple beneath his skin. His broad shoulders taper into powerful arms, chest sculpted like something out of myth. Then, with a gentleness that contrasts his strength, he drapes the shirt around me. It smells like him, that mix of pine and ink. It's hardly decent, but I'm beyond caring.

"Thank you. The miller always warned us that the millpond is haunted by a water spirit, but I thought he was just trying to keep people away."

"That was a nixie, and she most definitely is real." His frown deepens. "Later, you can tell me about this miller's nixie, but right now, we need to get you home where your vicious birds will keep you safe."

I manage a weak smile to keep him from worrying. While he packs his sketches and charcoal, I peek at my hands. They look normal. No talons, no claws. Whatever I saw the water was merely a hallucination brought on by nearly drowning.

*You're safe now.*

◦◦◦

Over the next few days, the memory of the millpond clings to me, dark and persistent. But just as vivid is the memory of being held in Jacob's arms. I tell myself I only want to see him again to return his shirt, but he hasn't come back. So I throw myself into overseeing the harvest instead. Thankfully, with Mother's jewelry now funding our efforts, I'm able to hire ten fieldhands to work the land. It means rising before dawn and working until the sky fades to dusk, but if we can keep this pace, we might finish before the first snowfall.

This morning, I stop by the kitchen to fill a basket of fresh-baked rolls and pretzels for the harvest crew.

"You aren't going to eat all of those in one sitting, are you?" Cook grins at me as I break off half of a soft pretzel and stuff it into my mouth. The sweet and salty taste warms my insides.

"I'm not that selfish. I'm planning on sharing one or two with the fieldhands," I tease and then give her a quick hug. "Thank you for keeping us all fed. I know it can't be easy."

"Nonsense." She bats me away with floured hands, but there's a brightness to her face I haven't seen since Mother died. The two had been close. Maybe we're all healing, one sunrise at a time.

I push open the back door and step into the garden. Leaves are scattered across the path, and the roses need pruning before winter. It's been neglected since Kurt joined the others to work in the fields.

"Ella!" Jesse calls out to me, waving a letter. A thrill of hope shoots through me. *Father wrote! Finally.* She hands me a smooth, creamy envelope. "Master Grimm stopped by and asked me to give you this."

"Did he?" Even though it's not from Father, my heart flutters as I remember how Jacob carried me in his arms like I weighed nothing. "How unexpected."

Once she leaves, I settle onto the garden bench and open the letter. A sketch of a raven, wings stretched out in flight, is tucked inside along with a letter. The paper crinkles as I open it. Desperately, I read the smooth, flowing script.

*Ella,*
*I drew this sketch and thought of you.*

*Perhaps our paths will cross again. In the meantime, stay clear of the forest and the millpond. I recommend you keep feeding those feisty birds of yours. They seem to like you.*

*Ever yours,*
*Jacob Grimm*

"Ever yours," I whisper, and my heart takes off racing.

I trace the outline of the raven, gray eyes filling my thoughts. Even though I know I shouldn't, I tuck the letter into my bodice, close to my chest, and hike out to the sun-drenched fields. A little dreaming can't hurt, right?

# CHAPTER 10

## JACOB

### HONAU

"This town is seething with stories," I say as I enter the bookshop after another day scouting the area. Wilhelm turns to face me from where he's writing at the desk.

"The villagers are suspicious of us," he warns.

"Can't exactly blame them," I say, hanging up my cloak.

"Especially since there have been three reported deaths and another person missing since we've arrived. We need to be more careful."

"We don't have time to be careful." But really, all I can think about is it's been weeks since I last saw Ella.

Wilhelm stokes the fire. "A letter from the king arrived while you were out. He's responded to our report and wants us to hunt down the wolves in this area."

He tosses the letter and bag of coins from King Frederick onto the table. The king's seal glows in the firelight. I pick up the letter, skimming over our latest orders.

"Appears he's annoyed that the wolves have been eating all his game." I pour myself a cup of coffee. "Here I thought he sent us to keep the villagers safe, but all he cares about is keeping his belly full and hunting guests entertained. He's hardly any different from the wolves."

"And we're so much better?" Wilhelm shoots back. "Who are you to say who's the better man? After all, we're out there hunting down people and sending them to who knows where."

The coffee is cold. I grimace.

"There's nothing natural about the Forbidden," I remind him, "if they're even people."

"Speak for yourself, Grimm," Rumpelstiltskin grumbles as he tromps down the stairs. "With those charming skills, it's no wonder half the town despises you."

"He has a point." Wilhelm nods as the old man stomps over to his spinning wheel that we set up for him in the corner of the shop. Wilhelm went to Rumpelstiltskin's house and retrieved it to keep him occupied. Spoils the old man, if you ask me.

"What would you have me do?" I throw up my hands. "How many times are we going to have this conversation? I'm sick of it."

"My one life isn't worth the hundreds on that list."

"We're sending them to a better place where they belong, not killing them," I remind him, plopping into the chair by the fire. "We're saving our world from the plague they're bringing."

"Listen to you talk." Rumpelstiltskin chuckles. "You want magic without consequences? Cute."

"Enough of your commentary," I warn him. "This conversation is between me and my brother."

"Are you sure we're sending them to a better place?" Wilhelm's red-rimmed eyes narrow on me. "How can you know the Enchantress is telling the truth? She tricked us into this life, and you know it."

"He's got a point." Rumpelstiltskin clucks his tongue and

picks up a blade of straw. "Freebies and magic don't get along."

I clench my fists and look away. I can't win this fight. I'll always be the villain, always the murderer. Finally, in a whisper, I say, "I couldn't let you die."

"You should have. It would have been better than this." He waves his hands at the manuscript he's working on. "A curse is what you've given us. How many more times will you have to save my life? And is my life really worth theirs?"

"I'll do it for the rest of my life if I must."

"I wish you wouldn't."

His words hit hard, taking all the fight from me. Shaking with anger, Wilhelm grabs the Enchantress's quill lying on the table and tosses it into the fire. Blue flames erupt from the hearth, and then the fire returns to normal. He curses the flames and storms outside.

I stand there by the fire, listening to the wolves howling into the crisp night and the whirl of Rumpelstiltskin's spinning wheel. The crimson liquid drains through the narrow funnel of the hourglass on the mantel. The urge to find the Forbidden, hunt them down, sinks its teeth deep into my heart.

"An impossible task." I run my hands over my face.

"Quite the snare you two are in," Rumpelstiltskin agrees.

"Indeed." I plop into a chair. "Hundreds of stories we're tasked to write. There must be a way out of this life, this madness. If only we could break her curse as simply as guessing your name."

"Guessing my name wasn't easy," Rumpelstiltskin says, but then he pauses, rubbing his long beard. I spy that glint in his eyes.

"What is it?" I ask darkly. "You've got that look."

"Perhaps we make another deal?"

I glare, but who am I to be picky? "I'm listening."

"I help you look for a way out of this curse, and you let me live."

We study each other, wary as thieves. "As much as I don't trust you, it's a deal I'm willing to make."

"That makes two of us." He grins.

"I'll let you live until you've nearly reached your last breath before I finish your story." I rise up and shake his cold hand.

I return to my desk and flip my sketch to my drawing of Ella. I trace the curve of her jaw, an idea forming in my mind. When dawn arrives, I'll visit Ella von Maier's forest again. There's no doubt something lurks in its woods, and maybe this time, I might see Ella.

"Pretty thing, but heaps of trouble," Rumpelstiltskin says, suddenly appearing at my side, gazing at her portrait.

I snap my sketchbook closed. "Mind your own business."

"Ah, but your business is now my business, right?"

Grumbling under my breath, I snatch the story Wilhelm had been working on and toss it onto my desk with a thud. Then I stalk to the fire and drag the quill out with the poker. It's still cool to the touch and completely unharmed. No surprise, I think irritably.

I dip the quill into the ink and furiously scratch the words onto the parchment.

"The sooner the stories are written," I say, "the sooner the curse will be lifted."

At least, that's the lie I tell myself.

# CHAPTER 11

## ELLA

MAIER MANOR

I *did it.* The thought buzzes in my chest as I sink onto the parlor settee, a satisfied smile tugging at my lips. Sure, I made plenty of mistakes and the work was exhausting, but this afternoon I completed the servants' payments and sold the grain.

It's hard to believe that only six months ago, I'd been that girl overwhelmed by my father's abandonment and still mourning the loss of my mother. When Father returns, he'll be pleased with the progress I've made. I'm sure of it. Now that I've proven I can run this estate, he'll see I'm not a burden to marry off like Herman keeps reminding me of.

I pull out Jacob's sketch and the note he left behind, the paper soft and worn from all the times I unfolded it. My fingers drift over the lines, like touching them might bring him closer. He's been the only solid and safe part of my life. The memory of him rescuing me, arms tight around me, the steady beat of his heart beneath my cheek, clings to me even though I tell myself we don't have a future.

He's the king's hunter, traveling from village to village, while I'm the daughter of a noble, raised to marry someone of

equal station, not a man who lives by the sword and disappears with the dawn.

"Ella." Cook bustles into the parlor, round face flushed
and graying hair tied neatly into a bun. Quickly, I slip the note
and sketch into my pocket. "Came to thank you for all you've
done. The reward money will go a long way for my family. You
know, with my husband unable to work anymore, I've been
worried sick. And now? Well, we're going to be just fine, that's
what."

"You're like family." I rise and pull her into a hug. She
smells like fresh-baked bread and honey. "Family sticks
together, yes?"

"Yes, yes, but where's your fire? A lady like yourself can't
be sitting in this parlor soaking up the dreadful cold. I just
won't have it. The servants really must be spoken to."

"It's fine. Seriously. You, of all people, know how understaffed we are. Besides, most of them have been doing extra
duties between working in the fields and their normal responsibilities. I'll take care of it myself."

"That's ridiculous. I insist on fetching someone this very
instant."

She hurries off despite my objections. Sighing, I stare at
the hearth and pile of wood. I've seen it done before, but I've
never actually made a fire. Still, how hard could it be?

I roll up my sleeves, tucking in the white lace so I can get
a better range of motion, and pick up a fine-sized log, setting
it into the fireplace. If only I could rip my corset off, that
would help. I suck in a deep breath and gather up a handful of
kindling and light it. The flame sputters out within seconds.

"Must you be so uncooperative?" I ask my unsuccessful
fire.

Outside, a horse's whinny and the rumble of a carriage
draw my attention to the front window. Who's coming here
this late? Not that we ever have callers.

Unless...it's Father. My heart squeezes. It makes perfect sense. He's returning in time for Christmas. It will be our first Christmas without Mother, but we'll spend it together, sharing in our sorrow but remembering the good times.

I rush to the window as a sleek black carriage parks in front of the house. A footman hops down and opens the door with a flourish. Three fine ladies step out, one after the other. My heart sinks in disappointment. Who are these people and why are they here?

But then another person climbs out. *Father*. He tips his tall hat back, surveying the house and grounds.

Joy surges through me. He came home! I face the front door, heart racing. Quickly, I try to make myself presentable. I push a stray curl out of my face, but frown at my ruined dress. Soot streaks across the front of the blue-flowered pattern, and somehow, I've managed to get ashes on my chest. I try to wipe them off, but it only makes it worse, creating black streaks.

But who cares? Father is home! Thankfully, the footman comes to the door, opening it to allow the travelers in. A gust of late fall wind blusters into the room.

My eyes are blind to the others. All I can focus on is Father as he enters. I rush across the room, not caring that tears are spilling down my cheeks.

"You're home!" I cry, throwing my arms around him. "I was so worried about you."

The welcome arms I'd been expecting push me away. Confused, I stare up into his face. Sure, he was angry when he left, but that was because of Mother's sudden sickness and death. And I understood his need to get away from a place that always reminded him of her.

Yet as I look at him, confusion swirls through me. I stumble backward. My father is so changed, I hardly recognize him. His hair has whitened, and the full beard is gone, leaving his face cleanly shaven. Those once cheerful corn-flower eyes are now cloudy blue. Lines crisscross his face like the world has stretched him out too thin.

As if he lost everything.

"This house of yours, Karl dearest, is rather disappointing," a voice cuts through the ringing in my ears. It's a distinct city accent, sharp with a haughty tone. Bristles rub against my skin. "Do tell me this frigid shamble is not the grand home you spoke of. Also, when does the help run about like savages and embrace you?"

"Hilda." Father steps away from me and turns to the woman speaking. "Please meet my daughter, Ella. Ella, I'm pleased to introduce you to your new mother, Frau Hilda von Maier."

I drag my gaze from Father to take in the woman who apparently is now my stepmother. She's tall and thin as a willow with a sharp chin that juts out like a bird's perch. Her mahogany-colored hair is coiffured into the latest fashion, and her gown is utterly stunning for someone to travel in. A midnight blue with silver ribbons that weave around the skirt, a tight bodice interlaced with silver threads, and a collar that rises to her neck like a choker. Every detail of her appearance is sharp and deliberate.

"Well, you are far inferior to what I expected." Her thin eyebrows tilt as she gives me a good look over and obviously finds me lacking. Her eyes travel specifically to the places on my dress where the soot still clings. "I see she needs some good upbringing. It appears as if she's been playing in the fireplace."

"I knew you'd be the perfect woman to teach Ella the fineries of life," Father says with a firm nod. "She will grow to be as elegant as your two daughters."

"And your daughters now, too," Frau von Maier reminds him, beaming brightly at the two young women standing off to the side. "Ella, meet Marianne and Bertha. I hope you'll take them in as your very own sisters."

I clamp my hands behind my back, desperately trying to process everything. This must be a nightmare because what I'm seeing and hearing is utter madness.

"Good to meet you," Marianne says with a kind smile as if she understands what I'm going through. She's wearing a shimmering chestnut-colored gown with lace framing her chest and the sleeves at her elbows. Her dark, glossy brown hair is neatly tucked into a frilly bonnet with blue ribbons tied in a perfect bow beneath her chin. "I'm sure we'll be the best of sisters."

Her true sister is the exact opposite. Where Marianne was dark, Bertha was light with pale blonde hair and rose-tinted cheeks. Her soft pink gown is all frills and an abundance of lace, like a flower in full bloom.

"What's wrong with your face?" Bertha's mouth puckers into a frown as she points to my cheek. "Is that a blackened scar? Or are you just dirty?"

"It isn't polite to point out others' faults," Frau von Maier reminds her loftily. "You must model for Ella how to act and dress. Remember, always take the higher ground."

"It must be soot from the fire," I mumble, suddenly feeling self-conscious. I wipe my cheek. "I was lighting a fire to warm the sitting room before you came."

"You? Lighting a fire?" Frau von Maier titters. "Whatever for? That's for the help. Oh, mercies. Karl, please tell me you have servants, and I haven't brought my daughters into desolation."

Father glowers at me as if I just ruined his entire existence. I slink into the shadows. The trembling in my knees won't let up. The father I once knew died the same day as my mother.

I'm utterly alone in the world.

# CHAPTER 12

# JACOB

## HONAU

The first snow drifts down, clean and bright, dusting the world in white, but all I can think about is Ella. It's a problem. Especially with the life I live. After that run-in with the nixie, it became clear my curse isn't just about writing stories for the Enchantress. It's that I can never have love. Whomever I'm with will always be bait, always a victim, always a pawn.

Even knowing this, every day this week, I rode by Ella's manor to check in with the servants to see her, but each time they said she wasn't available. A blatant lie. At least I wanted to believe she'd want to see me.

I leave the stable where I've been keeping Storm. Pulling my cloak tighter around me, I make my way down the cobblestone street toward our bookshop. Wilhelm comes racing up the street toward me, panting furiously. "Jacob!"

"What's the matter?" I ask, lifting an eyebrow. Wilhelm is always panicked these days. It's starting to get under my skin. Then again, what isn't annoying me? "Did you spy another wolf?"

"No, not that."

"Someone left us a fortune so we can live in leisure while we hire out our dirty work?" I tease.

"Nope." He points behind him, still unable to breathe.

"Someone's dead then."

"It's the house...the books."

That gets my attention. I break into a run. If someone took our books, it could mean many things—none good. Not only would our work be lost, but it would also be time we can't afford to waste. My heart thunders at the thought of someone discovering what we really did. But worst of all would be us not meeting our hourglass timeline.

Wilhelm and I are the ones taking care of the family, but the Enchantress warned us she wouldn't hesitate to take a step further to hurt them. Images of Mother, Louis, Lotte, Friedrich, and Georg flash through my mind. Ever since Father died, I've been the one who keeps the family together, alive and safe. They're my responsibility.

The door hangs slightly ajar, like it's been kicked open. Snow blows in, eager to overtake our living quarters. My steps slow, and I withdraw my blade, gripping the hilt tight. The moment I step inside, my heart sinks.

Precious books litter the floor. Paper flutters about in the wind. Chairs are knocked over, some broken, the legs splintered as if someone smashed the chair in anger. The sound of a steady drip, drip, drip from the spilled inkwell dispels the silence. Wilhelm rushes in after me.

"Did they take it?" I ask, holding my breath.

"I didn't look yet. Do you think Rumpelstiltskin is okay?"

"That rascal is off either selling his gold or stealing the king's latest newborn. Whoever did this was searching for something." I kick the door shut and drag a hand through my hair. I need to get things under control. "Someone knows the truth of who we are."

"We don't know that." Wilhelm beelines to the fireplace.

He yanks the stone from the side, revealing the hiding place we set up our first night. At every place we stayed, our first task was to create a secret place for our supplies so they would never be discovered.

"It's all still here."

Panic flows off me as he pulls out the quill. The hourglass —half full—the cat and mouse story, and our latest notes on the wolves. I sag against the wall.

"Well, that's a terrible relief," a voice says, sounding like chimes on a clear winter's day. My heart drops to my toes. That's a voice I hoped to never hear again. "I was afraid your family would have to suffer for your carelessness."

I swallow the lump in my throat and slowly face the Enchantress. Snow flitters from our ceiling above her, powdering the aged floor. She's wearing a bright silver gown that twinkles as if it had been soaked in diamonds. Emerald gems wink sporadically from the material as she strolls around the room. Evergreen branches are woven into her snowy hair, and the room fills with the scent of alpine.

She's breathtaking. I'm sure she's stolen many mortals' hearts only to leave them to wallow in misery at knowing they would never be good enough for her.

"Enchantress." I bow. "A pleasure to be graced by your presence. What do we owe this gift?"

"I came to check in on my two hunters," she purrs and steps up to Wilhelm, running her icicle-sharp nails along his cheek. He stiffens.

"Don't touch him," I growl, clenching my sword tighter, ready to strike if she hurts him.

She laughs. "As if you could do anything about it."

Frustration clogs my throat. She's right.

"Why didn't you finish Rumpelstiltskin's story?"

"That was my fault," Wilhelm begins.

"And a smart choice on his part, too," I add, determined

not to let him take the fall for this. I sheath my sword, trying to act indifferent. "Once we began interviewing the old man, we realized he knew more about this area and these villagers than anyone. So we struck a deal. He got to stick around a little longer as long as he helped us. Strange things are happening in this town, especially with the wolves in this area. Plenty of opportunities for new stories for you, Your Greatness. As you know, our lives are dedicated to serving you."

The Enchantress studies me carefully, but her face is stone hard and unreadable. Cold fear pricks at my skin.

"Clever boy," she finally says, and Wilhelm lets out a breath of relief. "I see you've learned some charm. I'd say spare the fawning and flattery, but they are rather nice to hear from time to time. No one understands the sacrifices I make." She sighs and looks around, grimacing. "What a rat hole you wallow about in. Is this how you always keep your supplies?"

"No, no, absolutely not," Wilhelm chokes out. "We were both gone, and when we returned—"

"Are you saying you're careless with my supplies and the gift I've granted you?"

"He's saying our assistant hadn't cleaned up by the time we returned." I wave my hand, hoping she doesn't notice how it shakes. I snatch Wilhelm's latest work. "Let me show you our progress on the latest book."

I lay *Cat and Mouse in Partnership* on the table with a slight flourish of my hand. We planned on putting it in her library tonight. Frosty eyebrows arch as her silver eyes drift across the words. A lift of her hand and the page turns, then all the pages flip at a shocking speed.

"Impressive reading skills," I say.

And terrifying.

The book slams shut. She cocks her head, narrowing her

eyes at me. She's trying to intimidate me, but I simply stare back.

"You both had decent talent in the art of the written word when I first found you wasting your lives away." She sashays around the table, lightly touching her icy fingers across my shoulders, nails scraping along my jacket, leaving behind a trail of snow. "Still, you have surprised me. Talent is hard to come by, but work ethic, determination, dedication. Now that combination is practically unheard of. What a lucky pair you are. After finding out about your little stunt with Rumpelstiltskin, I was determined to come here and kill you both, but I've decided to let you live yet another miserable and magnificent day serving me."

"I want out of your contract," Wilhelm says. "I didn't sign up for any of this."

"Really?" She gasps, and a chill whooshes through the room. "Because you most certainly did. Don't you have a mother and siblings? What are their names again? Louis, Lotte, Friedrich, and Georg?"

Wilhelm pales and drops into a chair, but anger roars through my veins.

"How dare you bring them into this?" I slam my fist on the table.

"Sometimes one needs to do what one must," she says matter-of-factly. "This isn't my fault, you know. It's all the work of the witches. They're the ones who sent the Forbidden into your world. I'm just trying to help you humans out. Unless, of course, you'd rather me find someone else?"

"No," I growl. "We're honored that you chose us."

I hate how she's manipulating us, using our family against us and twisting her words to meet her ideas. Now I'm even more determined to find a way to stop her.

"If that's the case, then I suppose I'm pleased with your work. For now. I don't like to be disappointed."

The wind rushes around us in a flurry of snowflakes and emerald starlight, dreadfully blinding and utterly intoxicating. Then she's gone, leaving behind snowflakes and the sickly-sweet scent of magic.

I let out a long breath. "That went better than expected."

"Are you serious?" Wilhelm gapes at me. "She just threatened our family."

"Considering we're both alive, I'm going to take it as a win. Now we just have to figure out who pillaged our house."

Wilhelm stares at me, green as pea soup. Then he rushes outside, barely making it out the door before I hear him retching. I don't blame him. I sit at my desk, clenching the hourglass in my hands. This is our lifeline, the blood pumping through our veins. For my family's sake, I must succeed.

No matter the cost.

## CHAPTER 13

# ELLA

### MAIER MANOR

How is it possible that breakfast could be quieter
with five people sitting around the table than it
had ever been when I was alone? I push my spoon
through my porridge, but my stomach aches too much to
eat. A quick glance at Father, mouth drooped into a frown as
he browses through the estate books, warns me he's in no
mood for chatting.

If I were to pass him in the village, I'd hardly recognize
him. He lost so much weight, and I admit, I miss the beard.
Mother adored his shaggy beard. Even the style of his clothes
is different now. Finely cut, tailored, expensive. Something
I'm sure we can't afford now that I know the state of our
coffers.

"The food is tolerable," Stepmother says, interrupting the
silence. She sneers at her brioche roll as if it were infested
with maggots. "That is a consolation, at least. I plan on hiring
another cook as soon as possible."

"But we have a cook," I say. "She's excellent and has been
with our family for my whole life."

"Marianne and Bertha must be given the finest foods as

they are of age to marry," she carries on, completely ignoring me. "No husband wishes for a scrawny, malnourished wife."

"I don't think you should worry about Bertha, Mother." Marianne giggles as she sips the special herb tea she brought with her. "*She* would never be mistaken as scrawny."

"How dare you!" Bertha's spoon clatters to the table, her face blooming red. "At least I'm not bone thin. Men won't even notice you with—"

"Enough!" Stepmother lifts her hands. My stepsisters go silent, shoulders stiffening. Even seated, the woman radiates authority. "I wish to meet the entire manor staff. You'll ensure this happens, won't you, darling?"

Father jerks his hand up from the accounts and frowns even deeper.

"Herman!" Father bellows, slamming the book down.

I jerk in my seat as if the book physically hit me. I know exactly why he's angry. But he can't be too upset. With the harvest sold and those jewels, we got further ahead than he should've expected.

"Whatever is the matter?" Stepmother asks.

Herman rushes into the room, bowing. "You called, Master Maier?"

"What's the meaning of this?" Father rises from his seat and hefts the books, shaking them in Herman's face. "Where did the money from the crops go? There should be more than is listed here. Have you been stealing from us?"

"We were desperate." Herman swallows. "The servants demanded their pay, and when the money ran out, I used the funds from the crops that came in."

"But you paid the servants double, you idiot," Father points out. "Why would you do that?"

Herman glances over at me. The choice is mine. Play dumb and let Herman take the fall. He'd do that for me, and it'd be the smart thing to keep Father's wrath from flowing my way. But it was my choice to give the servants double wages. I stand, looking Father in the eyes.

"That was my decision," I say.

There's a momentary silence as Father turns to stare at me, confusion furrowing his brow. A strand of his perfectly combed hair falls over his eyes.

"Clarify," he growls.

"There was no money to pay the servants." I grip the side of the table. "The coffers were empty as you took everything when you left. As time passed, servants started leaving since we couldn't pay them. I sold some of Mother's jewelry, but it wasn't enough. Our only hope was to sell the land off to Dr. Wissen or pay the staff a reward for helping harvest the crops."

"Lucky servants," Marianne murmurs.

"Please, tell me there's enough money for new dresses," Bertha begs.

"Who do you think you are to pay the help double?" Stepmother demands.

"If I hadn't, there would be no help left and the grain would still be on its stalk buried under this morning's new snowfall," I shoot back. "There would be no food in that bowl if it weren't for me."

"Good heavens." Her eyes widen at my insolence. "Such a high opinion of yourself."

I stiffen and look away, trying to keep my anger in check.

"You had no right, Ella," Father says.

"Before you left," I counter, "you told me to let the estate go to hell for all you cared. Do you remember that?"

"Mercies." Frau von Maier presses her handkerchief to her mouth.

My two stepsisters look utterly stricken. Understanding floods me. Hilda married my father believing he was wealthy, for he surely dressed the part. Perhaps he told them about our magnificent manor, portraying it as a castle and painting a mirage of wealth and protection for a woman with two daughters. That would explain their disapproval upon arrival.

We were never a wealthy family, always living on meager means year after year. Father used to promise someday we'd have enough money to host huge parties and gain the king's notice, but Mother hadn't minded. She'd say we always had what we needed.

"Those were tough days after your mother's passing," Father says, rolling his shoulders. "I was not myself."

"The crop brought in enough money to pay expenses," Herman explains stiffly. "If we are careful with the funds, I believe we should be able to survive the year."

"Careful with the funds?" Stepmother says in a strangled voice. Her hand touches her throat. "Survive?"

"Are we destitute, Mother?" Bertha asks, her large blue eyes blinking in worry.

"Now I understand why you were attending the fire, Ella," Marianne says slowly. Turning to my father, she says, "Ella may be fine with servants' duties, but that's simply beneath my highborn status. How am I to find a proper match with ash-covered dresses and rough hands?"

"No one is going to be destitute," Father barks. "I will get this household back in line. And I will start with you first, Ella."

I tremble as he points a thick finger at me. I've never seen him like this, so I've no idea what he's going to do. This man with a snarling mouth and cloudy eyes can't be my father.

"Bring your mother's jewels to my study. That will be a starting point."

Tears threaten to escape. I dash out of the room, needing to be as far from those eyes as possible. It doesn't take long to pull out the case of jewels I kept in my dresser drawer, but the thought of going back downstairs and facing them all is too hard. I just can't. I pull out Mother's sapphire necklace, glistening in the pale morning light, and curl up on my bed holding it. It holds memories of a different life.

Like the nights Mother and I climbed the hazel tree's boughs. We'd sit and count the stars and make wishes on those that fell across the sky.

Shouting in the hall drags me back to my harsh reality. I clutch my own bluebird necklace Mother gave me as I peek out my door. Stepmother is standing at the threshold of Mother's room with two servants. Last night, Father and Stepmother stayed in the guestroom since Mother's room hadn't been touched since the day she died. I creep into the hallway, but remind myself that this was my house before it was hers.

"I want this room scrubbed down," she's ordering the servants. "Everything of value will be sold. All curtains, bedding, and garments must be burned."

"Yes, Frau von Maier," Jesse says.

"The news of our family's state of affairs was rather shocking." Marianne appears at my side. "We weren't prepared for this reality. Mother is on one of her rampages, and I'm so sorry, Ella, but it appears as if everything of your mother's must be destroyed or sold."

She gives me a look of pity that makes my heart twist tighter.

I push past her and storm up to Stepmother. "You can't burn my mother's dresses and sell her possessions."

"I most certainly can," she replies, lifting her eyebrows in shock at my forwardness. "Who knows what kind of sickness she had? We can't risk contamination. As for her possessions, it's the least we can do after you nearly sank this household into ruin. In fact, how do we know you aren't sick, too?"

It takes a moment to register her threat and the dangerous ground I'm on. Clenching my fists, I watch as Jesse sets Mother's jewelry box into the basket along with a portrait of her.

"My mother died a year ago." I march to the basket and begin picking out items I want to keep. "If I had her sickness, I'd be dead by now."

"What do you think you're doing?" Stepmother's gaze cuts to me as if she's measuring me and I come up too short. "Everything must be sold, not given to you. Listen, young lady. You don't want to cross my path. I can make your life miserable."

Her gaze should've sent dread through me, but she doesn't know I already lost everything when I buried my mother.

I lift my chin, tucking the painting under one arm and pressing the jewelry box and a dress against my chest. "I'm keeping these."

"I think not." Stepmother's laugh grates my nerves like fingernails scraping stone.

I set my jaw and bolt from the room. The servants dart out of my way, mice fleeing a cat fight. When I reach the door, Marianne hovers by the entrance, wringing her hands. I try to brush past her, but she grabs my arm and pulls me into her room.

"Good for you, Ella," Marianne says. "I can only imagine how hard this must be for you. Losing your mother must have been devastating. I'm terribly sorry you have to go through all of this."

"It has been hard." I sigh and rest the painting against the wall. "Sometimes it feels like it was just yesterday."

"But now you have us." Marianne hugs me. "I know Bertha and I fight terribly, and Mother is stern, but we're your family now. You don't have to be alone anymore."

My heart tightens, and despite my best efforts, tears push their way down my cheeks. These past months have been lonely. Sure, I kept busy with the harvest and spent the evenings with the servants rather than eating alone in the dining hall, but it's not the same as having a family.

"If we sell your mother's items, it'll save us from destitution," Marianne continues. "It's all been so stressful. Mother and your father were just a little shocked, that's all. If you could do this for us, it'd calm everyone down."

She's right. I sold off one of my mother's necklaces for the very same reason. "Perhaps the jewelry box," I offer. "I suppose it's not that important."

"But the painting and dress you should keep." Marianne squeezes my hand. "It'll be the perfect way to always remember your mother."

"Yes, the perfect way." I pass the box to Marianne.

She smiles warmly and hugs me again. "Poor little Cinderella. You don't mind me calling you that, do you? I knew when I first saw you covered with ashes that we'd get along. I think it was destiny that brought us together."

A headache starts pounding. This is all too much. "I didn't sleep well last night," I say dimly, pressing my fingers to my temples. "I think I'll take this to my room and lie down for a little while."

"Do you need me to send up tea for you? I have the perfect concoction for headaches."

"No, thanks. I'll be fine."

When I enter my room, I place the painting against the wall. Leaves flutter off my shoulder. Strange. I don't know where they came from, but they remind me of Mother and our fall picnics under the hazel tree, leaves raining down on us. We'd gather them up and make wreaths with them.

"Everything's so wrong," I whisper to Mother in her portrait. "I don't know how to fix it."

My eyes swivel to her jewels on my bed. I planned on selling them before. What's stopping me now? Marianne's right. We are family, and with time, we can learn to get to know one another. Maybe even become friends. Besides, I still have the bird necklace she gave me when I turned sixteen.

I snatch the jewels and head to Father's study. Standing before his desk, my hands tremble. A part of me desperately wants to give him these jewels, and yet another part screams to never let go of what is left of my mother.

I place them on the desk.

"I'm glad you made the right choice to bring those to me." Father's voice stings cold and heartless against my chest. "You made many poor decisions while I was gone, but that's to be expected, as you have your mother's blood running through you."

"My mother's blood?" What's that supposed to mean?

"Ella, your mother was evil. Hilda suspects your mother was a witch of some sort, which is why I was so distraught after her death. It took time for me to be released from her spell."

"A witch?" I gape at him, horrified. And then fury rushes through me. "You're wrong. If anyone is a witch, it's that woman you married."

"Now, Ella. Be wary of the witch-blood that may have been passed on to you. We must watch you carefully."

The room tilts slightly as the memory of my hands in the millpond swims through my mind. The heat from the fireplace curls its talons around my neck, choking me. Could he be right?

No. What he's saying is impossible and a complete lie. Still, my world feels upside down. I backpedal toward the door. Father calls out final words of great wisdom, or perhaps a warning.

I just run.

# CHAPTER 14

## JACOB

### HONAU

T lift my head off my desk. I must have fallen asleep last night writing. The dawn is too bright and cheerful for my dark thoughts. My back aches as I shamble to the window and peer outside. The sun is spilling a lemon-yellow glow across the snow-covered cobblestones. Villagers are already out and about running their errands. I mentally kick myself for wasting precious hours sleeping.

"Thought you were so eager to get out and slay those dragons," Wilhelm says, coming downstairs.

"Couldn't sleep with Rumpelstiltskin's snoring. So loud, the menace likely woke the dead."

I splash my face with icy water and push aside the cabinet, revealing our weapon collection filling the wall. I attach my sword to my waist, then reach for the ax, but Wilhelm snatches it from me.

"What are you doing?" I ask. "It's one thing for you to disagree with me, but quite another to stop me."

"I'm helping you, brother. After our encounter with the Enchantress last night, I've decided we need to be on the same side. Besides, I can't let you get ripped to shreds by bloodthirsty wolves."

"You should stay here. Maybe do some research on those witches she talked about."

"That makes me feel needed." He rolls his eyes, but relinquishes the ax, picking out a bow and quiver full of arrows instead. "While you were snoring the morning away, I did some reconnaissance work."

"Do you even know how to do such things?" I tease.

"Hilarious." He checks to make sure the steel tips are on the arrows. "I've learned a lot about these wolves of yours."

"Now they're my wolves?"

"Some townsfolk say they're men in daylight and wolves by moon. Others talk about how they hunt humans and eat them whole. Sounds like the king called upon the right brothers to set things right."

I stop my preparations to stare at him. He really wants to help. This changes everything.

"Indeed, the king did." I grin, slapping my hand on his shoulder. "With so many potential hits in one place, we might complete our list before the year is done."

"When did my older brother become such an optimist?"

"Optimist? Hardly." I snort and pick up the hourglass. A new ember name glows on the top: Little Red Cap. That usual panic starts pumping through my veins. "Looks like a new story is ready for us."

The blood trickles with its usual slow drizzle, but I know better than to be lulled into thinking we have plenty of time.

"Red Cap, huh?" Wilhelm rubs his ear. "The word little makes it sound like a kid."

After asking around town for anyone with the name or nickname of Red Cap and coming up empty-handed, we decide to investigate the wolves while it's still daylight.

Snowflakes drift from silver-threaded clouds as we ride

out of the village toward Ella's manor. We debate over the villagers' rumors of the wolves.

"I can see the stalking of clueless wanderers," I admit to Wilhelm, "but swallowing a man whole and transforming into wolf? Sounds a bit far-fetched."

"And Rumpelstiltskin spinning straw to gold and a goose laying gold eggs doesn't?"

"Fine, you win," I grumble.

The snow-laden trees give way, revealing the Maier Manor with its white stone walls and lone turret. It reminds me of our childhood home in Steinau before Father died.

"So there's nothing special about this Maier family?" Wilhelm asks as we plod down the manor's main drive. "The place has an odd feel to it."

"You and your premonitions," I scoff, studying the place closer. A few of the shutters hang loose, and dormant ivy covers the front of the house. "The manor needs repair, but that doesn't mean it belongs to the Forbidden. It must be the birds you sense. See them in the distance by that massive hazel tree? There's something strange about them for sure."

"Once we deal with the wolves, I want to investigate this place next."

I'm not going to argue with him about spending time at Ella's house. The cold air bites at my lungs, and snow clings to the land, creating the illusion we are riding through silver fields. The birds swoop above, back and forth, cawing as if warning us.

"You're right," Wilhelm says. "These birds seem smarter than what makes me comfortable."

The wind shifts, rustling the leaves. And that's when I hear it. Soft feet padding on the dirt path up ahead. My heart thumps against my chest, and I look over at my brother. He nods in understanding.

Ever since we began working for the Enchantress, it's as if

our senses had been awakened. My sight is sharper, especially in tune with the Forbidden. I can run faster and fight better than anyone. We aren't immortal, but we're nearly impossible to kill.

At the forest's edge, we dismount and tie up the horses. Then we creep into the thick, gnarled trees, senses alert. A dark form swishes through the bushes, merely a rock's throw. I pause, but it moves on, so we follow. A prickling sensation scurries along my skin. Something is different about this hunt. Almost like we are, in fact, the ones being hunted.

I don't like it.

A low rumbling growl shatters the heavy silence. A beast bounds out of the thick bramble, claws outstretched, and green drool flinging through the air. Its fur spikes up sharper than knives. Red eyes looking hungry.

This isn't a wolf. This is something straight from hell.

## CHAPTER 15

# ELLA

### MAIER MANOR

I race out of the house, needing the cool air to calm my anger. The cold nips at my cheeks and nose. I'm glad I grabbed my cloak hanging on the kitchen hook before I left. I tuck it tighter around me as I march to the barn, needing to distract myself from my new stepmother. That's when I spot the Grimm brothers entering the forest on foot.

A wild, rebellious urge to talk to Jacob again swirls through me. Sure, it's hardly proper for a young lady to be visiting men in the forest, but if we crossed paths by chance, that wouldn't be wrong, right?

I grab a pitchfork from the barn—because you can never be too prepared—and yank my fur-lined hood over my head. The moment I enter the forest, a howl curdles the air along with shouting, growling, and snarling. A tingling scuttles through my body, warning me to run.

Jacob rescued me from the nixie. I need to help him if he's in trouble. I gather my skirts and take off toward the sounds.

More calls, human this time, sound along with a shout. Fear pierces my skin like thorns. My palms are slick against the pitchfork as I weave around the thicket of brambles and branches. When I finally stumble into a grove, my heart seizes in shock.

A giant wolf paws at the snow inches from Jacob's feet, where he lies, his blood staining the snow crimson. I'm not sure wolf would be the correct word. It boasts long claws poking out from massive paws. The body is three times larger than a man, and its coal-black fur consumes the light. The red eyes are bright as hot coals. Its mouth opens in a roar that trembles the earth and reveals a row of spiked teeth. Arrows litter the ground at the creature's feet. Any second now, this beast is going to pounce and kill Jacob. Jacob's brother stands off to the side, face pale as winter. His arms shake as he aims another arrow with a focus so single-minded he hasn't noticed me.

It's a ridiculously stupid move on my part, but I leap into the thick of the situation, holding out my pitchfork like I can actually face this giant-sized wolf. I plant myself between Jacob and the creature.

"What are you doing, Ella?" Jacob yells. "Get out of here!"

"Just repaying the favor," I explain, crouching in preparation for an attack. The wolf looks at me with calculating, crimson eyes. "Shoo!" I shove my pitchfork at the beast.

The creature leaps forward. I jump backward, but not before the beast tears off a portion of my cloak. Jacob grunts behind me. He's trying to get up.

"You're in my way!" the brother calls from behind. "I had the perfect shot."

"Just like all these others." I nod at the ground peppered with unsuccessful arrows.

The monster bounds at me again. I plant my feet and point my weapon at it. Its massive body smashes me to the ground, and I scream. The fork's spikes plunge into the creature. Blood sprays everywhere. My dress. My face. Paws pin me to the ground. Hot, reeking breath grazes my cheek. The fangs are inches from sinking into my skin like it can't decide if it should eat me whole or just rip me to shreds.

My body shudders.

But then the monster is lifted off me and flung through the air as if it weighs nothing.

*Jacob.*

His dark hair is tousled, and his chest rises and falls beneath a sweat-damp shirt that clings to every carved line of muscle. His sleeves are rolled to his elbows, and his forearms flex as he draws out a blade from his belt.

He's beautiful. He's lethal.

The beast growls and launches again. Jacob doesn't even flinch. With reflexes startling fast—too fast to be human—he meets the beast. The two tumble across the snow, the wolf swiping with its sharp claws while Jacob wields a bloody knife, stabbing into the thick coat of the wolf repeatedly.

"Jacob," I cry. "Be careful!"

But then it's over. The strange wolf is deathly still on the cold earth. Jacob rises to his feet. The wind shudders once again through the barren trees. Sweat drips from Jacob's brow, and between his wild hair and set jaw, it's as if he, too, is a dangerous creature. I crawl backward on the ground, horror keeping my body trembling.

Jacob turns to me, eyes like a winter storm and fire swirling together. "You all right?" he asks, his voice low and rough.

My lips part, but no words come. Who is this man? I take in his broad shoulders and the sharp blade clenched in his hand. Blood still drips from the tip. How can I speak after that? Not to mention the way he's looking at me. Wild and reckless as if I'm the one who might devour *him.*

"Ella," the brother says with a worried look as he pulls out a long rope from his pack. Jacob must have told him about me. "It's too dangerous here. You need to leave immediately."

I swallow my fear. "I was just trying to help."

He starts to tie up the wolf's legs until they're firmly bound, while Jacob comes to my side.

"Are you all right?" he asks again, softer this time. "What you did back there was very brave, but my brother's right." He picks up my pitchfork, handing it to me. "You should go back to the safety of your land and those wretched birds of yours. The scent of blood tends to call to evil."

"That's no ordinary wolf," I whisper. "The rumors in the village are true, aren't they?"

The brothers look at each other like they're communicating without words. Finally, the brother rolls his eyes and says, "Fine. You won't see reason anyway."

Victory flickers across Jacob's face, and he helps me to my feet. "This is my brother, Wilhelm. He loves to tell me no, but I'm older, so I get the final say."

"It's an honor to meet you," Wilhelm says, offering a quick bow.

"To answer your question," Jacob continues. "Yes. This wolf has magic in its blood. Which means these creatures lurking in the woods are very dangerous. Are you sure you want to stay?"

"It's happening!" Wilhelm exclaims. "Get her out of here."

"Last chance to run," Jacob warns me with a devilish grin.

"I'm staying."

Horror fills me as something unfolds before us, so impossible, it shouldn't exist outside of nightmares.

## CHAPTER 16

# JACOB

### THE BLACK FOREST

I tried to warn her. Confound it, Ella shouldn't be here in the first place. It's my fault for not sending her away, but selfishly, I wanted her to stay. She clings to me, and her body shakes in my arms. It's wrong and despicable, but all I notice are the soft folds of her body and how perfect she feels against my chest.

"Don't just stand there!" Wilhelm yells at me. "Get your sword!"

The massive beast's dark fur is transforming into the smooth skin of a lady with long red hair. It's shocking, even for me.

Could this be Red Cap?

"She shouldn't be seeing this." Wilhelm waves his hands about with frustration.

"She has every right to know what's happening in her forest," I say.

Dirt smears Ella's cheek, and despite the wolf's blood on her, she smells of lavender and dreams of what could've been. Her lips are trembling. I'm tempted to brush my finger over them, tell her I'll protect her, but these thoughts will only lead to trouble. Besides, for Wilhelm's sake, I need to pull myself together and focus. We've found our next story to write, and I've a brother to keep alive.

"What's happening?" Ella demands. "How is this possible?"

"It appears as if the wolves in this forest are shapeshifters," I explain, reluctantly releasing her. "Half-human, half-wolf."

"Werewolves," Wilhelm says bitterly, pulling out a leather-bound book and quill from his satchel.

Ella gasps. "If I didn't see it with my own eyes, I'd never believe you."

The wolf-woman's eyes flutter open. I press the tip of my sword to her neck, right where her mark as a Forbidden is located. "Don't even consider moving," I order. "You'll answer our questions quickly and honestly, or I'll happily kill you."

Wilhelm glares at me. "Can we for once do this without threats?" he asks, clearly not happy with my tactics. I'm sure when we get back home, he'll give me an earful.

"Wait!" Ella shouts, coming to the woman's other side. "I know her."

"You do?" I ask, startled.

"This is Scarlet, the baker's daughter." She crouches beside the woman.

"I wouldn't get so close," I warn, my muscles tensing. If this Forbidden so much as puts a scratch on Ella, by all that's holy, the creature will pay.

"Ella," Scarlet whispers. "I'm sorry. I didn't want to hurt you. The wolf inside me made me do it."

"Don't believe it," I warn.

Ella scowls at me. "It's not an *it*. This is Scarlet, my friend. Is it safe to touch her?"

"No," both Wilhelm and I say.

Of course, she ignores us. Promptly, she rips her own dress

into strips and, with shaky hands, tries to stop the blood. "You're treating her like she's a monster."

"Maybe because she is," I point out. I don't like where this is going.

"Please." Scarlet's eyes are cloudy. "Don't tell anyone about this or about who I am."

"How did this happen to you?" Ella presses. "Did someone make you this way?"

I glance at Wilhelm. He gives me a nod and then continues writing as fast as he can. *Good*. Maybe Ella can uncover some of Scarlet's story for us.

"You should never have helped these men," Scarlet scolds. "They're the enemy."

"Says the person who tried to kill you," I half-growl.

"By working with them," Scarlet continues, "you have angered the pack."

"Angered the pack?" Ella's voice hitches. "There are others like you? Are they the ones responsible for your mother's death?"

"How do you know it wasn't these two?" Scarlet's eyes drift to me. A sinister smile twists on her lips.

Damn it, this is going foul fast. Ella leaps to her feet and drags me off to the side. I allow her, but keep a close eye on the monster.

"Is that true?" Ella demands. "Did you kill her mother?"

"What do you think?" I snap because even though I'm not the one who did the deed, I'm capable of it. And given the opportunity, I would do it. "You saw the battle. I was defending myself. She was attacking me, and, if you remember, she'd have ripped you to pieces if given the chance."

Tears spring to Ella's eyes. I hate that I'm the one to cause it.

"You're right," Ella whispers as if she doesn't want to admit the truth.

I sigh. "I know she was your friend, but if we don't find out what's going on, more villagers are going to die. Will you help us get her story so we can stop this madness?"

She swallows hard, searching my face. Finally, she nods, face white as ash. "Yes. I'll help you."

"Thank you." I lead her back to Scarlet's side. "Why don't you ask her some questions?"

Slowly and carefully, Ella quizzes Scarlet over locations and people until she gets Scarlet to admit that when her mother refused to join the pack, they killed her. They were going to kill Scarlet next, but she decided to join them rather than die. I stand by, ready to strike the creature while Wilhelm continues to write as fast as possible. It's amazing how easily Ella draws information out of the werewolf. Perhaps my tactics are all wrong, or maybe it's just Ella and her gentle spirit.

"But I didn't mean to hurt you," Scarlet says. I don't like how much stronger her voice is. "You must believe me. Everything we do is for a greater purpose."

"Who's your leader?" I demand.

"I'll tell you nothing." Scarlet spits on my spurred boots. My glare deepens. "We've been watching you."

My heart sinks. They were the ones who ransacked our house. How much do they know?

"This greater purpose," Ella continues smoothly. "It sounds wonderful. Can you tell me about it?"

"Our lives are more than just existing," Scarlet says eagerly, sitting up. I grip my sword steady, ready to pierce her skin. "We have a greater calling, and even though Mother died, her body was taken to the sacred grounds. Just like yours will be."

In a rushing tide, her skin ripples. Bristles of fur break through. Her face contorts and her body twists, bones snapping and reshaping. Claws stretch out toward Ella as if to cut her.

I drive my sword straight through her heart. Wilhelm leaps to his feet and tosses me the ax. With a quick slice, I cut off the beast's head.

Ella's screams echo through the forest.

And then there's silence. The three of us stare in shock as the beast returns to Scarlet's body—beheaded.

I'm not sure I'll ever get used to that.

"That went sour fast," I say.

"No kidding." Wilhelm lets out a long breath and wipes the sweat from his brow.

"She's gone," Ella says in a trembling voice. "She was evil and horrible, and yet I can only hope God took her soul. Is that wrong?"

"No, not at all," I say. *Because you still see the good in the world.*

I unfurl the blanket I keep in my pack in case a Forbidden dies in front of humans and cover Scarlet. Now I just need to get Ella away so Wilhelm can write "the end," and she doesn't discover who we really are. I hate hiding the truth from her, but if she knew what we actually did, I doubt she'd be so ready to help us.

"I'll escort Ella back home while you deal with the body," I tell Wilhelm, who promptly lifts his eyebrows.

"Or I could take her back while *you* deal with the body." Wilhelm grins.

Ella shudders and wraps her arms around herself. "I don't need any escorting, thank you." She grimaces at her torn and bloodied skirts, and her face pales even more. "Both of you have injuries that need tending to, and I can't allow you to return to the village bleeding and soiled. Stop by my house, and I'll make sure your needs are met."

I walk her to her property line, intending on declining her invitation, but the words just don't seem to come out before she stiffly marches across the field to her home. I watch her go, amazed at her inner strength.

"Did you forget our rule about getting too close to the locals?" Wilhelm asks me when I return.

He's right. It's how we got imprisoned after getting too friendly with a blacksmith. If Wilhelm hadn't snagged the key, we would've been executed.

I stomp about as I gather the arrows and yank off the blanket. "We wouldn't have gotten Little Cap's story so quickly if it hadn't been for Ella."

"She did seem to know exactly the right things to say." Wilhelm scribbles the last of the words for the werewolf story. The words spiral up into an inky funnel, swirling around and then sucking up the body into its blackness before returning to the book. He shuts the tomes, and color returns to Wilhelm's face.

"She's bewitched you." Wilhelm snatches up the blanket and straps his bow to his back. "You sure she's not one of them?"

"You're implying she's a witch? Or one of these werewolves? That's ridiculous, and you know that. Besides, she doesn't bear the mark on her neck."

"Maybe hers is hidden in a place we can't see. Have you thought of that?"

"I am now." I grin.

He huffs and storms down the path.

## CHAPTER 17

# ELLA

### MAIER MANOR

My body won't stop trembling as I trek home. What had I been thinking, going out into the forest alone like that? It was foolish. Hunters, Jacob said they were. But they're so much more than that. I just hope no one saw me with them. I can't imagine what Father would do if he knew. Scandalous, the whole business.

My flesh burns like it's on fire, a thousand prickles stabbing, trying to poke through my skin as I enter the house. The whole experience is enough to make me want to crawl into bed and try to forget every moment of it. I slip inside the manor through the kitchen door and pour myself a cup of cool water.

"You all right, Ella?" Cook asks, not once slowing down as she kneads her dough. She has been working twice as hard ever since Stepmother threatened to find a replacement.

"I don't know," I say, sinking onto the wooden bench at the table.

"You look flushed...and what's all over your dress?"

Slowly, I set down the mug, the cool water clearing my thoughts. I forgot about the beast's blood—Scarlet's blood—

staining my clothes. My pulse starts pounding all over again. What do I say? No one will believe me. I hardly believe it myself. What if the servants think I killed someone?

"I fell on a rocky section by the forest edge," I lie, rising from my seat just as the head housekeeper, Gertrud, enters, giving me a raised-eyebrow scowl. "Scratched myself up dreadfully. Think I'll clean up. There are some men who should come by soon. Gertrud, if they call, make sure they're comfortable with refreshments, and let me know the instant that they arrive."

"As you wish," she says. "I wouldn't let the mistress see you in such a state, though."

I duck out of the kitchens and race to my room, closing the door behind me. I've always been the perfect daughter, followed the rules, and never had a reason to lie or hide the truth. Mother's last request to me was to promise to be good, and that has never been hard until now. Everything is changing and changing fast.

I yank off my dress and toss it into the fire. I don't need anyone questioning where the blood came from. Especially my new stepmother.

I pour fresh water into a basin on my dresser and wash myself down. Then I quickly brush out my long hair and slip on a new dress, robin's-egg blue with gold ribbon edging along the sides. I stare at myself in the reflection glass. Pale skin and blue eyes stare back at me.

I look like I saw a ghost.

Except what I saw is far worse.

A flash of fingers stretching out to talons shudders through my mind. Scarlet transforming back into the beast. Jacob slicing off its head.

Those brothers are hiding something. But what?

As I head downstairs, a million questions chase me, begging for answers. I gather bandages and ointments from the kitchen pantry and ask Cook to prep refreshments for my visitors. I'm hurrying down the corridor when I find Marianne coming out of Father's study.

"Where are you going, looking so fine?" she asks. "Expecting someone?"

I bite my lip. What was she speaking to Father about? A knock on the front door interrupts us.

"Well, well." Marianne grins, brown eyes glittering. "You are waiting for a visitor. Who is it?"

I ignore her and hurry to the front parlor. I barely sit down when the footman ushers the two brothers inside.

My eyes are drawn to Jacob. There's a rugged dangerousness to him. Blood stains his shirt and trousers. Strands of his hair hang over parts of his face, and those eyes, they're piercing blue, sharp as the tip of his sword when he focuses on me. My chest stumbles for a heartbeat, screaming to tell him to leave and shut him out of my life forever. But the stronger part craves to be near him. I stand and curtsy politely as if we hadn't been out in the woods slaughtering beasts that should never exist.

"Greetings," I say in my most dignified voice.

The brothers bow as Marianne comes in to join us. She smiles sweetly, curtsying.

Once introductions are made, I explain the situation. "My father recently returned with the great news that he has wed, and through it, I've gained two sisters."

"Congratulations are in order, I see," Wilhelm says, while Jacob merely scowls at Marianne, looking anything but congratulatory.

"It's a pleasure to meet you both," Marianne says.

"If you will excuse us," I tell my stepsister. "We have some business to discuss privately."

She lifts her eyebrows at my audacity to be unchaperoned with two men, but then a mischievous smile breaks across her lips. "Don't be too naughty," she whispers into my ear and squeezes my hand before leaving.

I want to call her back and explain this is purely a non-romantic meeting, but I can't tell her the true purpose of why they're here. Wilhelm settles into the chair opposite me while Jacob wanders, studying the paintings and bookshelves. Two servants slip into the room, depositing slices of cake and coffee.

"I need you to be honest with me," I begin, forgoing formalities. After what we went through in the forest, protocol seems trivial. "What exactly do you do?"

Wilhelm starts heaping his plate with food. "We're commissioned by the king to make your village safe again."

"Jacob mentioned that," I say darkly. "But something tells me that's only part of the story."

Jacob snorts in agreement. He picks a book off the shelf, flipping through the pages. I expect him to be rough with it, but he handles it with the touch of one who's in love with the written word.

"You have quite the collection here," he says. "Someone in your family reads?"

"Those were my mother's and now mine." I swallow, hating that I'm speaking about her in the past tense. It sounds so final, so real. "My parents met at a festival. She was a performer in the show. The two fell in love. They always said they were destined to meet."

At the word destined, Jacob's head snaps up. "Do you believe in destiny? In true love?"

My face burns at such a personal question. How do I respond to that? Earlier today, Father accused Mother of being a witch. Where is that love now?

"I want to believe in it. Even if it was only for a short time. And you?"

"Love isn't part of my fate." Jacob gently closes the book

like he's shutting away a dream. "Our father passed a while back. Maybe there was love in their life, but he left my mother penniless with Wilhelm and me to take care of the family. It's a sorry situation. One I don't plan on repeating."

"How dreadful. I suppose I understand a little of what you're both going through."

Jacob nods, but moves to stare out the window.

"Well, this is getting uncomfortable." Wilhelm clears his throat. "Let's get back to the matter at hand."

"Excellent idea," Jacob says, coming round to sit next to his brother. "You have our gratitude for your help in the forest. We have a list of creatures we're trying to seek out that we believe are endangering your village. If there was a time when we needed your assistance again, would you be willing?"

I stare between the two. Ever since Father returned home with a new family, I've felt like I don't have a place anymore. But these brothers are offering me something that sparks life in my chest again. "If it means I can save people, I want to help."

"Wonderful." Wilhelm grabs a slice of cake and devours it. He snatches up another, grinning. "For the road."

"Of course." I laugh, but then dare ask the question that's been haunting me ever since the millpond. "Do you think this transformation process of human to wolf is contagious?"

"Absolutely not," Wilhelm says. "We believe people are born with it."

I let out a long breath. "That's a relief."

The two exit into the hallway, tossing on their cloaks. On a whim, I grab the book Jacob had been looking at and hurry after him.

"Jacob." I touch his shoulder, trying not to notice the firm muscles rippling beneath his coat. "Would you like to borrow it? It's one of my favorites, and well, you seemed interested."

"It would be an honor." He takes the book and then wraps his fingers around my hand in a reverence that has me gasping. His lips brush my skin, lingering longer than is appropriate. A shiver rolls through me, slow and sweet. And I swear, for a heartbeat, it's like the world is holding its breath with me.

Wilhelm clears his throat, shattering the silence. "Ready to go?" he asks briskly.

Jacob nods, releasing my hand, but his gaze never wavers from mine. With a bow, the two leave. Breathlessly, I peek out the window, watching them slip onto their horses and ride down the lane. Soft white snowflakes flutter from the gray sky.

"Ella, who was that?" my stepmother's voice booms from behind me. Fear clenches my chest. Slowly, I face her, swallowing hard. "Did we have callers?"

"Just business I needed to attend to."

"Business? What sort of business?"

"Hunting. I've been allowing the Grimm brothers to hunt on our lands in exchange for money. Herman collected it."

"How utterly shocking. A woman isn't to conduct business."

Marianne slips in beside her mother. "I'm sure Cinderella didn't realize what she was doing. After all, she's been without a mother to guide her."

"True," Stepmother says, softening. "But from now on, I insist that your father take care of all business with those men. Your meddling has caused us enough problems."

I want to scream at her, but manage, "Of course, Frau von Maier."

"Call me Stepmother." She lifts her chin, eyes running over my figure in a calculating gaze. "Your father said you're twenty years old." At my nod, she continues, "The perfect time to marry, and not to poor commoners like those two men. You're pretty enough to do better. Perhaps pretty enough to bring in a nice dowry."

"Marry? But—"

"Don't vex yourself over trivialities," she interrupts. "I'll look into the matter. We can't wait too long. You're practically a spinster. Now go away. I don't want to see you until dinner."

# CHAPTER 18

## JACOB

### HOHENZOLLERN CASTLE

Jacob Grimm,

Your presence is needed. I sent my son to ask Prince Hermann for his daughter's hand in marriage, but I received a letter from Prince Hermann telling me his daughter chanced upon a frog at her pond. She claims it is my son. I have no idea what this folly is about so I leave you this task.

Find my foolhardy son. Tell him to stop this nonsense and agree to marry this girl, or suffer the consequences.

~ King Frederick of Württemberg

The ride to the castle is grueling for Wilhelm, Rumpelstiltskin, and me, and my muscles ache, so it's a relief when my eyes finally land on Prince Hermann's home. Perched high on a mountain peak, Hohenzollern Castle rises before us with its towers and battlements cloaked in a swirl of mist. I'm eager to get the task finished, edgy from being taken from our hunt for the leader of these werewolves.

The only consolation is that I'm hoping to spend some time in the prince's library. It's supposed to be the most prestigious in the land. Perhaps it may tell us something about our Enchantress. I clutch the letter from King Frederick, requesting our services, as I dismount my horse.

The palace gates slam behind us as Wilhelm, Rumpelstiltskin, and I step inside a corridor with a ribbed arched ceiling that soars above us. Torches are set into the walls, flickering like dragons' tongues on the flagstone floor. The air is cool, heavy with a musty scent.

"Being dragged along is what I am," Rumpelstiltskin grumbles. "Hate this place. Reeks is what. Or maybe it's just our escort."

I fight to keep my lips pressed together as the servant escorting us halts to glare at Rumpelstiltskin, who smiles toothlessly back at him.

"What do you make of this frog business?" Wilhelm whispers in my ear. "Do you think the prince really turned into a frog?"

"Hardly," I say. "The princess is probably being difficult. I heard she's immensely spoiled. As for Prince William, he's probably in the woods with his dogs having an entertaining hunt."

A lingering chill clings to the stone hallways, even with the tapestries and banners. The corridor stretches ahead, and its checkered floors echo our every step. Antlers line the walls, each mounted above a small plaque like silent trophies.

"Your prince is quite the hunter," I point out to the servant.

"Prince Hermann is a great hunter, well-feared for his fighting prowess," the servant agrees before a set of doors. "The prince waits for you in his throne room."

I've no idea what to expect from this prince. My only hope is that we can find Prince William quickly and get back to Honau by nightfall.

A pair of waiting guards opens the entrance. I draw back my shoulders and set my jaw. *You can do this*, I tell myself, and then march into the room, head held high as if I'm royalty myself.

Prince Hermann lounges in a large wooden chair. His white wig tilts askew on his head, and the rolled curls that are supposed to be tucked under look frayed. His tired eyes shoot us a fleeting glance, and he gives an indifferent sniff with his long nose, which seems to pull his whole face into a frown. His skin is pallid like he rarely sees the light of day.

"The great hunter, eh?" Rumpelstiltskin mutters. "More like a sniveling rodent."

I crack a smile, but say, "Not so loud."

Beside him must be his wife. She straightens in her chair as we enter. Her wig is elaborate, and her face is powdered snow-white to match. After one glance at us, she returns directly to her embroidery, clearly unimpressed.

"King Frederick said you could be of assistance to me," Prince Hermann drawls, barely bothering to utter the words.

"We are, my lord." I bow deeply.

"The issue concerns my daughter, Princess Maria. Completely distraught. This frog won't leave her side, you see." He takes a slug of his wine. "Says it demands to sleep and eat with her. Apparently, the frog told her he's Prince William of Württemberg. Pure silliness, don't you think?"

"Highly unusual," I say. And alarming. This all is starting to sound too much like the Forbidden. "May I have a word with your daughter?"

"Guards!" Prince Hermann waves his hand as if the effort is exhausting. "Bring in my daughter."

We wait in silence, shifting from foot to foot. Finally, the doors swing open, and a young woman who must be Princess Maria strolls into the room. A portion of her long blonde hair is plaited around the top of her head like a crown, while the rest cascades down her back. Her dress is of the finest purple silk with gold printed leaves scattered on it and a short train that slinks across the floor behind her as she strolls into the hall.

"Pretty as a petal, sharp as a thorn, I'll wager." Rumpelstiltskin's eyes pop from their sockets. "Still, perhaps this trip wasn't such a bad idea after all."

I kick him for his comment, even if he's right. Everything about her is perfect except those red lips dipped into a pout and the disdain in her eyes ruin her complexion. Held between two fingers, she dangles a frog.

"Saints help us," Wilhelm whispers.

"This is it." She marches to me. "Meet Prince William of Württemberg. Quite the catch." Then she giggles as if her words were immensely entertaining.

"The prince of Württemberg, my boots." Rumpelstiltskin spits on the floor. "More like prince of the pond."

I clear my throat, studying the wiggling frog. "Please set him on the table for inspection."

"With pleasure." She drops him onto the table and then demands a handkerchief from her lady-in-waiting. "Tell King Frederick, I refuse to marry a frog. It's simply repulsive."

The frog sits still on its haunches, staring at us with beady eyes.

"I don't understand," Wilhelm says. "Why do you think this frog is Prince William?"

"I was playing with my ball by the pond," she explains. "It slipped from my fingers, and then this frog appeared, offering to retrieve it if I gave him a kiss."

"And you agreed?" It's hard to keep my lips from twitching.

"I needed my ball!" Her brown eyes widen like she's stated the obvious. "But there's no way that I, a princess, could ever kiss such a slimy thing. Besides, how was I to know it would follow me here and make such demands? Take it away at once so I can sleep without it trying to crawl into my bed again. Horrid creature."

Wilhelm picks up the frog, which makes no move to resist. He begins inspecting it and then holds it in front of me, pointing to the tiny mark, showing it's a Forbidden. Blight it all, I think sourly.

"It's as green and slimy as a frog will ever be," Wilhelm acknowledges, clucking his tongue. "Definitely not prince material."

Prince Hermann shrugs like he can't be bothered by this nonsense. I don't blame him.

"Exactly. Not princely in the slightest." Princess Maria picks up her skirts and tosses her head with a harumph. Wilhelm gasps. I follow his eyes to the princess's neck. Bleeding stars, she's got a Forbidden mark, too. She storms out of the throne room, her lady-in-waiting rushing after her.

"I'm too old to play these kinds of games," Prince Hermann says, interrupting my scattered thoughts. "Tell the king we have yet to see his son, but we will make every effort to keep a lookout and notify him should he come our way. He's not the only one who needs to marry off a spoiled child."

"I'd be delighted to take your daughter off your hands," Rumpelstiltskin says with a grin that's little teeth and all trouble. "She's a pretty thing. Easy on these old eyes."

"Dismissed!" Prince Hermann announces, sitting straighter. "And take that inferior thing with you."

"Of course." I bow. "Thank you, your Royal Highness."

"He's talking about the frog, right?" Rumpelstiltskin asks as we exit.

"Hard to tell," I say. "We need to lose our escort. This is where you come in. I need you to distract him."

"Do this, do that. The demands never end, do they?"

"Either that or I finish your story when Wilhelm isn't looking."

Rumpelstiltskin glowers. "Fine, you tyrant."

As we round a corner, the corridor opens into a four-way intersection. The perfect spot to split up. I nod to Rumpelstiltskin. He huffs and rolls his eyes dramatically. Then, with a shrieking sound, he takes off down the hall.

"Where's he going?" our escort blurts, panic flaring in his eyes.

"You'd better catch him," I warn. "He has the habit of collecting shiny things."

"Stop!" Our guard races after him. "Come back, by order of the king!"

The only orders Rumpelstiltskin follows are tricks and schemes. Quickly, I find a small room and wave Wilhelm inside, shutting the door.

"Set the cursed frog on the floor," I order Wilhelm.

"You're not going to step on it, are you?" he asks before complying. It croaks up at us.

"Reveal yourself in the name of the Enchantress," I demand.

Wind rushes through the room, and in a funnel of magic, the slimy frog morphs into a handsome man with wavy ginger hair, chiseled features, and green eyes. His clothes are a bit of a tangled mess. The shirt is wrapped around one leg, and his jacket hangs from his neck like a bib.

"Prince William," I say darkly.

"This is the prince?" Wilhelm asks, bowing.

"Hello, there." Our frog prince shoots us a bemused look as he unties his shirt from his leg. "Do I know you? You look familiar."

"Jacob Grimm." I cross my arms. "We met at the village square of Honau. This is my brother, Wilhelm."

"It's an honor to meet you, Your Royal Highness," Wilhelm says.

"Ah, yes. Now I remember. My father's hunters."

"How convenient for you to show yourself now that the princess utterly despises you."

"It was a clever trick, wasn't it?" Prince William slaps us on the shoulders. "And I have you to thank for rescuing me from that spoiled princess. But how did you know to unturn me, or even how? Did Claude send you? I was getting worried when my servant didn't show up to command me back to my human self."

"This servant of yours doesn't sound all that dependable." I rub my chin. Now that we know he's a Forbidden, it changes everything. "That was risky what you did."

"Risky indeed, but a valuable gift to discover a person's true intentions. Claude has always been there, should things go wrong. It's my test, you see. If the girl loves me despite my condition and isn't scheming to take over my throne, then I'll know it's a good match. After my last wife, I refuse to make the same mistake again."

Nothing is ever simple with these creatures we're hunting.

"Why didn't you explain the situation to the princess?" Wilhelm asks.

"I can't very well reveal my secret to the entire kingdom,

can I? Imagine the uprisings that would follow if my subjects realized I was a shapeshifter! Besides, once I turn into a frog, I have trouble unturning myself, you see. But a kiss or a command works perfectly. I can't wait to tell my father Princess Maria wouldn't have me for the life of her. The look on his face will be priceless."

"I'm sure he will be thrilled." I massage my temples. This complicates everything.

"You act as if you've done this before," Wilhelm says, and I realize he's already cataloging notes in his head for this frog prince's story. My brother might be too kind, but there's no denying his brilliance.

"Indeed." Prince William grins deviously. "It's how I avoided marriage with Archduchess Maria Amalia, the Grand Duchesses Alexandra, and Maria Pavlovna. Quite clever, isn't it?"

"Ingenious." I resist groaning. "We should look for your servant before we leave. Any idea where he might be?"

"We agreed to meet at the stables if anything went wrong."

"Before we head there, I want to check out the library." I give a pointed look at Wilhelm. After seeing that mark on the princess, I wonder if we might find something of interest there.

"Excellent idea," Wilhelm agrees.

"Library?" Prince William scoffs. "Forget that. We need to get out of here before anyone sees me."

"We'll only be a moment," I say.

Back in the hallway, we discover our escort, who looks a bit dazed, along with Rumpelstiltskin.

"Ah, the frog sheds its skin." Rumpelstiltskin clucks his tongue. "Tell me, darling, how many kisses did it take to grow legs."

The prince scowls while I ask our escort to take us to the

library. The man merely stares off ahead. Rumpelstiltskin snaps his fingers and says, "You heard the tyrant. Take us to the library."

Our escort starts walking while I give Rumpelstiltskin a pointed look. "What did you do to him?" I ask.

"Why are you questioning me when you should be thanking me?" He huffs.

"I can't argue with that," I mutter.

As we stride into the library, my mind whirls, processing the fact that the king's son is a shapeshifting Forbidden. Does that mean the king is, too? Not to mention, Princess Maria. How did these Forbidden infiltrate our lands? How many are hiding in plain sight? I clench my fists as I realize the magnitude of what we are dealing with.

The library's opulence yanks me away from my worries. It's oval-shaped with built-in bookshelves tucked into white walls. Pedestals holding porcelain busts are placed with precision between each of the bookcases. Gilded bookshelves and gold fluted designs adorn the walls, with the far wall boasting a massive painting of Prince Hermann himself standing on a mountain top, gazing off into the distance. A second story circles above with more shelving and teal divans set strategically about for readers to sit and relax on. The arched ceiling is painted with cherubs holding gold harps flying around in a blue sky.

I couldn't care less about the gold or opulence. My eyes drink in the hundreds of books, and my hands tremble as I lightly caress the spines as I stroll along the bookshelves.

"Not a bad library," Prince William says after taking it all in. "But mine is far superior."

"You'll have to allow us a visit then," Wilhelm says.

"Ooohh, looky. Aren't these fine seats?" Rumpelstiltskin cackles as he flings himself onto a velvet couch. "Fit for a king, and perhaps a fine trickster, too."

I push out their voices and focus on scanning the book titles with speed I can only attribute to the Enchantress. Within minutes, I scan nearly the entire bottom floor, coming up with nothing about witches, enchantments, or shapeshifters. Wilhelm is working on the second story, but considering he hasn't said a word, I take it he's coming up empty-handed as well. Discouraged, I sag onto a couch in the corner when I notice a shift in the temperature. This section is cooler, almost as if chilled air is rising from the floor.

I crouch to the ground, pressing my palms to the cold tiles. Mist is creeping through the cracks.

"Wilhelm," I call out. "I think there's a secret room beneath this floor."

This gets both Rumpelstiltskin's and the prince's attention as well. I search for a doorway or lever to open it, but find nothing. It's when Rumpelstiltskin leans against one of the bust's heads that the floor rumbles. A large slab of tile draws back to reveal a spiral staircase sinking into darkness, a foul scent cutting through the library's smell of parchment and wax.

"Seems as if Prince Hermann has a few secrets of his own," I murmur.

# CHAPTER 19

## JACOB

### HOHENZOLLERN CASTLE

I snatch a candle from one of the tables and withdraw my sword before standing over the stairway that plunges into the floor.

"You can't possibly mean to go down there," Prince William says, plugging his nose. "Reeks like dead snakes."

"We could ask our escort." Rumpelstiltskin eyes the door. "He should be waking from his trance soon."

"Then we'll need to hurry." Taking a deep breath, I descend the stone steps into the thick mist.

Cool air embraces me. My spurred boots echo through the silence. There are no railings, so one misstep will send me over the edge. My candle wavers against the darkness as the stairs sink deeper and deeper. The scent of rotting meat assails me. Could this be a trap? Surely, the Enchantress has enemies, and in turn, her enemies are ours.

The stairs end on a cracked stone floor. The sound of creaking metal cuts through the air. My body tenses. I spin in a circle, lifting my candle and squinting into the misty gloom. To my right, there's a wooden table cluttered with dusty parchments, old books, charms, and jars filled with liquid that glows a wicked emerald in the candlelight. A five-prong candelabra sits in the corner. I light it with my waning candle.

Now I can see where the creaking comes from. Large, rusted bird cages hang throughout the room, swaying on aged hinges. A body is stuffed into one of the cages. I choke back bile.

Mist drifts out from a large kettle dangling in the fireplace. Chains drape from the walls, and bones litter the floor. My mouth dries up, pulse thrumming against my temples.

This is a place of death.

I edge back to the table. My hand shakes as I leaf through the pages. Dread fills me. The words are the same style as those in the Enchantress's contract, but I can't place the origins, even though I'm fluent in many languages. Footsteps pound against the stone stairs.

"Jacob!" Wilhelm calls out, holding a candle in front of himself. He's followed closely by the prince and Rumpelstiltskin. Once the three hit the ground, they pause, sucking in breaths of horror.

"All that is holy," Wilhelm gasps, "what is this place?"

"I don't know what to make of it," I admit.

"And here you thought I was trouble," Rumpelstiltskin says.

"Is that a body in that cage?" Prince William's voice trembles, inching closer to the swinging nightmare.

"Looks recent." Wilhelm grimaces.

The prince swears. "It's Claude. Those are his clothes. I don't understand. Why would they do this?"

"It means someone here knows more about you than they're letting on," I warn the prince.

"We need to leave." Prince William grabs my arm. "Now."

But I'm distracted by one of the scrolls. "Old Norse." I pick up the aged manuscript, edges frayed. Unlike the other books, this one holds words from our world.

Wilhelm draws to my side, examining it with the same curiosity. "What does it say?"

I point to the word *völva* at the top, fear clutching me. "I'll need time to translate it, but *völva* means witch." I tuck it into my bag along with a few others. "The prince is right. We need to get out of here, and quickly."

"I can't leave Claude in this dungeon." The prince starts to open the cage. "He deserves a proper burial."

Wilhelm holds him back, hushing him. "Someone is in the library above."

We freeze as dark forms stand over the entrance above. "You down there," a voice calls from above. "Come up this instant in the name of Prince Hermann. You've entered a restricted area."

"Now you've done it." Rumpelstiltskin wiggles his fingers, golden strands ready to fly. "Not to worry, I'll rescue you all."

"Please don't use magic in front of others," Wilhelm says, rubbing the back of his head like he might pull his hair out.

"You can't let them see me," Prince William says. "Princess Maria believes I'm a frog, and I mean to keep it that way."

"Or this is her room," I point out, "and she knows everything about you and your family."

A small, rounded door by the fireplace catches my eye. I crack it open, thrusting the candelabra into the gloom. Mist rushes past me, seeping into a long stone tunnel. It's either our escape or prison.

"This way," I whisper to our group.

Boots clatter down the steps. The prince hesitates by Claude's body. A guard races across the space with a sword and reaches for William, but Rumpelstiltskin's golden threads shoot out and wrench the sword from the man's grasp. More threads wind around the second guard's arms and ankles. They shout curses, but it gives us enough time to slam the wooden door into place. Rumpelstiltskin wraps more strands around the handle to keep it firmly in place.

"Don't say I never helped you," he says.

"Good work," Wilhelm says. "You did a fine job."

I roll my eyes. Nothing Rumpelstiltskin does is for our benefit. I look for the prince. "Where's Prince William?"

Wilhelm scoops up a small dark object from the ground. "I think I found him."

I'm about to unleash a lecture on how this isn't the time for shapeshifting nonsense when the door shudders as something slams into it. They're coming.

The three of us bolt down the musty shaft. A pale circle of light gleams ahead. Minutes later, we stumble out of the darkness and into thick pines and snow. I suck in a deep breath, realizing how close we came to being imprisoned again.

"I'll put on the disguise and get the horses," Wilhelm says, dipping his hand into his pocket and procuring a slimy green frog, plopping it into my palm. He pulls out the cloak and wig that have come in handy more times than I'd like to admit. When I open my mouth to object, Wilhelm holds up a hand. "The hourglass is still nearly full, and I have plenty of energy. This time, you can stay behind and rest."

"Leaving me to babysit the prince and trickster?"

A twinkle flashes in Wilhelm's eyes. "So it appears."

## CHAPTER 20

# ELLA

### MAIER MANOR

"**C**ome in, Ella," Stepmother says. "No need to loiter in the hall like an imbecile."

I swallow before stepping into my father's office. The room is visibly different after Stepmother packed up most of the books and oddities Father collected over the years and sold them off right before Christmas. Many of the shelves hold Marianne's potted plants now. Even though my new family members have been living in the house for some time, I still can't get used to it.

"As you are aware," Stepmother says, shoving aside a stack of papers and settling onto the settee. Her shiny brown hair is pulled into a severe low bun, not a single strand daring to slip free. "We're far overstaffed with our limited funds. I made a list of the help that must be let go."

She passes it to me. I scan it in horror.

"You can't release these servants," I say. "Who will take care of the gardens once Kurt is gone? And if Marie leaves, who'll do the laundry? And how will we run the household without Gertrud? Besides, these people are like family.

They've been with the estate for decades. We can't let them go."

I look at Father, waiting for him to agree, but he simply puffs on his pipe, watching the snow fall in thick flakes outside the paned window. I want to scream. If she hadn't insisted on new Christmas gowns for Marianne and Bertha, and Father hadn't thrown that extravagant party, we wouldn't be in this situation.

Over the past few months, I kept my mouth shut, but this is too much.

"It's best if you're the one to tell them they won't be working here anymore," Stepmother continues, her spine ramrod straight.

"You cannot be serious."

"And since they've already been paid a reward thanks to you, they won't need any severance. It's only fair."

"There's nothing fair about this." I toss the list into the fire, watching the flames hungrily consume the paper. "I won't do it. There has to be another way."

"We're all desperately working on saving the family name," Father says, joining the conversation. "Right now, Marianne is making the rounds, further introducing herself in society. After our grand Christmas party, she's already been invited for tea by several prestigious families. It's quite impressive."

"She's always been the admired socialite," Stepmother says proudly. "I've asked her to keep her eyes open for potential husbands for you, Cinderella. If we can get you married off to a wealthy man who can take care of your father's debts, maybe you can save some of your beloved servants' jobs."

"I'm not going to marry any man to pay off your party debts. That's absurd."

"It's your duty." She draws me to sit beside her on the settee, grabbing my hand between her cold palms. "Let's be honest. You're pretty in the country, simple sort of way. That's the most important asset you have. Remember your place, Ella. You've run wild here in these forsaken woodlands long enough. If you care for your servants and have any love at all for your father, you'll wed and help support this family."

I know her demands aren't unreasonable—if not expected—but Mother always said she wanted me to only marry for love. The room presses on me, stiflingly hot. I rip my hand free of Stepmother's grip and race out of the study, down the hall. With Mother gone, the only person who understands me is Cook. I really could use one of her warm hugs.

But when I enter the kitchen, it's oddly quiet without Cook's loud voice singing off-key as she worked. A stew is bubbling on the hearth, and the air smells of freshly baked bread. She must be at the market.

A light tap, tap, tap at the window draws my attention. A raven is perched on the sill, staring at me. Curiosity pulls at me. There's something about the gleam in its eyes, as if it not only knows me, but understands me. Finally, it flies over the snow-blanketed garden to Mother's hazel tree.

It's been a long time since I fed the birds. They're probably hungry since I'm the only one brave enough to get close to the tree. I grab my cloak from its peg and the basket of day-old bread that I always have ready and hurry out to the tree.

The boughs are barren, branches stretched out like bones. The words of my father, warning me I could become a witch by following in my mother's footsteps, haunt me. Even Jacob, a hunter, had been wary of the birds. Could there be something evil with Mother's tree?

No. My mother wasn't a witch. A tremor wracks my body so hard, I drop the basket. Breadcrumbs spill across the ground. Lately, it's been hard controlling my hands from shaking, not to mention the random heat flashes. Even my headaches have been increasing. The shock of my new step-mother and stepsisters has been tough.

The raven appears on the branch above my head. It caws as if it's trying to say something.

"I hope that was a thank you," I say, tossing the remaining crumbs onto the ground.

Once finished, I step back, expecting the bird to dig into the food, but instead it cocks its head to the side, watching me with one eye.

"Go on." I wave my hand at the crumbs. "Have at it. I'm freezing, and you must be starving."

The raven flutters to the ground to my right by a pile of crow feathers. The snow is tinged with blood. I bend down, inspecting it.

"You're trying to tell me something, aren't you?" I say, heart diving as I search the area, terrified a wolf is prowling about. "Do you know what happened to this crow?"

The raven flaps its onyx wings and flies into a hole in the tree. My body shakes, and my toes are numb. I should head back inside, but something is compelling about the tree.

"Ella," the wind whispers. Or is that the tree?

Curious, I creep to the tree's base. There's a crack along the trunk that I never noticed before. I trail my finger over the rough bark, and memories race through my mind.

*Mother holding my hand as a child.*

*A basket filled with seeds.*

*Singing to the birds.*

*A book of poems.*

*Feathers floating through the air.*

I jerk my hand back. Those memories are beautiful and terrifying at the same time. It's been over a year, and I'm still not ready to deal with the pain they bring. Tears trickle down my cheeks. Angrily, I brush them away and straighten my shoulders, breathing one simple breath at a time.

The tree groans, and I startle. The crack in the trunk swings inward, revealing a narrow stairway spiraling up inside the tree. I rub my eyes, completely confused and utterly shocked. This can't be happening. It's the grief. Or maybe I'm passed out on the ground, dreaming.

A breath of warm air courses out of the tree, smelling of fresh blooms on a spring day. I peer inside, wondering what this place is. Could it have anything to do with my mother?

I glance back at the manor with darkened rooms and a single trail of smoke winding into the dusky clouds. I don't think anyone is watching. With trembling fingers, I reach for the doorframe, testing to see if it's real or just my imagination. Solid bark scrapes my skin. I dare step inside. The wooden staircase is solid under my boots, and the walls are made of rough bark. Sconces blink to life, flickering like glistening knives. The narrow stairwell spins impossibly upward.

This place is dripping with magic. Indecision freezes me. Do I go up the steps and discover what's there or flee?

# CHAPTER 21

## JACOB

### HONAU

The tavern is practically bursting at the seams as Wilhelm and I enter. We find a table in the corner beneath a row of stuffed boar's heads, far from the roaring hearth, but at least it's out of the way of anyone listening. After we dropped Prince William off at the castle, we headed back to town for food, but Rumpelstiltskin refused to join us, saying he wouldn't come two feet from the tavern that serves watered-down swamp water.

"Everyone in Honau must be here," I say as the two of us settle into our chairs, shaking off the snow from our cloaks. "She does make the best bratwursts."

"Either that or something is brewing in town we're not aware of," Wilhelm says.

"Which is never good in our line of work."

"How did we miss that the prince was a frog? And that dungeon. I still can't believe my eyes."

"It was something from a horror story," I agree. "When we get home, I want to start a story about Princess Maria and our frog prince immediately. Their names will come up on the hourglass at some point."

"It will be a fun one to write, at least. Fetching her golden ball." He chuckles. "If I haven't seen everything."

I pull out the book labeled *Völva* and flip it open. "On the ride home, I took a look at the text," I tell Wilhelm. "Based on my initial translation of the Old Norse, it seems to be a book of spells. Except there's a section here on the Enchantress's Hunters."

"The witches know about us." Wilhelm groans. "That makes things exciting."

I rub my chin, studying the words carefully. "It looks like the Enchantress found a loophole in their spell. I think it says, 'She's gathered Hunters to send us all back to her foul land. They're nearly indestructible, but they can be killed.'"

"I suppose that's one way out of this curse." Wilhelm's mouth quirks into a wry half-smile.

"Then here it says, 'I have ideas on spells that will work. Just need subjects.'"

"Well, that's reassuring," Wilhelm says sarcastically.

I drum my fingers on the worn pages. "I wonder if there are others like us."

"I pray not."

A barmaid saunters over to our table, slapping down two huge steins, the brew frothing over the sides. "You two just here to enjoy my good company or to order some food?"

"Bring us cold vegetables and we wouldn't mind," I say. "We're that hungry."

She laughs. "Well then, I'll see what's still kicking and twitching in the kitchen."

"What's the occasion?" I wave to the groups of older men toasting and laughing. It's like they've forgotten all about the wolf attacks.

"You haven't heard? Ah, now, I expect you wouldn't, since you don't have marrying-age daughters in your house. The king has announced a grand festival and invited every girl of marrying age to attend the three balls he's hosting. Even commoners. Quite the gesture, isn't it?"

"Indeed." I frown. What is King Frederick up to? He only does things that make him richer or more powerful. And inviting commoners into his castle doesn't fit any of those criteria. "I wonder what has brought on this bout of goodwill from our king."

"Goodwill?" She sniffs. "He wants his son married. Rumor has it that it's the king's revenge on the prince for refusing to marry Princess Maria of Hohenzollern. He told his son he'd invite all the women in the land, and then the prince would see the error of his ways once he saw how dreadful commoner girls were. How's that for a king's confidence in his people?"

Now that sounds like the king we all know and adore.

"Fascinating," I say, sipping my drink. "We were left in the dark on this extraordinary news."

"The couriers are delivering the invitations this very moment. The king isn't wasting a moment. The first ball is in three days. I've a feeling tonight many young women will dream of a crown on their head and a prince on their arm. It's all quite romantic, except I worry many girls are going to come away disappointed."

Once the barmaid sashays away, my thoughts drift to Ella. What does she think of this ball? Will she attend? The prince would be a fool not to fall for her. She's not only beautiful, but the kindest, gentlest person I know.

"You're thinking of Ella," Wilhelm says, interrupting my thoughts as our food is brought to the table.

"I wasn't." I pick up my fork and dig into my plate of steaming hot bratwurst, thick chunks of cheese, brown bread, and cabbage. But the thought of eating doesn't seem as appetizing as before.

"You've got that look on your face."

I glare. "I don't have a *look*."

"A dreamy expression." He leans back with a smirk, enjoying himself too much. "You get it when you're thinking of her. It's the only time you don't look completely miserable."

"This is the most ridiculous conversation. Let's focus back on the task at hand."

"You want to attend the ball." Wilhelm sighs and stares at his cabbage gloomily. "I hate festivities. We'll have to wear itchy clothing and stand stiffly. Knowing our luck, we'll be one of the few bachelors there, and I'll be expected to dance."

"As revolting as it sounds, you know it's our best opportunity to find out what's going on, plus scout out the area for new story prospects."

"Don't call them that." Wilhelm pushes his plate away. "They may not be from our world, but they are real people and creatures with real feelings."

"Absolutely. Like that monster we killed in the woods had real enough feelings to rake her claws down my back and lick her lips as she imagined eating me whole." Wilhelm rolls his eyes. "Speaking of eating, better get to it. You'll need your energy because after our meal, you're going to write a letter to the king, reminding him that he's commissioned us to this region and wouldn't he wish for us to join the ball and make sure everyone is safe?"

"If you're so eager to go, why don't you write him yourself?"

"Because you're a better writer than I," I point out. "Your persuasion skills are impeccable. Besides, I need to make a trip out to visit Ella von Maier."

"I knew it!" He starts laughing.

"Your imagination is blinding you, brother. I'm simply

going to make sure Ella accepts the invitation to the king's ball and attends. After our struggle today, we obviously need her."

"I rue the day I supported the idea of her helping us," Wilhelm grumbles.

# CHAPTER 22

# ELLA

## MAIER MANOR

Frosty tendrils of breath escape my lips. Swallowing my fear, I start up the stairs of this strange tree. It's physically impossible, but it feels like I'm entering deeper into the tree rather than higher.

I'm halfway up when darkness swoops in. Blood pounds through my veins as I realize the outer door must have shut. I'm about to race back down when pinpricks of light shine through the bark, illuminating the stairwell in a soft glow.

*What is this place?*

I continue on, too curious to stop now. The stairwell spits me through a twisted, thorny entrance to an oval room. An onyx floor glitters with slivers of pearl. The walls are twisted roots winding around each other until they arch above my head.

A cry of shock escapes me. A creature sits on a throne of branches and glowing emerald leaves, studying me with bright hazel eyes. Is it a bird or a woman? I don't know, but I freeze in place. She's wearing a forest green dress, but two giant wings are tucked against her back. Their brown and blue feathers shimmer in the forest-green glow. Feathers flare out from the sides of her eyes, and a silver circlet rests on her forehead. Its sparkles reflect against her cheeks and forehead.

"Welcome, Ella von Maier," the bird-woman says. "It is about time you arrived. We were beginning to worry you'd never make it."

"We?"

She nods to the seven ravens perched on pedestals circling the room. They dip their heads in respect. I gasp. These are the ravens I feed.

"I must be dreaming," I say, backing away. "This isn't possible."

"I assure you this is not a dream, but the reality of your birthright." The bird-woman bats her long, thick eyelashes and smiles.

"I—I don't understand."

"Your mother is a descendant of the first of the bird folk," the woman explains. "He was a prince in love with a woman, but the malicious fairy, Mazilla, wanted to marry him instead. When the prince returned, she cast a spell on him, making him a bird to keep him from his true love. Yet, love found a way. We're living proof that true love is more powerful than a curse."

My knees give out, and I sink to the ground. I don't know how to explain it, but something warns me she's speaking the truth.

"My father was right," I whisper dimly. "My mother was a witch, and I have her cursed blood."

As if in anger, the ravens caw at my response.

"Cursed blood perhaps, but you are no witch," the bird-woman says. "The time has arrived for your transformation to begin."

"What transformation? What time?" I rise to my feet.

Horror washes my world into shades of gray. "You mean for me to turn into a bird? Like you?"

"Now you understand." The bird-woman taps her talons on the throne's armrest. I stare at them.

"No," I whisper, choking on the memory from the nixie pond.

"The moment you are called to enter the tree, it means your time of transformation has arrived."

"What if I don't want to transform? There has to be a way to stop it."

"There isn't."

"But my mother. She wasn't a bird. She didn't look anything like you."

"Are you sure? She was my sister."

I gasp. "So you're...you're my aunt?"

"Now you're thinking. My name is Fiona, named after our great-great-grandmother. I've been watching over you since the moment my dear sister flew into the heavens. Unlike her, I can't fully transform into a human. This is as human as I can be. As bird folk, most of us have the gift of being able to fully transform into a bird or take on a human form. Unfortunately, some of us can't shapeshift fully or even ever." She gazes off to the side, her face contorting as if in pain. "Or perhaps they don't wish to."

A million questions batter my mind. "Are you saying my mother was able to transform from bird to human? Why didn't she tell me?"

"She fell in love with a merchant, your father, but was too afraid to tell him the truth. I told her not to have anything to do with the man, but she wouldn't listen to reason. She was able to hide her bird form from him, but then she became pregnant. We didn't know how the bird-folk blood would affect you." Fiona rises from her throne and picks up a wooden goblet from a table. "When she moved here, I couldn't stand the thought of being separated from her, so she took a seed from the ancient tree of our family and planted it here for me to live inside."

"And who are you?" I stare at the ravens. "Are you also bird-folk?"

"No." Fiona begins petting one raven's thick black feathers. "These seven brothers have also been cursed. They were searching for their home. I invited them to reside here for as long as they wish, but theirs is another story for another time. Now I want you to drink this."

"Absolutely not! I don't have proof that what you're saying is true."

"I'll be honest with you. Everyone's transformation is different. For some, it's extremely painful. For others, it's a passing pain. Since you're a half-blood, I'm not sure what will happen, but it will happen soon. Tonight or perhaps tomorrow. We offer this drink to help with the pain."

"How do I know you're not trying to poison me?"

"It's a brew of pine needles, oak bark, and water from a fresh spring. Please, for your sake, take it."

She holds out the goblet. I eye it suspiciously. What if I never transform? Or worse, what if she's tricking me and that drink actually stimulates this horrible curse?

"You don't have to do this alone," Fiona says. "I'll be with you every step of the way."

"I don't want any of this." I shake my head. "You must be mistaken because Mother and I were very close. She would've told me. She wouldn't have left this world without telling me."

"Or maybe she did, and you just never listened." Fiona stares at the bluebird necklace hanging from my neck.

Her words stab me in the chest. Instinctively, I clutch the pendant that has always calmed me when I'm upset. I spin on my heels and stumble down the stairs, tears streaming down my cheeks.

I pound on the bark. "Let me out!"

Thankfully, the door swooshes open, allowing me to escape this horrid place. Once outside, the cold steals my breath, and the rain lashes against my cheeks, freezing my tears.

I sprint across the field toward the manor. My world is shattered. Nothing can fix that.

৩৯৩

I return to my room and claim a headache instead of having to do needlework with my stepsisters. The entire afternoon, I curl up under my covers, tormented. Will I get wings like my aunt? I touch my eyes, imagining the feel of feathers replacing skin.

Maybe I've finally lost my mind. Or worse, Fiona is trying to manipulate me like Scarlet did.

When dinner time comes, I drag myself out of bed and change into a midnight-blue dress. My hands shake so hard, I'm forced to call Jesse to help me button up the back. Jesse must sense my dismal state because she insists on braiding my hair and twisting it into a crown on top of my head with the rest cascading in curls down my back.

"You look positively divine." She kisses me on the forehead. I'm about to head downstairs when she takes my hand in hers. "Whatever happens, I believe you'll always be the true mistress of this house."

I stare at her sadly. Would she still say that if she knew I might transform into a bird? Or that she might not have a job tomorrow because I don't want to marry a stranger? Probably not, but I squeeze her hands. "Thank you, Jesse. You're like family to me."

"There's something I need to tell you." Jesse fidgets with the ties on my dress. "Frau von Maier won't be happy if I told you before she did."

"What is it?"

"Dr. Wissen stopped by," she whispers and glances behind her as if the walls themselves have ears. "I was curious about what he was like since some of the staff went to work for him. I pretended to be dusting outside your father's study. Dr. Wissen signed a contract with your father, and then the two shook hands as if they were making a deal."

My pulse misses a beat. "But that could be a deal over anything. Perhaps Father sold off our two cows? Dr. Wissen has plenty of land for cows."

"Dr. Wissen gave him a coin as a symbol of his pledge."

"He didn't." I sink onto my dresser stool. It's customary for the father and bridegroom to sign a contract upon betrothal and then for the groom to give the father a single coin as a symbol of his pledge. "He couldn't have pledged my hand in marriage without my consent. You must have misunderstood the situation."

"Yes, that must be it." Jesse nods quickly. But her eyes tell me otherwise. "Or perhaps one of your stepsisters is to be married. Wouldn't that be nice?"

As I head downstairs, I hear laughter and voices in the drawing room. One of those voices sends my heart racing.

"Jacob," I whisper, my steps quickening. If there's anyone who would understand what I just went through, it'd be him.

My entrance silences everyone. Stepmother takes in my hair and dress, frowning. Bertha, who is perched close to Jacob on the settee, gasps in annoyance when Jacob rises and bows. Meanwhile, Marianne lifts her eyebrows in amusement.

"You look lovely tonight," Marianne tells me. "I've gotten so used to seeing you wearing soot-smeared dresses or the help's cloaks, I was beginning to think you preferred servanthood."

The blood in my veins ices as I dip into a bow. Did she see me wearing Cook's cloak earlier? And if so, did she see me enter the tree?

"Hello, Ella," Jacob says. "I came to visit you and finally had the chance to meet the rest of your family."

"Good evening. It's wonderful to see you." I sit in an empty chair by the far wall.

"He was telling us he was studying at the University of Marburg, but the king commissioned him to hunt down the wolves in the area," Stepmother says. "Those beasts are a nuisance."

"I'm sure the king appreciates their work." I give him a raised look, wondering if the king knew what the Grimm brothers actually did.

A quirk of his lips tells me that no, the king does not. Warmth spreads through me as I remember the other day in the woods and the heat of his skin and the strength of his arms wrapped around me.

A sharp knock raps on the front door.

I jerk, now alert. What if it's Dr. Wissen?

The footman enters with a bow, allowing entrance to two grand sentries, regally dressed in red cloaks and armor with the king's coat of arms. Tall white plumes wave from their helmets. They both bow deeply.

"Greetings to those from the house of nobleman Karl von Maier," one sentry announces in a tired voice while producing a scroll. He sluggishly unravels it and drones out the words as if he's read it a million times. "The great, benevolent, and just King Frederick of Württemberg has cordially invited the household of nobleman Maier in three days to a three-day festival at his Lichtenstein Castle. Each night, the crown will host a grand ball for all the beautiful unmarried women of the

Kingdom of Württemberg so Prince William may choose a bride."

We all gasp.

"The prince will choose a bride?" Bertha exclaims. "I could be a princess?" She races to the sentry holding the proclamation and wrenches it from him. "It's true." She waves it about. "It's really true!"

"Now give it here." The sentry snatches the parchment from her. "That isn't yours for the taking."

Stepmother draws Marianne and Bertha to her in a hug. "Are you to tell me that the king has an interest in my daughters for his son?"

"I suppose," the second sentry says, taking in my two step-sisters. "Them and every other eligible maiden of the land."

Amidst the shouting and screaming, I glance over at Jacob. He's gone silent as the grave, studying my new family members intently. He doesn't look happy. I rise and move closer to him while the others dance around and scream in excitement.

"What has brought on that frown?" I tease. "Are you worried the prince will take all the beautiful women from you? Surely, he can't marry every maiden in the land."

This earns me a mischievous grin, and his eyes twinkle. "It is a concern, but I'm determined to endure it if you promise to dance with me at the ball."

"Ella at the ball?" Bertha frowns. I guess she was paying more attention than I thought.

"He did invite every *beautiful* young maiden," Jacob points out. "There's no doubt she qualifies."

My face burns at the compliment.

"That reminds me," Stepmother says. "Ella, we planned to announce the wonderful news to you over dinner, but now is as good a time as any, don't you agree, my dearest husband?"

Father nods. "Yes, of course. Ella, this afternoon, Dr.

Wissen visited, requesting your hand in marriage. We have drafted up a marriage contract and are waiting for approval by the magistrate. Which means there's no need for you to attend."

"A married woman," Stepmother gushes, clasping her hands together. "It's simply so exciting."

My heart sinks, and I gape at Father. Jesse warned me.

"Or Ella could go to the ball and secure a better match with the prince," Jacob points out.

"I'm sure you don't want to be a princess, right?" Bertha asks me, chuckling. "You'll be far happier with the doctor. *He* won't mind it if you build fires or run about in the fields like a wild animal."

"I'd love to attend the ball." My fists clench at my sides, but it's hard to stay calm. "I don't see why we have to rush me into this marriage."

The dinner bell rings. Father takes a final swig of his drink before bolting for the dining room. Stepmother, flanked by her two daughters, starts planning which dresses everyone will wear, and trails after him, too caught up in the excitement to realize they just left Jacob and me alone.

"Dr. Wissen?" Jacob picks up his hat, twisting it in his hand. "He's the doctor from the large manor at the edge of the forest, right?"

"He is." I find it hard to breathe. "A horrible man."

"The townsfolk are quite smitten with him."

"Yes, well, I seem to be in the minority on that point." I glance around, making sure we're alone. "I need to speak with you in private. It's too dangerous to say here."

"What are you proposing?" His eyes twinkle. "A midnight dalliance?"

"No!" I hit him on the arm with my gloved hand. "The walled garden behind the barn. Tomorrow midmorning?"

"Sounds clandestine, but if I might be so bold, I recommend meeting at night. Daylight reveals far too much for probing eyes. Besides, I have a proposition for you as well. Midnight perhaps?"

Tonight? It'd be even more inappropriate than what I suggested. And how much do I really trust him? But then there's my marriage proposal and what happened in my mother's tree. He's the only one who can help me. I held his secrets; he could hold mine.

"Midnight it is," I say.

"Excellent, until then." He bows and exits.

My heart patters in ways I know it shouldn't. I press my palm to my chest, trying to calm it down. I turn to discover Marianne standing in the doorway to the dining room, her eyes looking at me with pity. How much did she overhear?

"Sweet Cinderella. You like him, don't you?"

"Of course not." I bristle. "He's just a friend."

Marianne pulls me onto the hall bench, taking my hands in hers. "As your sister, I insist on watching over you and making sure you don't fall into this man's trap. He's a mere hunter and far beneath you in marriage. You are a *nobleman's* daughter. That's why Dr. Wissen is the perfect match for you."

"Except he isn't. Everything I know about the doctor, I despise."

She presses her lips together. "I completely understand. But Dr. Wissen is rich and secure. Do you know how important that is? When my father died, he left us alone with no money. We were practically out on the street. If Mother hadn't married your father, I don't know what we would've done. Love is fleeting, but security and safety, those are permanent. And for women such as ourselves, that's the only way we can acquire it."

It's futile to argue with Marianne. The two of us have very different views on love.

Thankfully, everyone at dinner is too preoccupied talking about balls and gowns and the hopes of becoming a princess to pay any attention to me. My eyes wander to the clock. Should I really meet Jacob at midnight? It's scandalous.

And if I do sneak out, can I trust him with my family's secret curse?

I have less than five hours to decide.

# CHAPTER 23

# JACOB

## MAIER MANOR

Clouds scuttle above. They shroud the moon and deepen the shadows. Tonight, I need the darkness. Ella's manor rises up on the other side of the field, lights beaming golden bars across the snow. I tether my horse and hurry toward the garden. It's borderline foolishness meeting Ella, but after what I saw earlier, waiting another day might be too late.

Not to mention that I'm haunted by the soft smile of her lips and the way her eyes twinkle over our shared secrets. Ella is becoming a distraction that's starting to burrow deep. I remind myself there's a line in our relationship, and I won't cross it.

Stealthily, I climb the back of the garden wall in case someone is watching the entrance. The moment my boots hit the ground, Ella ducks out of the shadows and points a fire poker at my chest. This woman and her weapon choices. My respect for her grows.

"Do you plan on piercing me with that?" I arch my brow. "Or are we having a dueling session out here?"

"I don't usually run about the gardens at midnight with

dangerous men." She doesn't put the poker down but places the ends in her two palms. "I wasn't about to leave my room unarmed."

A thick midnight cloak is wrapped around her, tucking her into the shadows. Her long hair tumbles in soft waves over her shoulders, catching the moonlight like strands of gold. This line I promised myself not to cross will be harder than I thought.

"Smart," I say. "But I think you're going to have to be more worried about the dangers of those running about in your house than out here."

"What's that supposed to mean?"

"It means you shouldn't trust your stepmother."

"Why?" She finally lowers her weapon.

I check the area to make sure we're alone and then pull her onto the stone bench.

"I need to tell you something that needs to remain between the two of us," I say.

"Now you're scaring me."

It should. "Remember when I told you I hunt for the king?" I begin, debating how much to tell her. "I'm actually hunting for what we call Forbidden. These are people, animals, creatures who all bear a mark. That's how we know if they don't belong here."

"Forbidden?" She gasps, her hand moving to her chest. "What does the mark look like?"

"Every Forbidden's mark is unique to them and appears on their neck right here." I skim a finger along the side of her neck. Her skin is soft, and she shivers under my touch. I swallow hard and pull my hand away.

Quickly, she presses two fingers onto the place I touched. "And you saw this on my stepmother?"

I nod. "What do you know about her?"

"Hardly anything other than her husband died, making

her and her two daughters nearly destitute. She met my father at a party. They married right away. What does this mean? Will she hurt me?"

Her voice is pained, merely a whisper. I slide closer to her and take her hand in mine.

"I don't know," I admit. "Pay attention to what she says and get any clues you can about her true identity. If you can get her full story, my brother and I can take care of her. We know how to get rid of these monsters."

"Monsters." She shudders. "You think that's what the Forbidden are?"

"Of course. Not only are they evil, but they're disrupting the balance of our worlds. You've seen how many people have died in your village alone."

"How do you know they're all evil?"

"You think your stepmother is good?"

"No." She looks away. "What exactly do you plan to do to these Forbidden? Because even though I don't like my new stepmother, she's still family."

And there it is. While Ella is kind and forgiving, I'm not. And I'll do everything I can to keep her safe.

"What happened to Scarlet was not ideal, but she was intent on killing all of us, and I couldn't let that happen," I explain. "Our goal is to send the Forbidden back to where they came from."

"And where's that?" she asks.

"I honestly don't know." I laugh darkly. "I'm just a mere hunter."

She studies me, while I find it hard to concentrate on anything other than the desire to feel her body pressed against me and her lips crushing mine. My hand moves like it has a mind of its own, brushing a strand of hair from her cheek. My fingers linger just long enough to feel her soft skin, warm in the cool night. Her breath catches, and she quickly stands. Cold air swoops between us like a slap in the face. It takes everything in me not to reach for her.

"Tell me more about these monsters," she says, stepping away. "If I saw someone who was a human, but could turn into another creature, say a cat perhaps, would they also be a monster? After all, cats are rather sweet animals, unlike wolves. Would you need to follow the king's orders and hunt them, too?"

"A perfect example." I follow her like a magnet. "I just encountered a man who could turn into a frog. He also had the mark, but I wouldn't consider him dangerous. Slimy, perhaps. I don't know all the ramifications, but even if they aren't physically threatening, they could have other ways of harming humans."

"I see." She backs up further like she's getting ready to run.

"Earlier, you mentioned you had something to ask me."

"You said you wanted us to work together," Ella hedges, biting her lip. "As you heard, my stepmother wishes me to marry Dr. Wissen, and soon."

The thought of him marrying her makes me physically sick. "I thought you despised him."

"Very much so. Which was why I was wondering if you could help me stop that from happening."

She has no idea the lengths I'd go to make sure he doesn't. "What if the contract were to go missing? I could arrange that."

She shakes her head. "That might delay things, but I doubt it will work. Dr. Wissen is highly connected."

"Give me some time," I tell her. "I'll think of something."

"Great." A smile tips her pink lips. "Then I'll continue doing everything I can in helping you with these monsters."

"You're attending the ball, right? We need you to be our eyes and ears."

"As long as I'm not married by then." She laughs, but the cold sucks it away.

"I'll do everything in my power to keep you from marrying him." I can't stop myself. I reach out and wrap my palm around hers. A cloud parts, allowing for a sliver of moonlight to skitter over the ground and illuminate her face. She's breathtaking. If I'm not careful, she'll be another man's wife. The thought scares me more than I'm willing to admit.

"Promise you'll be careful around your stepmother?"

"Only if you promise me a dance at the ball. You didn't give me an answer yet."

"A dance it is then."

Her lashes lower, brushing her cheeks, and my chest tightens like it's forgotten to breathe. I shouldn't. I *know* I shouldn't. But my eyes drop to her mouth anyway, and all I can think about is how soft her lips would feel on mine.

The air between us is charged, humming as if with magic. I lean in, slow, like I'm testing the edge of a cliff before jumping into a forbidden sea. Her breath ghosts against my lips. I wait for her to pull away, and yet she doesn't. For a second, I let myself believe I'm going to do it.

Kiss her.

But I stop, my lips a heartbeat away, because she deserves better. She deserves a prince, a hero. Not a hunter like me.

# CHAPTER 24

# ELLA

## MAIER MANOR

"You must tell him no," Aunt Fiona demands, stalking across my bedroom like she's known me all my life. Like she's not some stranger who appeared to me yesterday with a story about how I'm half-bird, half-human. "How can you work with him? He's our enemy."

"He's not our enemy!" I snap as I slip into my nightgown. "He's my friend. Lately, they've been hard to come by."

"If he truly is a friend, then why didn't you tell him the truth about the ravens and me tonight? Why didn't you tell him about your family curse?"

I keep silent at that, remembering Jacob's words about the poor, innocent frog-man. If he finds a frog dangerous, a bird fits in that category, too.

"I'm going to tell him," I say tightly. "Last night wasn't the right time."

But that's a lie. I sit in front of my mirror and stare at my reflection, remembering how the world hung still just for the two of us. Even now, I can taste the promise of his kiss. I wish he hadn't stopped. Wish that I had leaned in. Instead, I'm left suspended in time, craving the impossible.

No, I can't ever reveal my secret. He'd never look at me again like he did last night. Now I understand my mother's choice not to tell Father.

"Perhaps it's because if he knew the truth about your lineage, he'd hunt you, too," she continues, staring at the fire. The flames flicker over her feathered dress. "I don't know who these Grimm brothers are, but one thing I am certain of, you must stay away from them at all costs. Some of our flock have gone missing, and those two are at the top of my list of culprits. The ravens and I are trying to find out who they are and why they hunt our kind."

"I saw blood and feathers in the snow," I say, remembering how gentle he'd been with my mother's book. "Jacob would never do that to an innocent creature."

"You know nothing of the capabilities of a killer," she says.

The image of him slicing off the wolf's head rushes back to me. I swallow hard, telling myself if he hadn't killed that werewolf, it would've killed me. My hand shakes as I brush my hair. Finally, I give up the task entirely and clamp my palms together, begging them to stop. Fear curls in the pit of my stomach as that burning, pricking sensation under my skin roars to life, fiercer than ever.

"Drink it, please." Fiona sets the goblet she brought me on my vanity. "You're trembling. The transformation is beginning. You need to lie down. I'd feel better if you'd let me take you off into the woods and let this transformation take place where humans won't interfere. It'd give you time to adjust and understand your new body."

"It's nothing." I wave my hand and stalk to my bed. "I'm cold and tired. That's it. You should go before someone sees you."

My aunt gazes at me, face switching from worry to a distant smile. "You remind me so much of your mother. She was my little sister. Ten years younger than me, in fact. I loved her more than life itself. Having her taken from me was like a part of my heart was chiseled away, leaving a gaping hole. But finally being able to speak with you has helped my grief."

Tears threaten the corners of my eyes. After Mother died, it's as if everyone forgot she existed. Father not only replaced her but now acts like she never was his wife. Now here's a woman I don't know—a woman who looks almost like a bird —that misses her. *Heavens*. This is bad.

"Please leave," I say again. I don't want her life and definitely not her curse.

"Of course." Fiona opens the window and slips onto the sill, nimble as a dancer. "If the pain gets too bad, drink from the goblet. It will help."

In a rush of wind, she transforms into a bird, flying into the darkness. I dart to the window, letting the cool air chill me as I watch her fly to the hazel tree, before closing it and drawing the curtains. I pull out my treasures tucked beneath my pillow. Jacob's handkerchief, the raven sketch, and a new drawing I found tucked in the pocket of my cloak last night. I smile. Jacob must have slipped it inside.

It's a single heliotrope flower, the lines soft and simple. I trace them with my finger.

The thought of him thinking I'm one of the monsters he hunts makes my heart sink. The way he looked at me sent a flame of fire down my core. No one has ever made me feel like he does. I can't lose that.

I can't become one of them.

࿇

A scream rips from my throat. I wake in bed, gasping in agony. Fire prickles my skin like tiny knives cutting their way from the inside out. I blink against the darkness. What is happening to me? I clutch my sheets. Sweat drips down the sides of my face. Another surge of pain wracks my body. I scream again.

Doors in the hall bang, and voices call out. Footsteps pound against the creaky wooden floors. A sliver of light slices across my room from beneath my door, and then I hear a knock.

"Ella." It's Stepmother's voice, cranky and annoyed. "What is the meaning of this? What's going on?"

My senses sharpen, and everything rushes back to me. My supposed aunt, who's in fact a bird, telling me I, too, will happily join the bird family and fly about on wings. Utterly ridiculous. But I can't pretend this pain away. It's real and altogether terrifying.

Stepmother can't ever know about this. It's a dangerous secret. I grind my teeth, ordering myself under control just as Stepmother steps inside. Her candle flickers, casting her face in ghastly shadows that elongate her chin and make her eyes look sunken.

Knowing she's a Forbidden like Jacob warned me about makes perfect sense now.

"Hello," I say in my most steady voice. "I'm fine. Truly! I just had a nightmare about my mother's death, but now that I'm awake, I realize it was just a bad dream."

A fire builds under my skin. There's no way I can sit calmly in bed when the pain hits me again.

"You must learn to control your outbursts, Ella. You're a young woman now. Your father claims your mother came from a highborn family, but seeing the way you go on, I seriously doubt the accuracy of this statement."

*Just leave, you dreadful woman*, I want to shout, but instead I manage through gritted teeth, "Yes, Stepmother."

"Don't wake me again. The girls and I need our beauty

sleep. We can't go to the upcoming ball with dark circles under our eyes."

Finally, she leaves with a huff. Darkness swoops across the room, leaving me alone with my pain. Another surge wracks over my body. I stuff my sheets inside my mouth and bury my head into my mattress.

When the pain subsides, I lie on my back panting. Moonlight trickles through my curtains, offering a ghostly glow on my vanity and Fiona's goblet.

I promised not to drink it. But I'm desperate. I don't know how many more episodes I can suffer through without waking the whole house. The last thing I need is for them to find me with feathers for skin and talons for fingers.

With shaky hands, I tip the cup to my lips and drink. The brew tastes like pine and sweet spring water. Visions of trees and honey blossoms tumble over me.

I barely manage to drink half of it when another spasm hits me, causing the goblet to slip from my fingers and rolls across the floor in a horrid clatter.

The pain overtakes me again. I sink to the ground, clenching my fists.

Stay quiet.

Don't scream.

Keep the secret safe.

Someone shakes me awake. I lift my head from the floor to discover my maid, Jesse.

"Oh, Ella," Jesse says. "Whatever are you doing on the floor? Are you hurt?"

"No, I'm fine, thank you." I lick my lips. They taste like sap. Groaning, I rise to my feet. "Jesse, whatever happens, don't tell Frau von Maier you found me on the floor. Please?"

"I think that's a good idea," Jesse whispers. "A warning, though. She's in a foul mood today."

Jesse fetches me a simple, comfortable gown. Once she's gone, I check my face and body in the mirror. No feathers in sight. I'm safe. Perhaps it was just a bad dream.

And yet, the goblet lies at my feet, taunting me with its engraved bird etchings. I don't touch it and leave for breakfast.

Stepmother is at the table sipping coffee, a scowl on her face, when I enter.

"Good morning," I say, sitting at the table.

Stepmother doesn't acknowledge me, but Cook offers a strained smile as she practically throws the platter of sausages on the table.

"Mercies," Marianne exclaims, walking in gracefully with Bertha behind, dragging her feet. "What was all that racket last night? Was that really you, Cinderella?'

I grab a hot buttery roll from the basket. "Bad dream. I'm sorry if I woke you."

"Bad dreams?" Bertha raises her eyebrows, filling up her plate. "You were howling like a cow. I'm surprised you didn't wake the entire village."

"That's more than enough food for you, Bertha," Stepmother says. "You must keep your figure slim and delicate to look presentable for the prince. We may need to put you on a strict diet."

"Not that it will matter," Marianne says. A devious expression tugs on her lips as she delicately cuts her food. "The prince will only notice me anyway."

"You're truly horrid." Bertha throws her fork down. "I hate you!"

"Girls!" Stepmother commands. "Stop squabbling. I have news. I released Marie, one of the servants, so we can hire a tutor to prepare you for the ball."

"But she was my maid!" Tears fill Bertha's eyes. "How is that fair? Why did you get rid of my servant?"

"You let Marie go?" My fork clatters to my plate. "She's been with our household for her whole life. She's like family."

"All the more reason to get rid of her," Stepmother says. "She was taking advantage of her status by hardly working. Don't fret, Bertha. You'll get a fleet of servants once you're the new princess. We must sacrifice for the future. Always remember that."

"I suppose I can." Bertha perks up and starts buttering her roll. "She was a sniveling idiot anyway."

"Sniveling idiot?" Now I understand why Marianne's always so snippy to Bertha. She's despicable. "How dare you say that about Marie?"

"Be careful, Ella," Stepmother warns. "Perhaps you wish to take Marie's place as Bertha's maid?"

I open my mouth to let loose another remark when I note Stepmother's cutting gaze narrowed on me. She's serious. I swallow my remark and instead say, "We could share maids. You know, split our time. You have Jesse one day, and I, the next. We could work it out to wear the dresses that don't require extra help on the days we don't have her."

"I suppose." Bertha stares forlornly into her pile of food. "Mother, you said things would get better once we moved here, but they haven't."

"Don't be so quick to judge, because I've wonderful news," Stepmother says. "Last night I sent an invitation to Dr. Wissen to come for dinner tonight. We just received his acceptance this morning."

My blood chills colder than ice. "Did you know he tried to steal our manor and take everything we have while Father was gone?" I sputter. "He's not the hero you believe him to be."

"He's to be your husband." Stepmother wags a finger at me. "Are you sure you want people to think that about him?

Make sure you wear something nice to dinner tonight and be on time."

I grip my silverware, determined not to let my temper get the best of me. Mother's last words to promise to be good are becoming harder than I think she ever imagined.

"The tutor should be arriving within the hour," Stepmother continues. "Marianne and Bertha, be sure to put on your dancing shoes because I've asked her to start off reviewing the dances. You must know them to perfection."

"I'd love to join," I say. As much as I enjoy running the estate, I've missed doing fun things like dancing. "It's been a while since I practiced."

"If all goes well tonight," Stepmother's lips twist, "you won't have to bother learning a dance."

"The invitation says all unmarried women are requested to attend the ball," I say. "Maybe the prince will choose to marry me."

"How ungrateful! I'm trying to secure a safe and successful future for you, so you don't live your days cleaning the house or becoming a spinster. Today, you'll help Cook in the kitchen. She has much work to do to prepare for tonight's dinner, and since it's in your honor, it's only right that you help her."

My eyebrows rise. "You want me to help in the kitchen?" I can hardly believe it. It's not that I can't do it—Mother and I used to cook up dishes and cakes for fun—but even I know a kitchen isn't a place for a lady.

"Yes, I do," Stepmother says firmly. "Now run along."

Somehow, I rise from my chair, trying to ignore Bertha, who's pressing a napkin to her lips to cover uncontrollable giggles. As I make my way to the kitchen, Marianne catches up to me.

"I'm sorry you have to work in the kitchen," Marianne

says. "Later, come to my room and I'll review the dance steps with you. In case you wish to dance at your wedding."

"Thanks, but I'll pass."

"Are you sure?" Marianne clutches me harder, furrowing her brow. "Because I have an idea that would surely make him not want to marry you."

"Really?" Now she's got me interested. "What is it?"

"Ruin the night. Make it a complete disaster. What man wants to marry a disaster for a wife?"

An ache pinches between my eyes, but I push the pain aside. "What are you saying?"

"Be sure you look your very worst. That'll do the trick. I'm sure of it."

"That's a perfect idea." I hug Marianne. "Thank you."

When I step into the warm room, Cook is in a furious mood.

"She expects me to cook a grand meal," Cook complains, waving her hands about and showering the air with flour. "All by myself, mind you. What does she think I have, a magic wand?"

"She's expecting I'll be your assistant," I say.

"What?" Cook stops kneading the dough to stare at me. "You're the lady of the house. You'll do no such thing."

I grab an apron, and as I tie it on, I realize I've got leaves stuck to my dress. I toss them aside. "This is supposed to be a meal to impress my future husband."

"Is it now?"

"Which means we must be diligent and make the worst meal in history."

"That makes no sense, Ella. Unless—"

"Unless I want him to never come back here again. That it's such a terrible visit, just the thought of seeing me again would make him sick to his stomach."

Cook sighs and wipes her hands on her apron before coming to me and drawing me into a big hug.

"Your mother would never force you to marry a man you despised," she whispers, and then holds me out at arm's length, studying my face. "How about this? We make a meal that fits the character of the man we're serving. Then you'll go to the ball and meet the prince. He won't be able to resist you."

"I'm sure the prince can resist even my charms." I roll up my sleeves. "In the meantime, we have a dinner to make."

We get right to work. Cook shows me how to roll the dough for bread and let it rise above the stove where it's dark and warm. But like wicked little cooks, we don't let the bread rise, but bake it immediately. It comes out flat and—since we unfortunately let it sit in the oven a few minutes too long—blackened.

Next, we work on the stew. Cook teaches me how to chop the vegetables into perfect slices, nice and thick and hearty. We toss them into the pot while I hum one of my mother's favorite songs. Next, she shows me the array of spices for the perfect flavor, but of course, we don't add any of those. Instead, we toss in chili powder, lemon rind, and pine bark for a guaranteed hot-sour taste.

By midday, my dress is soiled and sooty. My feet ache from being on them all day, but I'm in a great mood. Even Stepmother doesn't bother me when she stops by to check on our progress, frowning when she finds us laughing.

"This meal better be perfect," Stepmother warns, brushing off non-existent lint from her dress.

"Trust me," I reply gleefully, stirring the bubbling stew. "It will."

"I hope you're making the right decision, Ella," Cook murmurs once Stepmother leaves. "That woman is as vicious as a snake."

# CHAPTER 25

# JACOB

### HONAU

After leaving Ella, I try to sleep, but all I can think about is how she's living in danger. When dawn crests the horizon, I'm perched on the windowsill, coffee cupped between my palms, a plan brewing in my head.

"Did you sleep at all last night?" Wilhelm asks as he clambers into the main room.

"No." I set my coffee down and strap on my sword and knife. "Rumpelstiltskin! Come down here."

"Where are you going?" Wilhelm asks. "It's too early to be prowling outside. You'll look suspicious."

"I'm heading to Dr. Wissen's house." I toss my cloak over my shoulders.

"You're not going to the doctor's house alone. I'm coming with you. No name has appeared on the hourglass yet, so there isn't an excuse to leave me behind."

"Rumpelstiltskin!" I yell louder this time. "I need you down here."

"You're going to wake the neighbors," Wilhelm warns.

"It's too early to be shouting like a flock of chickens,"

Rumpelstiltskin grumbles as he shuffles down the stairs. A single hair sticks up on top of his head.

"I need you to go to the Magistrate's office," I tell the trickster. "There's a contract that must be approved between Ella von Maier and Dr. Wissen. Destroy it immediately."

"So demanding."

"And make sure no one sees you while you're at it."

"What do you take me for?" he scoffs. "A petty criminal?"

Outside, frost hugs the eaves of the houses and spiders across paned windows. To a passerby, this Bavarian town nestled in the mountains appears quiet and unaffected by evil creatures.

"Remind me again why we're visiting this doctor," Wilhelm says.

"Ella's stepmother is planning on marrying her off to this man. She asked me to help stop the marriage. I promised I would."

"I'm sure you did. You're becoming far too invested in Ella. What will happen when our work is done and it's time to leave? How will you feel about that?"

"Let's just deal with one problem at a time."

We finally reach the house settled on the outskirts of the village, hugging the foothills of the Swabian Alps. It's an old manor with worn stone walls and a brick-colored slanted roof pocked with windows that leer down on us. A balcony juts from the tallest point of the home like a watchdog. No flower boxes welcome visitors. Only dead vines clamber across the house, even over the windows, reminding me of spider webs ready to trap those who dare enter its lair.

Steps crawl up to the massive wooden doors where a giant stone-carved wolf clings over the archway. The eyes look so real, they send a chill down my spine.

"Is it just me, or is the statue staring at us?" I whisper to Wilhelm.

"The manor is clearly cursed. Why do you always pick the worst places to visit before we've even eaten breakfast?"

"Would you prefer to come here at night then?"

Wilhelm glowers. "Let's get this evil task finished so I can enjoy my warm bowl of porridge and return to my books."

"I'm with you on that, brother."

We march up the stairs, and that itchy sensation of being watched heightens. Two bulging eyes and a toothed mouth serve as the knocker's handle. The scent of decaying animals hits my senses. I let the knocker boom against the wooden door, and we wait. Slowly, the door creaks open to reveal a large man with an untamed beard, trailing to his belly. He's wearing a tunic and breeches smeared with blackened streaks, along with boots coated in sawdust. He smells of sweat and rotting meat.

Lovely.

"Good day to you," the man says, sounding more like he's bidding us a curse than a good morning. "What's your business?"

"We're here to speak to the esteemed Doctor Wissen," I say. "Our business is for him and him only."

"Harrumph," the man grumbles, but opens the door wider.

"I'll take that as an invitation to enter," I say, and we step inside.

"Wait here," the man growls and strides off, footsteps booming and creaking along the wood flooring.

"Well, isn't this homey?" Wilhelm says sarcastically, looking around.

Dark oak paneling lines the entry's walls all the way to the top third of the wall. That's when the images take over, circling the room. Warriors in battle, maidens sacrificed on altars, and villagers' heads chopped off. The ribbed wooden ceiling is free of chandeliers, keeping the room dark and dank, other than light filtering from the two adjoining rooms. The hallway to the back of the house remains shrouded in darkness.

"I'm quite partial to the beheadings," I joke morbidly. "But I'm not sure if the villagers would appreciate a painting like that in the bookshop."

I decide to do a little snooping while we wait, so I step into the room on our right. A giant fireplace fills one wall, the sides arched into what appears like demons with sharp teeth cutting out from snarled lips and eyes curling upward. The blackened logs remain cold and still.

"There's something dark about this place," I mutter and yank at my collar.

"You think?" Wilhelm asks, trailing after me. "This was your idea. If anything goes wrong, I'm blaming you."

"I deserve that."

There's not much light in this room thanks to the heavy maroon drapes. An ornately carved wooden bench sits against one wall with portraits of young women, none whom could be older than twenty above it.

"That's an odd collection of portraits, don't you think?" Wilhelm muses. "They all look different. They can't be family members."

"Greetings," a man says, entering the room.

I turn to find Dr. Wissen, handsome even with the three long scars that run down the side of his face. His presence fills the room, and his blue eyes twinkle as if amused to be seeing us here.

"I'm Dr. Wissen. What do I owe the pleasure of the great and renowned Brothers Grimm?"

"Great and renowned hardly meet our humble description," I object. "We are merely two booksellers helping the king out as he sees fit."

"From what I'm told, you are much more than just book-sellers. You also hunt and write. An odd combination."

A servant rushes in and sets a tray of bread, cheese, and meat on the coffee table.

"If you're ever in need of a good book," Wilhelm says, trying to veer us into safer waters, "come stop by our shop."

"I see your land borders the wilds." I get right to the point. "The king commissioned us to rid the forest of the wolves. Have you had any trouble with these creatures?"

"Troubles indeed, but my men work tirelessly to rid our village and the surrounding forests of them. What I want to know is how you two went from prestigious law students to working as hunters."

"And booksellers. You must not forget that." I cross my arms, surprised he knew so much. It's also a bit alarming.

Dr. Wissen picks up a chunk of meat and begins gnawing on it. "Our village is rather unimpressed with the king sending mere amateurs to save us. It's as if he doesn't take our problems seriously."

"You can rest assured we're taking this very seriously," I say.

"Perhaps a better question would be why you? The two of you should be studying and writing books. Yet here you are. Highly unusual."

He suspects us. Not good.

"Some of us are not as fortunate as you." I narrow my eyes. "I heard you were once the town carpenter. What I find *highly unusual* is for a man of a carpenter status to rise to such a station of a manor like this one and a title of a doctor."

"I've worked hard for my success. You know the old saying, the Devil's favorite piece of furniture is a long bench." Dr. Wissen waves to the tray of food. "How rude of me! Do eat and relax. I can't have you come all this way and not feed you."

"We just ate breakfast, but thank you," I say, ignoring my growling stomach. "How do you feel about us riding around your land to check for tracks? I'd hate for you and your household to be attacked by these wolves."

"You're far too generous." Dr. Wissen smiles thinly. "But my men are well armed. I have a crew of men who are always cutting down new trees in the forest for my carpentry work. You see, even though I've taken up the office of councilman and doctor, I've not given up my love for carpentry."

He moves to the large cabinet and pats it lovingly, explaining each detail and carving. I don't hear a word he says because the flame from the candle flickers across his neck. A white saw like those used to cut wood appears. I stiffen. Ella had been right to suspect him. He's a Forbidden.

"Your carpentry is truly magnificent," I say. "But what intrigues me is this wall packed with portraits of beautiful young ladies. Sisters, perhaps?"

"I'm afraid not." The doctor sniffs and clears his throat, touching the corner of his eye as if to wipe away a tear. "Those are my lovely wives. They have entered the realm of death, but they live on in my memories."

"All of them? Dead?" Wilhelm studies the portraits closer. "That would be six wives."

"Indeed." Dr. Wissen nods sagely, clasping his hands together. "Some from childbirth, others from disease, one from a drowning. Wretched luck I have."

There's no luck involved here. This is madness. Ella's bridegroom-to-be is a murderer.

# CHAPTER 26

# ELLA

## MAIER MANOR

I really want to look despicable. But I've discovered Stepmother can be attentive if she wants to. She made sure Jesse assisted me, much to Bertha's annoyance. So when I finish dressing in my finest gown—a pale lavender that, according to Stepmother, made me look slimmer and not so short—Bertha's wail could be heard from her room down the hall.

"Tuck that strand back," Stepmother instructs Jesse, pointing to a stray curl that always tends to fly loose. "She must be perfect when Dr. Wissen meets her. And give her some powder on her cheeks. Her skin looks dreadful. Too much time in the sun."

While Stepmother orders Jesse about, I keep my lips sealed. She needs to believe everything is perfect when we sit down to eat. If she suspects I'm going to ruin her plans, she'll somehow manage to turn the tables on me.

But tonight, I'm going to win.

"You look lovely, Ella," Jesse says, patting my cheeks after Stepmother leaves. "I heard you crying last night. I know you miss your mother, but maybe having a husband at your side will ease your pain."

"I do miss her." I spin in a circle, watching my dress flounce about, and sigh. "It is such a lovely dress. Too bad I'll never wear it again."

"What do you mean?"

"Thank you, Jesse, but I think you should help Bertha before she breaks out in hives from all that crying."

"I suppose I need to, but Bertha isn't easy to deal with," she says and shuffles out of the room.

I linger at my window, staring down at Mother's tree. It's been warmer lately, so it won't be long before buds show up. So many memories with Mother are tied to that tree, like nursing a thrush with a broken wing. Or how she taught me to mix the salve, bind the bandage, and build the bird box. We cared for it until it flew into the sky, free and alive.

She'd want me to be free, too.

As I head downstairs, I tug out my curls from my perfectly coiffed hair and dart to the unlit fireplace. I scoop up a handful of soot. I pat a handprint on the side of my lovely dress and smear the rest on my hem. Hopefully, I look frazzled and wild, a terrible combination for the wife of an esteemed doctor.

As I enter the room, all eyes focus on me. Can they hear my heart pounding? Stepmother's placid face pales, and her mouth falls open. Bertha bursts into giggles, while Marianne gives me an appreciative grin. But it's Dr. Wissen's expression that pleases me most. His face darkens, and those bright eyes narrow in disapproval.

"Good evening," I say triumphantly, curtsying in the most unsatisfying way before plopping into the chair across from Dr. Wissen. "I hope you'll excuse me for being late. I was reading and completely lost track of time."

"Good evening, Ella," Dr. Wissen replies smoothly. "It's good to see you again."

"I'd forgotten you two have already met," Stepmother says, finally recovering from my despicable appearance.

"This is true," I jump to answer. "He came by and offered to buy our harvest for below value. He said I should take that offer before we were forced to sell the property to him for below the price. I told him absolutely not."

"Good," Father mutters. Hearing his voice startles me. I can't remember the last time I heard him talk. "These lands aren't for sale. They've belonged to my family for generations."

"I wouldn't dare dream of taking your family's land from you." Dr. Wissen squirms in his chair.

"Really?" I tilt my head to the side. "Is that what you told the family of your first wife?"

"My first wife?" The three long scars on Dr. Wissen's face flame up.

"You've been married before?" Marianne leans in, obviously loving this uncomfortable gossip.

"I have. A most unfortunate death. God rest her soul."

"Which of your wives' deaths was unfortunate?" I tap my fingers to my lips. "You've been married more than once if I recall the village rumors."

"You shouldn't listen to rumors and gossip, Ella," Stepmother admonishes. "A young lady must only focus on truth and compassion."

I want to ask her where her compassion was when she fired our three servants last month.

"I wasn't born into wealth," Wissen says. "I came from an appallingly poor family and would still be poor today if I hadn't made a wood delivery to a certain doctor. Seeing how the doctor lived, I asked how to emulate his success. The doctor showed me how to make my dream come true by handing me an ABC book with instructions. Here I am, transformed from complete poverty to one of the richest in the land. Not only that, it's empowered me to help those in need in our village."

"You must feel quite indebted to this doctor," Marianne says.

He clears his throat. "But of course."

"Quite the rags to riches story," I say blandly. "That must have been a very special ABC book to make such a transformation."

Marianne clears her throat. "Dinner is likely getting cold. Shall we make our way to the dining room?"

Stepmother nods, rising to her feet. "Absolutely."

Bertha shoots me her you're-doomed eyebrow waggle and smirk while Marianne winks at me.

"I never thought you could be so entertaining, Ella," Marianne whispers into my ear. "Do remind me to take you with me to all social functions, for you're wildly out of control."

Then she hooks arms through mine, and the two of us stroll into the dining room.

Before I sit down, Stepmother holds me back with a grip of iron. "I don't know what you are up to," she says through gritted teeth. "But if you mess up this marriage proposal, you'll wish you groveled at the doctor's feet, begging him to marry you."

My muscles stiffen, but I grind my teeth together. She might be determined to be victorious, but I'm determined to fight the whole way.

"I don't know what you're talking about," I say in my most innocent voice.

Unfortunately, Stepmother has arranged for the doctor and me to sit across from each other. I fiddle with my napkin, trying to look anywhere except at him. As Cook and Jesse serve the soup, Wissen studies me as if I'm a block of wood ready to be carved into a creation of his choosing.

"We have Ella to thank for this dinner," Stepmother says as Cook finishes serving the soup. "She helped prepare it. I'm sure you have a cook of your own, but a good wife must also be prepared to cook and feed her family if the need arises."

"Absolutely." Dr. Wissen's beautiful face flashes a dimpled smile as he dips his spoon into the soup. "I always appreciate a woman who can cook."

"I made this soup especially for you," I said, eagerly awaiting his expression as he ate.

The others in the room begin choking, and spoons clatter onto the table. Dr. Wissen's face screws up like he tasted spicy lemons. I dig my fingernails into my palm to keep myself from laughing out loud at his expression.

"So what do you think, doctor?" I ask naively. "Does it pass your palette test?"

He chokes into his napkin and gulps down his water, unable to answer.

"Ella," Stepmother says, her tone thick with rage. "What did you do to this soup?"

Oddly, Dr. Wissen holds up his hand. "It's fine. I don't expect a wife to cook with expertise for her first meal. It's an acquired ability, but I'm sure you have other talents. Besides, I have such great wealth. I hardly require my wife to cook. She shall have a full kitchen of chefs."

"How truly fortunate for your wife," Stepmother says, releasing a breath.

I stare at him, trying to understand this man. Did he guess my intentions? Or maybe he did change and is now a kind and generous man.

"Unfortunately," I admit, "I've no other talents. I spent most of my childhood sitting around and doing nothing."

"Ella!" Stepmother gasps. "What has gotten into you?

How rude! I must apologize for my stepdaughter. She hasn't been formally trained in etiquette."

He focuses on brushing non-existent lint from his starched white shirt, but his jaw tightens. My comment rattled him. *Good.* But when he looks back up at me, his eyes have chilled to a calculating intensity.

No, I didn't rattle him. I angered him.

"It doesn't matter, Frau von Maier," the doctor tells my stepmother. "I promised her mother a long time ago I'd take good care of her daughter. These scars, as ugly as they are, are a daily reminder to me of that promise."

I suck in a shuddering breath. Did my mother give him those scars? Could those marks be from talons? Understanding fills me. He'll marry me, not for love or even to raise his station in our community. He wants vengeance so he can hurt me like he wanted to hurt her.

"I won't marry you," I finally choke out, rising from my seat.

"Sit down right now!" Father bellows from his chair. "You will not disrespect me here."

Father's words snap me back into my chair. My body shakes, I'm so furious. My plans are falling apart because I let the doctor get to me. I'd been so worried about my stepmother trying to win this battle, I didn't have the foresight to understand how deeply Dr. Wissen hated my mother. I need to pull myself together and think this through.

"I brought a gift for you, my dear sweet Ella," Dr. Wissen says. "I hope you don't mind me calling you that since we're betrothed."

"I do mind, actually," I counter. "We haven't received notification from the magistrate that the betrothal is approved."

"This is a token of my affection for you," he continues as

if I hadn't spoken a word. He extends a small wooden engraved box. "I hope you'll accept it."

"Of course she will accept a gift from her future husband," my father says, snatching the box from the doctor and holding it out to me.

I clench the sides of the table but rise to my feet and take the box. Inside, I discover a single bird's feather, sky blue tinged with sunlight yellow. My pulse halts in dread. This feather must have been my mother's.

Dr. Wissen's lips curl into a wicked smile as my gaze meets his. *He knows*, I think in terror. *He knows what I am.*

## CHAPTER 27

# JACOB

## MAIER MANOR

I pace the outer fence of the Maier manor as the sun sets and the lights in the house flicker to life, glowing like eyes pocked along the walls. He's in there, Doctor Wissen, wooing Ella and probably solidifying his marriage proposal. I grasp my sword's hilt tighter.

"I'm going to kill him," I tell Wilhelm. "Murdering scoundrel."

"We don't know that he murdered his wives. If he's truly a Forbidden—"

"He is. I saw the mark. It was faint, but when the light hit his neck, I could see it."

"Then we'll get his story and get rid of him the proper way," Wilhelm says, then mutters under his breath, "If proper is what you'd call it. Come on. I'm starving for supper."

Wilhelm has a point. I can't prove he killed his wives, but something is wrong about him. I can feel it in my gut.

"Give me a piece of paper," I demand. "And a quill."

"Why must I be the responsible one? You should've brought your own writing kit."

"Hurry."

Sighing, Wilhelm digs through his satchel, withdrawing the parchment, quill, and ink. I scribble a note for Ella.

> *Ella,*
>
> *We need to talk. It's about the matter that concerned you last night. Meet me tonight. You know where and when.*
>
> *Yours*

I pause. Is it wise to write my name? I glance at the windows on the upper floor. They're dark, so the dinner party must still be underway. I decide to keep it blank and fold it up.

"You're going to meet her again?" Wilhelm chortles. "Truly, you're smitten."

I glower at him. "Go home and get yourself some food. I'm going to give this to their cook. Ella trusts her."

"Fine, but if you get caught, I'm not coming to rescue you this time."

I duck under the fence. A motion to my right catches my attention, onyx wings taking flight. It's one of those ravens. Knowing my luck, they work for Dr. Wissen and are on their way to warn him. I withdraw my sword, steel disrupting the silence, and take off again.

As I round the garden hedges, sounds of laughter and talking escape from an open window. My stomach twists. They're having far too good a time. Perhaps Wissen is a warlock and is bewitching Ella. Shoving those thoughts aside, I steal along the stone walls until I come to the servants' door and slip inside.

I creep down the hallway, following the scent of food until I reach the kitchen, bright and warm from the fire crackling happily in the hearth. At the table sits a plump, rosy-cheeked woman, humming a tune as she picks beans from their pods.

Before she can scream, I press a gloved hand over her mouth and hold up the letter.

"I need to ask you a favor," I say, then slowly release my hand. "Give this to Ella. It's important she gets it tonight. Can you do that for me?"

"You sneak in here like a thief and ask me for favors?" She snorts and continues cracking pea pods. "A lot of nerve you have."

"More like desperation. Ella can't marry Wissen. I need to warn her."

Her hands freeze. I've gotten her attention. She eyes the letter. Noises erupt from the hallway, the clattering sound of footsteps.

"She will pay for tonight's dinner!" a voice screeches. "No one crosses me. No one!"

"Hide!" the cook tells me, snatching my letter and tucking it into her pocket. "Under the table!"

A quick glance tells me there are only two ways out. The door where the voices are coming from or the window that my shoulders will never fit through. I scramble under the table while the cook slides the crate of potatoes and a basket of onions to hide me, so I'm firmly huddled up like the idiot I seem to have become. At least Wilhelm isn't here to see me and laugh.

The kitchen door bangs open. Peeking through the thin space between the potatoes and onions, I watch Frau von Maier swoop into the room, wearing a flowing gown of silver, hefting a plate in one hand and a knife in the other.

"How dare you?" she screeches, her hand gripping the knife as if she's ready to use it on the cook. "Here I provide a job for you. I keep you over all the other servants I've let go, and this is what you give me in return! The most shameful dinner ever served in the land."

The mistress drops the plate. It shatters across the wooden floor along with a roast, potatoes, and peas. Apparently, she didn't like the dinner.

"I'm sorry, mistress." The cook's voice trembles. "I'll make you another meal right away, that's right. Just real quick-like."

"You'll do no such thing," Frau von Maier says with a growl.

Her lips snarl, and she raises her knife. Frantic, I go to push out of my hiding space and defend the cook, but Ella bursts into the room.

"No!" Ella screams, grabbing the mistress's arm. "Please, leave her alone. This is my fault. I ruined the meal. She didn't do anything."

Frau von Maier slams the knife, point down, into the wooden table beside her so it remains upright. It wavers from the impact. I debate whether to reveal myself or wait and assess the situation. Wilhelm would tell me to wait.

"You will leave this house this instant," Frau von Maier tells the cook. "A cook who cannot manage her kitchen is no cook of mine."

"I'm sorry, Ella dear," the cook says, her voice choked.

"No, it's I who should be sorry." Ella presses a hand to her mouth as if to hold back a sob. Tears trickle down her cheeks. "I should never have brought you into this."

"Get out now or I'll have one of the men haul you out," Frau von Maier orders.

"Yes, mistress." The cook shuffles across the kitchen, grabs her cloak hanging on the door peg, and leaves.

I clench my fists. There must be something I can do rather than hiding like a spineless toad. Yet coming out could ruin Ella's reputation, so I remain where I'm at, seething.

"You!" The stepmother wags a thin finger at Ella. "You'll

pay for what you've done. You think you can outwit me? You're wrong. First, you can start by cleaning up this dish." She points to the broken plate on the floor. "Then you'll clean all the dinner dishes and scrub the pots. From now on, you'll take over the cook's responsibilities. And tonight, I won't have you keeping me up all night with your wailing. I'm moving your sleeping quarters to the room in the turret. Maybe then I'll finally get some peace."

With that, she storms out of the kitchen, screaming for the servants to follow her to Ella's room. I lean my head against the crate, now fully understanding the situation Ella is in. My troubles pale in comparison to what she's going through. Sobbing pulls me back to Ella. She collapses into a heap on the floor and starts picking up the plate's fragments, one by one.

I shove aside the crate and scramble out. Ella gasps and drops the pieces in her hand.

"Ella, it's me," I say, hating how I must have scared her. Leaping out from behind a crate of onions is hardly the act of a knight in shining armor.

My chest aches at the sight of her. Soot smudging her dress, curls spilling loose from her braided crown like they gave up fighting. Every muscle in my body screams to pull her into my arms and kiss away her tears. Wilhelm is right. I'm smitten.

"Jacob?" She wipes her tears away and stands. "What are you doing here?"

I creep to the door, peek around the corner to make sure the hall is empty, and shut it, turning the lock.

"I came to warn you."

"Warn me? By hiding under the table." She shoots a pointed look at my hiding place. "With the onions."

"Which are excellent for masking the smell of humans from wicked stepmothers. Highly recommended."

She crosses her arms, my attempt at humor falling short. "You should leave. If my stepmother discovered you, she'd have you guillotined or placed in the stocks in the village square."

"It's Dr. Wissen." I step closer to her, trying to ignore her intoxicating smell. "You can't marry him. I think he's murdered every one of his six wives."

"Only half a dozen?" She grabs the broom and begins sweeping up the mess. "And here I thought there'd been more."

"So you already knew." I can't hide my disappointment. I guess I wanted to be the one who came in and rescued her. Saved her from the monsters in her life. But seeing her pull herself back together, I see a strength in her that inspires me.

Bleeding stars, it makes me fall even harder for her.

"Yes, well I suspected," she admits. "But I had no idea there were *six*. That's why I tried to ruin dinner and the entire evening. I was so determined to win the battle tonight and show him what a wretched wife I'd be. But in the end, I got my dear cook fired. Meanwhile, Dr. Wissen gave me this vile grin and handed me a disturbing box as an engagement gift. That's when I realized he meant to marry me no matter what. At all costs."

"But why?" I pick up the knocked-over chair and start stacking the dishes.

"I could be wrong, but I think something happened between my mother and him." She frowns and presses her hands on the tip of the broomstick, staring at the floor. "I think the scars on his face are courtesy of her."

"She must have been a fighter, like you," I say. "What you say makes sense. Now that she's gone, he wants to have his revenge by using you. We won't let him win."

"We?"

I touch her cheek, rubbing away the smear of soot where

a tear cut through the blackness. "Tonight. Come with me, and let's discover the truth about who this doctor truly is. We'll go to his house, gather the evidence, and produce it to the village constable."

"You can't be serious." She backs away. "I can't just run off with you. Besides, I have dishes, and apparently, I'm moving to the turret. Quite busy. No time for dalliances with handsome and mysterious men."

She blushes then, like she hadn't meant to say the last part.

"I do hope you're referring to me," I say in a low voice.

I inch closer to her. She steps backward until her spine is pressed against the wall. I plant my palms on either side of her head, not to trap her, but to keep myself from doing something reckless. Like tasting her lips. Or finding out if she'd melt against me the way I've been imagining since the moment we met.

Her breath hitches. I clamp an iron grip on myself, not sure how much longer I can resist her.

"Let me help you," I finally say. "I'm an expert dishwasher. One of the perks of growing up a commoner."

"Truly?" She smiles, and my heart—oh, she has no idea what she's doing to me. "Fine," she concedes, ducking away. "But you must stay hidden while I get the rest of the dinnerware from the table."

"Your word is my command."

A wisp of a smile ghosts her lips. We work for a good hour. Wilhelm will be giving me an earful when I get home, but I'd take a lifetime of lectures to spend an hour with her. We are on the last dishes when Ella cries out in pain and doubles over.

"Ella!" I grab her arms, searching her face. "What's the matter? Sit down and rest."

I guide her to the very chair the cook sat in.

"Please," she says weakly. "You must go."

"I'm not leaving you here in pain." I wrap my palms around hers.

"I'm just tired." She pulls away, and my heart rips a little. "How about this? You head home so I can recover from this wretched day, and I'll come with you to Dr. Wissen's house tomorrow night."

I debate whether to go or not, the war in my chest pulling me in two. I want to respect her wishes, but it kills me to leave her like this.

"Don't worry about me," she says. "I'll be fine. Please go."

"If that's what you want." I drag myself away from her. "Meet me at your outer fence at midnight. Wear the color of shadows."

I leave then, but every step I take away from her feels wrong.

## CHAPTER 28

# ELLA

### MAIER MANOR

The moment Jacob leaves, all the laughter and brightness go with him. Never did I think I'd be standing beside a man washing dishes, much less Jacob, a fierce hunter. But the way he makes me feel, it's like I matter. He doesn't look at me like I'm a pawn to be sold off for money or used as a servant. My heart flutters as I replay how close our bodies were. How I almost fisted his shirt and kissed him hard, scraping my lips across his stubble. Even his scent of pine and spice still clings to me.

A light tapping draws my attention to the window. It's a bird. My aunt, in fact. I let her inside. A flurry of feathers and a rush of wind churn around me as my aunt transforms into her half-human and half-bird form. My stomach constricts thinking of becoming like that. My thoughts fly to Jacob and the look of pure admiration on his face. He won't look at me like that once he knows what I really am.

"You didn't drink your tonic," Fiona lectures. "The transformation is nearly unbearable without it."

"I spilled some of it accidentally and haven't had a chance to ask you for more."

Her eyes skim over me and narrow. "What happened to you? Why are you here in the kitchen?"

"My stepmother replaced the cook with me. I'm supposed to move to the turret tonight but I'm too weak to attempt the stairs at the moment."

"What's this nonsense you speak of? Where are the servants?"

"Most of them were let go." I sag into a chair. My whole body shivers, probably from shock. "I don't want to become a monster."

"A monster? Do I look like a monster to you? Those are lies that Grimm has been feeding you. Transforming is about becoming who you are meant to be. Being half-bird is a glorious gift. You'll see. No matter if we are half-bird, half-human, or fully human, the choices of what to do with your talents and your life are what determine whether you're a monster or a hero."

She goes and fetches me another cup of brew. The liquid is cool as it slides down my throat. I sigh and close my eyes, telling myself I'll rest for a moment.

ॐ

Someone shakes me awake. My eyes pop open to find Jesse staring at me, a horrified expression on her face. My heart slams into my throat. Why does she look at me like that? Have I finally turned into a monster?

"What is it?" I sit up, frantically touching my skin, terrified I'll feel feathers, wings, or—Heavens help me—a beak. But all I feel is me. Smooth—if not dirty—skin and arms and legs. I let out a sigh of relief.

"I just..." Jesse stumbles on her words. "I wasn't expecting you here. We came to eat breakfast, but Cook is gone and you're here...lying on the kitchen hearth."

I rise to my feet, my cheeks burning. But oddly, my muscles feel stronger, and my vision is sharper and clearer. Maybe sleeping on the floor isn't so bad.

Until I realize Jesse and I aren't alone.

Herman, Peter, and Kurt crowd around the door, twisting their hats as if unsure what to do.

"Is it true the mistress let Cook go?" Kurt asks.

"It's true," Herman says gruffly. "And if you wish to keep your job, you'll do your work as quickly and silently as possible."

"But what about our breakfast?" Peter stares at the kitchen, clean and tidy, but there's no sign of the usual hearty breakfast Cook usually prepares for the staff and family. "We can't be late to our duties."

"Well." I start digging through the cupboard. "I'm sure we can whip up something real quick. Cook must have baked rolls yesterday. Sausage can't be that hard to make, can it?"

We work together to create breakfast. It turns out to be more fun than I expected. We laugh over Kurt's burnt toast, and Jesse teaches a new song she made up. Once we're finished eating the breakfast we cooked, I set the rest of the food on the table for the family who haven't even woken yet. Then, taking a deep breath, I head upstairs. Pale morning light clings to the stairs, and birds sing outside. For a moment, I imagine Mother is still sleeping in her bed and Father is out walking the fields, preparing for the spring planting.

But Mother is gone, and Father is probably locked away in his office as he's become accustomed to doing. When I go to open my room, the door is locked. Numbness washes over my body as my new reality settles in.

"Ella," Marianne calls, peeking out of her room. Her long brown hair is unbound and sways at her waist, smooth as silk.

She rushes to hug me. "I'm so sorry Mother moved you to the tower. It's terrible!"

"She really did it," I say, dazed. "I'd thought she'd been exaggerating last night."

Tears stream down my cheeks as anger, sadness, and fear well up in my chest. Marianne's warm arms wrap around my shoulders.

"I made sure Jesse moved as many of your things into the turret as I could manage under Mother's watchful eye. Jesse worked hard to make it cozy. I even had her put fresh sheets on the old bed."

"Some of my things?" My tears dry up as anger wins my emotional battle. "How could she decide what I kept and what I didn't?"

"I know this must be so hard for you." Marianne touches my shoulder, staring at me with her rich brown eyes. Then she hooks her arm in mine and begins walking me down the hall. "Before we came here, did you know we were about to move to the poor house? We sold nearly everything except for our finest dresses. We did up our hair and went to our last party. That's when Mother met Father. Just think. If she hadn't met him, our lives would've been ruined forever."

"I didn't know that." I pause mid-step. "So my father literally saved you from destitution?"

"That's why we adore him. That experience showed me it's when things are the worst that hope comes."

When I clutched my mother's hand, cold and lifeless, that had been my darkest hour. Except ever since my new stepmother arrived, things have only gotten worse. Jacob warned me she was a Forbidden. Should I let Marianne know as well?

"Mother said she's going to sell off the rest of your things to pay for the needs of the family," Marianne continues.

"What?" I gasp. This isn't happening. I must be dreaming.

"Trust me, I know it's hard, and I know what it feels like. But we're sisters now, and sisters stick together."

A bell rings from Bertha's room.

"What's that?" I ask.

"It's Bertha." Marianne rolls her eyes. "She got sick last night from the dinner and is too weak to walk so she's using a bell to let me know when she needs something. I'd better see what she needs before she starts screaming and wakes Mother."

Marianne rushes off, leaving me standing there, mouth open in shock. Slowly, I shuffle down the hall toward the turret, dreading to discover what Stepmother took from me. We always keep the door to the turret's stairwell shut since the tower is drafty and cold.

The door groans as I open it. Thankfully, Jesse must have come through with a broom and brushed the cobwebs away when they brought up my possessions last night. A candle sits on the small table by the door. I light it and begin my climb.

When I was younger, I'd sneak up here, imagining I was a princess locked away in a tower. I'd pretend to fight my way out, battling against ogres and trolls. Except now I realize I'm far from a princess, maybe even becoming the very monster I once tried to slay.

At the top of the stairs, I open the second door and step inside the round room with its domed ceiling. Three tall, narrow windows spill beams of sunlight into the room, bathing the floor with a glittery glow like fairy dust.

My wooden chest sits at the foot of a tiny bed. An end table is set beside it with a vase of fresh sprigs of lavender. I trail my fingers over the herb, knowing it must be from Jesse. She knows it's my favorite scent.

A vanity with a tall looking glass is cushioned against the wall beside my bed. I stare at myself. I look horrible. Soot is smeared on my chin, my hair is tangled and wild, and my dress is ruined. The flowers that once danced across the lavender skirts are only a memory, burnt and covered with ashes.

I pick up my brush on the vanity and desperately start combing my hair. Once finished, I set the brush beside the small, beaded jewelry box Father bought me two years ago. But then my eyes land on the box beside it. My skin crawls. Dr. Wissen's gift.

I snatch it up and, after gently placing the smooth feather in my drawer, unlatch the tall glass pane and swing it open. I toss the box out the window. It hits the cobblestone pathway, splintering the wood into pieces. I smile.

That felt really good.

A spring breeze tickles my cheeks and tugs my hair. Maybe this turret isn't so bad. Now I don't have to worry about being quiet, and I have a place all to myself. My gaze trails up the mountainside to where Lichtenstein Castle is perched on the cliff, its pale tower spiking the sky, morning mist pooling around it.

Tomorrow night is the ball. I lean my elbows on the windowsill, wondering what it would be like to marry the prince and become a princess. He wouldn't be as exciting as Jacob. He'd never look at me or touch my face like Jacob had last night.

A raven sails up to my window and clings to its edge. It gives me a side look with its wide black eye, but there's something comforting about it, like a brother protecting me.

"What do you think the prince is like?" I ask. "Tall and handsome?"

The bird begins pecking at the side of my window, hunting for bugs.

"You're right," I agree with a sigh. "He's probably cranky and altogether disagreeable. Still, a girl can dream of escape.

He can't possibly be as horrible as Dr. Wissen. Plus, if I were a princess, I could rehire all my servants."

I take one last look at the castle, glistening in the morning light, and turn back to my new room. Stepmother thinks she can control me, but she's wrong. Anticipation dances across my skin as I dig through my chest, hunting for my black dress for tonight's adventure with Jacob.

# CHAPTER 29

# JACOB

## LICHTENSTEIN CASTLE

" I'm sure of it." Prince William slams his fist on the gilded chair's armrest and then rises to pace before us. His tiny poodle trails after him, wagging its tail. "I don't know who it is, but we have a mole among my staff. There are always rumors of someone trying to usurp the throne. If I were to get a golden coin for every threat, we'd be able to fill our coffers. This is different. It's as if someone knows my father's and my every plan."

Inwardly, I sigh. The king gave us access to his library today. I hoped to spend the entire day searching for clues about our curse, who these witches were that the Enchantress hated so much, and some idea of where the Realm of Candora was located. Especially since the spell book we found at Hohenzollern Castle didn't offer anything else useful. But the moment Prince William got wind we were here, he summoned us.

"Maybe if you explained the situation more, it would help," Wilhelm says, polite as ever.

"Last night, the weapons delivery was ambushed on the

hillside. It's the second order I've made that's been stolen. No one knew about it other than the men delivering it."

"Perhaps your mole is one of your soldiers?" I offer.

"Considering that every soldier from each delivery is dead, I think not."

"Sounds like someone wants you to be defenseless and weak," Wilhelm points out.

"Or they're amassing a large weapons collection for a keepsake," I joke. The prince shoots me a fierce frown. I suppose I deserve that.

"Someone is attempting to overthrow the crown," the prince repeats.

"Of course, Your Highness," I say, and then hating my next words, offer, "How can we be of service?"

He brightens. "What you two do is very special. You know things and see the world in a different way."

If only he knew.

"To add to the fact that you're aware of my...err...condition," he adds.

"Of course." I try not to think of him in his frog form, otherwise, I might start laughing. A guaranteed trip to the dungeon.

"I'd like to take a short trip before my ball," the prince continues.

"A trip, Your Royal Highness?" Wilhelm pales. "You wish for us to accompany you somewhere?"

"On the contrary!" The prince plops back down into his chair, throwing his hands up. "I wish to accompany you."

"How intriguing." I adjust my collar, which is currently constricting my throat. Wissen's name appeared at the top of the hourglass this morning. We don't have time for princely escapades.

"I want to see my kingdom in its purest form," the prince

continues. "To know what the commoners say about me and how they feel. And more importantly, I want to keep my ears open for any signs of the mole trying to overtake my future throne. With the two of you as expert hunters, I'm sure we'll discover the culprit, and then I'll bring him to my father's throne. He'll see me as a true prince and hopefully he'll let me cancel this lunacy of finding a wife through, not one, but *three* balls."

"I like this plan," Wilhelm says. "We'll have a great chance to get to know each other better."

What he means is we'll get his full story so we can send him back to the realm of the Forbidden. *Clever.*

"I knew you'd see things my way." The prince slaps his hands onto his knees and rings a bell for the servants. The door flies open, and an entourage enters the room. He waves his hands, indicating for his servants to come closer, saying, "I've decided to go on a short trip before my grand ball tomorrow night. I need time to reflect on my life before I choose the woman I shall marry. Make preparations. I leave within the hour."

The servants bow. The head servant escorts us out of the prince's quarters.

"This could be a problem," I tell Wilhelm as we head back to the stables. "What will we do with him tonight? We can't lug him along with us to the doctor's house. We need every minute to focus on Wissen's story."

All morning, my thoughts were on Ella, dirt smeared across her face, and that fierce look of determination storming in her eyes. She's all I can think of, and truth is, I'm counting the hours when I see her again.

Tonight.

She promised.

"If my memory serves me correctly," Wilhelm says. "You were the one who offered our services. This is your fault."

"Fine. Isn't everything?"

Why didn't I kiss her last night? I should've. That's my fault too.

"Maybe he could come along with us," Wilhelm offers. "He might be able to help."

"As a frog?" I snort. "I think not."

The castle bustles with activity, preparing for the festival of balls. Servants load chairs and long tables into the banquet hall while carts piled with fruits, vegetables, cheeses, and jugs of wine clutter the courtyard. We duck around a long line of servants parading in armloads of roses and sidestep past baskets overflowing with ribbons and lace.

"This looks like it will be quite the event," Wilhelm says after we clear the mayhem. We stroll out along the bridge that hovers above the chasm below. "But you're right. The important thing is to finish this next story."

I think about Ella and clench my fists. "We'll find Wissen's story. You can be sure of that."

Once we prepare our horses and one for the prince, we ride to the courtyard to wait. A servant races outside, waving a letter. Bowing, he hands it to me. I find a note inside.

I'm in the garden by the fountain. Do not bring me a horse.

"Thank you," I tell the servant and hand him the reins of the prince's mare. "Take this horse back to the stables. We don't need him anymore."

"As you wish." The servant dips into another bow and leaves.

"Did the prince cancel?" Wilhelm asks.

"He's waiting for us in the garden."

Sure enough, a small frog sits contentedly on the fountain's stone border, waiting for his escort.

"I think this will be a first for me," I say.

"I'm getting tired of firsts," Wilhelm says with a sigh.

"Good afternoon, Your Highness," I say, and scoop him

up, dropping him into my pocket. "You can stay safe in there. Can't have you falling off the horse now, can we?"

"Can he understand what we're saying?" Wilhelm whispers as we ride out of the garden.

"I imagine so. Let's visit the site of the robbery and assess the situation."

It feels good to be riding, the sound of the horse's hooves beneath me and the wind in my face. Buds are showing up on the trees, spring daring to cut through winter. The path steepens in a sharp downward slope as it works its way down the mountain. About halfway, I spy wheel tracks cutting through the path, angling sideways.

"This is where the carriage went off track," I point out.

We dismount, and a few strides off the main trail, I find that the bushes are twisted and bent. Though the attack was only last night, the bodies have been taken care of, but dried blood is on the grass. Flies buzz about.

I scramble through the bushes while Wilhelm wrenches aside the broken carriage door. A forgotten arrow is buried in a bush, and I bend to pick it up.

"Nothing in the carriage," Wilhelm calls out, his face blanched. "Except a bloody arm that reeks. Doubt you'd want to smell that."

A glimmer of light just to the left of the carriage catches my attention. A shiny ax with a smooth wooden handle is embedded in an oak trunk. I yank it out, twisting it in my palm. A glint shimmers across the silver blade, and an eye stares at me. A chill shudders over my body. I drop the ax, leaping backward.

"What's wrong?" Wilhelm steps to my side. "What happened?"

The eye vanishes, and the blade becomes just silver again.

"No, everything isn't all right." I mount my horse. "Whoever attacked this caravan used some sort of mirror magic to do it. It also means they now have a large supply of weapons."

We discuss our options as we head down the mountain. When we arrive at the village, it's hard to ride through the streets with the added visitors here for the king's festival. We visit several shops, and I make sure to have my pocket open so our Frog Prince can have a good view of what's happening.

Guests fill up every vacant room and there isn't a table free at the tavern, so we order food and take it back to our shop.

Once the door is locked and the shutters closed, I set the frog onto the floor and command him to his human form while Wilhelm arranges our dinner on the table. Rumpelstiltskin arrives with news he's managed to burn Ella's marriage contract, but when his eyes land on the prince, he hisses, leaping back.

"Who let *him* in here?" he asks. "Why does no one consult me on these matters? He's going to imprison us all."

"Don't worry." Prince William waves his hand dismissively. "As long as you're not trying to take my kingdom, you're welcome to stay here."

"Can't promise that," Rumpelstiltskin mutters only loud enough for me to hear.

A knock raps at the door.

"Let me get that," the prince offers, holding his shirt in one hand while he uses the other to throw open the door before I warn him otherwise. "Oh, hello there. I'm afraid we don't require any lady kissers as the brothers seem to have got that part all squared away, but you have my thanks."

"Excuse me?" An all-too-familiar voice gasps. "I'm hardly a lady kisser."

My heart sinks as I step to the door to find Ella standing there, scowling at the prince.

# CHAPTER 30

# ELLA

## HONAU

A half-naked scoundrel stands before me. I avert my eyes, face heating, but not before noticing his tight red curls and bright green eyes, a wide smile spreading across his face. He looks vaguely familiar.

"I'm sorry." Wilhelm pushes the man backward. "We have a guest who um..."

"Needs to work on his decorum," Jacob says gruffly, stepping forward as thankfully the green-eyed man tugs a shirt over his head. "Come in."

I stare at my boots. "I know we agreed to meet at the edge of my field, but lately I'm so tired at night I figured earlier would be better." What I don't say is that my attacks are worse at night, and I wanted to avoid the embarrassment of possible screaming.

When I look up at Jacob's face, he's smiling like I'm the best thing he's seen all year. Warmth floods my cheeks.

"Come in," he says, stepping back to make room. "Stay for dinner."

My stomach knots, and not because I'm hungry. His voice is rich, easy, like the offer is no big deal, but to me, after feeling isolated and alone at home, this is everything. The air smells like roasted sausages and fresh-baked bread, along with beeswax and aged parchment.

"This man is...a relative of ours." Wilhelm clears his throat awkwardly. "Distant."

"Fritz." The curly-haired man introduces himself and then kisses my hand.

"You look oddly familiar." I wrench my hand away. Lady kisser, indeed. "Wait! I know why. You're the merchant who bought my mother's necklace. Did your stepmother like it?"

"Really?" Jacob's eyebrows rise.

"Ah, that's right!" Fritz brightens. "You have an excellent memory. And yes, she most certainly did."

Once Jacob introduces me as simply Ella, my muscles relax. The last thing I need is for the villagers to realize the daughter of nobleman Karl von Maier is running about town unescorted. I'm thrilled to find Otto here, though. In a whisper, he tells me how he destroyed my marriage contract, and I'm so happy, I nearly hug him.

"Thank you for doing that," I say. "You've given me extra time."

"Now you're free to marry me instead, if you've got the nerve for it," he says, eyes glinting.

"I'm quite happy to *not* marry right now." I turn and take in this shop of the Grimm brothers.

It has a cozy air to it, a mix of shop and living space. The hearth glows with a crackling fire, and a copper kettle hangs over the flames. Bookshelves are tucked against two of the walls, tomes lined with perfection and care. An oak desk is cluttered with an inkwell, papers, and stacks of books. A honey-yellow spinning wheel is set up next to the large window overlooking the cobblestone street.

We all gather at the large wooden table in the center of the room, where sausages, sauerkraut, and piping-hot, buttery rolls are set out. Wilhelm adds a plate to the table for me.

"So when do we leave?" I ask as Jacob passes me the platter of sausages.

"She's coming, too?" Fritz frowns, but then suddenly brightens, and he winks at me. "Ah! She's for the kissing."

"Kissing?" I drop my fork. This is scandalous!

"Ella, could I have a word with you in private?" Jacob draws me to the far side of the room. "This man is one of the you-know-whos we talked about."

"The Forbidden?" I choke out the word. "How do you know?"

"He has the mark." Jacob sighs and glances back at the three. Fritz is digging into his sausages as if he hasn't eaten for days.

"I don't see a mark."

"Only Wilhelm and I can."

I shudder and adjust my cloak higher around my neck.

"Don't worry, he's harmless," he says. Clearly, he misinterprets my shaking because he takes my hand, squeezing it. "He works for the king. We're trying to discover who stole a weapons delivery. He's the one who can turn himself into a frog. The only way he can return to his human form again is if he is kissed by a maiden or if commanded out of him."

"He thinks I'm going to kiss him?" I'm horrified.

"It doesn't matter what he thinks because you don't have to kiss or worry about him." He tucks a stray curl behind my ear. It's far too intimate, and yet, every fiber in me wants to lean into the touch. "Also, how are you? I couldn't sleep last night. I was worried about you."

"Right now, I just want to stop my marriage to Dr. Wissen. Otto said he destroyed the contract, but that'll only slow things down, not end them. If my stepmother has her way, she'd have me married to him by morning without a formal wedding."

"You're not marrying him. Not while I'm breathing. Tonight, we're going to get his story and rid him from this world once and for all." He takes me to the back corner of the shop and pulls back a bookshelf, revealing a wall packed with weapons—knives, axes, bows and arrows, daggers, and the sword I always see him carrying.

"This is...a lot."

"Take this." He plucks a dagger, deadly sharp, from the wall. He presses it into my hand. It bites cold against my skin. "Just in case."

"I don't even know how to use it."

He steps in behind me, the heat of his chest warming my back. "Like this," he murmurs, wrapping a callused hand around mine. My pulse thrums dangerously.

"Keep your thumb here, tip up like a hammer. If an attacker comes at you, target the areas that will disable them, like the eyes, heels, or hands."

His voice is low and deep, more intimate than it should be for a lesson in violence.

"And if I miss?" I swallow, the air thick between us.

"You're strong, stronger than you give yourself credit for." His mouth hugs the shell of my ear. "But don't worry, I'll be there if you need me."

I look over my shoulder, up at him. His mouth is there, waiting for my lips. If I just lean in closer...

"Are you sure you should give a weapon to a woman?" Fritz asks, interrupting us. I stiffen. "She might hurt herself, or worse, hurt us."

Jacob releases me, shooting Fritz a glare as he hands me a belt for the dagger and reaches for his sword. "Ella is not only capable of taking care of herself, but a whole village, if necessary."

Then he turns to me and asks, "Do you wish for any other weapons?"

"This should suffice," I say, hiding my smile as Fritz sputters, trying to recover from his statement.

"Excellent," Jacob says. "Let's go."

Jacob, Wilhelm, Fritz, Otto, and I ride through the village without so much as a glance from the locals, thanks to the excitement for the royal balls. When we reach Wissen Manor, I suck in a horrified breath. To think this could be my home makes me sick. Its tower and stone walls loom dark against the slate sky, illuminated by a thick cream moon. It belongs to a nightmare.

"Tell me you have a plan to enter this forsaken abode," Fritz tells Jacob. "Surely, we can't go about knocking and inviting ourselves over for a midnight supper."

"Hardly," Jacob says. "And even if we were, it appears Dr. Wissen has company himself."

"Now that makes things exciting," Otto says, winking at me as a carriage rumbles up to the house. "Looks awfully familiar, don't you think, Ella?"

My heart plunges. It bears the Maier crest. "My father must be here to rewrite the marriage license."

"This complicates things," Wilhelm says.

The carriage halts at the front steps, and Peter, our driver, rushes to open the door. I gasp when a woman steps out, wearing a simple gown of midnight blue and a hat with a mesh drape covering her face. I clench my reins. It's my stepmother. She must be here to fix the marriage contract. It makes sense. She's conniving and desperate enough to risk sneaking into another man's house at night.

"Looks like your intended is having a midnight rendezvous," Fritz says.

"He's not my intended." I bristle. "And I couldn't care less who he's with."

Except that's a lie because my stepmother's appearance changes everything. The woman strolls confidently to the front door and waits, not bothering to knock. The door creaks open, and she slips inside.

There's no question now. I must sneak inside and destroy that contract. Jacob's eyes meet mine. He nods once like he knows what needs to be done.

"This is actually perfect," Wilhelm says. "The doctor will be distracted, and we'll do our search without him even knowing."

"We'll go through the back of the house then," Jacob decides, dismounting. "And leave the horses here."

"I'll stay here with the horses," Otto offers. "I'm not setting a toe on Dr. Wissen's cursed property."

I can't blame him.

"You do know that means we'll have to enter the forest," Wilhelm points out, tying up his horse.

"What's wrong with the forest?" Fritz asks, peering into the dark woods tentatively.

"I suppose you'll just have to see for yourself," Jacob says with a wicked grin. Then to me, "Do you want to stay here with the horses?"

"And me," Otto pipes up, giving me a toothless grin. "Can't forget that."

"I appreciate the offer, Otto, but I'm going," I say determinedly.

Jacob leads us into the woods, skirting along the house's bordering wall. We duck under branches and skirt around the trees. Jacob's tall frame is graceful as he melds into the shadows, a beautiful wraith of the brittle night. I shake my head, reminding myself I don't have the luxury to even think about Jacob.

The sound of steel shivers against the silence.

"What was that?" I whisper, scanning the shifting boughs.

"One can never be too prepared." Jacob hefts up his sword. It gleams in the moonlight.

"Maybe we should wait until morning," Fritz suggests, his voice quivering. "I have a really bad feeling about this place."

"Makes my skin crawl," Wilhelm agrees.

Jacob pauses, hushing us. I freeze, listening. At first, all I hear is the sighing of the trees as the wind rushes through the pines, but then I catch something else. Maybe it's from the lack of other noises in the forest. The cicadas are silent, and the bullfrogs don't croak. Or maybe it's that bird-part of me emerging.

A pad of footsteps. Sniffing.

"Something hunts us," I whisper, my muscles screaming to turn around and run. "Wolves."

Jacob's eyebrow lifts as if in surprise.

"I hear nothing," Fritz says.

My heart pounds as the padding of paws breaks into a gallop. "They're coming and fast," I say breathlessly.

"Run!" Jacob orders.

We take off at a sprint, ducking under branches and leaping over logs. Twigs snap against my cheeks and tear at my skirts, but I refuse to slow my pace. My feet fly across the ground as if I'm lighter than air. I bound over fallen logs and duck under low boughs. A giant wall rises before us, blocking our path.

"If we can get over this wall," Jacob says, "we'll be safe from the wolves."

He holds out his hands before him, indicating for me to step into them. I comply and find myself catapulted upward to the ledge of the stone wall. My nails scrape along the surface, but I pull myself up. I turn around and reach over the edge, helping Fritz up next as Jacob shoves him toward me.

Shadows fly across the ground like phantoms, meters from Jacob and Wilhelm below.

"Hurry!" I call down as Jacob helps Wilhelm up. "They're coming."

Growls cut through the air. Once Wilhelm joins us on top of the wall, both he and Fritz reach down and yank Jacob up. One wolf leaps into the air. It clamps its maw onto Jacob's leg. As Jacob bellies on the wall, I stab the beast, and it lets go of Jacob's leg.

"Are you all right?" I ask, grabbing his arm.

"It was nothing," he says. "A mere scratch."

"That looked like more than a scratch," Fritz warns. "The wolf sank its teeth into your skin and then chewed on it."

Horror spears me. "Let me bind it up," I offer.

"I'm fine," he says, brushing his injury aside as if it's nothing. "Let's keep moving."

He drops onto the other side of the wall like it's not a fifteen-foot drop. Wilhelm follows effortlessly while Fritz lands with a crash in the bushes, grunting in pain. My boots touch the edge of the wall when it's my turn.

"I'll catch you," Jacob offers, holding out his hands.

My heart hammers, but I jump. Strong arms swoop around my body, pulling me against his solid chest.

"See? I told you I'd catch you." His breath is hot against my ear, his grip unyielding. There are wolves hunting us, we're in the backyard of a man I'm determined to never marry, and yet in his arms, I feel safer than I've ever felt in my life.

By the time he sets me on the ground, I'm breathless. It has nothing to do with the terrors on the other side of the wall.

"What kind of place is this?" Fritz asks. "And what's that dreadful smell?"

I rip my gaze from Jacob to see what he's talking about.

"I've no idea," Jacob says. "But I don't like it."

Mist slithers across the ground, masking our forms. We thread our way across what looks like once were gardens but now appear more like a graveyard. Thin, bone-white trees grow across an otherwise barren yard. There's something sinister about the grounds with hundreds of naked trees, boughs clawing for the moon as if begging for life. Brown grass crunches beneath my boots as I creep closer to the house. The stench of rotting flesh permeates the area, forcing me to press my handkerchief to my face to stop the wretched smell.

Wolves cry from the other side of the wall, and their claws scuff at the stone.

My foot stumbles on something. I fall to the ground. Jacob rushes to my side and reaches a hand to help me up, but my whole body is frozen. Right beside my cheek lies a bone, smooth and white as pearls.

My mouth opens in a scream, but Jacob's hand clamps over my lips with a gentle hush of a warning to keep silent. I nod, whimpering despite myself. He lifts me off the cursed soil. We take off running again, darting around the skeleton trees, moonlight illuminating their limbs so they look like dancing ghosts.

My hand squeezes Jacob's tighter. I don't want to ever let go. Finally, we reach the far end of the yard, panting and gasping for air. We're in a carpenter's work area, the ground littered in sawdust and the roof covered by a wooden slab. Saws hang in the workshop, and long boards are stretched out for the workers.

"Didn't Wissen mention he only dabbled in carpentry work now?" Wilhelm asks. "Looks as if he's in full operation."

"And these axes." Jacob studies a row of them dangling

from the roof. "Looks like the same make as the one we found by the attack on the weapons delivery."

"You found the culprit," Fritz says, his voice trembling. "Excellent work. I say we leave this instant and have the king send in his men at first light."

"When I fell," I say, "I landed next to a bone. There's something odd about a bone lying in the yard, isn't there?"

"Maybe. Or perhaps it was just one of the doctor's dog's bones," Wilhelm says, but his eyebrows are raised as he stares at my hand tucked into Jacob's.

It takes all my willpower to let go.

"Come," Jacob snaps at Wilhelm, clearly angry and annoyed. "For the entrance to Hell is just over there. Fritz and Ella, you two stay here. Fritz, if so much as a hair falls from her head, I'll kill you."

"You can't talk to me like that," Fritz says loftily.

"Seems like I just did," Jacob replies.

"I'm going in there with you." I plant my fists on my hips, mainly to keep them from shaking. "I need to destroy that newly made marriage contract they're making right now."

Jacob stares at me for a moment, the muscle line in his jaw tightening, like he's considering me. "Fine. But stick close."

He storms into the manor without a backward glance.

# CHAPTER 31

## JACOB

### WISSEN MANOR

T he door creaks against the silence as I enter a dark hallway, absent of any light except for one candle at the far end, flickering morosely.

Evil lurks in these corridors. It nips at my skin and coats my throat with its stench. I don't like the idea of Ella being here, but at the same time, I want her to find freedom. It's something I wish for myself and Wilhelm every day of this cursed life. Except if anything happened to her, I don't think I could live with myself.

"Perhaps we should split up," Prince William offers. "We could scout out the place faster that way. You take the stairs to the left while the maiden and I go down this hallway."

"The *maiden* has a name," Ella corrects him sharply.

"It would be best if *Ella* and I stick together in case," the prince says and winks. "Because. You know."

"You might turn into a frog and need a kiss?" Ella snorts and rolls her eyes. "You can find yourself another maiden for that."

"Sometimes it happens when I get frightened." Fritz tugs at the edge of his shirt, not able to look at us.

"It's a good plan," Wilhelm says. "We'll accomplish our investigation faster that way."

"If anything happens to Ella," I say, giving Wilhelm and the prince a hard look, "I'm holding you both responsible."

"I'll be perfectly fine," Ella says and pulls out the dagger I gave her. "I'll look for the contract while you find the evidence you need. We get in and out quickly."

Bristling, I withdraw my sword and spin on my heels, heading upstairs. I hate the fact that being with her makes life worthwhile. Makes breathing bearable.

It doesn't help thinking about her kissing the prince or even being near the guy. Sure, she doesn't realize Fritz is Prince William, but the more time he spends with her, he'll see how amazing she is.

And what woman can resist a prince?

Not that I care. I've no right, time, or position to offer her happiness. I've nothing to offer Ella other than a life on the road, hunting down the Forbidden. It isn't a life; it's a curse.

"You keep stomping around like that," Wilhelm whispers, grabbing me by the shoulder, "and you're going to get us both killed."

I swear under my breath, leaning against the stairwell wall. He's right. I need to get myself under control and focus on making sure Ella never sets foot in this place again. I set off, the floorboards creaking beneath my boots as I work my way down the hall. I begin opening each door, searching for clues for Dr. Wissen's story. I'm on my fifth one when I notice a brass plaque on it.

Gretel, Beloved 8th Wife

Eighth wife? And here I thought he only had six? Startled,

I glance back at the other doors. Just like this one, they all have name plaques.

"Every wife had her own room." I point to the plaques. The whites of Wilhelm's eyes grow wide as moons.

With dread, I crack open Gretel's door and peer inside. Darkness fills most of the room, other than a lone beam of light spilling from a tiny, barred window. A wedding dress hangs on the side of the wardrobe as if it were worn only yesterday. My boots crunch on the floor. I'm stepping on dried flower petals that had fallen loose from a forgotten bouquet.

I check the other rooms. They're all the same. Wedding dresses—some lying on the bed, others hanging from the ceiling beams—while forgotten veils, slippers, and bouquets are tossed aside as if dropped in a rush.

My mind reels, trying to understand what I'm seeing. Was Dr. Wissen that obsessed with his wives' wedding day that after they died, he hung the dress up in remembrance? Or were his actions darker and more sinister? I reach the far end of the hall, all the rooms boasting plaques except this last one at the end. This door has the face of a wolf carved into its wood.

"I don't like this." Wilhelm adjusts the grip on his dagger.

Swallowing hard, I twist the doorknob. Instead of opening, the carving on the door springs to life. The eyes of the werewolf blink open. Its teeth gleam moon-white, and drool drips down the door. Heart thudding, I leap backward, while Wilhelm holds out his dagger.

"Who tries to enter the abode of the master?" the carved werewolf rumbles.

"Hello, there," I say, trying to sound nonchalant. "We thought we'd pop in for a moment."

The creature howls. Instantly, a howl echoes outside as if in reply.

"Guess we just lost our element of surprise," I say.

I pull out my knife and stab the carving in its wooden eye. The knife in my hand sinks into the door as if it's being swallowed whole. I let go and stare in shock as it disappears into the wood.

"It just took my best knife!" I exclaim.

"That's the least of our worries," Wilhelm says, eyeing the hallway behind us as the howls outside grow louder. "We need to hurry."

Heart pounding, I kick the door open and rush inside. A large wooden desk sits in front of floor-to-ceiling glass doors that open to a balcony overlooking the village. It's not quite as prestigious a view as from the castle, but not bad. One stone wall is filled with names. I don't want to know what that means.

Warily, I inch closer to the desk. One of the boards sinks inward. A trap.

I leap backward just as daggers plummet from the chandelier above into the carpet, inches from either side of my spur-tipped boots.

"Hurry!" Wilhelm barks from the doorway, drawing back an arrow in his bow. "We've got company."

The sound of arrows whizzing in the hall warns me that Wilhelm is already shooting. I suck in a deep breath and bypass the dagger-riddled floor to the desk. I scan the letters and lists of names and materials. My heart sinks when I spy a giant book with a picture of a rooster on it. Its title tells me everything I needed to know about who Wissen really is. *ABCs of Witchcraft and Sorcery.*

There's also a map of the Swabian valley filled with arrows, x's, and circles. But when I pick it up, the back section of the desk morphs and twists, coming to life. A branch-like hand snaps out and wraps its wooden fingers around my wrist. I cry out in pain.

"That's not yours," the desk's deep voice booms.

Refusing to drop the map, I begin hacking at the wood with my sword. Chips fly into the air, but its grip remains firm.

"Jacob!" Wilhelm calls from the doorway. "I need your help!"

"Little tied up right now!" I glare at the wooden fingers only to discover more hands pushing themselves out of the wood, reaching for me.

This isn't how I planned for tonight to go.

A scream from below vibrates through the air. My heart starts to seize. *Ella!* Wilhelm rushes into the room, slamming the door shut. He pushes a large cabinet in front of the door.

"You may have sealed us in a prison," I point out.

The cabinet shakes as someone on the other side tries to break down the door.

"Thought I'd delay our demise for a moment," Wilhelm says. "Besides, it looks like you need help."

"Forget me. Find Ella. I heard her cry out. Try the window. Be careful of the traps in the floor."

Wilhelm ignores me. He pulls an ax off the wall and begins chopping at the wooden hand gripping me.

"You nicked my wrist!" I growl, trying to block out the pain and blood.

The branch snaps. The fingers let me go. I'm free and still holding the map.

"You're welcome." Wilhelm snatches a few papers off the desk and stuffs them into his pouch. "You'll heal. You always do."

Frantically, I search for another exit as the cabinet scrapes outward. The far wall is filled with jagged, knife-edged saws as tall as I am hanging vertically. There's an odd glow to them, and as I step closer, I realize they're like a moving picture.

"Is it just me, or does that look like the throne room in the palace?" I ask, dread filling my chest.

Wilhelm whistles. "It does. And this one looks like the inside of the tavern in town. People are...moving? What is this?"

"Sorcery," I say.

I turn only for my foot to trip on the rug. My eyes narrow. I toss the carpet aside to find a ring on the floor. I pull on it. A section of the floor lifts up, revealing a set of stone steps spiraling downward.

"Rather risky." Wilhelm grimaces. "Reeks, too."

The cabinet finally moves enough to allow a guard to squeeze through. His face contorts and then twists into a snout. Fur spikes on his skin. Eyes burn red.

"The guard is transforming into a werewolf," Wilhelm chokes out.

"Everything is starting to make a whole lot more sense."

I practically throw myself down the staircase.

# CHAPTER 32

# ELLA

## WISSEN MANOR

Watching Jacob walk away feels like someone doused the only fire keeping me warm, leaving me behind, shivering in the dark. But Fritz has a point. Splitting up is better. Fritz and I tiptoe down the hall, following the sounds of laughter and the clinking of glasses.

I peek around the corner. A fire roars in a hearth flanked by stone wolves. Two wing-backed chairs face the fire. I can't see the faces, but a full skirt billows out from the sides of one chair. A paper and an inkwell sit on a small round table by the wall. That might be the contract.

"To infinite power," Wissen's recognizable voice says as he raises a wine glass. The woman in the other chair clinks her glass to his, finalizing their toast. "They'll fight, of course. And lose."

The woman chuckles. "They always do."

"Looks like your intended is having a fabulous time with his lady friend," Fritz whispers from my side.

"Shush," I scold him. "I'm going to get the contract."

Holding my breath, I creep along the shadows on the

walls as the two talk. The pounding of my chest drowns out their conversation. The fire pops, and I freeze.

"You'll be at the ball, yes?" Wissen asks.

I let out a breath and continue. I'm reaching for the slip of paper on the table when a clanking fills the hallway. Heart pounding, I vaguely hear Wissen saying it's just his servant. I snatch up the paper and duck back into the hall, victorious.

"Someone is coming," Fritz whispers to me.

A servant is shambling down the hall, holding a candle in one hand and a platter covered with a large metal lid in the other. His glassy eyes are focused on the floor. The jangling comes from chains binding his ankles.

"Hide," I order Fritz and drag him with me into an alcove, except I realize the servant will still see us when he gets closer. We're doomed.

Something hard and round pushes into my back. A door-knob! Quickly, I open the door, and the two of us tumble into the darkness. I barely push the door shut when the clanking passes by.

"That was close," I say, releasing a breath.

"This was a bad idea," Fritz says. "You just locked us in here."

Sure enough, there isn't a doorknob on this side of the door. I try to push and then dig my fingers under the crack in the floor to pull it open, but it's no use.

"It's unfortunate, but at least I got the contract," I say, trying to stay calm as I stuff the paper into my pocket. "I'm sure there's another exit."

"I like your positive outlook," Fritz says, "but I'm not so convinced."

I turn to discover we're standing on the top landing of a rickety wooden stairwell that leads into a stone-lined hallway. Unlike the other corridors of the house, this one has lanterns hooked into prongs on the walls.

"Such a bright and cheerful home," Fritz notes as we begin our descent. "And to think this will all be yours."

"Not funny, Fritz."

"Why did your father agree to this marriage?"

"Because my father and stepmother need the money," I explain. "Personally, I think my stepmother is determined to have me married off so I can't go to the ball."

"That doesn't make sense. Most mothers would go to extreme ends to be a part of the royal family."

"It's all about my stepsisters. She wants the prince to notice them. I don't know why she's worried. He won't give me the time of day anyway."

He's silent for a moment, and then, "No, it isn't. I'm sure all other maidens would pale in the sight of your fierceness. You might be the bravest girl I've ever met."

"That's very sweet of you." I flash him a kind smile. "I wouldn't say I'm brave, just desperate not to be married off like a piece of property. If we can find evidence to lock Dr. Wissen away, then I'll be free. I want more than to be married off to a wealthy man. When my father was gone, I managed our property. I really enjoyed that."

"You and I have more in common than I first thought."

"That said, a part of me just wants to go to the ball for fun. I've never been to a dance."

"I wouldn't exactly categorize the king's dances as fun. More like a battlefield of silk and champagne."

"At least you've been to one." I chuckle despite our dismal surroundings. "It feels cooler down here, doesn't it? I'm guessing we're below ground."

The sound of fluttering wings catches my attention. A dove, scrawny and molted, flutters about in a cage dangling from a hook in the ceiling. It squawks, and I rush to it, trying to push my fingers through the bars to console the poor thing.

"You shouldn't be caged," I coo to the creature.

"Turn back, turn back, young maiden dear," it says. "'Tis a murderer's house you enter here."

I freeze and turn to Fritz. "Did you hear that?"

"Squawk, squawk?" He grimaces. "If it keeps up the ruckus, it'll alert the doctor we're here."

"He said we've entered a murderer's house."

"He said that, did he?" Fritz chuckles.

I press my lips together. He thinks I've lost my mind. *Might be true.* Regardless, I can't allow the bird to stay locked up. I unlatch the cage and hold out my hand. The bird hops out and perches itself on my finger quite happily. He cocks his head, assessing me.

"I think the bird likes you," Fritz says.

"Turn back, turn back, young maiden dear," the bird sings the words this time. "'Tis a murderer's house you enter here."

"Thank you for the warning, friend. But you must free yourself, too, if you can."

The bird flies off down the hall and around the corner. The flapping of its wings echoes against the stone.

"We should follow the bird," I say. "I think it knows its way out."

"This is utter madness, but we have no other options," Fritz agrees.

The hallway turns, and we stumble into a room only to find it occupied. I scream in surprise, and Fritz grabs my arm, as if to hold himself up. But as my terror subsides, I realize it's only an old woman, stirring a bubbling mixture in a giant kettle. A few strands of hair dangle at her shoulders. Her skin is weathered like dried-out apricots, and dark warts pock her face.

Her head snaps at attention. "What are you doing here?" she asks in a rusted voice.

"I—I came to see where my betrothed lives," I manage, trying to calm the drumbeat in my chest.

"Alas, poor child," she says. "Why did you ever come? You should've turned around and run far from this place. You have come to a murderer's den, a place of horrors. Yours will be a marriage of death. Your bones will rot in the garden, giving magic to the trees in the Death Forest."

"Death Forest?" Fritz gulps.

"She must be talking about those white trees we passed through," I whisper to him.

"Listen, my dears. You seem like nice, sweet folk. You must leave with haste while you're still free and alive."

She points her spoon to the shackles attached to her ankles. It's just like the ones the servant upstairs wore.

"I've been forced to cook for Wissen's army. They'll be hungry and will be here soon. Run away, and fast, before the master comes. Bride or no bride, it won't matter. He's married many a wife and none live to tell the tale I've just told you."

"But why?" I ask, needing to know. "Why bother with the marriage ceremony if only to kill me?"

"The murderer believes the body of a wife gives the trees magic. A sacrifice of a loved one brings ultimate power, yes?"

"We should go!" Fritz begs frantically, peering around the edge of the room.

But I need answers. "Power?" Wingbeats clatter against my ribs. "How can bodies possibly give trees power?"

"Ah, you're smarter than the others." She starts stirring with her wooden spoon. "The trees soak the power of the dead into their roots. The doctor uses that wood to build chests, doors, chairs, and such. Then he carves them with faces of animals or humans. The magic inside the wood enchants the lumber."

"Are you saying his carpentry pieces are magical?"

"He can see through the eyes of the carvings using the saws he cuts the wood with."

"The box he gave me." My eyes widen, and I turn to stare at Fritz, who is swaying a little. "It had a face on it. He was planning to spy on me. I bet that's how he gets information on everyone in the town. He's been spying on all of us."

"Perhaps even the king," Fritz says and clutches my arm like he's about to pass out.

A clomp of footsteps echoes in the hall.

"Quickly now!" the hag whispers. "Hide! Slip behind this hogshead where you won't be seen."

I move only to find Fritz has vanished. There's a croak at my feet.

"Oh, you didn't," I grumble. Quickly, I sweep up the plump green frog and tuck him into my pocket.

"Be still as a mouse," the hag whispers as I dart into the hiding place, hoping she's not tricking me.

I hunker in the dark silence, praying every prayer I know while trying to ignore the foul stench of the hog's head and the sticky floor.

"What was that sound I heard?" Dr. Wissen's voice booms into the room.

"That silly bird," the hag says. "What a ruckus it was caus-ing. Flew right in here and scared the death from me."

He grunts.

"The bird is missing," another man's voice says. "Should I go find it?"

I peer around the edge even though I know I should remain completely still. The doctor is staring into the pot, sniffing at it, while the other stands by the door, thick-corded arms crossed.

"No time for that," Wissen says. "Find the intruders."

"Yes, doctor."

I listen, fear trembling through me as the footsteps tromp down the hall. Quickly, I scramble out of my hiding spot.

"Thank you for keeping me a secret," I tell the hag.

"Did I not tell you you've come to the house of death? Now go, and make sure you never return."

"But what about you?" I ask. "How can you stay here?"

She looks down at the chains binding her feet. "Nothing to be done about it."

"I can't leave you knowing you're chained against your will. He must keep a key around here somewhere."

"Don't waste your pretty life on me," she grumbles.

But I refuse to leave this woman. I scour the room for a key until I discover one above the doorframe. My hands shake as I slip it into the key lock. It clicks open.

"There. You're free," I say as the chains clatter to the ground.

"How peculiar." She rises from her stool, looking a bit lost. "What should I do with myself?"

"Take this." I pull off the bird necklace my mother gave me. It had been my backup plan to sell it to pay for my escape. But if it were not for her, I would already be in Wissen's hands. As much as it pains me to part with it, I couldn't live with myself leaving her here helpless. "The sapphire is valuable. Find a convent or a master in need of a... a good cook."

"Bless you, child," the hag says, eyeing me with this strange look. "May the favor be returned to you. Now hurry!"

Before I go, I toss the contract I found in Wissen's study into the fire and then race into the next section of the hall when more footsteps, quicker than before, come stampeding down the hall. Terror roots me in place. I'm too far from the hogshead to get there in time. But then Jacob and Wilhelm's faces emerge, running toward me. Not caring for decency, I throw myself into Jacob's arms. He practically lifts me off the ground, holding me tightly.

"I thought we were too late," he says, voice trembling.

"Fritz," Wilhelm says. "What happened to him?"

"Oh!" I extract myself from Jacob and pat my cloak pocket. "He's safely here with me."

"Excellent." Jacob nods. "Let's go."

We careen out into the hall and tumble down the dark corridor the way the bird went. As we push open the door and stumble outside, the air fills with the sound of howls.

*They haven't eaten yet. They'll be hungry.*

"Werewolves," I whisper, realizing what the hag meant. "Wissen's hunters were the wolves."

# CHAPTER 33

# JACOB

## WISSEN MANOR

Moonlight casts our shadows into twisted contortions on the soft dirt as I lead Wilhelm and Ella across the orchard, ducking around the holes scattered about, which Ella explains will soon be graves. The ghost-like tree branches claw out as if to stop us.

A grinding creak at the other end of the manor's grounds draws my attention to the gate at the far end. Guards are swinging it open. A pack of werewolves waits, growling on its other side, jaws frothing, eyes glowing crimson in anticipation to break into a sprint.

"Over there!" a voice cries out from the manor. It's a group of guards, armed to the hilt.

I swivel left and make for the wall closest to the trees. Ella's breathing hitches, which only heightens my panic. I was a careless fool to bring her here. This is by far my worst experience with the Forbidden. The second we get to the tree closest to the wall, I grab Ella, nearly throwing her up into the branches. Meanwhile, Wilhelm spins around and releases two arrows. It does nothing to slow the pack hurtling toward us.

A werewolf leaps through the air, aiming its paws at my

face. I swing my sword, decapitating the creature. Not that it matters. There are at least twenty more, along with five guards.

"Almost out of arrows," Wilhelm wheezes.

"Climb the tree," I command. "I'll hold them off until you can cover me."

He tosses me his ax and swings up on the closest branch. I grip both my weapons and ready myself. They attack. A cry erupts from my core. I cut, slash, and twirl in a reckless dance. My arms move faster than I ever remember them moving before. Blood coats my boots and arms, spraying my face. The hot stench of the creatures' breath chokes my lungs.

When the arrows ping down onto the werewolves, it gives me a second to leap into the tree with Wilhelm while Ella scrambles up on the wall, her black skirts snapping against her legs in the harsh wind. She pelts the creatures with rocks. The werewolves spring up, jaws snapping inches from Ella's skin, but her blade strikes fast. I ready myself to leap to the wall when the branch I'm standing on slowly lowers, trembling as if the tree purposely wants me to fall into the hands of my enemy. Wilhelm crouches to jump onto the wall with Ella, but his bough twists, sending him tumbling to the ground.

I belly myself over my branch and grab hold of his cloak. He grunts and cries out in pain as a wolf's jaw clamps onto his leg.

"Wilhelm!" Ella screams. "Jacob, do something!"

Sweat makes my grip on Wilhelm slick. I will not lose my brother. My senses and muscles kick into place. With my free hand, I grab my ax, and with a calculated aim, throw. It plunges into the beast's back. The creature's jaws loosen from Wilhelm to howl in pain, allowing me to slowly heave my brother up. A cry breaks from my throat from the effort. Wilhelm gets high enough to pull himself up.

"The tree is working with them," I say, panting. "We must jump now."

Wide-eyed, Wilhelm nods, and the two of us launch ourselves off the tree just as the branches fall away beneath us. My body crashes against the stone wall, but I slap my hands over the surface until I find a stone jutting out to cling to. Then I pull up to where Ella is helping Wilhelm. A wave of dizziness rushes over me, and I nearly fall off the wall. Thankfully, Ella clamps a hand on my arm, pulling me closer to her.

"I'm not losing you now," Ella says. "Stay with me."

I must have lost a lot more blood than usual. Below, the werewolves whine and turn, sprinting back for the exit, the men joining them.

"It won't be long until they're after us on horseback," I say, my tongue thick in my mouth. But Wilhelm's shoulders are dipped from where he's kneeling. His ankle must be wrecked. "Can you make it to the horses?"

"Do I have a choice?" He eyes the drop below warily.

We're in trouble.

"This way." Ella waves for us to follow her along the wall. "There's an easier drop up here."

Once back onto solid ground, relief hits me when Rumpelstiltskin comes riding up with our horses in tow. I hate to admit it, but I'm thankful the rascal came. Even with our healing abilities, Wilhelm and I have both lost a lot of blood, and I'm not sure if we'd have made it back fast enough before they caught us.

"The great and mighty Grimm brothers having a bit of trouble?" He cackles like this pleases him. "Good thing I popped by to rescue you. Like usual."

"You're a lifesaver," Wilhelm says.

"Where's the other horse?" I snap, scanning the forest for creatures.

"Got spooked and took off," Rumpelstiltskin says. "But never fear. The lady can ride with me."

"The lady will be riding with *me*," I announce as Wilhelm and I climb on our steeds. I reach out a hand to Ella, and she swings up behind me. "Tell me you still have the frog."

"Tucked safely in my pocket," she says.

Relief floods me. If we lost the prince, it'd be an utter disaster.

"Hold on tight," I tell her. The moment her arms wrap around my chest, my heart pounds louder than it ever did in battle. I let Storm loose as fast as he can go with two of us on him, but as we career around the bend in the road, we discover it lined with men holding weapons.

"When did the doctor get so many people working for him?" I mutter.

"I think we've discovered where all of the village's missing young men went," Wilhelm says.

"And the king's weapons," I add, pulling on the reins. "Looks like the road is off limits for us."

"I vote we go deeper into the forest," Rumpelstiltskin says. "Wear them out."

"It's our best chance," I agree. Except as fast as our horses are, the werewolves are having an easier time, ducking and racing through the old woods.

"The river," Ella says. "It's not far from here. If we cross it, they'll lose our scent."

"Excellent idea," I say, eyeing Wilhelm, who's gotten far too quiet for my liking.

I allow her to guide us to the riverbank. The water is fairly deep, and the rushing current makes the horses nervous, but we manage to cross. By the time we reach the other side and slip into the shadows of the trees, the horses are tired and lathered. Wilhelm is sagging on his horse. He needs to get home and rest.

"We're far from the village now, aren't we?" I ask. "My brother needs to rest."

"I think I know where we are," Ella says. "There's an old fortress, perhaps a half-an-hour ride. We could hide out there."

I nod. "If they do manage to track us, it will offer a good defense until the horses are rested. I admit I'm not used to being hunted. Usually, it's the other way around. The doctor was far more equipped than we were. We underestimated him."

"Yes. I had no idea such horrors could exist," Ella whispers. She lays her head against my back. It melts my pent-up anger.

"I'm sorry you had to see that," I say.

"I'm not," she says. "If I hadn't seen the doctor for the true man he was, I wouldn't have known what he was capable of."

Then she tells me what she discovered from the old woman and how Wissen uses the trees to create magic in the wood.

"That makes sense," I say. "Upstairs in his study, he had saws that looked like mirrors into other places. He is spying on the town."

"It also explains how he knows everything that's going on," Ella finishes.

"To think you thought I was the wicked one." Rumpelstiltskin chuckles from behind us. "Clearly, you've been setting your standards far too low."

As we ride, Ella's arms tighten around me. The horse's steady footfall creates a rhythm around us, making me wish I could just take Ella with me and ride far away from reality. Finally, we arrive at the ruins. The full moon gives us a clear view of the abandoned area. I let my muscles ease, tension slipping from my shoulders at the sight of shelter. Only a single turret still stands whole while a thicket of vines trails up the crumbling walls. The courtyard lies barren except for a few scraggly shrubs and rocks.

Ella slides from the saddle but crumples before her boots hit the ground. My chest seizes, and I'm at her side in an instant.

"Ella." Her name scrapes from my throat. "Are you hurt?"

Her skin is damp with sweat, lips pale, but somehow she still gives me a faint smile. "I'm fine. Just need a moment."

"Today was horrifying," I breathe. "And yet you were braver than I ever thought anyone could be."

She fumbles for the flask at her belt, hands trembling as she tries to lift it. The sight twists something deep inside me, and it takes everything in me not to pull her into my arms. I catch her fingers, steadying them.

"Here," I murmur, taking it from her. "Let me."

After I help her drink, I assist Wilhelm to a smooth rock to rest while Rumpelstiltskin grumbles about being hungry. I tie up the horses, glad to find my wounds are healing quickly as usual, and set off to scout the area. I find a whole portion of the wall still standing, strong enough for me to walk along it and get a clear view of our location.

The valley below stretches wide and hushed beneath the silvery glow of the moon. It's so peaceful, as if none of the horrors we experienced even existed.

"We're higher than I thought," I call down to the others from the top of the wall. "I imagine the view is quite stunning in daylight."

Wilhelm grunts but remains lying on his slab of rock. I scramble back down to join the others. Relief pours through me at the sight of Ella, steadier on her feet, as she bends beside Wilhelm and lifts his flask to his lips.

"I'm going to find myself a snack," Rumpelstiltskin says. "This little outing of yours is turning out to be exhausting."

As he trudges off, complaining about always rescuing us, I turn to Ella. "This might be a good time to take out our frog and see how he's doing."

Ella opens her pocket and carefully pulls out the frog. His eyes bulge, and with a ribbit, he tries to hop away, but Ella closes her hand over his body.

"Not so fast, little guy." She giggles. "I just don't see how this little creature could be Fritz. I feel a little bad for him. He was terrified in Wissen's house."

Guilt stabs me. I haven't been quite so truthful about how Fritz is actually the prince of Württemberg. "I suppose I should turn Fritz back into a man."

"If I were to kiss him, he'd really turn back into human form?" Ella asks, inspecting the frog.

"Don't worry, I can—"

Before I finish, she lifts those perfect lips to the slimy frog's face. In a burst of emerald-green glow, the frog bulges, growing larger. Its body twists and writhes. Ella screeches and drops him.

"Oh!" she says. "I'm terribly sorry. The transformation just surprised me."

The green slime vanishes along with the black spots until the frog has become the prince once again. The only semblance of his previous appearance is the large green eyes. His tunic hangs from his waist, and his pants are stuck to one arm. Though his left eye is ringed blue, like he got punched, he looks in far better shape than the rest of us.

"Appears as if you're still alive," I say.

But the prince's eyes are only on Ella. "Thank you. Your kiss was enchanting."

"Oh." She looks away, clearly flustered. "I'm not really an expert kisser."

"Trust me." The prince takes Ella's hand and kisses it.

"I've kissed my share of maidens over the years, but yours surpassed them all."

I grind my teeth in annoyance. Am I jealous that the prince got a kiss from Ella? Definitely. Am I proud of it? Not one bit.

"You don't look so good." Ella steps closer to him. "I wish we had ice for your eye."

"Must have gotten a little beat up in the escape while in my...er—frog—form. Nothing that another kiss wouldn't fix."

Ella laughs, rolling her eyes.

"We need to set up a barrier in front of the turret's door," I say, darkly, eager to change the subject. "So we can be ready in case the werewolves decide to cross the river and follow our trail."

"Werewolves?" the prince asks and then looks around. "Where are we exactly?"

"The ruins of Hohenurach," Ella says. "North of the village."

"What happened?" The prince rubs his head. "It's a bit of a blur."

"Before story time, let's focus on creating a barrier," I suggest.

The prince frowns, clearly not used to being treated like a common merchant, but thankfully, he merely grumbles and follows. Once we get the turret's doorway barred to my satisfaction, the prince and I help Wilhelm to the first floor. Ella brings in some pine boughs for him to lie on and holds up his flask of water for him to drink.

"He doesn't look good," Ella says. "I wonder if the wolf's bite is poisonous."

"He'll survive," I grumble.

"Don't remind me," Wilhelm says through clenched teeth.

"How can you treat your brother's illness like it's inconsequential?" Ella asks, aghast.

"It's fine." Wilhelm waves us away. "I'm just so valuable, you can't kill me. Right, brother? Now go away and let me sleep this wound off."

I cross my arms and scowl. The last thing I want is to be reminded of how hard it is to kill us thanks to the Enchantress's power flowing through our veins. He's simply weaker because we haven't finished Dr. Wissen's story yet.

"That doctor is responsible for the wolves?" the prince asks.

"I've got bad news for you and then more bad news," I say. After I share with him how the saws look into the castle and that Wissen seems to be in control of the werewolves, I pull out the maps and papers Wilhelm and I snatched from the doctor's desk. "We found some information you're going to want to look at."

The prince, Ella, and I head to the roof of the turret in hopes of using the moonlight to see the documents. Once we're settled on the dusty stone, I spread them out and we begin trying to discern what exactly we're looking at. One map shows the location of the orchestrated attack on the weapons delivery.

"These are payment letters," I explain. "This one is another map with sketches that appear to be a planned attack on the castle."

"This material is treason!" The prince tosses the map to the ground and begins stalking back and forth across the turret.

"Looks like the doctor has bigger plans than just marrying me," Ella muses as she unstraps the belt and sets the dagger beside her. "Based on these documents, he's preparing to overthrow the throne."

"Well, let him try!" The prince goes to withdraw his sword, only to find it must have gotten lost in the transformation. "I'll have him and all of his underlings beheaded."

"I've got to say," Ella says, studying him carefully. "For a mere merchant, you have a great loyalty to the king."

"Great loyalty?" Prince William snorts. "There's much about the king that I question, but he's still the supreme ruler of the kingdom."

"True, but if we were to bring him this information, I doubt he'd listen to us," she presses. "It's not as if we're anyone of consequence. Jacob, you could use your influence as the king's hunter to try to gain an audience with the king."

"She has a valid point," I tell the prince. "Especially considering your station."

I can't help but push him to reveal who he really is. Ella deserves to know the truth.

The prince stares at Ella, as if debating whether to spill his secret with her. "There's something you should—"

"Besides," Ella interrupts. "Tomorrow, the king's hosting a ball for his son. I'm sure he's far too busy deciding which royal boots to wear and if fowl or venison should be served."

"My vote would be for both," I say, not bothering to hide my smile.

"Yes, a dilemma to be sure," the prince says distractedly. Then he gathers up the documents and folds them neatly under his arm. "Thank you both for this. I will never forget what you did for me tonight. I must take time to mull this over."

Once he leaves, I'm acutely aware it's just Ella and me. Night stretches around us, the valley bathed in silver moonlight. The air tastes like pine, sharp and clean, but all I can breathe in is her. She shifts closer, her thigh brushing mine, and the world tilts. My chest tightens with the pure joy of just sitting beside her, but also this need to be as close to her as I can.

"Mull this over?" She imitates the prince's haughty tone. "Do all merchants act so entitled?"

"Only the slimy ones." I grin, and she returns the smile.

"Thank you for what you did for me back there," she says. "You risked a lot to go into that lair. Now that we know the truth of who Dr. Wissen is, will you write a story about him and send him back to his land?"

"Absolutely. My only concern is we don't know his intentions. We'll try to write the story based on what we know. If the story is complete, then the process of his removal begins."

"Process? What sort of process?"

How does one explain the magical funnel and portal that leads to the Enchantress's library? "One of us writes the story. Once it's finished, the Forbidden is transported back to their world."

"Just like that? Even if they aren't evil?"

"What do you mean?"

"Like Fritz. He may be a shapeshifter and easily terrified, but he's a good man, don't you think? You said that all these creatures were monsters, but Fritz isn't a monster. Will you send him from this world because he isn't normal?"

I rake my hands through my hair, unable to look her in the eyes. "There's something I haven't told you yet. This quest of Wilhelm's and mine is not as simple as I may have led on." I swallow hard, wanting desperately to stop myself, and yet on the other hand, I want her to know the truth about who I really am. "Wilhelm was dying when an enchantress arrived at our house. I was willing to do anything to save him. Anything."

She blinks at me. "An enchantress?"

"She's the ruler of the Forbidden's realm, called the Realm of Candora, where these creatures belong and where we must send them back to."

"But I thought you were hunters for the king."

"We are, but it's more of a disguise for us to hunt for the Enchantress."

Shock ripples across her face. "Why would you do this?"

"There's a group of witches who hate the Enchantress and her laws, so they attempted to overthrow her. They formed a curse that sent all the inhabitants of the Realm of Candora into our world. That's why the Enchantress enlisted fools like Wilhelm and me to write the Forbidden back into their world."

"This all sounds like something from a storybook." She looks away as if she's trying to process my words.

"Right?" I sigh and rub the back of my neck. "I made a deal with the Enchantress. She would save my brother, and we would work for her, writing these stories, until we finished her list. Once we're done, only then will we be free of her command. Truth is, it's a curse."

"I didn't know." She reaches out, grasping my hand in hers. I should pull away. I don't. "I'm so sorry."

"There are some positives. Our vision and hearing are incredibly acute."

"And your movements are faster than humanly possible." A smile plays on her lips. "I wondered if I'd been losing my mind when I saw you fighting."

"I hope you were duly impressed."

She laughs, shaking her head at me. But then she pulls her hand away, and a painful expression passes over her face. "How do you know the Enchantress is telling you the truth? What if the witches did the right thing by saving these Forbidden, and the Enchantress is the villain? Maybe these Forbidden are innocent and can co-exist with humans."

"I think about that every day, but then I'm reminded of people like Dr. Wissen. He's a Forbidden. Would you call him innocent? Or how about the werewolves chasing us? As far as creatures like Fritz, we don't know what the consequences of having him here in our world could be. They don't belong here. They belong in their world."

My muscles tense, thinking about the guilt that plagues me every time we write another story. Were we making the right decision? But then what choice did we have?

She presses her lips together as if she wants to say more but decides against it. I study her silhouette, the shape of her nose, and the curve of her jaw. Every fiber in me yearns to reach out and pull her into my arms, feel her body pressed against mine. My lips hunger for hers in ways I never experienced.

Before I can think better of it, my hand lifts, cupping her chin. My thumb drags along the smooth line of her jaw, and she shudders, eyes closing like she's memorized. I ease closer to her.

I shouldn't. I'm nothing but a cursed man. But then her eyes find mine. They're soft and luminous in the moonlight. All my reasons crumble. Stopping isn't an option. Not when she's looking at me like that.

# CHAPTER 34

# ELLA

### RUINE HOHENURACH

T daydreamed about kissing Jacob more times than I can count. But when he leans down and our lips collide, it surpasses every one of those fantasies. The kiss is soft and gentle like the times he touched his precious books. His fingers gently push my tumbled curls aside as his lips brush across my skin to my neck. Warm, safe. Despite my inner warnings, my body sinks into his. A fiery passion races up and down my core, lightning forking through me, kindling my heart. I never knew a kiss could be so magical, so life-changing.

A whisper warns me to stop. If he knew the truth of who I am and my family, would he still kiss me like this? Or worse, what if he isn't in love with me, but is trying to find my story so he can send me back to this Enchantress's lands?

I pull away.

"What is it?" he asks, dark eyes searching mine.

He tilts my chin to face him. I bite my lip, trying to find a way to explain to him that I'm everything he shouldn't want.

"It's okay. I get it. I'm not the guy a girl dreams of," he

says so softly that the wind cutting across the fortress wall nearly sweeps his words away.

"It's not that." I reach up and place my palm on his cheek. "You're everything I've dreamed of."

I shouldn't want him. Shouldn't want there to be an *us*. He's a man carrying a curse, and according to my aunt, my enemy. Except since my mother's death, I've felt like a shadow, but with him, I've found my shape again.

I shove aside all reason and say, "Kiss me."

His lips find mine again, and his palms capture my face between them, enveloping me back into a world of perfect harmony. The kiss deepens, stealing the air from my lungs and igniting my entire body in flames. The ruined fortress falls away. The chill of the night vanishes. There's only him and his hand cupping the back of my neck, anchoring me as the world tilts. His scent cocoons me in a world of pine, secrets, and stained ink.

A strange tickling sensation creeps up my spine. I try to ignore it, but it only intensifies, moving from my neck all along my entire body.

Sharper. Stronger.

I jerk away from Jacob, startled. Pinpricks race along my palms. I stare at my hands in dread. Something is trying to poke through my skin and break free, and it's stronger than it's ever been. Is my body transforming into bird form right now? Dread knifes my soul. What if it happens in front of Jacob?

I peer up at him. Gone is the fierce, callused hunter. His eyes are soft as molasses. A smile curves across his face, warming his eyes.

"I shouldn't have pushed," he says, but he doesn't pull away. His thumb brushes over my knuckles, sending a shiver of desire through me. "But stars, it's hard to keep myself in check with you. You're the most intoxicating woman I've ever met."

"It's not the kiss," I say, fear ripping my hands from his. "That was perfect. I just need some time alone."

"I don't recommend you going anywhere alone. We're in the wilds, far too dangerous for anyone to be by themselves."

The prickling intensifies. I gasp, clutching the stone wall for support. I need to get out of here. Being this close to Jacob is dangerous.

"I must go." I rise to my feet, mind whirling.

My aunt transforms from bird into half-bird, half-human. My mother could choose between bird and human whenever she wished. I'm not sure what I'll become, but the one thing I do know, I don't want to find out with Jacob Grimm standing in front of me. He can never see this side of me.

I stumble backward, wiping the sweat that now coats my brow. I reach for the flask of medicine my aunt gave me to deal with the pain. It's empty.

Jacob comes to my side, steadying me. "Are you all right?" he asks. "Let me take you inside the turret. I can't imagine how difficult today has been for you, and then I went and overloaded you with all my problems. Today has been more than taxing."

Every muscle in my body aches. More than anything, I want to do just what he offered, but I need to get away, far from prying eyes. I straighten my spine and grind my teeth as a spasm of pain wracks through me.

"Don't worry," I finally manage breathlessly, trying to smile, but I'm sure it comes out more like a grimace. "I'll be just a moment. Then I'll join you in the turret."

I scamper along the wall, stopping every few seconds as pain sears my skin. Tears stream down my cheeks, and my vision wavers. Soon, the wall veers close enough to the ground that I'm able to drop onto the soft earth, but my legs crumble beneath me, and I fall, my head hitting the grass.

"Ella!" Jacob cries out, watching me from the top of the wall.

I scramble to my feet and manage a weak wave as if to indicate I'm fine. "Please," I say. "I need a bit of privacy to take care of some lady business. Would you kindly turn around?"

He crosses those thick muscular arms, concern stretching across his face. I back toward the thicket of woods, twirling my finger to indicate for him to follow suit. The moment he turns, I dart into the trees, breaking aside the boughs and stumbling over logs. I'm not sure how long he'll give me, but I know he's fast. Otherworldly fast. I saw how quickly he ran at Dr. Wissen's manor. That thought alone quickens my steps.

But then another spasm cuts through my body, so strong it sends me flying to the ground. I hit the earth once again, smashing my lip against a rock. I taste blood. With my fingers, I try to wipe it away, but freeze as I stare at the talons that my hands have become.

Razor sharp, dangerous. Feathers poking through my once smooth skin.

My pulse thumps against my ears like a drum. It's happening. The transformation. A sob escapes my chest. I'm becoming a monster.

"Ella?" Jacob's voice rings through the forest.

Too close.

He can't see me like this. I won't let him.

Scrambling to my feet, I break into a run. I push my legs faster as if that will take me away from this destiny I wish I could escape. Away from the man who awakened my soul.

Jacob's footsteps thud across the ground, sure and quick, darting through the forest like he doesn't need the moonlight to guide him. He isn't far behind.

"Ella!" he calls. "Please. Come back. I promise I won't kiss you again."

*Run! Faster!*

A small ravine, maybe four feet across, blocks my path. I search for another way, but he's only a few yards back through the pines. Trembling, I face the ravine, and with a slight running start, I leap across the space. I reach out for the thin bough dangling within a finger's grasp on the other side.

Wish for escape.

Pray for flight.

An explosion erupts from the deepest, darkest, truest part of me.

And I soar.

Wings beat to the rhythm of the wind. My vision widens as I twist and weave through the tree branches until I break free of the last bough and I'm flying into the great night. The wind brushes over me, and I breathe in cool air that causes every fiber in this new body to shudder in pure delight.

The ground falls away, and with it, all my fears of becoming a monster. Up here, away from the pain and heartache, away from the horrors at home since Mother's death, I'm free. I just entered a whole new world I don't ever want to leave.

Beating my wings feels as natural as if I'd been doing the act a thousand times. This is what I'm meant to be. There was no reason to fear this transformation. It's as if a part of me was waiting to be unlocked.

The rolling expanse of the forest halts at the sharp cliff. A castle spikes into the air, lanterns glowing in the courtyards and torches lit on the battlements. There's something important about that castle, but it's hard to concentrate on that thought when the wind is rustling over my feathers and the elation of pure freedom soars through me.

Soon, my wings ache. I need to land. A new image pops into my mind—home.

I scan the ground, wondering where my father's manor might be located. After a few rests in the treetops, I find the house, bordering the forest, just as the first ribbons of light strain amber bands across the horizon.

A tall hazel tree seems to extend its boughs as if reaching for me, calling me home. I flutter wearily and land on a branch, sinking my talons around the firm, rough surface. That feeling of belonging seeps through my bones as I sink my weary beak against my chest and drift off to sleep.

"I see you've found your bird form, Ella." A bird flutters over to me, waking me up. "This is wonderful."

I blink and cock my head. There's something familiar about this bird. "Who are you?"

"Your Aunt Fiona," the bird says with a twitter of a laugh. "Surely you recognize me?"

"Oh." I wrack my brain until slips of human images piece together. It's rather confusing. Besides, I'm ravenous. How can I concentrate when I'm this hungry? That flight worked up my appetite. The bird seed in the feeder practically calls to me. "I need food."

I flutter my wings, trying to remember how I did that flying thing earlier, except when I try to beat my wings, my body twists and contorts. My limbs flail, and then I hit the ground with a hard thud. Every bone and muscle aches, especially my arm, which I land on. Groaning, I roll over on my back, blinking against the pale morning, feeling incredibly disorientated.

A buzzing thrums through my head. My mouth tastes like I stuffed it with batting. What just happened? I sit up, trying to remember why I'm outside under the hazel tree. I'm wearing my black dress, but my cloak is missing, as is one of my boots. Soot covers my entire body. I brush it off, and small black flecks flutter into the air.

Feathers.

Dread pools in my stomach like cold rain.

I transformed.

"You all right, dear?" a voice asks from the tree above. I rub my head and realize it came from the bird perched on the bough. "That was quite the fall. Now get up, and let's have a good look at you and see if you're part bird or fully human."

"Aunt Fiona?" I push to my feet but sway a little as if my body can't quite figure out what it is. "What happened? Why am I out here?"

"Bless me if I should know. Only moments ago, you flew in bird form onto this tree. You were spouting off something about being hungry and then fell. I should've warned you that hunger, tiredness, or sudden fright can cause one to shift out of their form. Happened constantly to your mother when she first started transitioning. Don't worry about the leftover feathers dusting your skin. They brush off easily."

My stomach rumbles. I push a hand against my belly as the events of the previous night flash through my mind like my brain is catching up with my human form. Dr. Wissen's monstrosity, the flight to the woods, Fritz transforming into a frog, Wilhelm getting injured, and Jacob.

*The kiss.*

I suck in a deep breath, touching my lips with trembling hands. I kissed him. Just the memory sends my pulse racing and fire coursing deep into my core. His lips were so soft. And our kiss was full of hopes and dreams. When he wrapped his arms around me, I didn't want to ever leave.

Except then I became this. A monster. Something he's cursed to hunt.

"Are you even listening to me?" Fiona asks. "This is one of

the most important moments of your life, and you're just standing there daydreaming."

I shake my head, forcing myself back to this moment. "Why didn't you ever speak to me before in your bird form?" I ask.

"I did. You just never understood me. Just like the door to the tree has always been there, but you never saw it until you were ready. Such are the ways. But as I was saying, it appears as if you are now completely human. I'd think you'd be happier."

*She's right!* I hold up my hands, recalling the image of them morphing into talons and feathers. Even though I'm relieved to be fully human, I shudder from the pain-filled memory.

"There's nothing about this that makes me happy," I say.

"You have dual transformation abilities, which means you can be completely bird or completely human. Very helpful. I'm quite jealous, but happy for you, my dear."

"It was extremely painful."

"The first time always is. According to your mother, it gets easier with every switch. And with experience and time, the confusion after shapeshifting will improve. Go ahead and get some rest and food. Then I want to test you to see if you can transform upon command or if it's accidental."

Fritz popped into frog form the second he got scared at Dr. Wissen's manor. I really hope I can control this ability. It could become quite awkward otherwise, to say the least.

"Uh, oh!" Aunt Fiona cries and begins hopping back and forth on her branch. "We have trouble coming."

I follow her line of sight to the house. My stepsisters, stepmother, and father are all standing by the back door. Stepmother's arms are crossed, a firm scowl on her face, but it's my stepsisters and Father who walk out toward me.

## CHAPTER 35

# JACOB

### RUINE HOHENURACH

S he simply vanished. How is that even possible? I scour the forest until the first hints of dawn claw across the sky like skeletal fingers. Finally, I drag my exhausted body to the turret, collapsing alongside the others. Even Rumpelstiltskin's loud snoring doesn't bother me. I'm woken at dawn by someone shaking my body. I crack my eyes open to see a frazzled prince, red hair sticking up on its ends, a dirt-smeared tunic, and a very black eye.

"Where's Ella?" the prince asks, grabbing my shirt with both fists. "I haven't seen her since we were talking on the roof."

I wipe the sleep from my eyes. "Don't know," I say wearily, pushing his hands away. "She left. I looked for her all night. Even tracked her footprints. It's as if she disappeared."

"Or Wissen's men captured her," he exclaims. "We need to rescue her."

What he means is I need to rescue her. I join my brother and Rumpelstiltskin in the courtyard. Wilhelm is tending the fire, his body healed, ready to hunt monsters. Meanwhile, Rumpelstiltskin is turning a roasted rabbit on a stick.

"That smells good," I tell him, and my stomach agrees with a rumble.

"You think you're going to get a bite of this, tyrant?" he asks me as he rips off a piece and hands it to Wilhelm.

I grin. I deserved that comment.

"You did well last night," I say, settling on a rock by the flames to warm myself against the cool morning. "We'd have been in trouble if you hadn't shown up with the horses. Thank you."

He snorts a huff but remains oddly quiet. Or maybe he's just too busy licking his fingers from the rabbit juice.

"So the girl is gone, huh?" Wilhelm says.

"We need to return to Wissen's manor immediately and look for her," Prince William says, pacing the courtyard. "You saw how dreadful a place that was."

"Look at you," Rumpelstiltskin tells the prince. "All doe-eyed over that girl."

"What do you think?" I ask Wilhelm.

He stares at me with a look that makes my insides itch.

"It's not what you think," I tell Wilhelm hotly. "There must be another explanation."

"Normal people don't just disappear under a starry night," Wilhelm says, and starts picking up our few belongings. "I wouldn't worry too much over the girl, Your Highness. I'm sure she's made it safely home. The important thing is for you to get back before your ball tonight."

"The ball! How could I have forgotten?" Prince William fists his hands into his curls, clearly distraught. "Good point. What we should do is return to the castle and arrest Wissen now that we have evidence he was behind the weapons crime."

My whole body wishes to abandon the prince and race back to Ella's house to make sure she really is safe. I refuse to believe Wilhelm's insinuation that she's a Forbidden. Besides, she can't be. She doesn't have a mark.

"You're completely right, Your Highness," I say as I prep the horses. "Wilhelm will escort you back to your castle while I pay a visit to Ella von Maier's manor and see if she found her way home."

"Really?" Wilhelm shoots me an exasperated look. "Why am I never involved in these decisions?"

"At least he acknowledges your existence," Rumpelstiltskin points out.

"Excellent idea!" Prince William slaps me on the shoulder as I mount Storm. "I will make this a royal decree. Once you have something to report, alert me as soon as possible."

"You're out of your control, Jacob," Wilhelm warns me. "Watch yourself."

I refuse to listen to his lectures this morning. With a quick nod, I flick Storm's reins and take off, retracing our tracks from last night back to the Echaz River. Storm must sense my urgency because once we reach the open road, his hooves break into a gallop, never wavering. I lean low, allowing the wind to wake me as I set my sights on Maier Manor.

When I arrive, I knock on the door, pacing as I wait. When no one answers, I head around the back. Maybe I can sneak in through the kitchen door. It's hardly appropriate, but the moment I signed the Enchantress's contract, I forfeited every rule of society.

When I reach the back of the house, my steps falter. She's here, standing beneath the hazel tree with her family. Relief floods over me that she's safe and unharmed. It must have taken her all night to walk back without a horse. It takes every ounce of control not to rush over and speak with her, but my arrival could only make things worse.

Why did she leave? None of it makes sense. Unless she's afraid of me. A stone settles in my stomach. I never should've kissed her.

## CHAPTER 36

# ELLA

### MAIER MANOR

My legs tremble as I stand before my family. I need to be strong in case I'm like Fritz and transform when afraid.

"Cinderella!" Marianne holds out her hands and grabs mine. "We were so worried. No one was there to help with breakfast. We didn't know where you were."

"Been everywhere searching for you," Father says in a gruff voice. "Where have you been?"

"I've been out here by my mother's tree." It's not quite a lie, but there's no way I can tell them the truth. Did Stepmother discover I'd been at Dr. Wissen's house? "I was missing her."

"Blasted tree," Father says, stuffing his hands in his pockets while frowning at the branches.

"You shouldn't sleep outside." Marianne pushes a strand of her brown hair behind her ears. "It's still too cold."

"We were imagining all sorts of horrid things that could've happened to you," Bertha explains. "I suppose we never considered you'd been sleeping out here by this old tree all

239

night like some kind of—" She wrinkles her perfect nose and finishes, "Animal!"

I grin, deciding this might not be a good time to tell her she's close to the truth. "That's very sweet of you to be worried about me. I didn't know I'd be missed."

"This tree has nothing but evil memories." Father kicks at a pile of crow feathers scattered on the ground. "Cursed is what it is."

I frown. Could that be from another missing bird Aunt Fiona was talking about?

"No, it's not. It was Mother's tree. Don't you remember the picnics we had beneath its boughs? Or how high you pushed me on the swing?"

His face softens like the memory has brought back the old him. He reaches into the feeder and scoops up a handful of seeds.

"Father, you're right about this tree being cursed," Marianne says, placing a hand on his arm. "There's an odd feel to it. Seems as if it would be best to chop it down, don't you think?"

My heart falters, missing a beat. Chop down my mother's tree? The tree my aunt and the ravens live in? Thunder rolls inside me. That won't happen as long as I'm alive.

"No one is chopping down this tree," I say, crossing my arms.

"What's taking so long?" Stepmother shouts from the edge of the garden path, her toes pressed to the border as if she doesn't dare step into the fields. "Ella needs to make breakfast. The ball is tonight, and we're wasting valuable time. The girls' dresses need pressing, and their hair must be done."

Father's head snaps up, and he tosses the seeds to the ground. That hardness forms back on his face as he faces me. "A lady never sleeps outside like a wild animal or servant. But if it's a servant you want to be, then a servant is what you'll become. Now get inside and help your sisters get ready for the ball. For once, we will be a *civilized* family."

"Come along, Cinderella." Marianne hooks her arm in mine as we head back to the house. "I have the best of news! Dr. Wissen sent over a letter this morning. Apparently, the marriage request was approved, and he already booked the church for tonight."

I freeze, pulling away from Marianne. How did it get approved? Otto said he destroyed it.

"We'd attend," Bertha says, practically skipping at my other side, "but we'll be at the ball."

"I won't marry him." I clench my fist. "I refuse."

"You will marry him." Stepmother dares to march over and drag me toward the house. "I can't afford to feed another mouth or dress another daughter. Besides, Dr. Wissen is paying all the expenses for Marianne's and Bertha's ball gowns. He can't have his wife's sisters looking like they're trying to escape poverty."

Panic squirms in my stomach, knotting into thick ropes. Heaven save me, he wants to marry me today. What's the hurry? Unless he knows I was at his manor last night and discovered who he really is. I need to delay the wedding until Jacob can write his story or find a way to escape.

"What if I come with you all to the ball, too?" I feel like I'm trying to hold snowflakes in the heat of summer. "Maybe the prince will choose me. Then I wouldn't have to marry Dr. Wissen, and our family worries would be over."

The odds of that happening are impossible, but it would give me time.

"Prince William, fall in love with you?" Stepmother laughs. "Look at you. Sooty and smelly. Besides, what would you wear to the ball? You destroyed your best dress."

"It's not like I think the prince would marry me," I

whisper to Marianne, trying another tactic. Stepmother always listens to her. "I just want to go to the ball before I'm a married woman."

"There must be a way you could convince Mother," Marianne whispers back. "What if you helped us get ready and did extra chores? I'm sure that would put her in a good mood."

If she promises to allow me to go to the festival of balls, that will last three days. Three full days to find a way to escape the doctor or maybe even this house. I can't help it, but my thoughts turn to Jacob. The way he looks at me like I'm the most incredible thing he's ever seen. How his arms fold around my waist, strong and protective, while his lips press against mine with a desperate, hungry need.

I shake my head. His destiny is to write people like me from this world. If anything, he's my enemy and one I can never trust.

"Please let me go to the ball," I call after Stepmother as we enter the house. "What if I did extra chores and helped my sisters out with preparations? Then would you let me?"

Stepmother marches into the kitchen, where the staff pretends to be waiting for their breakfast, but considering the window is open, they were obviously eavesdropping. They leap to their feet, bodies straight as boards. Stepmother clenches her fists as she takes in the situation and then spins on me.

"Enough!" She waves her hand at me like she's shooing away a fly. "Your whining grates on my nerves. Cook breakfast for the lazy staff, and then I want you to help Bertha and Marianne with their hair and dresses."

"And then," I push, "will you let me go to the ball?"

"I don't have time for your nonsense." Stepmother says. "Dr. Wissen will be here soon, and the girls must be dressed before you leave."

She breezes out of the room with my stepsisters, leaving

me alone with the servants. I stare at them, unable to move. My head is fuzzy with hunger, and I'm so tired. I can barely keep my eyes open.

"Ella, dear, you look as if you are about to pass out." Jesse grabs my shoulders and helps me sit down. "Take a rest. We'll all work together and make something good to eat, won't we?"

The others agree, patting my shoulders.

"I'm just going to close my eyes for a moment," I tell them and tuck my head against my arm on the table.

I'm not sure how long I slept, but the ringing of bells wakes me. I startle and nearly fall out of my chair.

A bowl of porridge is set on the table beside me, which Jesse must have made. I need to thank her. My hands tremble as I eat as fast as possible. Then I hurry to Bertha's room to find her perched in front of her looking glass, a snarl on her face. Inwardly, I cringe. She's never fun to be around when she's in one of her moods.

"Where have you been?" Bertha exclaims and throws her brush at me. I duck. "My hair isn't done yet, and we leave for the ball in four hours!"

In the next room, Marianne has Jesse running about, sewing on extra ribbons and brocade to her dress. I pick the brush off the floor and set to work on Bertha's hair, an arduous task since I have to listen to her practice a series of lines their culture instructor had given them.

"How do you do, Prince William?" Bertha cocks her head to the side and bats her eyelashes at her reflection. "It is *such* an honor to meet Your Highness. Dance? With your royal Highness? I'd be obliged, Your Royal Highness!"

"Can you not move your head about?" I ask.

"Ow!" Bertha yells. "You're hurting me!"

I lift my eyebrows. "I didn't even touch you."

Marianne rushes into the room. "What's happening?"

"I was just finishing her hair," I say through gritted teeth.

Unlike sweet Jesse, who is peeking her head around the doorway, worry stretched over her face. I honestly don't have the disposition to tolerate such a brat.

"Of course, you were." Marianne smiles kindly. "I know this must be dreadful to watch us get ready for the ball, but we must focus on one of us marrying the prince. Just imagine. You could visit me at the castle. We could have tea. Wouldn't that be lovely?"

An image of Marianne as the princess of Württemberg swims through my mind. A glistening crown on her head, a mountain of tulle and lace, and her neck swallowed in jewels. She'd be a fine enough princess, but by that time, I'm hoping I'll have run away, forgotten and safe from the doctor.

Peter, our footman, bursts into the room, startling all of us. "Your Royal Highness and Greatness." He bows before Marianne. "It displeases me to disturb you."

"Your Royal Highness?" I furrow my brow. "Why is he calling you that?"

"We were merely practicing it in case the prince marries me." Marianne huffs. "Having a little fun, that's all."

"Frau von Maier told me to come get you at once."

"Why?" Marianne crosses her arms. "Is something wrong?"

He focuses on me. "Company has arrived. For you, Ella."

"Who?" My whole body numbs, cold and lifeless.

"Dr. Wissen, of course."

The brush falls from my fingers, clattering on the floor. Somehow, I manage to lift my head and march into the hall. Jesse tries to stop me, tears streaming down her cheeks, while Marianne hurries after me, probably eager to watch the drama. Bertha remains at her dressing table, returning to the recitation of her lines.

Two men stand in the hall as if they're guarding it, or perhaps they're preparing to drag me away if I resist. At the doorway, I pause, trying to still my beating heart. Dr. Wissen is sprawled out on the settee in the parlor with Stepmother and Father. Usually, servants bring out coffee and sweets for our guests, but there's no one left other than Jesse and me.

Dr. Wissen is wearing a fine embroidered jacket and the latest styled silk pants. A hat sits beside him on the end table, and his cane lies on his lap. Bile fills my mouth, knowing what he does to his wives. When I step inside, he rises to greet me. The left corner of his lip curls up.

"Ella!" Stepmother exclaims. "You should've changed. You can't wear a torn-up black dress for your wedding."

"Father, there's something you should know about Dr. Wissen," I say, deciding to see if he'll believe me when I tell him about Wissen's past wives.

Jesse barrels into the sitting room. Marianne's ball gown lies in her arms, billowing up so it's hard to see her face.

"Ella!" Jesse cries out. "What do I do? Marianne's gown for the ball tonight has been ruined. The hem must have gotten too close to the fire and singed it."

"What?" Marianne screams, snatching the dress from Jesse and holding it up.

Sure enough, the entire front hem of the dress is ruined. I press my lips together, glancing at Jesse, giving me hopeful eyes. My heart squeezes. She did this purposely to save me.

"Idiot! You've ruined my ball gown!" Marianne yells at Jesse and then slaps her across the face, leaving behind a fierce mark. I gasp in shock. "Get out of my sight before I throw you into the fire like you did with my dress!"

"How dare you hit her?" I march up to stand between Marianne and Jesse. "Next time you have an issue with one of the servants, you come to me first." Then to Jesse, I say, "I'll get some poultice for you as soon as I'm done here."

Her hand trembles as she touches her cheek. Marianne throws the gown at Jesse. "Why are you still here?" Marianne demands. "Get out!"

Jesse races out of the room. I suck in a deep breath, knowing she just gave me a gift. I can't waste it.

"This is terrible, Marianne. Now you don't have a gown for the ball," I say, adding panic to my voice. "I'd offer to help, but I can't since I must get married. Unless...we delayed my wedding." I pause, carefully choosing my next words. "Step-mother, Marianne needs me to stay here and fix her gown. With the ball only hours away, she might not be able to go unless we hurry."

"She's right, Mother," Marianne says, rubbing her temples. "I need her to stay. This is a disaster."

"And I need my wife," Dr. Wissen counters. "I cannot wait another day for her."

I'm stunned by the doctor's urgency. It means he wants to murder me tonight. Feed me to his trees to gain my magic.

"If I'm a princess," Marianne says, eyes sharpening on him. "All will be well. My positioning is the key, and nothing can jeopardize that. You can wait."

"*Your* positioning?" Wissen scowls. "This isn't just about you."

I step back, letting the two fight it out.

"Oh, but it is," she retorts. "Father, I need Ella."

Father wipes his forehead vigorously, rising from his seat. "Marianne's right, my dearest Hilda. We can't jeopardize her chances of marrying the prince. If she needs Ella, she must have Ella."

Stepmother sighs in resignation. "I'm sorry, doctor, but it's true. We're severely understaffed. And with the loss of Mari-anne's gown, we can't lose our beloved Ella quite yet."

"I understand your urgency." Dr. Wissen glowers at Mari-anne. "How about we compromise? You have Ella today. At dawn tomorrow, I'll send a fleet of servants, so we don't have this issue. They'll work all day on your daughters, leaving Ella free to marry me."

"That is only fair," Marianne says triumphantly.

I don't like this. I've only managed to buy myself one day. It's not enough time, but it'll have to be for now. He bows politely to my father and stepmother and heads into the hall. Strangely, Marianne follows him. Curious, I slip into the shadows and duck behind the clock to listen.

"Let's hope the fool of a prince falls madly in love with you," Wissen says in a light growl. "You've put me in a difficult situation."

Marianne glares as he slips outside like oil roiling across a marble floor.

"What was my future husband talking to you about?" I challenge her, stepping out of the shadows. She startles.

"I didn't see you there." She touches her throat. "It was nothing. Just reminding him of my eagerness for him to be a part of our family."

She's lying. Why?

"Of course." I smile, hoping she can't see its falseness. "I'm going to make a mid-day meal. Can't have you go to the ball hungry, can we? Meanwhile, why don't you look through your dresses and see which one you wish for me to work on?"

I hurry into the kitchen, thoughts churning. Something is in the works between those two. But what? I need to tell Jacob. The door bursts open, and Marianne rushes into the kitchen.

"What exactly did you hear between Dr. Wissen and me?" Marianne demands.

"Nothing. You two just seemed like you had a secret." I look away, setting a mixing bowl onto the table, and then drag a sack of potatoes toward me. I decide to play dumb. "Listen, if you're having an affair with him, I don't care."

She jerks, eyebrows lifting. "An affair? No. I'd never come between you and your fiancé."

When she says fiancé, I slam my knife sharply through the

potato. "I just want to go to the ball, Marianne. It's that simple."

Marianne studies me intently. She moves to the table, digging her hands into a bowl of dried lentils, sifting them as if in deep thought. "I truly wish to be a good sister to you, Cinderella. I want to be the sister you've always dreamed of. Let's keep this whole thing just between the two of us."

Her voice is as sweet as honeysuckle. It's alarming. She's worried about something. But what?

"Of course." I flash her a tight smile.

"Mother!" Marianne calls down the hall. "Mother!"

Is Marianne really going to help me, or is this a trick? It doesn't take long for my stepmother to find us, even if a little breathless.

"Whatever is the matter?" She holds her hand to her chest. "What has Ella done now?"

"It seems only fair to let Cinderella go to the ball. She needs one last night of bliss before she marries," Marianne says, flashing me a smile. "Perhaps after she's helped Bertha and me, does some extra chores, and doesn't cause any trouble, we could let her go."

"If that would make you happy." Stepmother's nose lifts disdainfully as she assesses me. Then she snatches the bowl of lentils on the counter and throws them into the ash-filled fireplace. "How about this? Pick every lentil out. Once you finish your chores and dress your sisters, then you can go."

It's an impossible task, but I need to try. "Thank you, Stepmother."

"You're so generous, Mother." Marianne kisses her on the cheek and then winks conspiratorially at me. "Sounds like we have a deal, don't we, Cinderella?"

"That we do," I say, hoping I haven't fallen into another trap.

# CHAPTER 37

# JACOB

## LICHTENSTEIN CASTLE

"This whole marrying business makes me itchy all over," Prince William mutters as we step into his quarters. "One wife was more than enough for me, let me tell you. I got out of that one, but Father is furious at my insistence on never marrying again. There must be heirs and a name to carry on, apparently."

"So it seems," I say. "Perhaps tonight you'll find a wife worthy of you."

"I'd rather be chained in the dungeons than subject myself to another dreadful oath." The prince throws himself onto the couch, leaning his head back on the cushions, groaning. "It is wonderful to be back in the world of comfort. I don't know how you two do it, running about like savages in the wild."

This is more than comfort. Silk drapes cover stained-glass windows while paintings and tapestries cling to stone walls. Intricate carpets, ornate lamps, and artifacts clutter the room.

My eyes land on a wooden chest tucked beneath the bay window. The intricate carving of the wolf sends chills straight to my bones. I step closer to inspect the chest. Its bulging eyes seem to stare right at me.

"What is it?" Wilhelm joins my side only to suck in a deep breath.

I glance around the room and rip a tapestry off the wall, tossing it over the chest.

"What are you doing?" the prince cries. "That was woven by my great-grandmother."

I press my finger to my lips and lean to whisper in his ear. "The chest looks exactly like something from where we visited last night."

The prince stares at me, eyes widening as he realizes that chest has allowed Wissen to spy on him. "I'll have it removed and burned immediately."

"A wise choice," I say. "In fact, I recommend having the entire castle checked."

Once the chest is taken away, we pull out the maps and lists we stole from Wissen's study.

"Reading through these leaves me no doubt the doctor's men ambushed the weapons delivery. Which means our doctor is well armed," I say uneasily. "Between his werewolves, the wooden chests scattered about the castle, and the addition of weapons, I'd bet he's planning to overthrow your family."

"And what better time to do that than at the ball amidst the chaos of so many guests and people coming and going." Wilhelm adds. "The castle will be hard to defend. You should consider cancelling the ball."

"That sounds too good to be true. I'll bring this information to my father," the prince says, but he doesn't look hopeful. "I doubt he'll cancel. In the meantime, I'm going to send soldiers to arrest the doctor and have him questioned immediately."

"Let's hope he doesn't suspect anything and run," I say.

"Plus, if the doctor is locked up, he won't be able to hurt or marry Ella."

"Exactly," the prince says and leaves to search for his father.

Wilhelm and I find a seat, and a servant brings us drinks along with an assortment of fruit, cheese, and bread. Between Wilhelm and myself, we devour the food in minutes.

"Hardly enough food," Wilhelm mutters as he pulls out the pen and book. "You took more than half."

Probably true. I lean back, staring at the book. "Whose story are you writing?"

"The doctor's, of course. I'd hoped the story would be finished by now, but the words "the end" haven't appeared.

"That's not good."

"In the meantime, I've already started on the prince's story. It's only a matter of time before his name shows up."

"Ella had a good point last night before she disappeared," I admit. "The prince may be a Forbidden, but he's not evil. Not like the doctor or his army of werewolves. What if the Enchantress is actually the villain here?"

"How many times have I said the same thing? You're just considering it because of Ella." Wilhelm begins writing letters in his flowing script. "But like you said, what choice do we have? We signed a blood oath."

I sink my head into my hands. The magnitude of our task and the feeling of hopelessness weigh on me. "We live in a life without choice, don't we?"

"You never told me," Wilhelm says. "Did you find Ella?"

"Yes. She was at her manor. By the tree. Her family was there, so I couldn't speak with her without drawing attention. It's not normal for callers to be visiting betrothed ladies at the crack of dawn."

"Yes, that might have been awkward. Do you think—?"

He stops there, unable to speak about what sits heavily on

both of our minds. That Ella is a Forbidden. My chest tightens.

"I'll find out tonight," I finally say.

"If her stepmother will allow her to come to the ball."

"She'll come. I'm sure of it." I tap the sides of the chair, unable to control my emotions churning inside of me.

"You've fallen for her, haven't you?"

"What? Of course not!" I scowl, rising to pace before the window.

"I warned you. You should've stayed far away from her."

"There's no room for love in our lives." I stare outside. A stone's throw away is the edge of the cliff where the castle is perched, plunging into the valley below. I can see how living up here, one might feel powerful, untouchable. "All we're guaranteed is death."

And yet, our shared kiss lingers on my lips, tasting of life and the fullness of what could be. I'm desperate for that.

Desperate for her.

# CHAPTER 38

## ELLA

### MAIER MANOR

Today has been torture getting my stepsisters prepared for the ball. First, preparing Marianne's dress and then her bath, which required multiple trips to the kitchen to boil water. She even sent me to the garden to find flowers. Impossible this early in spring. The most frustrating part is returning to Marianne's room to discover flower petals floating across the bath's surface.

"Where did you find those flowers?" I ask her as she sinks beneath the water's surface.

"I have my sources." She smiles coyly at me. "My skin needed them to soak in their essence."

"Then I suppose you don't need these flowers." I set the ones I gathered onto the vanity.

"Those useless weeds? Hardly!"

I don't have time to mull over Marianne's strange behavior or the source of her roses because Bertha is in the next room screaming for me. I pause at Marianne's mirror, realizing I need to find time to clean up and dress. Bertha screams my name again. Letting out a frustrated breath, I rush into her room only to watch her throw all her jewelry out the window.

"What's wrong with you?" I demand and peek over the ledge. Jewels are scattered on the ground below.

"Wrong with me?" Bertha tosses her shiny blond curls over her shoulder. "You're the one who threw all my jewelry out the window. I hope nothing is broken."

Fear winds up in my chest. "You're not blaming this on me," I say.

The sun is dipping low in the sky. Time is fleeing. I've minutes at best to gather up the lentils. An impossible task.

"Darling Bertha, why aren't you ready yet?" Stepmother breezes into the room in a dazzling crinoline gown.

"It's Cinderella's fault." Bertha points a shaking finger at me, tears trickling from her blue eyes. "She didn't want me to look beautiful, so she threw all of my jewels out the window."

"Cinderella!" Stepmother cries. "What's the meaning of this?"

"I'll fetch them immediately," I say, and dart out of the room. There's no use arguing. To my stepmother, her daughters are always right, even when they aren't.

I gather up the jewels in my apron but stop at the kitchen first. If I hurry, there's still a chance I can go. Dropping onto the hearth, I start digging through the ashes and picking up the lentils. After a few moments of listening to the ringing of the bells for me to return to my stepsisters' rooms, I decide I'd be happy to never see another lentil again. Stepmother knew this was a hopeless task when she tossed them into the ashes.

"She's won," I grumble. "Again."

A twitter of a bird, and then a *tap tap* on the window catches my attention. I open it, discovering the ravens and Aunt Fiona in her bird form perched on the small tree.

"What's going on?" she asks.

"It's the ball." Then I explain the impossible task my stepmother gave me.

"My poor dear," Aunt Fiona says. "My sister would peck my eyes out if she knew I allowed such nonsense to happen to you. And she'd insist you went to the ball. Don't worry. I'll call the pigeons and turtledoves. They are excellent at such things. Then you can dazzle the prince and be free from your nonsensical stepmother. Now hurry! Go get dressed. Once you come back here, you'll find your task complete."

"Thank you, Aunt Fiona!" I kiss her feathery forehead.

By the time I scurry upstairs, sweat soaking my dress, I find the three already dressed and exiting Bertha's room. They look like queens, strolling down the hall with gossamer tulle, shimmering lavender bodices, honey-dipped skirts, and brown-sugar brocades. All my hopes and dreams of attending a spectacular ball melt away.

"I brought the jewels." I hold out the box filled with glittering rocks, now looking too fine for my callused hands.

"Never mind those old things," Bertha scoffs. "Mother found a far finer set of jewels. Aren't they simply enchanting?"

With her satin-gloved hands, she points to her neckline where a large ruby pendant hangs over her chest. Then she shakes her head, allowing the matching ruby earrings to catch the fading sunlight in their crevices.

I frown. "Those are my mother's jewels. I thought you needed to sell those."

"They're the household jewels," Father says, coming up from behind the group. "Since you threw Bertha's out the window, I decided it's only fitting she should have the best. Now let's be off. If we don't hurry, we'll be late."

Panic seizes at my throat, threatening to cut off my air. "Wait! You can't leave yet."

"I'll take those." Stepmother snatches the box from my hands. "Can't have you trying to steal the family jewels. I know how you think, Cinderella."

"I wouldn't." Or would I? They'd let me start a new life, wouldn't they?

I trail after the group when Marianne touches me lightly, careful to hold her skirts away from my grimy-covered ones.

"I'm sorry you can't come," she says. "I promise to tell you every juicy detail tomorrow."

My heart squeezes tighter. I know it's silly to want to go to a ball. I should focus on finding a way to escape. Except Jacob is also depending on me coming to help him.

"You promised," I call after Stepmother.

She spins on her satin slippers, her gown swaying off the ground like a bell. "Cinderella, you knew our deal."

"Please, just wait." I rush down the hall into the kitchen. Sure enough, the bowl is filled with lentils, cleaned of ashes. A lone feather lies beside it. "Thank you!" I whisper into the air, before snatching up the bowl and racing back to Stepmother.

"See." I present the lentils. "The task is done. I've fulfilled the agreement."

"Let me see those." Marianne peers into the bowl, first studying the lentils and then me, a frown puckering her forehead. "How did you gather these so fast? It's as if you used magic."

My heart stutters at her words. Like she knows about such things.

Stepmother tsks. "Wonderful work, but have you seen yourself in the looking glass? You can't wear that gown. You're hardly fit to walk about our manor in such a state. You'd only bring shame to our family and whatever strands of nobility the Maier name has left."

With that, she joins the others climbing into the coach. I can't move, gripping the bowl as if it's the only thing that keeps me from losing it. Peter flicks the reins, tipping his hat forlornly to me. No one gives me a glance from inside the coach, too busy fluttering fans and giggling in anticipation.

In that moment, it's as if I'm dragged back to the night of Mother's death. Though there isn't a drop of rain in the sky, I feel like I'm drowning.

I stumble down the steps, dropping the bowl of lentils onto the grass. What did they matter now? I wander, not really knowing where to go or what to do. Sunlight filters through the trees, and I gaze at the castle resting on the cliff. The sunset illuminates the tower into gold, a lofty promise of hopes. The sounds of music and laughter waft down from the castle on the wings of twilight's breeze.

If only I could fly away and leave everything behind. Clenching my fists, I try to imagine myself transforming. When that didn't work, I take off running, holding my arms out as if to trick my body into the act of flight. Instead, I only manage to look like a fool.

It's then that I realize my feet took me to the one place I feel wanted, needed. Mother's grave beneath the hazel tree. I drop to my knees, and a single tear trickles down my cheek. I brush it away, determined to be strong.

"Why are you crying?" It's Aunt Fiona back in her half-human, half-bird form, sitting on the tree bough, kicking her legs as the wind brushes over her feathered arms. "You should be off to the ball."

"I wanted to, but Stepmother is right. I can't exactly wear this. You know what Mother's last words were to me?" I ask her. She shakes her head. "Be good and pious, and then the good God would protect and look down on me from heaven and be near. But what has that gotten me? I'm nothing but rags and soot. I'm a slave in my own house and betrothed to a monster. I even tried to transform into a bird so I could fly away, but even that didn't work."

"Well, that's a terrible predicament indeed."

I rise to my feet, brushing the dirt from my skirts, which

is laughable. "I need to pack. I have only a few hours to escape before they return and notice I've gone missing."

"Escape?" Fiona laughs. "I thought you wished to go to the ball. The ball is where you must go because that's your future, not this place." Then Fiona switches to a sing-song voice, saying, "Shiver and quiver, little tree, silver and gold throw down to thee."

She flourishes her hands. A golden gossamer dress lined with silver ribbon floats through the air, landing in my arms. Silver slippers appear at my feet.

"How? How did you do this?"

"There might be a touch of magic in our family line." Fiona titters as if she's telling a good joke. "Maybe you'll be lucky and inherit that as well. Come inside. We'll get you all polished up and wipe those tears away."

The doorway appears in the tree, and I step inside. The scents of fresh wood and earth flow over me, rich and deep. Fiona directs me to a side room tucked behind branches where there's a basin of scented water. I clean up and slip on the shimmering gown. Then Fiona brushes out my hair, and with a few twists and pulls, braids and curls it into an intricate design.

She whistles and doves carry in snowdrop flowers, which Fiona tucks into my curls. After I slip on the silver slippers, she directs me over to a full-sized looking glass, larger than even Marianne's.

"Now if that isn't ever the prettiest girl in the land." Fiona squeezes my shoulders.

I blink at my transformation. The dress shimmers as if it holds starlight. My hair looks like spun gold, free of dirt and soot. I touch my chest. The dress reveals more skin than I'm used to.

"Your mother's jewels are gone," Fiona says, misreading my actions. "But I have the blue star jewel passed down in our family for generations. I wanted to give it to you earlier, but I feared Frau von Maier would take it."

She opens an old wooden jewelry box and, from its velvet-lined depths, withdraws a deep sapphire-blue pendant. She clasps its gold chain around my neck. It sparkles against my skin. Then she lifts a brush and sweeps powder over my face so my skin glitters too.

"How can I ever thank you?" I spin around, enchanted with how the dress moves like a stream rippling over rocks.

"You can thank me by having the most glorious time. The powder has a masquerading spell to keep others from recognizing you as long as you're wearing it. Now off you go. Take a horse up the mountain path. It's the shortest way. I'll have the ravens escort you and make sure no harm befalls your trip."

# CHAPTER 39

# JACOB

## LICHTENSTEIN CASTLE

The castle reminds me of my favorite play, *A Midsummer Night's Dream*. Garlands and scarlet roses from the greenhouses drape above the walkways and arches, drenching the air with a floral aroma. Star-studded lanterns sway from the ceilings while additional candelabras are set along the corridors and tucked into alcoves, creating a fairy-world atmosphere. Servants rush about, carrying trays laden with more food than most villagers see in years.

My thoughts go to my family at home, scraping by. If only Wilhelm and I could forget this nasty business and sneak out the back door with a bag stuffed with food and race home. It'd be like Christmas in the old days when Father was alive.

Golden candlelight pours through the tall windows and glitters across the gardens like stardust. Laughter and heady perfumes permeate the air as eager guests stroll through the entrance.

"I want to say we're ready," I tell Wilhelm. "Except Wissen has shown to be a formidable opponent."

"What I don't like is the fact that he's gone into hiding

the day of the ball," Wilhelm mutters as we make a final round, checking each entrance for security. When the king's army arrived at Wissen's house this afternoon, it was empty. I put Rumpelstiltskin in charge of the front gate with a firm reminder not to leave his post. He refused until Wilhelm promised him punch and treats.

"Ready?" Wilhelm asks as we step inside the ballroom full of glistening gowns and black suits.

"I must mentally prepare myself for the onslaught of supe-riority." I clear my throat. "Very well, I'm ready as I'll ever be. Should we make a direct beeline for the punch and food? I'm starved."

"Excellent choice," Wilhelm agrees eagerly. "I'll need to pilfer a few for Rumpelstiltskin while I'm at it."

Decked with streams of tulle and clusters of roses, the ballroom is already filled to the brim, dancers performing their moves to perfection and maidens flapping their fans and giggling in hopes of catching Prince William's attention from where he's standing beside his father's throne on the raised dais. He's hardly recognizable with the powder dusting his face, the wig, and the embellished uniform. The scowl on the prince's face speaks volumes to his feelings about finding a new wife.

"Our Fritz looks as if he's having a fantastic time." Wilhelm grins as we pile plates full of sliced meats, skewered vegetables, berries dusted in sugar, and tiny cakes spread with white whipped frosting.

"Indeed. If he continues with this mood, not a maiden will have him, and he'll have to resort to marrying one of the garden frogs. Any sign of our doctor?"

"No, but I've spotted Ella's family. She isn't here."

My stomach turns. Is she avoiding me after that kiss, or is it just because her family won't let her come? The cake I popped into my mouth suddenly tastes dry. A noticeable shift stirs the room. Conversations falter, leaving only the string quartet to fill the void. I reach for one of my daggers, scanning the floor and the guests' faces, which are filled with a mixture of surprise and awe.

"Something is happening," I say, readying myself for an attack.

The crowd parts, revealing the most beautiful woman I've ever seen standing at the ballroom entrance. She's wearing a billowing ball gown that sparkles under the chandeliers. It clings to her body like it was made for her, every fold catching the light as if it were spun from the sun itself. Golden hair piles in intricate braids on top of her head, tangled with snowdrops, with the rest cascading down her back like wings of a dove. She looks like a princess.

The prince's head whips in the direction of the commotion, and his slouched shoulders draw back at attention. He steps off his platform and strides through the crowd, guests parting for him like a curtain until he reaches the princess.

"Looks like the prince doesn't need a distraction anymore," Wilhelm says.

"Let's hope it's not too much of a distraction. We need him to be prepared for a potential attack."

The prince bows to the golden woman and says something. She nods and gives him an endearing smile that, for some reason, tugs at my chest. He takes her gloved hand and escorts her to the dance floor.

My eyes narrow. "There's something strangely familiar about that woman. Have we seen her before?"

"Knowing our luck, she bears the mark," Wilhelm grumbles as he loads his plate high with food. "Big surprise there. At this rate, we'll never leave this village."

I frown, tossing my plate onto one of the servants' trays

and begin pushing my way closer, intently noting how the prince has wrapped his arm around the golden girl, whisking her across the ballroom dance floor like he's enchanted. Everyone's staring at the couple, probably in shock at the sudden change in the prince.

"I heard her speak," one lady gossips to the lady next to her. "She's from the Southlands."

"Do you think she's a Southlander princess?"

"Oh, to be sure. But a foreigner? Really, the prince should know better. We know how dreadful that went for Prince William last time."

"But a wise choice to gain the Southlands' approval."

"I heard from a neighbor that the king of the Southlands himself might be attending."

I pass near Ella's stepsisters, both decked out in the most extravagant gowns in the hall.

"Oh, Jacob Grimm," the thin, elegant one says. Marianne, I think her name is. "What are you doing here?"

"The prince needed my services," I say vaguely, focusing on the prince and the golden woman as they spin around the dance floor.

"I'm surprised they let a commoner such as yourself in." Frau von Maier sips from her glass as if to swallow her detest.

It takes every ounce of my restraint not to snap back at her. How Ella manages to live with such a monstrous stepmother is beyond me. Mentally, I make a note to start writing this woman's story and immediately get rid of her once and for all.

"Where's Ella?" I ask.

"She couldn't make it," Marianne says and plucks a canapé from a dish. "She wasn't feeling well today."

My mind tumbles. If she's home alone, I can speak with her and find out what happened last night. Except I can't leave the ball, not with the possibility of an attack. For her safety, Wissen is my top priority."

"That's unfortunate," I say, and then, unable to help myself, continue, "She's truly the most beautiful maiden of the land. The prince would snatch her up in a heartbeat if she were here."

My comment strikes exactly where I want because Frau von Maier chokes on her champagne.

"It doesn't matter anyway," Marianne says carelessly. "Cinderella's to be married tomorrow."

"Cinderella?"

"It's Ella's pet name we gave her." Marianne whips out her fan and cools herself. "She's always lying about in the ashes. You must have noticed how she's determined to be covered in soot."

"No," I say in a low, threatening voice. If she continues this sort of talk, Marianne might need to run for her life even if she's not a Forbidden. "I haven't."

"It doesn't matter." Bertha's petite mouth pouts at her plate of delicacies. "The prince is far too enraptured with that Southland princess to give any of us the time of day."

"Stop eating!" Frau von Maier grabs the plate from Bertha. "You won't be able to fit into tomorrow's dress."

Bertha gazes forlornly at the plate as it's handed to a servant. But I'm distracted when Prince William and the golden woman waltz past us. Her gown shimmers in the candlelight, swaying as she spins past me. She tilts her head to the side, and her eyes catch mine. Eyes as startlingly blue as a summer day.

Drumbeats pound against my chest.

Abandoning Ella's unfortunate relatives, I follow the couple around the perimeter of the dance floor, skirting by hooped gowns, giggling onlookers, and whispers behind fans.

I probably look like a hound on the hunt, but I don't care because I know those eyes and the curve of her jaw.

The shape of her ear and those plump lips.

But that's impossible. Unless I don't recognize her because I've only ever seen her in mourning clothes and sooty dresses. I need to get close enough to be sure.

"Excuse me." I step up to where the prince and this mysterious maiden are standing, having just finished their dance. It's incredibly bold and terrifyingly rude, but when has that ever stopped me?

"May I have your next dance?" I ask her.

She turns then, a smile spreading across her face, lighting her eyes. The tiny scar on her forehead, small and unnotice-able to anyone else, calls to me. My heart stops beating.

This is Ella von Maier.

The rest of the room falls away as she presses a gloved finger to those full, red lips as if to tell me to keep her identity a secret. But then my eyes trail down the smooth curve of her neck.

Where a mark is.

Wings of a bird in flight. Screaming at me that she's a Forbidden.

There isn't enough air. A buzzing hums in my ears. I'm frozen in shock and terror and horror.

How did I not see it before?

Prince William frowns, patting my shoulder, jerking me back to reality. "Sorry, Jacob," he's saying. "She's my partner. Besides, don't you have important things to be doing?"

My words catch in my throat. Then the prince whisks her away into another dance. Her eyes stay on mine, pleading for me to understand. But I don't. This can't be happening. It's a nightmare. Dancers swirl around me, but my feet remain rooted to the floor.

I can't look away. I don't even want to try. If only I could cross the space between us. Take her hand. Pull her into me. Tell her I'm going to find a way for us to be together.

"Brother." Wilhelm drags me off the dance floor. "Are you unwell? You look as if you've encountered the Devil himself."

Sweat beads across my brow, and my hands tremble. He hauls me across the room against the wall. A servant passes by with a tray of drinks. He snatches a glass, passing it to me. I down it in one gulp.

"Jacob. You have me worried, which is saying something. What's the matter?"

"The princess is Ella," I say in a gasping, choking sound, nodding to them as they whisk past us. "She's a Forbidden. Dancing with the prince."

"Are you sure?" Wilhelm turns to study the infamous couple.

"Without a doubt."

"Ah, I see it now. How did I not before? Of course, that's her. And there's the mark, yes. How unfortunate."

"Unfortunate?" I sputter. "I can't do this anymore. She represents all that is good in this world. I can't write her story."

"You fell for her, didn't you?" He rubs his forehead. "You promised not to get involved with her. How many times did I warn you?"

I start pacing along the wall, racking my brain for ways to fix this.

"Jacob, you're losing it," Wilhelm says. "We need to focus on more important things, like how Dr. Wissen could be forming an attack on the castle."

None of that matters anymore. All that matters is that Ella is a Forbidden, and I must find a way to save her.

"Excuse me," a sweet-sounding voice says from behind me. My throat tightens like there's a noose around my neck. I turn to face her.

"Ella, you made it," I manage. "You look...stunning."

"I managed to escape the prince, for a moment." Her eyes search mine. "I wanted to thank you for what you did for me last night. And apologize for leaving so suddenly."

Last night. The kiss. My eyes drift to her lips, soft and inviting. "You left without saying goodbye."

"I know. Something happened. I just... I can't talk about it right now." Her chest heaves as she takes a deep breath. I drag my gaze from the curves of her breasts to her face. It's no safer there. Every part of me aches to trace the line of her jaw, touch her trembling lips, and sink my hands into the tumble of her long, honey curls.

She's devastating. Enchanting in a way that steals the ground from beneath my feet. Maybe she's a witch. Maybe she's an enchantress sent to ruin me. I don't give a damn. Because whatever spell she's cast, I'm already hers.

A quick glance warns me people are staring at us while the prince is looking about the room, obviously searching for Ella. We don't have much time.

"I'm glad to hear you're safe," Wilhelm says, breaking the awkward silence. "We were worried."

"And I feel terrible about that. Last night was..."

"A nightmare?" Wilhelm offers kindly.

"Dance with me," I demand.

Her eyes widen. "Are you sure that's a good idea?"

"It's a terrible idea," Wilhelm warns.

But I slip my palm around the small of her back and grab her hand, thrusting the two of us into the next dance. It's almost as if magic binds us together when our hands meet, telling me we're meant to be together no matter what comes our way. The music swirls around us, a mesmerizing melody that threatens to destroy everything I've been fighting for to keep my oath to the Enchantress. But as I pull her closer, I don't care.

I want to cling to last night and the kiss that left me completely intoxicated. To the night we washed dishes in her cold kitchen, and the afternoon in the woods when she hefted that pitchfork to save me. To the morning when I showed her my sketches, and even when her arms wrapped around my waist as we galloped away from the house of a monster, chased by a pack of werewolves.

"I'm glad you aren't married to Dr. Wissen," I say.

"Barely," Ella says. "But I've only managed to delay it."

She tells me what happened. I'm shocked at the lengths Frau von Maier went to make sure Ella didn't come. But when she asks me if we've finished Dr. Wissen's story, I shake my head.

"The prince sent men out this afternoon to arrest Dr. Wissen, but he and his werewolves have vanished. Don't worry. Wilhelm and I will finish his story, and then you won't have to deal with him ever again."

The candlelight flickers over her neck where the feathery blue mark is. I swallow down my fear of its implications. She's one of them.

"You know, don't you?" Her voice is a whisper only for me. "That I'm one of your For—" She breaks off as if she doesn't dare say the word.

"Yes," I admit. "You have the mark, but it's the first time I've seen it on you. Did something happen?"

She shivers, and her feet stop moving. She's slipping out of my arms. I want to take it all back and somehow fix this, but as her eyes stare into mine, the chasm between us widens impossibly far.

Prince William steps up, holding out his hand. "There you are," he says to Ella. "Care to dance again?"

Her eyes don't leave mine, but she nods. "I'd be honored, Your Highness."

"I know this sounds strange," he tells her. "There's something about you that's so familiar. Have we met before?"

Her eyes drag from mine to the prince. "I hope I'm not that unmemorable," she says with a coy smile.

"Hardly. Perhaps I've been dreaming of you. Let's dance." He gives me an annoyed glance. "Any problems, Jacob?"

"Not a one," I lie. My heart wrenches in half as the prince sweeps Ella away.

# CHAPTER 40

## ELLA

### LICHTENSTEIN CASTLE

Tonight should be the most magical night of my life. The prince, who looks oddly familiar, is dancing exclusively with me. My family has no clue about my true identity. And my dress is the talk of the ball. Fiona really outdid herself.

Except I'm miserable. Those brief minutes with Jacob ruined me. How can sitting on a ruined fortress wall, wearing tattered rags, be more special than this? But last night's kiss haunts me. And now all I can think about is how I want to do it again.

It takes every ounce of self-control not to search for Jacob, but despite myself, I spot him while dancing the allemande and nearly mess up the entire procession. He's glowering off to the side, looking like he's ready to murder a Forbidden monster. I swallow hard. Now I'm on the Grimm brothers' list for termination.

I lift my shoulders back and smile brighter up at the prince, determined to make the most of the night and enjoy myself. By the time we take a dancing break, my mood improves. The prince hands me a glass of punch.

"You and the Grimm brothers seem close," I say, unable to purge Jacob from my mind.

"They work for me from time to time." He shrugs. "This morning, we returned from a horrifying adventure. The good news is I was able to uncover who has been conspiring against me."

I freeze mid-sip. "You were with them last night?"

"Now don't you worry about me getting hurt." He winks. A sickening feeling settles in my stomach. I know that smile. *Wait.* I definitely recognize those sparkling green eyes. The prince is wearing a freshly powdered wig, and his face is powdered white, but if I lean closer...a red curl peeks out from the side and his right eye is tinged blue. I gasp, jerking backward. It can't be.

Except, it *is* him. Fritz is Prince William.

He turned into a frog, and I turned him back to a human with a kiss. I press my fingers to my lips.

I feel dizzy.

"What's wrong? Is the punch too strong?" Then his smile widens, and he waggles his eyebrows. "Or did you want something stronger?"

He's a Forbidden. Jacob knew all along, the scoundrel.

What if the magic powder my aunt gave me wears off, and the prince recognizes me? I lightly touch my cheeks to see if it's still in place because if not, it could be disastrous. A lady gallivanting about the countryside unchaperoned and kissing the prince would be the scandal of the kingdom.

"You do look a little flushed," the prince says, brow knitting. "Perhaps we should find a quiet corner to chat. Just the two of us."

I back away, heart tumbling. "I need to go home. Now."

"Please don't go," the prince—the frog, no Fritz—begs. "I'll walk you out and keep you company."

I plant on a smile, acting as if not a thing in the world

bothers me, nor that I'm imagining him as a frog. "Actually, some one-on-one time with a drink would be nice. I'm going to freshen up, and then we'll have our chat."

"Brilliant." He beams.

It's the same expression he had standing half-naked in the Grimms' house. *Heaven help me.* I spin on my heels and make for the closest exit possible, pushing through the crowd. I'm nearly there when I plow into a man, laughing with two others as they swig from steins of brew.

"Excuse me," I say.

"Ella?" the man asks. "Is that you?"

I stare into the face of my father. His eyes narrow into suspicion. My pulse pounds against my temples.

"You have me confused with someone else," I say and hurry away.

Desperately, I exit the castle but pause at the fork in the path. My frazzled brain can't remember which direction the horse stalls are.

"Hello, there," the prince calls out as he races out of the castle, chasing after me. "You took a wrong turn."

Behind him, I spy my father, barreling through the archway, his tailored black coat billowing like wings. I dart away and hurry into the first building I come across. I slam the rickety wooden door shut and drag a crate in front to keep it secured. Spinning around, I'm met with squawking and feathers flying.

"The pigeon house?" I whimper at my idiocy. There isn't time to give myself a lecture because someone begins pounding on the door.

"Please, princess!" the prince says. "I don't even know your name."

And then an even more terrifying voice says, "Give me an ax. I think that's my daughter."

*Father.*

The sound of chopping cracks through the air as the metal head of an ax slices through the door, wood splintering around me. I jump backward and circle the pigeon house for an exit.

"Climb!" one of the pigeons cries.

"Fly, princess!" another says.

I press my hands to my ears. It's either thinking about the birds or my panic is forcing my secret identity to be exposed. Talons cut through my hands. Feathers nip at my skin. My heart pounds as fire rages through my veins. That's when Jacob comes climbing through the back window. Leave it to him to be resourceful.

"Ella." He holds out a hand. "Come with me. I can get you back home safely. Your father will never have to know."

"No." Tears edge at my eyes. I can't let Jacob see who I really am, see the monster breaking out of me. "Go. Just go."

My eyes land on a ladder that rises to the rafters. Desperately, I scale its rungs, ripping the material of my perfect golden dress. By the time I reach the tiny window in the rafters, the door crashes open, boards flying. Fear explodes inside me, and my chest bursts. I'm shoved off the ladder, and I fall.

Terror spears my stomach.

Now they all will know the truth.

But then my wings catch the air. *I've transformed.* With a few simple flaps, I lift my tiny body up and away from the chaos below.

"Where did she go?" Father asks. "Did you see her?"

"The fair maiden?" Jacob asks. "I scoured the place. No sight of—"

But his words fall away because I'm sailing out the window and into the endless night. Free. Unharmed.

Except now my secret is safe with the very man I need to keep it from the most.

❁

Back home, I land once again at my mother's tree, weary and a bit terrified. There must be something about it. It's like a homing beacon that calls me back to where I belong.

"How did it go?" Fiona asks, startling me so greatly I fall off the branch and thump to the ground. This is becoming an irritating habit.

Instantly, my feathers crumble to soot, the claws fall away, and the beak crushes into dust. I groan, rolling onto my stomach.

"You need to stop scaring me when I return," I say. "I can't keep falling like this."

"Sorry, I was just so excited." Fiona flutters through the air, morphing back into her half-human, half-bird state. Her brown feathered dress flaps in the evening wind. She reaches a hand to help me up. "Tell me everything. Did you dance with the prince? Did you get any compliments on the dress? How was the food?"

"It was the most magical evening ever." I throw my arms around her. "Thank you for giving that gift."

"Did the prince ask you to marry him?" she asks like she already knows the answer.

"What? No."

"What do you mean, no?" Fiona looks shocked.

"I had to leave. I think my father recognized me. What time is it?"

"Time? It's been so long since I thought about time."

"Has my family arrived yet?"

"I'll ask the ravens." She spins in a whirlwind of feathers and takes off into the night as a bird.

If only I could transform so easily. Fear nips at heels, chasing me. I hurry to the house. Time as a bird feels so different. I've no idea how long I'd been flying, but I've a vague sense it's longer than I would've liked.

When I step into the cold kitchen, I'm so tired and cold in my flimsy gown, I could collapse. I manage to get a fire going when the door to the house opens.

"Cinderella!" my father booms from the hallway.

That's the first time he's ever called me by that name. I sit up in terror.

"They're here," Fiona chirps, landing in the kitchen window. "You returned just in time."

"No, I didn't! I'm still wearing the gown you gave me and my hair." I stare at my dress. It's ripped and soot-covered from the transformation, but when they see me, they'll recognize the gown, and there will be no doubt I'd been at the ball without their permission.

"Your dress!" Fiona gasps. "It's a disaster."

The sound of footsteps clomp down the hall.

"Where's my old gray dress?" I ask. "I need it!"

The door flings open to reveal my father, along with Stepmother and my stepsisters, hovering behind him. He's still gripping the king's ax. I tremble at the sight. Would my own father use it against me?

"Cinderella," Father says, a little deflated. "Have you been here all night?"

I look down at my dress to discover I'm wearing my gray one. Except perhaps it's even dirtier than I remembered it being. How did Fiona manage that?

"Yes, Father," I lie, praying Mother would forgive me. "All night. Sitting by the fire, hoping you had a wonderful time. Would you care for some coffee?"

"Oh. So it seems." His eyes flicker in confusion.

"No coffee tonight." Stepmother steps forward, studying me intently. "The girls must get their beauty sleep to prepare for another important day tomorrow. The prince showed great interest in them, especially Marianne. If things continue, you may be calling Marianne, Your Highness."

Once they leave, I sag onto the hearth, noticing my silver slippers have vanished as well, leaving me barefoot and cold. From my spot on the floor, I gaze out the window at the castle, illuminated in the moonlight. The wind carries with it the sounds of music and laughter. Memories of the night assail me.

Spinning around the dance floor with the prince.

Being wrapped in Jacob Grimm's arms.

Flying on the wings of the night.

Sitting by the fire in a soot-covered dress.

I tuck my knees to my chest, trying to understand which girl I'm meant to be.

## CHAPTER 41

# JACOB

### LICHTENSTEIN CASTLE

"Where did she go?" Prince William demands, shaking my arm. "I saw her come in here with my very own eyes. You must have seen something."

I stare up at the loft's tiny window where moonbeams filter down to the sawdust floor. The truth of what she is rocks me to the core. I can't process anything other than that she can transform into a bird. I think about our conversations. She knew last night. Is that why she suddenly left? She had to escape.

From *me*. My heart tears at the thought.

"Jacob?" the prince prods. "You must have seen something?"

With a slight bow of my head, I say, "I'm sorry, Your Highness. I came in through the back window, but she slipped out before I could catch her."

"Damn it all." The prince kicks at the ground. "She was the one. I'm sure of it."

"Perhaps if you're lucky, she'll attend the festivities

tomorrow night. Try to focus on that. Keep yourself in good spirits and stay in human form."

"Yes, yes. Very good point," the prince mutters, and, clearing his throat, changes the subject. "Any news on an attempted attack?"

"Not a whisper."

"I still can't believe Wissen has evaded us. My men couldn't find anything at the house. Not even a finger from a dead body, or a live one, for that matter. Seems strange, doesn't it?"

I frown. "Quite. Almost as if they'd been expecting us."

Once he takes off, I pick up a lone sky-blue feather off the ground. It's soft against my skin, tickling my senses. I tuck it into the folds of my jacket, mind whirling.

"What is that you have?" a woman asks, startling me. She stands at the entrance of the pigeon house as if not daring to enter. Her dress glitters, a thousand emeralds stitched to create a galaxy of jewels. Even in the shadows, the Enchantress's eyes gleam wickedly, clearly enjoying herself.

"I want out of this madness," I snap.

"You know she's one of mine. Pitiful thing. She thinks she can outsmart you and me, but we know better, don't we?"

Her words knife me. My jaw clenches. More than anything, I want to withdraw one of my hidden daggers strapped to me.

"Ella is far smarter, braver, and kinder than you could ever achieve in a thousand lifetimes. She's nothing like the evil monsters you made me to believe these so-called Forbidden, the citizens of your lands, are."

"Perhaps I misguided you in that, but it's true that every one of my people who roam this land poisons the humans. You simply can't keep her for yourself. She doesn't belong here. Which reminds me." She holds up her razor-sharp nails, scrutinizing them. "I noticed how you've been searching for a way out of working for me. All those hours spent in the king's library are taking time away from what you should be doing. So I paid your mother a visit."

My dagger is in my hand in seconds. I plunge its blade straight into her heart. Except the emerald dress acts like a suit of armor. The metal bounces off its surface. The Enchantress laughs.

"So quick to betray me." She clucks her tongue and whips her fan out, batting it languidly. "She's fine. Just a little sick with a gift I gave her. Not sure how long she'll last under such conditions. Perhaps not through the night."

"You're a murderer."

"*Murderer*? Here I am spending the last morsels of my power to save the humans from a plague that will destroy their race, and you call *me* a murderer? I never wanted this. It was never my idea to send my people into this forsaken place. So dirty." Her nose crinkles as she assesses the pigeon house. "It was those conniving witches. They're your murderers."

"Then why don't you talk to them about this? Why bring us into your petty skirmishes?"

"You focus on your job, and I'll focus on mine. In the meantime, if you wish for your mother to last through the night, I'd hurry and finish another story. Let's see."

A scroll appears in her other hand, unraveling to her feet. She gives it a cursory glance. "You spent five hours at your university in Marburg, one hour at Prince Hermann's library, and five hours here at King Frederick's library scrounging around in my personal business. Quite a lot of lost time. Therefore, I expect at least one additional story for the next three nights. You have until the stroke of midnight each evening. I've made an allowance on the hourglass for you to choose each story. There. Now that that tedious business is finished, I think I'll have some of that delicious cake I saw being served."

She flicks her fan again and vanishes in a swirl of glittering emeralds. I rub my throat, trying to control the rage that's overpowering everything within me and stomp back into the ballroom. A woman screams when she sees me holding my knife.

"Not to worry." I tuck it away. "Just taking precautions."

The grandfather clock at the far end of the room points to ten. We have very little time. I hunt for Wilhelm, hoping whatever story he's working on is close to being finished. Still, the memory of Ella's father stalking out of the pigeon house, the scowl on his face, and the murderous fury in his eyes twists my stomach. More than anything, I want to mount Storm and make sure Ella is safe.

"Wilhelm!" I call out to my brother the moment I spot him. "We must leave this instant!"

❦

Back at our house, I drag out one of the books we've been working on, slamming it onto the table. "We have a problem."

"Just one?"

I stare at him and then the clock. "Good point. Tell me you're nearly finished with that story you were working on earlier."

"The doctor's story?"

"That's the only story you've been working on? The end hasn't even appeared on it yet. We haven't even sent him back."

"Obviously because he's still here." Wilhelm fidgets with his timepiece. "Why are you in such a hurry?"

I sink into one of the chairs and explain the Enchantress's threat, noting we have an hour remaining. "So you see our situation? What other stories do we have in play?"

Wilhelm withdraws his small notebook from his pocket

and begins reading through it. "The last one we finished was Elise. On deck is the boy and girl who, according to their parents, got lost in the forest last week. No one has seen them since. I have a note here to ask Ella what their names were. Then we've got Prince William and Dr. Wissen. There are those ravens at Ella's manor that seem awfully suspicious. Ella's stepmother. And then—" He clears his throat. "Ella herself."

I glower at him. "Take Ella off that list."

"You know she belongs there."

"No, she doesn't."

Wilhelm taps his pen against the table and then yanks the brick out of the fireplace. A hiss and a curl of smoke stream into our humble room as the door to the secret room opens. Wilhelm slips inside and returns with the scroll in his hand. I flinch as he unfurls it across the table. The list of names screams at me to stop this madness, or perhaps they're begging me to save them all.

He points to a single name that flickers like a flame caught in the breeze. *Cinderella.*

"The stepsister's nickname for Ella," Wilhelm says.

"Always covered in soot, Marianne said," I mutter, heart sinking. "Cinderella."

"What if we gave Ella a happy ending?"

"We can't just dole out happy endings. It's our job to relay our stories exactly as we see them or from what others have relayed to us. The Enchantress warned us it's essential to maintain the whole truth for it to work."

"What if we gave Ella the happy ending she needed by nudging events in her life in the right direction?"

I stare at the books, my thoughts moving to Ella. Could we do that for her? Somehow, find a way to give her a happier life than the one she has here in this realm?

No. I can't do it. I won't write her story.

"We can use this story." I pull a book from my shelf. "This recounts a story of the nixie from the millpond. I'd been waiting for the hourglass to illuminate the name, but we're running out of time, but now we can choose the story."

Wilhelm skims through my story. "This will work," he says excitedly.

"Then let's ride to the nixie's pond." I grab my coat. "We don't have a second to spare."

When we arrive at the millpond, I call out to the nixie, reminding her of her generous offer to take me for her own. She steps out of the water and onto the shore just as I expected. Wilhelm writes "the end," and she's spiraled into the air, screaming obscenities at me, minutes before midnight.

"Good work, brother." I sag onto the shoreline in relief. "I wish I could ride to Kassel and make sure Mother is safe and well."

"We still have two more nights to write two more stories," Wilhelm reminds me. "It's not over yet."

I hate it when he's right.

"Do you ever wonder where they go after they vanish?" Wilhelm asks, packing up.

I stare out across the still pond, no longer haunted by the nixie. "Every single damn time."

# CHAPTER 42

# ELLA

## MAIER MANOR

I 've run out of excuses, and there's nothing to stop me from slipping on the wedding dress.

"You can just fly away and leave this all behind," Fiona offers as she helps me with the back buttons. "If he's a monster, no servant's job is worth your death."

"He promised to pay a year's salary to every one of the servants we let go." I frown at myself in my looking glass, hardly recognizing the woman who stares back at me. My dress billows up at my ankles, and the sides don't even touch my waist since it's one of Bertha's everyday dresses. Dark circles rim my eyes, and my face looks as ashen as Dr. Wissen's trees in his orchard.

Not that I care. If I'm to marry Dr. Wissen, the last thing I want is to look beautiful.

"You need to find a way to see the prince again," Aunt Fiona insists. "If you're worried about your servants, he has more money to pay them than Wissen ever will."

"Don't worry, Fiona. The moment he pays the servants, I'll transform myself into a bird and fly away. It's the perfect plan."

"It's not a perfect plan, Ella, and you know it. Not once have you transformed on command. Also, I flew by the house last night while you were dancing with your prince. It was as silent as a grave, chilling abomination of a place."

"Perhaps the Grimm brothers managed to get rid of him. Also, he's not my prince." I smile thinking of Fritz—I mean the prince—turning into a ribbiting frog the second things got scary at Dr. Wissen's house. If I hadn't tucked him into my pocket, who knows what would've happened to him. "But it was fun going to the ball. Thank you for that."

"You should go to the ball tonight. Hide in the forest until it's time to leave." Fiona's eyes flash with excitement. "I've an idea for another gorgeous gown. It would make this dress look like a burlap bag in comparison."

The summons bell rings, yanking me back to reality. My heart patters with nervousness.

"I can do this," I tell my aunt, willing my words to be true. "I can be just as sneaky and conniving as him."

"You are the master of your future," she says as she cups my face between her two palms and stares into my eyes. "Never let others determine who you are or what you should be. Do you understand?"

My heart stutters. Why am I *really* marrying this monster? To fill my father and stepmother's coffers? To ease the guilt of watching my former servants be sent off with nothing but the clothes on their backs? To ensure my stepsisters are well-presented to society?

"Yes, I understand," I finally say and kiss her on the cheek, her soft feathers tickling my face.

I slip on my boots, feeling secure in their sturdiness, and hike up my skirts as I face the door Fiona opens for me, bowing to me as if I'm a princess. A wobbly laugh escapes me, but I step out onto the long spiral stairway and head downstairs.

When I enter the main hall, my stepsisters and stepmother are decked out in even more stunning dresses than the night before. True to his word, Dr. Wissen had sent a fleet of servants parading in with boxes filled with dresses and accessories to help my stepsisters prepare for the ball.

"Your dress—" Marianne pauses from clipping on an earring to make a face of disgust, only to compose her complexion. "Looks...clean."

"Why, thank you." I suppress a laugh. Leave it to Marianne to find a positive thing to say in an impossible situation.

"I still don't think it's fair she stole my dress," Bertha pouts as she adjusts her slippers.

"We all must make sacrifices." Stepmother waves her hand dismissively. "Besides, one of you will marry the prince, and then you'll not need that old dress."

"Where's Father?" I ask, trying to ignore the emptiness threatening to swallow me as I prepare to marry a monster.

"He's outside by the coach." Stepmother slips on her fox gloves, muttering about how chilly the air is.

I push past the haze of perfume to find Father in front of the coach, speaking with Peter.

"Father," I say.

"Ah, Ella." He smiles, but when he takes in my dress, pooling up on the dirt road, he frowns. "What's wrong with your dress? Are you really such a small stunt of a thing?"

"I didn't have time to hem it." The memory of the golden gown I danced in last night floats through my mind, sending a pang through me. "Are you escorting me to the church?"

"Herman will," Father says, just as my stepmother and stepsisters sashay past me. Peter opens the carriage door for them. "I'm needed at the ball. With Marianne catching the eye of the prince, we can't risk missing such an opportunity. You have your man wrapped around your fingers already. You'll be fine."

"But I don't want to do this alone." I search his face for the father I once knew.

"It's quite easy." Father shrugs as he adjusts his hat. "I've done it twice now. Just stand by Dr. Wissen, say yes, and that's it. So simple my horse could do the job. Now, be a good girl and go with Herman. Jesse will be your escort."

He climbs inside, closing the door firmly behind him. Marianne and Bertha wave from the window as the carriage jerks into motion, sending a splatter of mud across my white gown.

I stare down at the mud and can't help but chuckle. "How fitting."

"Ella," Herman says from the doorway. "Let me know when you're ready."

Standing here, my determination to be selfless wavers. What if my aunt is right and I can't transform into a bird? Or what if that's exactly what Wissen is expecting me to do and has a plan?

*You are the master of your future.*

It's a long shot, but the prince could choose me, right? Aunt Fiona seems to think he will choose me. Plus, he only danced with me last night, no one else. Fiona had a point. If I married him, I could not only pay all my servants but also hire them to work at the castle. I'd escape my family and Wissen. Besides, if I don't marry the doctor tonight, what will my father do? He's already done his worst.

"Would you be so kind and wait?" I ask Herman and point to my mud-streaked dress. "I need to freshen up."

"Of course," he says.

Picking up my dress, I race to Mother's grave. I search for Fiona, but she's nowhere in sight. I bite my lip, knowing time is running out. I decide to sing the tune she used last time. "Shiver and quiver, my little tree. Silver and gold, throw down over me."

Falling from the branches like a blanket of leaves, a gown and slippers, even more stunning than yesterday, drop into my arms. The tree opens for me, and I hurry inside and slip into the dress. It's pale as starlight with dove-white feathers edging the hem and a long train that flows as if it had wings. The sequin bodice shimmers like ice on a cold winter's day with sleeves hanging off my shoulders.

"Oh my," Aunt Fiona says after fluttering into the room and transforming into her half-human form. "I'm so pleased you changed your mind. The prince will choose you, and you'll live happily ever after in the castle, far from your stepmother."

"I hope you're right, but I was thinking I'd be an idiot to waste this opportunity."

"Pssh." She waves her hand. "You're smarter than you give yourself credit for. Now stand very still while my friends assist you with your hair."

A flock of doves swirls into the room, landing on my head. Their beaks tug at my strands and yank so hard that tears pick at my eyes.

"Tell them not to poop in my hair," I say, and when a beak nips at my scalp, I flinch. "Ouch!"

"Don't move!" Fiona scolds, brushing that magical powder over my face.

"This powder isn't foolproof, you know. The Grimm brothers recognized me."

"Did they now?" She purses her lips. "Hmm...I suppose anyone could if they were looking beyond the surface of a pretty face and sparkling dress. You know how I disapprove of those boys. Stay away from them. They'll only break your heart."

My spirits soar as I stroll through the castle doors and into the grand ballroom. To think that right now I should be at the church, marrying Dr. Wissen, and yet here I am in disguise, dancing among the most powerful lords and ladies in the land. I wish I could see Wissen's face when he realizes he's been stood up.

I scan the room. Whispers ripple behind opened fans and gloved palms.

"She's back! And that dress. It's unlike anything I've ever seen."

"The prince won't dance with her again, will he?"

"How did she do her hair? It's simply divine."

That last comment causes my lips to curl into a smile. If they only knew. On the dais sit the king and queen on their thrones, looking quite pleased with themselves. At first, I don't spot the prince, but then I see him dancing with Marianne. He has this glazed look, but Marianne is positively glowing.

A tinge of worry tugs at me that Marianne is thwarting my plans, but then I feel bad. Marianne deserves happiness, too. What woman here wouldn't want to marry a prince? My dress takes up so much space, especially with all the layers of my train, but I don't need to worry. The crowd parts for me, and my silver slippers take me closer to the dance floor.

The prince's eyes catch mine as I hover at the edge of the dancers. A smile bursts on his face, and warmth fills me. He can be endearing at times, I decide. I may never love him, but we could be friends. Not to mention he'd be a far better husband than Wissen could ever be.

The bigger question is, will he still feel the same for me once I take off this dress and clean the powder from my face?

"Ella," a deep voice says from behind me. "Would you be so kind as to dance with me?"

My heart stutters. Jacob Grimm. His dark, silky hair is

swooped back and tied at the nape of his neck in an attempt to keep it tame. His stubble is freshly shaven away. As he takes my hand, his eyes glint, and I'm sucked into his piercing gaze. I know I shouldn't, but I can't stop my feet as he draws me onto the dance floor, circling his arm around my waist. Pulling me so my chest is pressed against his.

I drink in his scent of deep forests and forbidden moments. It takes me back to the times I should forget. Scandalous midnight rendezvous in the garden. A horseback ride beneath the moonlit forest. Kisses on top of a forgotten fortress as the winds of temptation nearly swept me away.

He whirls me with perfect grace around the dance floor. The two of us are one with the music, leaving me breathless and my pulse racing.

"Last night," I dare speak, even if it breaks the magic. "You saw who I really am, didn't you?"

"Yes." His steps slow, and he focuses on my face, searching me until his eyes land on my lips. My heart soars on wings I know I shouldn't fly on. We're on dangerous ground.

"Then why are you dancing with me? Why are you looking at me like that?"

"I shouldn't. My brother warned me to stay away from you."

I stop mid-stride. "Then perhaps you should."

"Perhaps I should." But his grip only tightens as he glances over his shoulder. I follow his line of sight to where the prince is still dancing with Marianne. She's glaring at me while the prince gazes at us, forehead crinkled.

The dance continues, but when it's time for Jacob to spin me, he twirls my body, propelling me forward and then whirling me out into the garden. He drags me into the shadows, away from the silvery moonlight. Roses climb the stone wall behind me. Their scent drenches the air, but all I can breathe in is him.

We're alone.

His gaze rakes over me, sending a delicious shiver coiling through my stomach. My heartbeat pounds in my ears, wild with desire as his body looms over me. Large, callused hands clasp mine. Raw need flashes in his eyes, sucking my breath away.

Everything about him is dangerous. My chest rises and falls, too fast. Frantic as a hummingbird. Instinct warns me to flee as his hand slides around my waist, pulling me to him so my breasts are pressed against his chest. Except my body thrills in it, betraying me as it melts against his.

Fiercely, his hand cups the back of my neck, and then our mouths crash into each other's. A groan escapes him like he's been dreaming of this moment, and it's finally here. That shatters every barrier inside me. I fist his shirt, dragging him so our bodies are intertwined, because I need more. My lips part, and he sweeps his tongue against mine until I'm dizzy and breathless. His lips skim down my neck, leaving behind a heated trail. He slides his hands down my sides like he's memorizing me. I moan at his touch, loving every gentle stroke.

My knees tremble, but his strong arm tucks me to him like we're meant to be together, no matter what. Or maybe because he's afraid to let go.

"Ella," he whispers into my ear. "My perfect Ella."

My heart soars as my body surrenders to him. There's no more doubt in my mind. Jacob, wandering nomad, cursed writer, is what I want. Not a prince.

Except...he screams of unyielding power and magic, dripping off him like something from another world. And my heart breaks in two.

"You can never be mine, can you?" I whisper, dragging my body from his. "And I can never be yours."

"No." He pushes me against the stone wall, his face

contorted in agony as he places his hands against the wall behind me, caging me in. "Ella, you torture me. There must be a way."

I stare into his eyes and find pure adoration but also unbridled desperation. It undoes me. My fingers reach behind his neck and pull him down to me once again. He kisses me harder, like the world might end, and this is all we will ever have.

And maybe it is.

Finally, he steps away, and my world is cold and empty without him in my arms. He's panting heavily and tugging at his collar as if he just fought off a horde of werewolves. It takes everything in me not to reach for him again.

"I'm to write your story," he admits.

"I know."

"I can't do it." His eyes lower to my neck, and he traces an imaginary line along my skin. I shiver at his touch, never wanting him to stop. "I can't imagine a life without you."

"There must be a way for us to be together," I whisper.

The sound of footsteps and someone yelling erupts in the garden. "She can't be far."

"Fritz," I whisper. "He's looking for me."

Jacob's lips curve into a devious smile. "The *prince* is quite captivated with you."

"Find her and bring her to me this instant!" the prince yells to his guards. "I won't dance with another maiden until I've danced with her."

"Yes, Your Royal Highness," a guard replies frantically.

The footsteps fade, and I sag against the wall.

"You should make him love you," Jacob says. Even in the darkness, I feel his mood changing as he pulls away, retreating into his hunter facade. "Marry him. He can be your escape from your stepmother. He may turn into a frog from time to time, but it's nothing that a kiss can't rectify."

"So that's what it's to be?" I challenge, advancing on him. He takes a step back. As if *I'm* the dangerous one. "For us to have nothing but stolen kisses? For me to marry this frog prince so you can write us away to your Enchantress's realm?"

He runs his hands through his hair, cursing under his breath. "Do you think I want this life? Do you think I find joy in it? I live a cursed existence. It's only fitting I should never find happiness."

"We make our lives, not live them," I snap back as fury rises in my chest. "Today I was supposed to marry Dr. Wissen. I didn't show up to the wedding. My family will suffer for it, my servants won't get their wages now, and Claire's two children, Hansel and Gretel, might even starve because of it. I could be out there, wooing the prince, but no. I'm here with you because I've fallen for you."

His face tightens, and he turns away. "I'm the last man on earth you should fall for."

My heart stutters, and something inside me breaks. "What are you saying?"

"That you deserve to be a princess." His eyes are storm clouds. "I can't give you what you need."

"When do you get to tell me what I need? You know what?" I throw my hands up, frustration raging through my veins. "I'm tired of being the doormat, tired of pleasing everyone, tired of trying to do the right thing and failing. Don't come to me for stolen kisses. You've made it very clear that your curse is more sacred to you than our happiness."

With those words, I storm out of the garden, bursting into the brightness of the hall. My hands shake as I feel traces of Jacob's hands and lips lingering on my skin, but he can only promise me death in this world. I smooth down my skirts and set my jaw tight. Then I stride into the ballroom, making a beeline for the prince. It's time to stop dreaming of love. Stop hoping for someone to come save me. I need to take my future into my own hands.

The moment the prince sees me, he abandons Marianne, whom he was speaking to without a backward glance, and hurries to me.

I curtsy, dipping low, and then look up at him with my most devastating smile. "Your Majesty," I say coyly. "I know I've had my share of time with you, but perhaps you'd dare risk dancing with me one more time?"

I don't leave his arms for the rest of the night. Or look for Jacob even once.

# CHAPTER 43

# JACOB

## LICHTENSTEIN CASTLE

"We scoured the countryside," Prince William exclaims the morning after the ball to Rumpelstiltskin, Wilhelm, and me. "Still no sign of Dr. Wissen or his wolves."

"This is a problem," Wilhelm says, rubbing his forehead as he scans through Wissen's maps one more time. "We need to find him before he decides to use those weapons. What do you think, Jacob?"

I startle at the mention of my name and push away from the window overlooking the valley. My thoughts are drowning in memories of last night in the garden with Ella. The taste of her lips, the way her body fit against mine, her soft skin under my touch.

"It's highly concerning," I agree. "He's up to something. I wish we knew what."

The problem is that Wilhelm and I need to capture him so we can complete his story. Ella isn't safe until we do.

"My father hired you because you were supposed to be expert hunters," Prince William says. "Not having this doctor chained and prepped for execution worries me greatly. Especially because I want tonight to be special."

"Special?" Rumpelstiltskin laughs. "Special is just another word for trouble dressed up in ribbons."

My heart stills at what I think he will say.

"It's the last night of the festivities," the prince explains. "Which means I'll choose my bride and announce her to the entire kingdom. I won't have this moment destroyed by a doctor and his dogs, do you hear me?"

Is it horrible that I want to write his story before he announces his bride? Yes, and I don't care.

"Perfectly," I practically growl. "Who's the lucky girl?"

"The beautiful maiden I danced with both nights." Prince William pours himself a drink and downs it all in one gulp. "I don't know her name yet, but she's the most beautiful woman I've ever met. Never has there been a person alive who has moved me like she has. She keeps running off before I have a chance to ask her name, which makes me worried she'll leave before I have a chance to propose."

"May I suggest a brilliant stratagem?" Rumpelstiltskin offers, tapping his fingers together excitedly. "Have your guards smear pitch on the bridge, so if she tries to escape, you'll catch her. Can't escape if you're stuck in muck."

"Quite the extraordinary way to woo a woman's heart," I say, rolling my eyes. Getting caught in pitch is the last thing Ella would want.

"Extraordinary indeed!" He smiles, quite pleased with himself. "Tonight, I'm going to discover her name and proclaim her as my future wife."

"It's quite the decision," I say. "Are you sure you don't want to take more time to think about it? At least know her name for a few days."

"This is true." The prince's smile wavers. "My first marriage didn't go so well."

"Who needs a name when love is on the line?" Rumpel-stiltskin asks.

Wilhelm scowls at me. "You're making the right decision, Your Highness. From the rumors I've gathered, she's the kindest, sweetest person you'll ever meet. She deserves the life you can offer her. I know you two will have a happily ever after."

"I say we drink to that!" Rumpelstiltskin says.

"Yes!" The prince's face brightens, and he pours everyone a drink. Then he lifts his glass into the air. "To happily ever afters!"

"To bargains struck and debts well kept," Rumpelstiltskin adds and gives me a meaningful look.

"To giving those we love everything they deserve," Wilhelm finishes, clicking his glass against the others while staring hard at me.

Why does even a toast have to be about me? I turn back to the window, leaning my arm against the frame, cursing every story I ever wrote and all the ones yet to come. The prince will marry Ella. It's the right decision. There's no escaping the inevitable.

I'm heartbroken.

# CHAPTER 44

# ELLA

## MAIER MANOR

I may have avoided my family at the ball, but when they returned last night to find me sitting by the fire, an unmarried woman, both Father and my stepmother were livid. Father dragged me up to my tower and locked me inside, telling me I'd stay there without food or water until I married Wissen.

That should've upset me, but all I can think about is the ache in my stomach knowing I can never be with Jacob.

When the first rays of sunlight skim across the floor of my tower, I get dressed only to find the door locked. I pace the room, waiting for the bells to ring or for someone to come and escort me to Dr. Wissen, but I'm only met with silence. It isn't until the sun is high in the sky that the stairs creak, signaling someone is coming. I stand by the far wall, bracing myself as the keyhole clicks and the door opens.

"Oh, Ella." Jesse slips inside with a tray of food. She sets it down and rushes to hug me tight. "I came as soon as I could. The family is taking a nap before the final ball. Your stepmother said to get you so you can help Marianne dress." She scrunches her nose. "Marianne still won't let me help her."

"That's not a bad thing," I say, gobbling up the porridge. "I wish you didn't ever have to deal with either of them again. Did Dr. Wissen show up today?"

"The master sent a servant to the Wissen manor, but no one answered."

"Jesse, I need your help. If my father locks me in here again, when my family leaves, I need you to sneak up here and unlock my door. Can you do that?"

"But your father. He'll be so upset."

"He'll never know. I'll be back in my locked room before they return. I just want to spend some time by my mother's grave."

Her face softens. "Of course."

Guilt slides through me for lying to her, but I need her to be as innocent of wrongdoing as possible if she's questioned.

"Thank you," I say, hugging her, and then scurry downstairs to Marianne's room.

When I step inside and close the door behind me, my stepsister is nowhere in sight. I check her bathing room only to find leaves laid out in a perfect circle with a bowl filled with crushed lentils. I frown. That's the same bowl I used to pick them up with yesterday. Pain sears behind my eyes as another headache comes on. When I turn around, I nearly jump out of my skin when I see Marianne walking across the room like she's been here the whole time.

"Oh!" I say, pressing a hand to my chest. "I didn't hear you enter."

"I was reading by the couch," Marianne says, smoothing down her dress. I frown. She definitely hadn't been sitting on the couch when I entered. "I'm glad you're here. Now help me with my hair. I must look perfect. The prince will announce his bride tonight."

"Really?" I help her undress and then slip into a shimmering lily-white gown, but all I can wonder is if I were to attend, would he choose me? And if he does, would I say yes? That shouldn't even be a question, I remind myself. It has to be a yes. Jacob isn't an option and I can't live here anymore. "Has he shown any preferences for any girls?"

"There's been this one, but after one look at me tonight, he won't be able to resist me. I've been working on this gown all night." She spins in a circle. The material swishes like the wind rushing over the trees. "What do you think?"

"It's stunning." There's something special about this dress, almost magical. Not that I know much about magic other than Mother's hazel tree. "But what do you mean you worked on it all night? Surely you didn't make it?"

"Oh, Cinderella, my sweet sister." She cups her hands around my face, staring deeply into my eyes. "You've no idea how I've come to care for you. Without you, I'd never even have a chance with the prince. I'll never forget what you've done for me."

I can't look at her. Guilt tugs at me because I don't want her to marry the prince. I want to. In fact, every time I've listened to her advice, things have only worsened for me. Not only has she used me to get what she wanted, but she's tried to make it seem like she's doing it because she cares about me.

"We have so much in common," Marianne continues. "Two women trying to survive in a world where our parents failed us. Perhaps marriage is the only way to freedom and power, but it's all we're offered, and so we must take what we can for ourselves. I know it's hard to marry a man you think is a monster, but what is love anyway? A fleeting emotion, that's what. Sometimes sacrifices must be made to get what we deserve."

Then she plops into her chair and pulls out her tiny mirror, staring at herself as I begin to brush her hair. "Curl my hair and then pin it up with this honeysuckle. That's what I'll use to bind his love to me. One whiff of it and the prince will be mine."

One whiff? It's like she's using magic. The headache pierces the back of my eyes again. I push back pain, gripping the brush tighter. She can try to tempt him with her dress and flowers, but it's going to be me whom he will choose. It's the only way I can escape this madness.

⚜

As soon as the carriage rumbles away and Jesse unlocks my door, I grab my meager pack of belongings just in case the prince doesn't end up choosing me and I need to leave my village forever.

"Good luck at the ball," Jesse says, squeezing my hands. "Maybe you'll even get to see the prince."

I promise to tell her all about it when I return and then rush downstairs into the hallway, but when I pass by Marianne's room, those crushed lentils haunt me. Could those lentils be the same ones I tossed to the ground last night? There was something strange about her last words to me. I peer inside, noticing once again those strange leaves scattered about. Pain pierces my forehead as I step inside.

Ignoring the ache, I follow the trail of leaves to the far wall where Marianne's large mirror stands. I stare at myself with neatly braided hair and a pale blue dress. Except there's something about this mirror. My headache pounds, and my stomach cramps so tight, I double over, reaching to the mirror for support.

Except the surface of the mirror isn't hard. It's fluid like the curtain of a waterfall. I fall through face-first, tumbling onto soft grass. Terrified, I scramble to my feet to find I'm in a garden enclosed by towering stone walls. The same mirror from Marianne's room rests in the center, surrounded by lavender, roses, and honeysuckle.

The sky is light purple, and the air smells like the herb tea Marianne drinks each morning. Hundreds of empty bird cages hang from twisted birch trees, swinging and creaking.

My heart clatters. What is this place?

Curious, I peek into a cage to discover it riddled with bones and a mirror. Biting back my dismay, I slip my hand inside and pull out the mirror. As I stare into it, an unblinking eye gazes back at me. I drop the mirror. It smashes into a million pieces on the stones at my feet.

*Mirror magic.* Just like Wissen used with his saws and carpentry.

A tiny chirp and a flutter of wings break the silence.

"Help, Ella! Help!"

Two doves flutter inside the cages behind me. I run to them.

"You poor things. I'm going to get you out of here."

My pulse kicks up in horror as I unlatch their cages and hold out my hand, which they promptly fly onto. These must be some of the missing birds Aunt Fiona was talking about. Which also means all these bones must belong to the other missing birds.

"How did you get in here?" I ask them.

"Witch, witch, witch," they sing.

Witch? This mirror leads to Marianne's room. Does that mean she is a witch?

"Are there any others?" I ask the doves.

"Gone, gone, gone."

Gooseflesh prickles across my skin. I need to leave and get these birds out of here. I'm about to return to the full-sized mirror when I notice a book bound in vines lying on a stone table. Dread fills me as I creep closer to it.

Reaching down, I touch the vines. My fingers tingle. A

sizzling sound fills the air, and the vines shrink away from the leather-bound tome. Hands shaking, I open the book. Quickly, I skim through the pages.

*There are rumors that magic from our world seeps through the shadows of the Black Forest. I cannot say if they're true, but with the coven's strength waning, and with it my throne, I can't afford to ignore them. If that magic could replenish my powers, it would change everything. An old friend lives in the area. He might be able to help us. He certainly owes me.*

Powers? Covens? My hands tremble. Is Marianne a witch? No, that can't be possible. Someone else's handwriting appears below that.

*Be careful. There are rumors that the Enchantress has been hiring hunters to search for us. And where there is magic, they are sure to find it.*

"This isn't just a book," I whisper in realization. It's a means of communication between witches.

*I was right. The Kingdom of Württemberg is perfect. I'll have to appoint servants to take the roles of my mother and sister, but sacrifices must be made.*

Stepmother and Bertha are Marianne's servants? My head spins as the pieces snap together.

*Sacrifices? You dare speak of sacrifices while I rot on this forsaken island, shackled to the whims of those slippery mermaids?*

I flip through the conversations between the witches until I come to the last page. It's a journal entry about me. My breath catches.

*I knew there was no way the cinder girl could collect those lentils in the time she did. Thankfully, the foolish girl has no idea the powers she holds.*

And here I thought she was watching out for me. She's right, I think angrily. I was a fool.

*Last night, I went outside and discovered them on the ground, laced with magic. I crushed them and infused their magic into my dress. Now the prince won't be able to resist me. Even that annoying Southlander princess won't come close to my beauty. The Kingdom of Württemberg and all its power will be mine. The Enchantress will rue the day she ever stepped in my path.*

My blood runs cold. The prince is being hunted by a witch planning to use him to control the entire kingdom. I need to warn him.

I'm about to close the book when I spy a single word scrawled in sharp, angry handwriting. The world tips sideways as terror claws at my heart.

## GRIMM

*Jacob.* She knows about him, which means he's in danger. Talons pierce through my hands as anger ripples through me. I take long, deep breaths and calm myself. Magic or not, I'm going to do everything in my power to stop Marianne.

I tuck the book under my arm and rush back through the mirror, running faster than I'd ever run in my life.

# CHAPTER 45

# JACOB

## LICHTENSTEIN CASTLE

T he room presses in on me, the sounds of the crowd ringing in my ears as I search for Ella.

"She still hasn't arrived," I tell Wilhelm. "This is the last night of the festival, and tonight the prince will choose his bride. Should I be worried?"

"Considering the fact that you always do what you want to do," he says, "I don't know why you bother asking me."

"The pitch trap has been laid," Rumpelstiltskin says, hurrying up to Wilhelm and me, rubbing his hands with a look of delight.

"Let's hope Wissen tries to attack," I explain. "It will slow him down. And if he's already here, it will hinder his escape."

On the dance floor, Marianne is dancing with the prince. His face has this weird, enraptured expression.

"I know I should be happy to see the prince occupied with someone other than Ella," I point out. "But I don't trust Ella's stepmother. Does the prince look enchanted to you?"

"Most assuredly," Rumpelstiltskin says.

"Ah, yes, that expression." Wilhelm taps a finger to his lips. "Where have I seen that before?"

"The Swan King. What was his name again? It's been over a year." I snap my fingers. "King Ludwig of Bavaria. He was obsessed with that one woman we suspected was a witch."

"You think Marianne is a witch? She hardly fits the profile."

"Which is why she worries me." I rub the side of my face.

A murmuring rises in the crowd. I follow the source of the commotion and find Ella standing at the entrance, looking as if she flew down on the wings of heaven. Her dress is the color of the bluest sky, with layers of light material. The sleeveless, brocaded bodice glimmers like stars, spilling down the center of her dress. Her curls are twisted into a nest of braids, and long golden tresses cascade down her back. A necklace studded with sapphires hangs against the smooth skin of her breasts.

I swallow hard. This woman has the power to send me to my knees.

"Glad to see Ella made it," Wilhelm says. "She'll get the prince back on track."

"Now that's a sparkly dress," Rumpelstiltskin says. "I wonder if she'd dance a jig with me."

"Don't push your luck," I say, loosening my collar as Ella glides toward the dance floor.

I run a palm over my eyes, needing a distraction. That's when I taste it on the edge of my lips, the metallic tang of magic stirring in the room, clashing like it's about to go into battle. I tense.

"Do you taste that?" I ask Wilhelm.

"Tastes sweet like cakes." His eyes widen. "Something's wrong."

"Split up," I say as the urgency grates against my skin. "You go down. I go up."

"I'll sample the cakes," Rumpelstiltskin says. "Wouldn't want anyone keeling over before the fun begins."

We bolt each heading in separate directions. As I pass by the guards and hurry upstairs, I realize I never checked the royal family's private quarters for wood that might've been carved by the doctor. Had the guards?

At the second floor, I pause, listening. A red carpet stretches down the ornate papered corridor with sconces lighting the way. I crack open the first door and slip inside, my heart pounding more than I'd wished. Digging into my belt, I withdraw a knife for comfort. Its smooth handle steadies my nerves. Moonlight streams through the windows, washing the floor in rivers of light. There's nothing here.

By the time I reach the fifth bedroom, I'm ready to give up. But a cabinet with a lion carving makes me pause. Curious, I open the door only to find rows of clothes. Still, something about the carving reminds me of Wissen's office. Grimacing, I press my palm against the lion's face, and sure enough, it sinks beneath my touch. A series of clicks echoes through the room. With a groan, the cabinet door swings inward, revealing a secret passageway.

I steel my nerves and climb inside the cabinet. A spiral staircase takes me down into a tunnel hewn from rock. I allow my eyes to adjust to the dark, an ability courtesy of my curse. What is this place? Did the king know about it, or is this Dr. Wissen's work?

A snarl and the sound of claws scraping stone cut the silence. Glowing red eyes and glistening white teeth shine through the gloom as a dark form bounds toward me. I spin and run, retreating the way I came, not waiting around to see if there were others. The last thing I need is to be ambushed in a dark tunnel. I scramble out of the wardrobe just as the beast lands on me, sinking its fangs into my neck.

Pain rages through me as its claws rake across my chest. With a cry, I plunge my dagger into the beast's skull, and it slumps onto my chest, slowly returning to his human form. A howl erupts from within the cabinet.

*Great. This one has friends.*

Before I can move, another beast emerges from the wardrobe, foaming at the mouth as it snarls. I shove the dead man off me and whip out my sword, hunkering down.

"Surprised to see me, huh?" I taunt the werewolf. "Don't worry, I promise to make your death quick."

The beast roars and leaps through the air, splintering the sides of the wardrobe to get its massive form out. I step slightly to the left. In one smooth arc, I slice off its head. The blood sprays across the ground, dousing me with its rancid stink. But it's not over. Unfortunately, another creature shows up from the wardrobe. I roll my neck, beyond annoyed as the room begins to spin due to my blood loss.

I stab the creature and kick the cabinet door shut. Then I push a dresser in front of it. It might not keep them out, but it's enough to slow them down and allow me to tend to my wounds. I stagger to the bed and rip apart the silk coverlet, wrapping it around my neck. I've just finished tying the knot when a sound like horse hooves thuds in the hallway.

Frowning, I throw open the door as a pack of werewolves races past me toward the grand stairwell. They're headed for the ball.

"I can't get a break, can I?" I grumble and race after them.

# CHAPTER 46

# ELLA

## LICHTENSTEIN CASTLE

As I step into the prince's arms, he has this glazed, trance-like expression that reminds me of my father since he returned. The hairs on my arms lift like a thousand tiny needles. Fear spirals in my stomach. No, it's as if he's under a spell.

My eyes trail to the bouquet and those familiar, sharp-edged leaves pinned to his jacket's lapel. The same leaves I keep finding around the house and on my clothes after talking to Marianne. The power of the bouquet wafts over me, clenching its tentacles of pain around my head. The headaches I've been having weren't from stress or my trans-formation; they were from when Marianne was trying to control and manipulate me.

She's had a spell on all of us since the moment she arrived.

Anger rolls through me. I rip the bouquet off him, tossing it aside.

"Those leaves were ruining your attire," I explain.

He startles and steps away from me. "Who are you? You still haven't told me your name."

"I need to warn you." I glance around. Everyone is watching, so I move us to the corner of the room. "Someone is trying to marry you for your position of power rather than love."

He blinks a few times like he's trying to focus. "Welcome to my world. This isn't news to me."

"The woman's name is Marianne." I point her out to him. "Whatever you do, don't get near her."

"I don't care about any other woman except you." He takes my hand in his. I try not to think about how slimy he was as a frog. "You still haven't told me your name. You promised to tell me tonight."

Do I tell him who I really am? Will he still accept me? Except if I'm to enter a marriage, I need to start with trust. No lies.

"You're right." I take in a deep breath. "My name is—"

A scream curdles through the air. Dark forms bound down the grand staircase, leaping over the heads of the guards and landing on the guests, sinking sharp teeth into flesh. Their howls echo through the room. Behind them, bloodied and holding a sword in one hand and a knife in the other, is Jacob, pursuing them. His jacket flaps behind him, and his hair is wild. He plunges his sword into one of the beasts. A choked cry breaks from me. There must be two dozen werewolves. Dr. Wissen's werewolves. Even with Jacob's prowess as a swordfighter, there's no way he can stop them all.

The room shatters into chaos. Rainbows of silk and tulle dresses tumble over each other as guests stampede from the room in a desperate escape. The king and queen slip through a secret door with their guards. Screams replace the lilting music. Tables that once boasted ice sculptures and tiered cakes crash to the floor. I even spot Otto running for the exit, loaded with cakes.

The prince draws his sword, which I think is more ornamental than anything. I grab his arm for support, only to find him shaking like a leaf. The last time we met these beasts, it was I who protected him.

"Don't transform!" I turn to stare into his eyes. "Stay with me. I need you to fight. You know how to use that sword, right?"

"Transform?" The prince gasps. "How did you know?"

*Even now, he still doesn't recognize me?* "Jacob told me."

A chorus of howls breaks through the screams. I spin around as Dr. Wissen treads down the stairs, determination pulling on his jagged scars. His curly hair is combed smooth. Those eyes, sharp as battlement spikes, search the ballroom until they land on me. Backing up, I quiver under his gaze, which never wavers as he picks his way toward me, stepping over bodies strewn as if they're cumbersome annoyances. He's wearing a dark velvet jacket edged with gold and shiny golden buttons that gleam along the center of his chest.

In one hand, he holds an ax, dripping with blood, and in the other, a ring. Terror rips at my chest.

"My beautiful bride," he says, calm and confident. "Yesterday, I waited for you at the church, and yet you did not come. Today, I searched for you at the manor, but you were nowhere to be found. To think you thought you could hide from me. Gowns and fairy dust, golden slippers and flowers cannot mask your true form."

"What in the devil's name does he speak of?" the prince asks.

"He thinks I'm his bride." I clutch the prince's arm as the Grimm brothers and guards battle against the pack of werewolves across the room. "You see, my prince, I had this dream. I visited the house of my bridegroom. A woman cooking soup warned me that a murderer lived there."

"Did she now?" Dr. Wissen reaches for me, but Prince William swipes his sword at him. Wissen snorts and grips his ax tighter. "As if you could stand against me."

"A place where he feeds his brides to a grove of trees," I continue. "To create a magic so wicked, so twisted that it could only be used for evil. But perhaps it was only a dream. A nightmare that haunts me in the darkest hours of the night."

"I know this place." Prince William's eyes grow wide.

"Release the woman." Dr. Wissen glowers at the prince. "She's betrothed to me."

The prince and I cling to one another, but with a single slice of the ax, the doctor sends the prince's sword clattering to the floor. The prince cowers as Dr. Wissen presses the slick, blood-smeared weapon to his throat.

The prince vanishes.

"What the—?" The doctor spins, searching for him.

Thankfully, the doctor hasn't thought to look at the floor where the prince now squats in his bright green, slimy skin. Swiftly, I step over the frog, hiding him beneath my gown, hoping my frog prince will stay hidden beneath its folds.

The doctor snags hold of my arm, growling. "Not to worry, Prince William isn't my concern. It's Marianne who wants him. All that matters is you. Once we have secured the castle, you'll marry me."

"Why bother?" I snap, twisting my arm to get free. "Just kill me and get it over with."

"Because the magic is always more powerful when you kill your loved ones. I know what you are. The magic runs strong in your family. Your blood will make me very powerful. The witch thinks after tonight, she'll be more powerful than me, but she hasn't figured out your true nature as I have."

I freeze. He's right. My family is cursed with magic. It runs in our blood, fills our bones. Except maybe I was wrong. Maybe it's not a curse after all.

"Let. Her. Go," Jacob growls, power coiling around him as he presses his blade to Wissen's throat. Each syllable carries the promise of a threat.

Wissen stiffens. I use the distraction to pick up the prince and pocket his slippery form. Wissen whirls, his ax clashing against Jacob's sword with a clang and sparks. Steel flashes as they drive strike after strike at each other. Wissen's ax slices across Jacob's side, and a cry rips from my throat. Jacob staggers, blood darkening his shirt, but he doesn't waver.

"Get out of here," he tells me. Then, with speed impossibly fast for being wounded, he cuts left, missing the ax, only to drive his sword deep into Wissen's leg.

"Someone help us!" I scream, scanning the area. A few soldiers are fighting off the werewolves, but most lie motionless on the floor. In the corner, I spot Wilhelm using his own weapon—the pen—writing frantically in his book, probably trying to write the doctor's story so he could be vanquished. Smart.

I dart across the room to the banquet table and seize a carving knife just as a werewolf dives through the air, teeth gnashing in hunger for a bite of me. I thrust the knife at it. Sharp, prickly fur skims along its body as the creature curves away from my blade. My hand trembles, and I send up a prayer of thanks that I'm still alive. Picking up my skirts, I race back toward the fight where the two dart in and out, circling each other.

But when I leap over a body, my golden slippers fail me. My foot slips, sending me skidding uncontrollably across the slick marble floor. I land in a heap, skirts snarling around me. Determination yanks me to my feet, and I advance closer to where Jacob and Wissen are battling it out.

"I told you to run, Ella!" Jacob commands.

Ignoring his order, I sneak behind Wissen and slice my blade across the doctor's calf above his boot. He howls in pain, and his knee buckles. He whirls around, shoving a hand against my shoulder. I'm thrown backward, slamming into the wall.

Someone starts clapping. Frantically, I untangle myself from my layers of material. Jacob presses his blade to Wissen's throat, standing over him with fire in his eyes, while Marianne lounges on the king's throne.

"Such entertainment," she says. "See? I told you, Wissen, she's the perfect wife for you. But it appears as if the Grimm will kill you for me. Thank you for that, Jacob."

His eyes darken, but he doesn't make the killing blow.

"Marianne," I say, snapping the last of the pieces together. "It was you in the carriage at the doctor's house. It was you who arranged my marriage to that monster. You've been working with him all along."

"Who do you think taught him the art of tree and blood magic?" She chuckles, deep and throaty, and lifts her mirror to check her hair. "Oh, Cinderella, it's endearing to see how innocent and gullible you are. I'm deeply grateful for your kindness. After all, it was your lentil magic and allowance to control your household that made my climb to the throne so simple."

"Then why did you try to destroy my life?"

"Because I've also learned that to survive, you have to be selfish. Sacrifice, love, and loyalty will only get you killed or heartbroken. Likely both. You believe in all those things, don't you?"

I swallow, clenching my fists. "What's life without them?"

"See?" She shakes her head, her eyes dripping with poisonous pity. Those same leaves she's been using to control us appear in her palms. She tosses them into the air. "When I'm still alive, powerful and radiant in youth, your shriveled body will die alone, only to be tossed back to the earth, forgotten."

"If you understood love, if you knew love, you'd know that was a lie." A pang hits my temples as the leaves fall at my feet. "You think you can control me with those leaves, but now I know the truth. I won't let them control me any longer."

"If that's the case, I suppose it's time for us to say our goodbyes." She wiggles her fingers and vines spring out of her palms, twisting and curling around the throne, hundreds of sharp-pointed leaves bursting into bloom. "Now that I can add the Kingdom of Württemberg under my control, you aren't necessary anymore. Goodbye, my little stepsister."

She raises her palms into the air. Instantly, her vines snake across the floor like serpents. The leaves rip off the plants and twirl in the air. My heart slams into my chest.

"Jacob!" I scream. "Run!"

Jacob abandons Wissen and instead reaches for my hand. The two of us race across the ballroom, leaping over dead bodies, sliding on blood. But we aren't fast enough. The leaves whirl through the air, cutting my arms, slicing through my golden locks, slashing my dress to ribbons.

We burst out of the ballroom, but the hallway is blocked by werewolves.

"This way!" I call and dive into the small chapel, slamming the door shut and bolting it.

Jacob stalks the chapel, blade ready at his side as he inspects the room. His clothes are shredded, revealing a toned and muscular chest. His hair hangs over his face, and despite the blood running in rivulets down his arms, he looks so alive, so wild. In this moment, I want him to be mine more than anything I've ever wanted before.

"Jacob. I'm so sorry. I came tonight to warn you about Marianne. I was too late."

"Nothing about any of this is your fault. I should've suspected something. She must have used magic to hide her mark."

He closes the space between us in a heartbeat, eyes burning with a fire that steals my breath and snatches my soul. His hand catches my chin, and then his mouth crashes into mine. The kiss is passionate, all-consuming, and my knees nearly give out as the world narrows to nothing but us.

It's a kiss that ends all things, and my soul aches for what we could've been.

"Stay here. I'm going to get you your happy ending." And then he's gone through the door, leaving me alone.

"No!"

No, no, no.

Marianne will definitely kill him. Wissen's likely planning on chopping him up as a snack for his beasts. My mind screams for a solution. Candles flicker around the chapel like tiny prayers of hope. The air sings with the rich scent of the woods beyond, calling me away toward freedom. There's a single window above the altar, so tiny that only a small person could get through it. I climb up the wall and push open the stained glass, revealing the dark plunge that dives into the valley below.

Jumping is suicide.

Fear spirals in my stomach.

I pull the prince from my pocket. "I'm sorry, Fritz, to leave you here like this, but you're safer as a frog."

I set him on a bench, hoping he'll remain unharmed. No one will give a second glance to a frog. The chapel door groans as vines twist through the cracks. It crashes to the ground with a boom. Dr. Wissen and Marianne step into the chapel. My heart sinks. Where's Jacob?

"There she is," Marianne says with a proud flourish. "Your lovely bride is waiting for you at the altar. How convenient."

"I'm not your bride, now nor ever." I crawl onto the windowsill. I'm small enough to fit inside. Perhaps being a 'stunt of a daughter' isn't such a bad thing, after all.

"Now don't go killing yourself," Wissen says. "You'll ruin everything. You don't wish to die a spinster, do you?"

"You're completely sick." I bite my lips, laced with salt

and panic, as I shimmy to the edge of the window. "You'll never have my magic."

The cool night breeze slithers across my bare shoulders as if begging for me to join it. I close my eyes, trying to focus. Hoping I'm right.

The doctor lunges, reaching for me. As his fingers scrape across my body, I throw myself out of the window. My body plummets. Air rushes against me, encasing me in the night. My heart screams in terror while I pray I'm right about my transformations.

Then it happens.

The fiery pain, the piercing of feathers through skin, the sharpening of sight and hearing.

In a swoop, I correct my fall to an ascent. Now I'm soaring toward the stars, soaking in the inky darkness. Free. Nothing but wings and wind. But then I remember I'm supposed to do something. What is it?

Marianne, sitting on the throne, clapping. Blood dripping off Dr. Wissen's ax. And the realization that Jacob might be dead. Rage rips through me like wildfire. It's time for me to use the magic of my family to save us. Not to hide from who I am, but to become my true self. I caw into the air, calling every bird of flight to me.

*Join me*, I cry out. *Avenge my attackers.*

As I circle the castle tower, I'm only met by silence. But then I see Aunt Fiona, the seven ravens, and the two birds I rescued flying toward me.

*Well, if you aren't full of surprises?* Aunt Fiona chirps. *You transformed at will.*

*That's one way of putting it*, I say, deciding not to tell her how I jumped out of the castle tower. *I found out where all the birds on our property have been going. Marianne, my stepsister, is a witch. She's been using their lifeforce to feed her powers.*

I tell them what I saw in the witch's garden, and the rescued birds pipe up with the rest of the story.

*I need to stop the witch while we have the chance*, I say. *Will you help me gather up others?*

*You're using your abilities to make a difference*, Aunt Fiona tells me. *Your mother would be so proud.*

They swoop into the trees, asking the others if they'd join us in our fight against the witch.

Soon the rustle of wings beat against the night, and the sky blots out the moonlight thanks to the birds of every kind.

I chirp my message: *Destroy the werewolves and any who attack the king.*

They don't hesitate. With a squawk of rage, they flood every gate, every window, eager to follow my directions. I bank left and follow in their wake. As I sail back toward the castle, glittering in a thousand lights, a part of me wishes I could leave it all behind and enter the thick, rich forest of forgetfulness.

But as I dart into the ballroom, the sounds of fighting and the smell of blood overwhelm my senses. I spot Jacob, sword flashing in the candlelight as he battles against a pack of werewolves. One beast lunges for his throat, but Jacob twists and slams a boot into its chest. The creature sprawls on the floor.

Another jumps, latching onto Jacob's arm, tearing at fabric and skin. I dive in, on wings that slice the air. My talons rake across the wolf's back. It whimpers and scurries away. Meanwhile, Jacob swings wide and cuts through another beast. Blood and steel blur together in his dance against the horde while my beak pokes at their eyes and my talons cut through fur until their howls echo against the stone walls.

One by one, they stumble and thrash. Together, Jacob and I fight against the pack. I'm a bird of prey with Jacob, my beloved hunter, at my side. The werewolves, now blinded, snarl and break into cries as their bodies shudder and twist back into human form. The castle guards seize the moment and surge forward, shackling Wissen's men in chains and dragging them away.

Only Wissen remains. He staggers in the courtyard's center, shrieking as birds swarm him, tearing at his flesh. Now that once handsome face is marred and bleeding. When at last they break away, he crumples to his knees, groaning, hands covering his once beautiful features like he's in mourning. Then, in a violent whirl of crimson, his body shimmers and swirls into a stream of ink that's sucked into the book Wilhelm is holding. It's like magic took him away.

*Grimm magic.*

Now I fully understand what Jacob and Wilhelm do. A mix of awe, fear, and pride fills me. I flutter to sit on top of the ballroom chandeliers, pleased with the success of my flock.

*Thank you,* I tell them. *You have done what humans couldn't. Go now and be free.*

With those words, the birds take flight, squawking in victory while I stay behind. Except there's no victory here, only death from greed and selfishness. I swoop into a dark alcove where no one can see me.

When my clawed feet hit the cold marble floor, I tug at the human part of me, allowing the transformation to take over, twisting my body until I'm human again. Sluggishly, I pick myself off the floor. The glitter from my dress drifts away like the magic can't hold onto it any longer. My gloves are gone, my necklace is snared in my ragged hem, and my slippers lie forgotten on the ballroom floor. Curls hang over my face, tangled and wild. Once I've tucked my shoes back on my feet, I survey the ballroom, blinking as my eyes adjust.

The hall is still as the stone it was hewn from. The guards have already dragged the prisoners away to the dungeons.

Nothing moves except for Wilhelm, hovering over a body by the grand staircase.

My pulse drums against my temples. Every fiber in me warns me to turn around and flee. Except my heart drags me across the silent hall. To the one my soul yearns for.

To Jacob, lying in a pool of blood, cuts and slashes ribboning his face. His neck is gouged by the werewolves' bites, and his body lies still as the marble floor. Raging sorrow slams against me, and it feels like my heart is being ripped out of my chest.

"No!" A sob escapes me. It can't end like this.

# CHAPTER 47

# ELLA

## LICHTENSTEIN CASTLE

"Jacob," I choke out, pressing my shaking fingers to my mouth as I fall to his side. "Look at me! Tell me you're alive."

His eyes blink once, and he shifts his head slightly to look at me. Eyes the color of a brooding storm, memorizing me like this moment will be his last. My heart shatters.

"Ella," he whispers. His face is gray, ashes falling from a dying fire.

My hand trembles as I tenderly drag my fingers along his jaw because suddenly I know. I'm in love with him. He's the fire of my life. It's he who brought me out of the cinders. It's he who told me I could be a princess even though no one believed it, not even myself.

"The creatures are gone." I wrap my palms around his. "As is Dr. Wissen. You did it."

"It was you," he whispers. "You saved us, my beautiful Ella."

A cry escapes my throat. This is not the aloof warrior I've always known. He's broken and torn to shreds, and yet, more beautiful than I ever imagined. I look at Wilhelm, sitting at Jacob's other side.

"Tell me he'll be all right," I demand. "His body will heal just like yours did in the fortress."

Wilhelm shakes his head. His eyes are bloodshot, and there are rivulets staining the battle grime on his face.

"The casualties are too great." He scrubs a hand over his face. "We can withstand greater losses than a normal human, but we aren't immortal. I tried to finish the story, but I wasn't fast enough."

"Then we change the ending," I say. "There must be something you can do."

"It is finished. You did it when you pronounced the truth of who Dr. Wissen was to the prince and then called your birds to defeat him. It had to be you, his future bride. You exposed him for what he was."

Wilhelm opens the book to show me a story: *The Robber Bridegroom*. I should find consolation that the doctor has been sent from this world. That the people of our village are finally safe. Except my heart finally breaks in half. It's suffered too much loss.

"But it's not too late for Jacob, right?" I gasp for air. It's too hard to breathe.

Jacob's hand squeezes mine. "I want you to have your happily ever after," he says.

"Then don't die," I shoot back.

"Wilhelm," Jacob rasps. "Write Ella her happy ending. Promise me? Make sure that witch doesn't get the prince. Ella must marry the prince."

"No!" I sob and press his hand to my cheek. "Please. We can find a way to be together. We will figure something out. Don't make me marry someone I don't love."

"I love you," Jacob says. "I think I always have."

And then his eyes glaze over, and his grip slackens. Life

slips from his lips, gathering into the candlelight. I collapse against his chest, unable to stop the sobs wracking my body. Wilhelm leaps to his feet, throwing down the book.

"This was not the deal!" Wilhelm yells, punching his fist into the air. "You can't let him die! If he dies, then I'm out. There will be no more stories. No more writing. Without him, I can't. Just can't."

Wilhelm's rage peters out until he slumps onto the floor. I don't have the strength to leave Jacob's chest to offer comfort.

That's when she comes. At first, I think we're being assaulted by fireflies, but then they swirl together, solidifying into a woman. She's terrible and beautiful with a gown spun from the coldest winter's snow and skin smoother than ice. Her crown, studded with gems the color of the rainbow, is so sharp, it could be a weapon.

"How disappointing." The woman clucks her tongue. "He was my favorite, you know."

"Enchantress," Wilhelm says with a growl, so similar to his brother.

"Oh, don't take it personally." She waves her thin wand flippantly. "I like you well enough. But this one, he had sass. Always liked to challenge me."

So this is the woman who has been torturing the Grimm brothers. I give her my fiercest glare.

"He's not supposed to die." Wilhelm's fists clench at his sides. "This should never have happened."

"Well, it happened, so I suppose it was meant to be," she snaps back. "Don't even think about blaming me. Now you." The Enchantress stops talking and glides to where I'm huddled next to Jacob, narrowing glacial eyes on me. "How unexpected. A mere bird-girl. You saved them, didn't you? You know they're your hunters."

"I was too late," I choke out. "Can you save my Jacob?"

Her eyebrows shoot up at my words. "Your Jacob? He's *my*

Jacob. And don't forget that. But the witch, she's afraid of you, isn't she?"

"Marianne?" I snort. "She's definitely not afraid of me. I suppose she hates me since Prince William liked me better than her. Not that it matters."

"Yes. Yes." The Enchantress nods, her eyes growing wider as her white lips curve into a smile that could dazzle anyone. "I like you, Cinderella, quite a lot actually."

"Ella," I correct.

"Fearless for such a little bird," the Enchantress coos. "I respect that."

I scowl. "This is your fault."

"It's for the best that he died. A pretty, bright thing like yourself can do so much better. Besides, your love was never meant to be. Star-crossed lovers, that's all you ever were."

Every muscle in my body screams to jump up and stab her with Jacob's sword. But then a desperately wretched idea forms into my mind.

"This witch, Marianne," I say, clenching my fists to keep my rage in check. "How long has she evaded and outwitted you? Because I think it's been quite a while."

The Enchantress studies the ballroom's carnage. "The witch's and my history are none of your concern."

"I've read her journal." I rise to my feet, empowered by the sudden hunger flickering in the Enchantress's eyes. "A fascinating read. In it, she writes about her plans, her desires, her allies. Riveting material."

"You lie," the Enchantress says, but her body leans toward me like she believes every word I say.

"There were conversations in that book between her and other witches. They all have grand plans, but their number one goal is to destroy you." The Enchantress is quiet. Her fingers drum against her wand. "I could give the Grimm brothers this journal and keep her from marrying the prince and gaining a kingdom to rule over. But I want something in return."

"The little bird is more clever than I gave her credit for," the Enchantress mutters. "What do you want?"

"Bring Jacob back to life," I say. "You can do that, can't you?"

She remains quiet, looking down at Jacob, still as forgotten stone. "There would be consequences. There always are consequences. But since he hasn't completely left this realm yet—maybe."

I suck in my breath, too much hope daring to spill out of me, and yet terror hovers there as well. Consequences? What did that mean? I think about Jacob's deal with her when he saved Wilhelm's life. Jacob said they lived a cursed life because of it.

"Ella!" Wilhelm grabs me and draws me aside. "Don't do it. Don't make any deals with her. Ever. There's not a day I don't regret the decision we made to be slaves to that wretched woman. Trust me on this."

"You would rather let Jacob die?"

"Yes, most definitely. In fact, his dying wish was to give you your happy ending. How can I do that if you're enslaved to this Enchantress?"

"I can't let him die." Tears spill down my cheeks. Now I understand Jacob's pain and why he chose his path.

"If you truly love him, you'll let him go. It's the right thing to do."

"But isn't love about holding on no matter what?" I counter. "Isn't love about fighting for each other, despite all odds?"

Wilhelm stares at me, swallowing hard. Mother used to tell me you could see a person's soul through their eyes. His are deep pools of sadness.

"Wilhelm," the Enchantress commands. "We must speak."

He leaves me to join the Enchantress in the corner where the two talk in whispered voices. I wring my hands, trying to keep them from shaking.

"The deal has been struck," the Enchantress says upon returning. Her face is hard and unreadable in the candle-light. "All that's required, Cinderella, is for you to keep your part."

"My part?" My heart feels like it's sinking into the depths of the sea.

"You must hand over the witch's book to Wilhelm," she says. I let out a breath, but she continues, "And complete your fairy tale. I suspect it's through your tale that we can stop Marianne forever."

*My fairy tale.* Wilhelm's book is open on the floor. The pages turn on their own accord to an unfinished story called *Cinderella.* My breath catches in my throat, and a gasp escapes my lips. Wilhelm races over and snatches up the book, but there's no more hiding the truth. Jacob and Wilhelm were writing my story this whole time without my permission? Of course, they were. I'd been a fool to think I might be differ-ent. Jacob got close to me only to use me to cross off another story from his list.

A smirk slides across the Enchantress's face as if to say, *What did you expect?*

I confront Wilhelm. "Jacob's and my relationship was only about completing your next story, wasn't it?"

Wilhelm blanches, clearly stricken by my words. "It's not what it seems. I mean, it is, but you're from the other realm, and that's where you belong. This is your chance to enter your own fairy tale where you can choose your own ending. I'll merely write out the events as you see fit. Or even better, forget this madness. Let Jacob die in peace and go home and live out your life."

"Yes, because my life at home is so lovely," I say dully.

She lifts her hands as if she's preparing to kill me. My thoughts whirl in desperation. Fear scrapes my skin.

"If you kill me," I say quickly, "you'll never get your book back."

Her hands lower. "What book?"

"The one in your garden," I say. Her lips part slightly, a sharp breath catching in her throat. "Yes, I know about your secret hiding spot and what you've been doing to my poor bird friends. And I found your journal full of information and communications that I'm sure the *Enchantress* would love to read."

"How do you know about *her*?"

"It's why I took your journal and hid it in my own secret place. If I don't return home alive, I've asked a friend to make sure the book is given to the Enchantress. You know, I was shocked at how much information you wrote in there. Plans, allies, *weaknesses*."

"You dare think you can bribe me?"

"Not think, I *know*." I throw on a smirk even as my knees tremble. "Also, get your hands off the prince."

She lets go of him and he startles as if coming out of a trance.

"Princess, you're alive!" he exclaims. "I saw you jump out the window. I merely kissed this lovely lady because I wanted to get out of my frog form and save you. You must believe me. It's a long story, but I can explain everything."

Backpedaling, I give the Enchantress a meaningful look. She lifts her chin but doesn't stop me. Urgency rails at my nerves. I need to hurry and get Marianne's book to Wilhelm. There isn't a second to lose; Jacob's life depends on it.

"Wait." Prince William starts after me. "Don't leave. I order you in the name of the king to stay."

"I have to go, Your Highness," I say. "I'm sorry. For everything."

Picking up my skirts, I take off down the hallway, heading to the back gate, blue feathers from my tattered gown fluttering in my wake. With every step, I expect Marianne to use her witch powers and stop me, but she doesn't. Concerning, but I don't have time to worry about it.

"Guards!" Prince William calls, running after me. "Close the gates!"

The castle corridors, once full of partyers, are silent as if holding their breath. Once outside, I rush to cross the wooden bridge only for my slippers to sink into dark pitch, making it impossible for me to move.

"Someone is on the bridge!" a guard's voice cries out from above.

"By orders of the prince," another guard says. "No one can leave the castle without permission."

Heart pounding, I manage to slide my feet out of the slippers and then mentally focus on turning to my bird-form. Except I'm still having trouble transforming upon command. Voices gather at the edge of the drawbridge. My heart pelts against my ribcage. Panic claws at my throat. But it appears once again my panic will save me. Maybe the frog prince and I have more in common than I thought.

Because I'm ripping, tearing, shredding from my human form. I lift into the sky, vanishing onto the wings of night.

# CHAPTER 48

## JACOB

### LICHTENSTEIN CASTLE

A rushing sound thunders in my ears like the crash of a waterfall. I gasp. *Need more air.*

I flicker between this world and another just out of my grasp. Faces blink. In and out.

Wilhelm.

And...oh no, the Enchantress. I scowl.

"Ah!" she says, her voice the sound of falling snowflakes, fleeting and cold. "There's the Grimm frown I've come to love. Appears as if he's perfectly fine. Back to his old self, to be sure. I can't wait to see how this story turns out. It's sure to be glorious."

With a flurry of starlight and a gust of midwinter, she disappears.

"Brother!" Wilhelm throws his arms around me. I groan from the impact. "Sorry for the tackle. I'm glad you're alive. You were dead. At least, mostly dead."

"Now we're even," I grumble, sitting up. The movement hurts, but not as much as it should. I inspect my body, expecting to see chunks of my skin ripped off and stab wounds in my flesh. I'm completely healed. "Why didn't you just let me die?"

"It was Ella's idea, and I agreed to it." Wilhelm lifts his chin. "We made a deal."

"You should never have let Ella make a deal with the Enchantress." Dread coils down my body. "That was the worst idea you've ever had. What was the deal?"

Wilhelm explains it all to me as I stand. My knees buckle, but Wilhelm catches me and holds me up. Blood begins to flow through my veins once again.

"My life wasn't worth hers," I say. My stomach twists at the thought of Ella vanishing into her story forever. To never hear her voice again or wrap my hand around hers. Never kiss her lips. "You should've left me to die."

"Actually, I would've," Wilhelm says, his voice laced with guilt. "But Ella refused."

"I'm glad you would've." I rest my hand on his shoulder. "I couldn't have asked for a better brother."

"Someone find her!" The prince's voice echoes through the halls, frantic. "Close every gate. Don't let her escape."

I try to run to meet the prince at the ballroom entrance, only to trip over my wobbly legs twice. Dying really can be inconvenient. "What is it, Your Highness?" I ask and then blink in surprise. "Are you all right?"

The prince looks wretched. His jacket and pants are inside out. His wig is gone, and his stockings are ripped, cloak tattered. There isn't a piece of his clothing not streaked with blood. Blood even stains his lips.

"It's the Southland princess." Prince William grabs my shirt, eyes wild. "She ran off. You must find her this instant!"

"Of course. I'll find her." Because I need to talk to her. I will get her out of this deal with the Enchantress. My life is an easy exchange.

Which exit did she use? I spot a trail of golden dust that

"Time is ticking," the Enchantress calls out. "He's nearly beyond my reach."

A queasiness settles in the pit of my stomach. Without Jacob, I wouldn't have found the truth behind Dr. Wissen. The monster would still be alive, and I'd be a married woman, perhaps already fed to his trees. He also gave me the strength to stand up for myself and made me believe I could do what I otherwise thought was impossible. For all Jacob's trickery, I owed him. I face the Enchantress.

"I agree to your terms."

"Excellent," she says, pulling out a contract and pen. "Prick your finger and sign your name in blood. I recommend you hurry."

A wave of dizziness washes over me after I sign. Then I spin on my golden slippers and dash into the hall only to run into Prince William kissing Marianne.

"Fritz—I mean Prince William?" My voice is strangled.

Marianne pulls away from him with a coy smile. Her hand still clutches his tussled jacket as if she's holding him up. Blood drips from her lips.

"What have you done to the prince?" I demand. "His blood is on your mouth!"

She chuckles, wiping the crimson off her chin and then licking it. "Don't you worry, stepsister. That isn't the prince's blood. It's yours. When I discovered the true reason for Crabb Wissen's obsession with you, I swiped some of the blood you spilled and tasted it. Sweet and tangy, full of magic. Deep, old magic. The doctor was keeping secrets about you from me."

"You speak like a madwoman."

"You must come from a very powerful family with ancient magic. The doctor and I drank a blood oath that you would be his and I would have the crown. But he's dead now, thanks to you, so I think I'll just take everything."

leads down the hall. I take off in a sprint, running faster than I've ever run in my life. But when I reach the back gate, I see I'm too late. A lone bluebird is flapping its wings, soaring off into the forest. All that is left are glass slippers etched with gold, entrenched in the pitch the prince had ordered.

"Don't know where the maiden got to." one of the guards calls from the top of the wall.

"Same here," a second guard says, joining me. "Saw her from the top of the wall, but by the time I got down here, she had vanished into thin air."

"Better keep quiet about what you saw," I tell the guard. "The prince would have your head if he knew you let her slip away. Leave this matter to me."

"Oh, yes. Of course." He nods vigorously.

I grab a board and toss it over the pitch, balancing my way to the slippers and lifting them out of the muck. I wash them in the moat until their glass glistens gold in the torchlight. They're so tiny. Memories of our last kiss haunt me.

"Did you find her?" the prince asks, running to the gate, breathless.

"Err..." the one guard says.

"We um..." the other stutters.

"Yes." I stride up to Prince William. "Unfortunately, she got away. But your stratagem for using the pitch worked in the end."

I hold out a glass slipper. His eyes widen. Reverently, he takes the shoe.

"This is the princess's," he says. "I'm sure of it."

"Perhaps it can help us find your bride." My tongue is thick in my mouth just saying that.

"Yes, I must marry her. Dawn will be here shortly. I'll ride the entire kingdom until I find who this shoe belongs to. I won't stop until I find her. No one shall be my wife except the girl who fits this glass slipper. You must ride with me, Jacob. I won't have it any other way."

"Of course."

He takes off into the castle, barking orders. I lift the other slipper out of the folds of my tattered jacket, holding it up into the air just as the first hues of marigold sunrays light up the sky. Love and happiness may never be destined for me, but that doesn't mean I can't bring happiness to the one I love.

◎❀◎

After the fifth house, I can barely keep my eyes open.

"We should just take him to the Maier manor," Wilhelm grumbles. "Then we can get this whole dirty business over. You can't delay this forever. We both know it's Ella's slipper. And I don't like the idea of Ella being alone with that witch."

I peek at the hourglass in my pack. The name Cinderella winks savagely at me. I've been delaying the inevitable, hoping I'll come up with some scheme to out-trick the Enchantress, but we're out of time. Every maiden we visited desperately tried to squeeze the slipper on to win the heart of the prince, but they all failed. I clench Storm's reins. Wilhelm is right. Again.

"Your Royal Highness." I move to the side of the prince's carriage. "Perhaps we should pay a visit to Lord Maier's manor. I've heard he has daughters."

"Lord Maier?" Prince William frowns. "Yes, I remember his eldest daughter. We should make way there with haste."

As Wilhelm and I ride behind the royal carriage and the entourage of guards, my heart begins pounding. I can't let her marry the prince. Except that's the right choice, isn't it?

Because true love gives the one you hold closest the wings to fly.

# CHAPTER 49

# ELLA

## MAIER MANOR

The cage swings from the tree bough, creaking as I work at the lock scrunched within the bars of my cage. A pile of broken hairpins lay scattered at my knees. None work. My fingers ache, blood dripping from them as I poke myself with the pins. My throat burns from the lack of water, and I blink back frustrated tears. I need to escape. It's only a matter of time before Marianne returns.

Last night, when I landed at the hazel tree and transformed into human form, my stepmother and stepsisters were there, waiting for me. Before I could process what was happening, Marianne tied me up and the three dragged me to Marianne's secret garden, locking me in this cage.

"Flee, Ella!" a dove calls from the cage beside mine. "Flee! She comes!"

"I'm trying," I say. "I can't—"

My words stick in my throat as the tall mirror in the garden's center wavers and Marianne steps through. Glee fills her eyes as she strides to my cage.

"Good morning, sweet sister," she says pleasantly as if we're having tea and cake.

"You're no sister of mine," I say in a menacing tone. "And I'll never tell you where your book is."

"I didn't expect you to turn so wild so quickly. No matter. I've got wonderful news. The prince's retinue just arrived in search of the girl who dropped her slipper at the ball. Whoever it fits will be his wife and live in the castle. Isn't that just wonderful?"

"Then I suppose you'd better cross your fingers you have the same shoe size as that girl." I flash her a wicked smile. We both know my feet are significantly smaller than hers.

"Cross fingers? What kind of witch do you take me for? I leave nothing to fate or whimsical wishes."

She pulls out a skeleton key and slips it into the lock of the dove's cage. With a twist, it clicks open, and she reaches her hands around the dove. "Come here, you pretty thing," she coos and holds the bird up. Her face is enraptured despite the bird's cries.

"Let the bird go," I demand, fear chilling me.

"Oh, don't worry. I will."

She pockets her key and then presses on the bird. Its pure-white feathers darken to gray. I scream, shaking at my bars, demanding she stop. The bird screeches, and then its body crumbles into ashes in her palms.

"Why?" Tears stream down my face. "You horrible, horrible witch!"

"Don't worry, sister. The bird's life still clings to these ashes."

She cups her palms to her mouth and pours the ashes down her throat. I choke in horror. Instantly, her hair deepens in richer shades of brown, and her skin smooths out, glistening like she was drenched in diamonds. She's utterly enchanting. I clench the bars of my cage, fury raging through me.

"I will end you," I promise.

"There. Now the prince won't be able to resist me. There's just one more thing I must do before I meet him. A precaution, because you can never be too prepared."

She withdraws a pair of shears from her pocket and slips it through the bars. "Cut off your hair."

I snort. "I'm not doing a thing for you."

"Then I'll have your father chop down that rotten hazel tree and capture every bird on the property and bring them to me. So, do we have a deal?"

I suck in a horrifying breath. This isn't a deal. That's when I realize this is just the beginning of her control over me until there's nothing left except my ashes. I scowl but take the scissors. In a few brief seconds, I chop off my long golden curls. Then I drop them on the floor, my final act of defiance. Greedily, she scoops up my hair and drops it into a pouch.

"By the way," she says, pausing before slipping through her mirror. "Your Jacob Grimm is here. Don't worry. I'll make sure he never bothers you again."

*Jacob's alive!*

But my joy is swallowed by fear. Gripping the cage bars, I push down the panic edging at my nerves. What's she going to do with my hair? Will she use it to hurt Jacob? And I can't let her marry the prince and rule the land. I need to get out of this cage now.

# CHAPTER 50

# JACOB

## MAIER MANOR

Ella's father, stepmother, and stepsisters are all waiting for us in the front room, but Ella is nowhere in sight. The father is slouched in his chair, passed out with an empty teacup tipped over beside him. When Prince William parades in after being announced, the women gasp, covering their faces with fans. Marianne glances at the two of us, her face peaceful as ever. As if she doesn't know who we are. I smile deviously at her, and she narrows her eyes back at me.

"Keep a close eye on the witch," I mutter to Wilhelm.

"Where's Ella?" Wilhelm whispers.

"Obviously not here." It's concerning. "Maybe she saw us coming and is going to get the witchs book."

"I have the most beautiful feet in the land," Bertha proclaims, promptly removing her own slippers and reaching for the glass one balanced on the pillow held by the footman.

"Let me try it first, Bertha." Marianne pushes her sister aside, who crashes to the floor. Marianne flashes the prince a stunning smile that chills my skin. In a purring voice, she says,

"I'll never forget all the lovely dances we had together, Your Highness."

"Err..." Prince William's forehead bunches in confusion. Waves of magic ebb from Marianne. Her spell wraps around our entire group, its tentacles clawing its way to my chest.

"Why aren't you writing this all down?" I snap at Wilhelm, fear suffocating me. "We need to get rid of this despicable witch before it's too late."

"Yes, yes, of course." Wilhelm shakes his head and rubs his eyes before slipping behind the royal guards at the desk.

Marianne produces her stockinged foot for the footman. He kneels before her and holds out the glistening shoe. The witch grunts, pushing her foot into the delicate slipper, a frown ruining her perfect complexion.

"Something isn't right, Mother." Marianne bites her lip. "My slipper appears to be too tight. What did you do to my shoe?" she demands of the footman.

"I—I did nothing," the footman stutters.

"Not to worry," her mother says smoothly, and then draws Marianne up from the chair. "We'll be right back. I need to see if something got stuck in her stockings."

"Of course," Prince William says, gazing rapturously at Marianne. "We're happy to wait."

The two hurry into the hall, whispering.

"What do you think that's all about?" Wilhelm asks, coming to my side.

"Perhaps she will cut her toes off." I grin wickedly. "Then her foot would fit nice and snug."

"Snug indeed." Wilhelm shakes his head at me.

We peer around the corner. Marianne is wrapping her foot in golden thread. Or is it yarn?

"I don't like the looks of this," I whisper. "It reeks of magic."

"Let me try!" Bertha demands and snatches the slipper

from the footman as we wait. She grunts and groans as she jams her foot into it until she's red in the face.

"It does not fit you," the prince says.

"No surprise there," Wilhelm murmurs.

"I'm just going to behead the witch and get it over with." I palm my sword's hilt.

"You can't do that," Wilhelm says. "I need to finish the story the proper way."

"Where is Ella?" I ask, looking out the window. "She should be here by now."

"You don't think the witch—" Wilhelm's words break off, and he swallows as if he doesn't dare say what he's thinking. Then he rushes back to the desk and starts writing again.

I pace along the wall. Do I go look for Ella or stay here and keep an eye on the witch? Bertha suddenly squeals in victory.

"It fits!" Bertha proclaims and displays her foot, beaming in triumph.

"Ah, yes!" the footman says with a relieved sigh. "Our hunt has finished."

A trail of blood drips over the edge of the heel of the golden shoe, and then it pops off Bertha's foot, smacking the footman in the face. He cries out, rubbing his nose.

"Oh, Bertha!" Marianne titters as she waltzes into the room, limping ever so slightly. "You are too cute, but you know that's my slipper. Truly, you didn't expect the prince to marry you?"

Bertha's face falls, lips pouting as she retreats to the couch while Marianne snatches the slipper from the footman's hand, who quickly darts backward as if to avoid another facial casualty. She tucks the glistening shoe right onto her foot and flourishes her hands over her raised leg.

"It fits!" Marianne claps her hands over her chest. "Oh, Mother! I'm going to be a princess. And then queen."

The stepmother beams. "As you have always been destined to be."

"My darling." Prince William rushes to her, arms outstretched. "How happy I am to find you."

I cross my arms, frowning, and go to Wilhelm. "I refuse for the story to work out this way. Ella needs to marry the prince so she can live the rest of her life in wealth and privilege. The witch must have put a spell on those threads."

I follow the couple outside to where the coach waits. Prince William announces to the entourage that he has found his princess. The trumpeter plays while the couple heads to the carriage. It's all happening so fast. I can't seem to think straight.

Swooping down from above, seven ravens line up on the bough of one of the trees, gazing down at the proceedings with their typical disapproving glare. Suddenly, one of them speaks as if it's human.

"Turn and peep, turn and peep," it says, shocking me. "There's blood within the shoe, for it's too small for her. The true bride waits for her prince."

"Wait!" I race to Prince William. "Your Highness, you've been tricked. Look at her foot. Blood is streaming out of the slipper."

Marianne's dress covers her feet, but when the prince demands she show him the shoe, it's no longer tinted with gold. A greenish tinge with veins of blood streak down its sides. Strands of golden hair fall off Marianne's heel. My stomach turns at the sight. It's the same color as Ella's.

"This is treason!" The prince pulls out his sword in anger, turning to the father, who had stumbled out of his half-slumber to send off his stepdaughter. "What's the meaning of your daughter's treachery?"

"I uh—do not know," the father stutters, clearly still incapacitated.

I clench my fists, anger burning a storm inside me. "But you have another daughter, do you not?"

"Of course not!" He pauses, confusion flickering in his eyes. "There is a little stunted kitchen wench who my late wife left behind after her death, but she cannot possibly be the bride you seek. She's betrothed to Dr. Wissen."

"Dr. Wissen is dead. Therefore, the betrothal is nullified. Where is she?" I yell. "Tell me this instant."

"In her room." The vile man points to the top of the turret. "Up there."

"I'll fetch the maiden for you, Your Highness," I said with a bow.

I take off into the house, hating every footfall, every stride, but I love her too much not to give her everything she deserves. And if it's a prince she wants, I'll move heaven and earth to give that to her.

# CHAPTER 51

# ELLA

## MAIER MANOR

I grit my teeth, determined I won't fail Jacob. Whether he realizes it or not, his life is at stake here. The agreement forged between the Enchantress and me teeters at a precipice.

The hairpins aren't working. Marianne said ancient magic is in my blood. She was so sure of it, she locked me up here and used my hair to empower her. The only power I know of is my ability to turn into a bird, which isn't very helpful in escaping from a cage.

My eyes land on the lone dove's feather lying motionless on the grass below. Could my bird form somehow help me? Could it have special powers? A bizarre idea creeps into my mind. It probably won't work, but I need to try.

I take deep breaths and visualize myself in my bird form. Soaring over thick forests. Coasting on cool winds over castle peaks. Diving through clouds streaking across the sunset.

Pain prickles across my skin and aches in my bones. It's happening! Instead of resisting the transformation, I allow it to scuttle through my entire body. I clutch the bars for support as my body convulses. Suddenly, my vision sharpens and widens so I'm able to see nearly the entire garden around me. The leaves on the trees are brighter, and the flowers deepen in an amplified variety of colors.

I'm a tiny bird, hopping in a cage. I begin scuffling about, searching for food, nipping at the sides of the cage, and testing out my surroundings. I preen my feathers, deciding I don't like this cage. It's very constraining. I'd much rather fly.

After a few moments, I pause, noticing a feather on the grass below. There's something about that feather. A memory tugs at me. I focus on it, and a vision of a human drinking from the ashes of the dove shoots through me.

Marianne. Locked in a garden. My name is Ella, and I'm a bird-shifter. I cock my head, quite proud of myself. I'm getting much better at focusing my mind on my bird form.

But why did I turn into a bird? There's a reason for it. I peck at the seeds. It had to do with a feather like the one on the ground. Yes, I need a feather to pick the lock. A lucky, magic feather. I twist my neck and, with my beak, pluck out a smooth blue one from my body and lay it beside me. Now I just need to turn back to my human self.

I try to think of human things from my human world. Birdseed, trees, sky—no, those are all wrong. I fluff my feathers and try again, this time focusing on a pain buried deep within the human part of me.

*Jacob.*

I must save him.

My body contorts and my insides rip, tear, grow. I scream. The pain of transforming again so quickly is almost too much for me to bear. Finally, the transformation finishes, leaving me panting and aching all over. I press my cheeks against the cold metal of the bars, tears streaming down my face, and wait for the pain to subside.

Finally, I push myself to sit, groaning from the effort, and search underneath myself for the feather I hope I hadn't imagined plucking. Relief floods me when I find it tangled in my skirts. My hands tremble as I gingerly fit the sharp quill inside where the key should go. Maybe it's wishful thinking, but I hope whatever magic my bird form might have will work on this lock. I wiggle the end and push the tip in all the way.

The lock clicks, and the cage door pops open. Relief floods me, and I cry out in joy and relief as I climb out of the cage. The moment my feet hit the soft grass, elation overwhelms me.

I snatch up my wooden shoes lying on the grass beneath my cage, then stumble on weak legs through the mirror and out into the hall. Desperately, I race to my room and grab Marianne's book that I hid under the floorboards.

But as I descend, footsteps pound up the stairs. I'm trapped. Marianne somehow discovered I escaped. I halt in my tracks, heart thumping against my chest. I don't have a weapon or any way to defend myself.

"Ella! Is that you?"

And there he is, rounding the corner. Tall, handsome, the prince of my heart.

"Jacob!" I throw myself into his arms, tears streaming down my face. "You're alive!"

I press my palms to his cheeks, soaking in his warmth. The life that sparkles in his eyes. The curls that hang haphazardly over tanned skin. "You died and I couldn't—"

His lips crash against mine, hot and passionate. I cling to him, falling into an endless abyss I never wanted to leave. His hand slides to the back of my neck, anchoring me closer, while the other presses against my waist, pulling me against him. The world fades until there's only the taste of him, the strength of his arms, and the desperate wish for a life with him, shining with possibilities. A life with love so deep, so real.

If only we could have *this*.

If only *this* could be my fairy tale.

I break away, breathless. "I can't. We can't."

His eyes search mine. Pain and desperation replace the sparkle. His hands lower down my arms, and I shiver at his perfect touch. My whole body craves him. Needs him.

How will I live without him?

"I know," he whispers. "You deserve so much more than the cursed life I can offer. I want you to have everything. The prince, the castle, the life that you were destined for. And I'm going to do everything to make sure you get that."

"Jacob." I run my hands along his shoulders, down to his hard chest, memorizing the feel of him. "*My* Jacob. You may think you live under a curse but never forget that you have a family who loves you. And these stories you write are saving our villagers from monsters and warning us of the dangers around us. And because of that, I want you to write my story to give others like me hope. You'll do that for me, won't you?"

"Anything you ask of me is yours." Tears well up in his eyes. He takes my hands, kissing them like he's sealing his promise. "I've been seeking a way to break our curse ever since I made the mistake of signing the Enchantress's contract. But perhaps you're right. Perhaps I've got it wrong."

"We will always have our story," I remind him. "No one can take that from us."

Tears escape from my eyes, streaming down my face. There are so many words to tell him. Too many, and I fear that if I let them loose, they'll hold too much power. He wipes them away and kisses my forehead, but pain is turning his eyes stormy blue.

"This is for you." I push Marianne's book into his hands. "The Enchantress is expecting it. It's Marianne's journal and communication source. Perhaps it can even help you with your curse."

"Thank you." He tucks it under his arm. His finger catches one of my locks. "Your hair. What happened?"

"Marianne is what happened. Now let's go find Fritz, I mean the prince."

"Are you sure? I've been frantically thinking there must be another way."

"When my mother died, I thought my whole world ended. In some ways, the old me died with her that day, too, because I'm not the same girl I was. Our family will never be whole again, but I like to think I'm stronger and a little wiser. So this new me is what will make my future, and that starts right now."

He nods in understanding.

Back outside, we're met by Stepmother arguing with the prince's guards. Bertha is wailing while Marianne hangs onto the prince's arms, whispering words into his ears. A glaze haunts his eyes. A sickening feeling rises inside me as I realize the hard truth.

The prince isn't my soulmate. Could we still be happy together? Would we be able to ward off the evils we surely will face in our happily ever after?

The answer hangs heavy on me.

"I'm here," I call out amidst the noise.

Everyone faces me and grows silent except for Marianne, who gasps.

"You have a slipper for me to try on, Your Royal Highness?" I ask, bowing to the prince.

"Ella?" Confusion twists his mouth. "You're the stunted daughter?"

Heat rises to my face. Father called me that in front of everyone?

"She never attended the ball," Stepmother says. "So you couldn't have met her."

"We didn't meet at the ball, did we?" Prince William steps closer. "All that time and I never saw it."

"Sometimes we only see what we wish to see." I settle primly on a stool that Wilhelm provides for me.

The footman groans, muttering under his breath, but carries a pillow with my slipper on it to me. I slip off my wooden shoe and allow the footman to replace it with the glass one. It slides on perfectly.

"It fits!" the prince pronounces, throwing his hands into the air.

"Of course, it does." I smile. "It's my shoe."

The prince's men clap politely, and the trumpet is blown, while my family is clearly not pleased. Father withdraws a flask and begins heartily drinking from it. Stepmother begins a rant about what a wicked girl I am to take away an opportunity from my stepsister, while Bertha launches into one of her fits.

Marianne remains serenely quiet. Too quiet. That worries me most.

To my left, Wilhelm sits on the stone steps, writing furiously. Dear Wilhelm, always dependable and kind. And then there's Jacob, pacing in front of his horse, hand on his sword. Impatient and annoyed. But his faithfulness and selflessness are deeper than I could've imagined.

"Come, my princess," Prince William says, kissing me on the hand. "It's time for us to announce our engagement to my parents."

Except the wind starts to rise, tugging at my skirts, gaining in strength. She isn't going to let me have my happily ever after. The guards are knocked over. The prince tumbles to the ground.

"Ella!" Jacob screams, pushing against the wind, trying to get to me.

Fear races through me. I turn to face Marianne, standing

with her hands at her sides, palms face out. Her bright green dress remains unmoving, a stark contrast to everyone else caught in a windstorm.

Wilhelm abandons his story to help, but the force is too strong. Desperate, I fight against the gale, trying to reach Jacob one step in front of the other, but the wind funnels around Marianne and me in a wall, a barrier that even the Grimm brothers can't get through.

"You can't have him, sister," Marianne says darkly. "He's my prince and I will be queen."

Leaves fly off the trees and shoot across the lawn, joining in the whirlwind funneling around us. Marianne flicks her wrist. Leaves slice across my neck and hands. I cry out as pain sears me. Marianne means to cut me so fiercely that I'll bleed to death. She waves her hand and another force of wind barrels through, knocking me to the ground. I try to crawl toward Jacob, but her powers are too strong.

"I won't move until I've watched your blood run like a river," she says.

Every fiber in me screams to morph into my bird form and fly away. It's what my body has done every time there's been trouble. But something warns me that it's exactly what she wants. A bird is so much easier to dispose of than a human.

Gritting my teeth, I force my battered body upright, every muscle screaming. My knees wobble, but I plant my feet firmly on the earth and spread my arms wide as if to embrace the very sky. Closing my eyes, I push past the pain, past the fear, reaching deep inside myself for that invisible thread I grasped last night at the castle.

*Help*, I whisper in my mind, hoping they can hear me even in my human form. *Please help.*

At first, there's only the wind and the thundering of my heartbeat. Then a rush of wings. The air shivers and the sky darkens with their arrival. Sparrows, crows, doves, ravens, and of course, Aunt Fiona. They descend in a flurry of wings, feathers brushing my skin as if to tell me that they're here to protect me. They swirl around Marianne and me, a whirlwind of flashing talons and piercing beaks. They squawk and shriek in a battle cry.

"Stop this instant, you vile creatures!" Marianne's shrill voice cuts through the wingbeats. She flails wildly, abandoning her leaf funnel. The spell falters. The wind dies with a groan, and the funnel collapses. Leaves scatter lifelessly to the ground.

Jacob rushes to my side, holding out his sword in protection.

But there's no reason for him to attack since the birds are diving at Marianne. Sharp beaks graze her arms. Talons rake her hair. Marianne screams in fury.

"Bertha!" she shrieks. "Help!"

Bertha swings a branch at them, but it's useless. The flock surges as one, an unstoppable tide, and attacks Bertha as well.

"My skin!" Marianne screams at me. "My hair! You don't understand the sacrifices I've made for them. You've destroyed me. You will pay for this."

"You'll have to come through me first," Jacob says.

"She's to be my wife," Prince William says, picking himself off the ground. "Any person who hurts her will be executed."

But there isn't any need because the birds are incessant. Holding their arms over their heads, my stepmother and step-sisters race away, screaming.

"Is it bad that watching them being chased by a flock of birds makes me happy?" I ask Jacob.

He glares at their retreating forms. The guards pursue them, finally catching and binding them up. When his gaze shifts to me, it softens. "A little exercise might do them some good." He pulls out a handkerchief and gently, slowly, wipes away the blood like he's memorizing the shape of my face. Like it's the last time he will ever look at me. "You were magnificent, standing up to that witch."

The air punches from my chest. I'm afraid to speak, because my words might ruin everything. I'm not sure I'm strong enough for what I'm about to do.

Prince William comes over to us. "Are you ready, my love, to join me in the carriage?" he asks.

A spark flares in Jacob's eyes, and his mouth tightens at the edges. He takes my hand and kisses it, hot lips against my cold skin. But it's not enough. I want more.

No, I want him.

"You'll always be my fairy tale," he whispers.

Then he steps backward, still holding my hand until our fingers slip apart. Prince William is talking to me, but my whole focus is on Jacob walking away, talking to Wilhelm, and then swinging onto his horse. My heart shatters as he gallops down the road, dust billowing in his wake.

Desperately, I want to race after him, but I made a vow in exchange for a life. It's a promise I will keep because I love him.

"I assure you I won't turn into a frog for the entire ride," I realize Prince William is saying.

"Oh, Fritz," I say, using his fake name. I turn to him and squeeze his hands. "I've grown quite fond of you, and for a moment, I believed I could find a way to make our fairy tale work. But I don't love you, and because of that, I'll never make you happy."

"I see." He swallows hard, clearly devastated. "It has to do with Jacob Grimm, doesn't it?"

I offer him a kind expression. "Can I ask a favor?"

"You saved my kingdom and my life from Dr. Wissen," he says. "And then from the hands of a witch. Your every wish is at my command."

"I ask that my father's name be taken off the land title and given to me and my faithful servants: Jesse, Cook, Herman, Kurt, and Peter. Also, that my stepmother and stepsisters are put on trial for their crimes."

"Consider it done." He turns to his guards. "Arrest the stepmother and stepsisters at once for the attempt to murder and overthrow the crown. From this moment on, ownership of the Maier manor will be held by Lady Ella von Maier and her servants. Furthermore, a monetary reward will be sent to your ladyship as a thank you for the great service you have given your king and prince."

I bow deeply. "Thank you, Your Royal Highness. You have brought me the fairy tale I could only hope for."

"If you change your mind, you know where to find me." Fritz kisses my hand and, of course, winks.

۞

As the guards deal with my stepmother and stepsisters, I join Wilhelm, who's waiting patiently for me.

"And here we are," I say. Sadness warps its tentacles around my chest. "Will you walk with me to my mother's grave before you complete the task?"

"Of course," Wilhelm says solemnly.

The spring air smells of wild roses and honeysuckle. The birds twitter from their boughs, and all seven ravens perch in Mother's tree, preening their feathers, quite pleased with their handiwork.

"Are you sure this is how you want your story to end?" Wilhelm asks as he pulls out his book and quill. "You still can marry the prince. Spending the rest of your life at your manor could get lonely."

"It won't be," I say brightly. "I'll find new friends. Make

sure you write in birds to keep me company. I'll take long walks through the forest—"

At that, I fall silent. The memories of Jacob's and my time together are still too raw.

"He's quite upset," Wilhelm says as if reading my mind. "Unfortunate, the whole business."

"Yes." Tears threaten to fall. I force the lump down in my throat. "I wish you the best in your life and pursuit of stories. I know writing these stories upsets you."

He nods, studying his quill. "Every day I pray for the madness to end."

"That's not a way to live." I touch his arm. "The work you're doing isn't only about keeping the world safe. These stories show the world in a new light and remind us not just who we are but who we can become. Don't ever forget that."

He looks up at me, pain in his eyes. "I'll try."

"Perhaps someday you'll find love and happiness like I have. And what a lucky girl she will be. After all, to love a Grimm was more beautiful and magical than I ever dreamed possible. You'll take care of him for me, won't you?"

"Always."

I suck in a deep breath, preparing myself. "I suppose it's time."

I turn my back to Wilhelm and his dangerous book and quill. I close my eyes and stretch out my arms. The prickling sensation isn't as painful this time, or maybe it's because my heart is breaking, and that is greater than any physical pain could ever be.

My wings flutter, and with a beat, and then another, I'm flying. Saying goodbye to my tree and my mother's grave.

Goodbye to love.

# CHAPTER 52

# JACOB

## ACADEMY OF THE SCIENCES

30 years later

Throngs of people pack the auditorium so that every chair is full, leaving standing room only as spectators gather under the stone arches of the hall of the Academy of the Sciences. My heart thumps in my chest as Wilhelm and I wait in the side room to be introduced.

"Why are so many people here?" I ask the professor introducing us, shocked at the crowd. "There must be hundreds."

"They're here to see you, of course," Professor Müller explains. "You and your stories have become famous."

"I don't believe it," Wilhelm says, gaping alongside me as Professor Müller strides out onto the platform and begins his introductions.

"Greetings, fellow students and scholars," Professor Müller calls out in a loud voice. "I'm pleased to introduce you to our newest professors, Jacob and Wilhelm Grimm. They're fluent in over fifteen languages and have been granted prestigious awards from countries around the globe. Yet they are most famous for their numerous book publications, including *Children's and Household Tales*. Without further ado, I introduce you to the Brothers Grimm."

As Wilhelm and I step up to the platform, hundreds of people burst into cheers. I'm stunned at this support, considering our years in exile, the hardships of scraping by for food as we hunted down monsters. If Mother could see us now. She'd be proud.

"Greetings, my esteemed colleagues," I begin. Instantly, silence rules the stone halls. I fumble for a moment with my papers, trying to pull myself together.

"Thought is lightning; speech is thunder. As I stand before you today, I'm reminded of a Saturday night long ago at a king's ball. Invaders attacked the castle, causing panic and mayhem. Amidst the chaos, it was a single woman who saved us all. She stood her ground when everyone else fled, found help in the most unexpected way, and was instrumental in defeating our enemy. It's stories like hers that inspire us to break free of our ordinary acts and give us the courage to take on extraordinary moments. Acts like hers belong at the bedside of our children and in the hands of those who need hope and strength for the day.

"And so the idea of our books was born, sharp and bright as lightning. Fairy tales."

I glance over at Wilhelm, tears in his eyes as he remembers that night that nearly took my life and the sacrifice of Ella.

"Fairy tales remind us of the place where once upon a time lives and thrives. Where witches charm kings, and wolves hunt the innocent. Where young men disappear from villages at the piper's tune, and a prince can transform into a frog. I'm sure you've read some of our reviewers who claim our fairy tales are nonsense, rubbish, and violent. But we believe these tales represent the most reassuring and refreshing of God's gifts to man: resilience, hope, love. They are reminders of who we are and the roots of our people. Every character, every act, and every choice in those tales is a part of us. They are the truth of us."

I pause, and for the briefest of moments, I think I spot Ella standing in the crowd, her dress soot-covered, eyes blue as summer, hair wild as a bird's nest. Even in this moment, she has given me purpose, life. I'm about to lift my hand to wave to her, but she vanishes, a mere figment of my imagination.

Once our speeches are finished, Wilhelm and I open it up to questions.

"What are you writing next?" someone asks.

"I hope to begin work on a dictionary," I say. "Except how often, as writers, it's when we are comfortable, we long to begin something new?"

Laughter rushes through the crowd.

"What about your love life, Jacob?" another asks. "There are speculations about whether you will marry or not."

"I'm convinced that love is like death." My voice trembles and my hands shake, forcing me to grip the podium as I speak. "It must come to us all, but to each in his own unique way and time. Sometimes it will be avoided, it can't be cheated, and never will it be forgotten."

Ella von Maier. Even now, she remains my one true love, forever, if only to live in the fairy tale of my heart.

Once the speech finishes, we're assaulted by autograph requests and invitations. It's rather overwhelming, and I'm eager to get home to my quiet study and return to my books. A mother stops us from leaving. Her daughter, with bright brown eyes and a tangle of dark curls framing her face, looks up at us. Our book of fairy tales is tucked under her arm.

"Excuse me," she says, showing Wilhelm and me her copy of *Children's and Household Tales*. She opens it to the tale of

*Cinderella*. My heart clenches. "I've read all your stories, including this one. As I do not believe the tale, I must pay you a thaler. Actually, I don't believe any of your stories. But since I don't have much pocket money, I can't pay you all at once."

"But they are true," I say, bending down to her. "Why don't you believe them?"

"Trees don't throw down dresses, birds can't speak, and witches aren't real. Even I know that."

She opens her pink purse and takes out a coin, handing it to Wilhelm.

"I can't accept this," Wilhelm says kindly. "Keep it and save it to buy yourself another book."

"Mama says I shouldn't accept money as a present." She pulls on her mother's hand and marches away, leaving the coin in Wilhelm's palm.

"I suppose we can't expect everyone to believe our stories," Wilhelm says.

"Sometimes I find it hard to believe myself," I whisper.

## CHAPTER 53

# HANS CHRISTIAN ANDERSON

### KINGDOM OF PRUSSIA

Honestly, I don't know what I expected, coming to the Grimms' house without any letters of introduction. But as I stand at their doorstep before the servant, asking me which brother I wish to speak to, I'm at a loss for words.

"My name is Hans Christian Anderson," I say. "I wish to speak to the Grimm who has written the most stories."

"Jacob is the most learned," she offers.

"Perfect. Take me to him."

My hands shake as she leads me to a thick wooden door that she knocks on. I clamp my hands together, reminding myself I've traveled too far and have too much to lose to mess up this visit.

"Come in," a voice calls.

The servant leads me into a study. Bookshelves line two of the walls with paintings resting on top of the shelves, while portraits clutter another wall. One massive desk stretches across the back of the room, teetering high with books and stacks of paper. Two smaller desks extend at right angles from the larger one, forming a half-circle around a single chair. In its center sits a man, enclosed on three sides by towering stacks of books.

"Jacob," the lady says. "This man is here to see you."

A man rises from his chair. The famous and renowned Jacob Grimm. His sharp, knowing features fix on me. In that moment, I understand why people find him intimidating. It's like his gaze strips me bare, exposing my every flaw and weakness.

"Who are you?" he asks abruptly.

"Hans Christian Anderson," I say, completely flustered. "I should've brought a letter of introduction, but I figured…to be honest, I hoped my name might be familiar to you."

"I don't remember your name, but I'm pleased to meet you." He shakes my hand, and I feel privileged to have met this legend. "So tell me, what have you written?"

"Well, there's "The Princess and the Pea" and "Thumbelina." Perhaps you've heard of them?"

"Can't say that I have. Tell me some of your other works. Surely, I've heard of them."

But when I name off the titles, he shakes his head, and I wish suddenly to disappear on the spot.

"What must you think of me?" I ask. "I come to you as a total stranger, thinking you must know me. The thing is, I published a story in Märchen of all nations, and I dedicated it to you. Perhaps you've read that?"

"No." He grins, blue eyes softening. "I haven't read even that, but it delights me to make your acquaintance. These fairy tales of yours sound intriguing."

"Yes, and actually that's why I came to see you. The thing is, your fairy tales and mine have commonalities. Even though I'm from the north, it's as if we have a similar story source."

He chuckles, rubbing his gray hair. "I highly doubt that."

"True as that may be, I still had to seek you out. I was hoping you could help me. I'm having some…you could say issues." I pause, swallowing hard. "It involves a certain woman who calls herself the Enchantress. Are you familiar with her?"

The blood drains from Jacob's face, and he leans against his desk as if the air has been pushed out of him. "Yes," he finally says. "That explains things."

Relief hits me. I haven't come all this way for no reason.

"I need advice. You see, I've fallen in love," I grimace, "with a mermaid."

Jacob chuckles, shaking his head. "Why don't you sit down, Hans? Sounds like we need to have a talk."

# CHAPTER 54

# JACOB

## KINGDOM OF PRUSSIA

*Many years later*

The trip from the Hartz Mountains might have left me with a persistent cough, but it also awakens emotions inside of me I've tried to forget.

Night is falling, but I'm not ready to sleep. I wave off my niece, Auguste, who's wringing her hands at my health, and plod past Wilhelm's office. His desk remains untouched since his passing, reminding me of our days writing together, hunting down stories. Even now, it feels like he might come striding through the door and plop into his chair, eager to get to work on our next task. I'd complain about the clutter, but he'd say the mess looked as if it was settling on our desks like snow in the countryside.

Every part of my body aches like it's remembering every battle wound. I sit at my desk, staring at Wilhelm's and my final project, Volume II of the dictionary. Even though I promised at his deathbed to finish what we started, I've only gotten to the letter E. My fingers skim the glass dome beside it. Inside sits the spool of golden straw Rumpelstiltskin gave me as a parting gift before we finally wrote his story. That old man drove me mad, but right now I miss his cranky charm.

The fragrant scent of the heliotrope flowers I picked this morning wafts through the room, distracting me.

Reminding once again of *her*.

I pick up the frame with Wilhelm's picture. It's one I sketched of him when we were young, fighting off witches, shapeshifters, and nixies, and I find myself daydreaming of those lost days.

"Uncle," Auguste interrupts, coming in with a tray. "I've brought your coffee and streusel. Do you wish for me to light the fire for you?"

"Thank you, but it isn't necessary." I smile wearily at her as she sets down the food, kisses me softly on my forehead, and leaves.

The moment I'm alone, I open the frame and pull out the hidden drawing of Ella, tucked beneath the picture of Wilhelm. The edges are worn and paper-thin, but the look in her eyes never changes. Long ago, I memorized every contour of her face and the curl of each strand of hair. It's a bit of an obsession, and often I find myself daydreaming of moments we could've had together.

Picnicking, long walks, and hikes into the mountains, just like the one I finished earlier. There are at least two new florals I discovered on my last hike that I'd never seen before. Ella would've loved them.

I let out a soft sigh, unable to resist any longer. Reaching into the velvet pouch tucked away at the back of my desk, I draw out the glass slipper. Its golden surface catches the candlelight like it's whispering my secret.

"Are you truly still mooning over that bird-girl?" I don't

have to turn around to know that voice. The Enchantress. "It's pathetic, if you ask me."

"I definitely wasn't asking."

"Your brother found a nice human from this world, didn't he? Why couldn't you? From what I've gathered, you're quite famous. People flocking to hear you speak, singing to you as you stand on your balcony, and yet all you can do is brood over lost love."

I set down Ella's portrait, annoyed. "What's it this time? I finished your list. We agreed that once I finished the tales, you'd leave me alone."

"Yes, well, there's one more piece of unfortunate business I must complete." She rolls her eyes, glitter sparkling on her lashes. "It has to do with a promise I made to your brother."

"A promise?" I don't like the sound of that. "What did he promise?"

"Remember that annoying time when you decided to die at Cinderella's ball? Quite inconvenient."

"I most certainly did not *decide to die*, and yes, it was rather inconvenient. Dying isn't something one forgets." I rise from my chair, coughing in agitation. "Now what have you done this time?"

"You don't look so good." She clucks her tongue, looking me up and down in pity. Her fingers swipe across the broken hourglass resting on the bookshelf. I will never forget the moment the last name on our list was crossed out and the curse was broken. The hourglass fell to the ground in a rush of wind, and the blood seeped out, returning to our bodies. We were free. At least, I thought we were until this moment. "The way you look, you might drop dead any minute. We should hurry."

"I'm not sure why you care about me. You never did before."

"Don't say such things. You were always my favorite, you

know that, Jacob. So when Wilhelm asked me to join you with your one true love, Ella, I agreed. As long as Ella kept her end of the deal, the two of you completed your work for me, and you never found love again."

"How can that be possible?" My heart begins pounding, hope daring to spark.

"Wilhelm never told you because that was a part of the deal. But Ella never married that Frog Prince. She chose to run her manor as her happy ending, but I have the power to alter the story. You'd have to enter the tale yourself and become one of my subjects in my realm. And then go find Ella and marry her."

"How do I even know if she's still alive?"

"Time works at a different pace than it does in this world. The choice is yours."

I sag into the chair, picking up her glass slipper, cradling it in my hand. "Yes." My words come out as a whisper, but there's a resoluteness to them. A knowing that somehow I'd been waiting for this moment my entire life.

She snaps her fingers, and a book appears in her hand, snowflakes falling from its pages like confectionery sugar. It's my favorite tale. *Cinderella*. As she cracks open the spine, the smell of spring wafts into the dreary, cold room. The sketch of a young woman standing by a tree feeding birds shivers on the page.

"She's waiting for her prince to come. That shoe might help you find her." The Enchantress studies me. "And since I am rather fond of you, how about I make you the prince in the tale. Would you like that?"

"I don't care what I am as long as I can be with her." The thought roots deep within me. She's the only thing that has made my life complete. And God help me, I'd give up everything if it meant I could spend a day with her.

"Then it's a good thing I like you, or I'd turn you into a pig or—"

"Don't say frog."

She laughs then, a thrilling, ice-shattering laugh. "Tell your ash girl I said hello."

The world shifts as if everything flipped upside down. The room spins, ice and fire, wind and unbending storms. My body rips from my chair and stretches in ways I can't understand.

And then darkness swallows the light. Silence suffocates the tornado.

Groaning, I blink. I'm lying on my back, staring up into swaying oaks. Birds chirp and the wind shifts, rustling the tree boughs. I roll to my side to find a chestnut mare munching on a patch of emerald-green grass.

"What's going on?" I ask the Enchantress, climbing to my feet, searching for her.

She's nowhere in sight. The horse nudges me. Instinctively, I grab the reins and that's when I notice my hands are smooth and wrinkle-free. My clothes are different, too. Breeches and a smooth silk tunic like a noble would wear. A red cloak drapes over my shoulders. A sword hangs at my belt, and my limbs don't ache anymore. There are even spurs on my boots, which causes a smile to crack on my lips. She remembered the spurs.

I look around, wondering if the Enchantress really sent me into her realm or if I've died and gone to Heaven.

Then I notice the pouch hanging from my belt. I pull at the binding, and a golden shoe tumbles into my palm. Its glass gleams in the sunlight like a promise.

Ella's slipper.

My heart beats so wildly, the whole forest must hear it. I mount the horse and pull on the reins, hoping I'm heading in the right direction. As I round the bend, I ride up to an adorable manor. Ivy climbs the stone walls in playful twists. A peaked turret rules the home, and red roses spill over the garden gate like a trail of kisses. A bird chirps at me from the garden wall, then flies through the arched gate. Something tells me I won't find the love of my life in the house.

Pushing the horse, I urge it to follow the bird, making my way through a garden. A woman with golden hair stands beneath a tree, tossing seeds to the ground.

As I draw up my horse, my voice traps inside of me. I don't know what to say despite all the words I wrote in my lifetime. She turns to stare at me with those sky-blue eyes that haunt me in my dreams.

"Do I know you?" Terrifying hope fills her voice, but her brow wrinkles in confusion.

Still, I can't speak, fearing my words might break the magic. Instead, I kneel before her, withdrawing the golden slipper from the pouch. She gasps, and I slip it on her foot.

"It fits," I finally dare to say. "Ella, my love."

She presses her hands to her mouth, tears streaming down her face. "Jacob. How is this possible?"

"My brother made a deal with the Enchantress. And this time, she had to fulfill her end of the bargain." I stand and take her trembling hands in mine. I press a kiss to her knuckles, slow and reverent. "Living without you wasn't living. But I've found you, and now that I have, I don't want to ever leave."

Her breath shudders, her eyes lifting to mine. "Then let's not ever say goodbye again."

The words undo me. I pull her into my arms, holding her like she's the only solid thing in my world. My mouth finds hers. The kiss starts soft, hesitant. But then it's like the years and separation fall away, and she melts against me.

Our kiss deepens, the emotions of every lonely night, every aching hour without each other pouring into this moment. Her tears salt my lips. My palms frame her face. And we cling to each other like we'll never let go.

This isn't just a kiss. It's a memory of what we lost and what we found. But it's also the beginning of our fairy tale.

"I love you," I tell her. "Madly, wildly, eternally."

### Did you like the book?

If you enjoyed this story, I'd appreciate your time and effort if you'd leave a review and share with other readers what you loved about the book.

### Want to find out what happens next?

You're cordially invited to attend the wedding of Jacob and Ella. Head over to my website and get the special bonus scene of their wedding and romantic wedding night.
https://christinafarley.com/romantic-adventures/

### Don't want the story to end?

Continue reading the Fairy Tale Hearts series with *To Love a Siren* about Hans Christian Andersen's and a mermaid's journey to finding love.

# TO LOVE A

# SIREN

## FAIRY TALE HEARTS: BOOK 2

Lose yourself in this sweeping
Little Mermaid retelling where
Hans Christian Andersen becomes
the hero of the love story he
longed to write.

# THE INSPIRATION FOR
# THE BOOK

The idea for this book came to me on my family trip in Germany. Our family stayed at the adorable village of Honau in an old manor run by a kind couple. The first morning there, we hiked up the mountainside and visited Lichtenstein Castle. We had so much fun touring the castle and walking along the castle walls. There was a hint of magic in the air, and it felt like we were stepping into a fairy tale with the mist swirling around us and the view of the valley rolling below.

That night back at the manor, while we were eating dinner in the garden, we could see the castle was all lit up, glittering on the mountaintop. Music was playing, and it drifted all the way down to us. We asked the owner what was going on. He said the duke was having a party. Apparently, he throws parties often for his wealthy friends. It instantly made me think of Cinderella, and how she must have longed to go to the ball.

In that moment, the kernel for *To Love a Grimm* was born. I began wondering about the Brothers Grimm themselves. What had inspired them to collect and preserve their stories?

That question launched me into a deep dive into their lives, writings, and world.

This book is the tip of the iceberg of all that research. For instance, in one draft, I wrote scenes based on the Grimm Brothers' time in Marburg based on the brothers' journals. That scene didn't make it into the book, but it did give me a lot of Jacob Grimm's perspectives.

Historical characters are mentioned in the story, such as King Frederick, Prince Wilhelm, Princess Maria, and Prince Hermann. This was a fun way to play with the idea of how real-life people might have influenced the Grimm Brothers and the famous fairy tales we know and love.

Another highlight of our travels was Hohenzollern Castle. It's breathtakingly beautiful, with a dungeon that sent shivers down my spine. And you probably guessed it. It inspired the dungeon scene in the book! Fun fact: I also had the best hot chocolate of my life there.

For some chapters, I pulled ideas from history. Chapter 53 is based on a real event where the Brothers Grimm spoke at the Academy of Sciences. I even adapted parts of Jacob Grimm's actual speech to fit the novel. The girl who interrupts them at the end really did show up, but she was talking about the tale of The Cunning Little Tailor, not Cinderella.

Chapter 54 was super fun to write as a preview for the next book in the series, To Love a Siren. The events and dialogue were based on Hans Christian Anderson's visit with Jacob Grimm in real life. I pulled everything directly from Anderson's diary but tweaked some of the dialogue to sound more modern and natural to today's reader. In fact, I chose to use modern language for this book to make it more accessible. Sprinkled throughout the story, you'll find nuggets of Jacob's actual life and lines he wrote in his journals about living at the Steinau home. And for my Grimm fans, there are twelve Grimm tales mentioned in the book. Can you name them all?

As you can see, this book really is my love letter to the magic of fairy tales, the history behind them, and the timeless power of the Grimms' legacy that we still celebrate today. There are 14 tales mentioned. Can you find them all?

# About the Author

CHRISTINA FARLEY writes romantic fantasy and thrilling adventures inspired by her travels. When not wandering the world or creating imaginary ones, she spends time with her family in Florida where they are busy preparing for the next World Cup, baking cheesecakes, and raising a pet dragon in disguise as a very furry cat.

**Visit her online:**
ChristinaFarley.com
Instagram: @ChristinaLFarley
Facebook: @ChristinaFarleyAuthor
YouTube: @ChristinaFarley
TikTok: @ChristinaFarleyAuthor

**Join Christina's Newsletter, the Travelogue:** Exclusive access to videos, book updates, giveaways:
www.ChristinaFarley.com

# STAY IN TOUCH

I hope you'll stay in touch by joining my newsletter group, The Travelogue, or Keeper of the Realms so we can continue to take more adventures together. If you sign up, you'll receive a free book as my way of saying you're awesome. Head over to ChristinaFarley.com.

**Christina's Newsletter, The Travelogue**: Reader news, writing tips, giveaways, and book updates.

**Christina's Keepers of the Realms**: Join Christina's VIP Reader Club called the Keepers of the Realm: This community is designed for passionate readers like you to not only dive deeper into my stories but also help spread the magic of my books. Gain exclusive content, have a say in my worlds, and join the monthly giveaway!

# THE
# IMMORTAL
# SECRET

Step into a world where immortals reign and power is everything. Estrella, an immortal stripped of her memories, is banished to live as a mortal at the mysterious Home for Girls in Florida. She begins to unravel the mystery of her past and discovers dark and terrifying secrets about her abilities.

But when she meets two immortal rivals for her heart, her life spirals further out of control. One offers protection from her past, while the other urges her to embrace it. She debates who to trust and unwittingly thrusts herself and her friends at the Home into a struggle against the powers who put them there.

Yet as memories resurface, Estrella realizes her forgotten past holds a secret more dangerous than she could have ever imagined. She must decide how much she's willing to sacrifice and who she can trust her heart with.

# THE
# IMMORTAL
# HEART

In a world where trust is a fleeting shadow, Estrella finds herself on the run from those she once called allies. Betrayed and hunted, she makes a daring escape with the one person she's been told never to trust. The Sabian prince.

Together, they journey to the Sabian Kingdom where Estrella must navigate a landscape of danger and intrigue. Determined to do whatever it takes to rescue her friends, she enters a world of glittering balls and whispered secrets of a lost tablet, rumored to hold the key to the immortals' power.

But amidst it all, her heart is torn. Should she open it to the prince who stood by her side? Or return to the one who held it from the start?

# THE
# IMMORTAL
# WARRIOR

Desperate to regain her immortal powers, Estrella journeys to Japan to be trained in the way of the Immortals by the legendary Eien master Conduit, the only one who can help unlock her dormant immortality and extraordinary powers.

But as she immerses herself in the rigorous training, she's caught in a web of emotions. Her heart becomes a battleground between two men, both with unique ties to her past and the Immortal kingdoms. This tug-of-war intensifies as her powers and memories reawaken along with hope for an elixir that could change everything for the future of all immortals.

Yet Estrella knows she has a greater purpose. The fate of the Immortal kingdoms and her friends hang in a precarious balance. This is a larger battle than she could have ever imagined, and one wrong decision could tip the scales between good and evil.

When Scarlett discovers her sister's heart was broken by the notorious Mr. Wolfe, she travels to Germany to expose this Big Bad Wolf and his Fairy Tale Tours. Disguised as a tourist, she explores magical castles and quaint towns while plotting Wolfe's downfall. But soon she faces new truths and unexpected romance.

Will she find love with the charming Hunter, mysterious Wolfe, or dazzling Movie Star? Choose your fairytale ending where the path to love is only one choice away.

# GILDED

Sixteen-year-old Jae Hwa Lee is a Korean-American girl with a black belt, a deadly proclivity with steel-tipped arrows, and a chip on her shoulder the size of Korea itself. When her widowed dad uproots her to Seoul from her home in L.A., Jae thinks her biggest challenges will be fitting into a new school and dealing with her dismissive Korean grandfather. Then she discovers that a Korean demi-god, Haemosu, has been stealing the soul of the oldest daughter of each generation in her family for centuries. And she's next.

Eighteen-year-old Aria Hale loves her job at her father's dream therapy company where she enters dementia patients' dreams to save their memories. But when their lab is ransacked, two technicians are murdered, and her father is kidnapped, everything changes for her.

Determined to find her father, Aria and her friends embark on a harrowing hunt across continents using the dreams of their enemies to guide them. But this dangerous journey plunges her into a world she never bargained for: deception, intrigue, and even love. As she races to save her father and hunt down her enemies, she soon realizes she's in fact the one being hunted. And her dreams are the greatest danger of all.

# ACKNOWLEDGMENTS

Each book I get to write is truly a gift. I'm so grateful to you, dear reader, for reading and joining me on this adventure. I wouldn't be able to continue writing without your support!

The heart of this book is the journey of becoming who we are truly meant to be. Our lives are beautiful and full of wonder, and when we embrace our unique gifts, they become wings, lifting us to heights we never imagined possible. I'm so thankful to God for showing me this in my own personal life and for inspiring me every day I sit down to write.

A special thank you to my Keeper of the Realm Group: Laura P, Mila C, Beth G, Andrea M, Ava M, Kendra P, Laziz T, Ana B, Amanda F, Jennifer A, Aziza E, Marisela Z, Eva M, Jenny H, Christina V, Amber J, Shana D, Kelli J, Bert B, Dianna B, Tez M, Bri L, Candi M, Julianne J, Amy P, Kris D, Sheree W, Jamie G, Jan W, Stephanie B, Ells, Heath W, Willa Z, Jerry N, Kate H, Joyce K, Tiffany L, Vivi B, Alison R, Callie T, Sarah W, Sunny B, Finely T, Margaret T, Billy F, Jocelyn M, Laziza T, Merry M, Megan B, Susan L, Emily I, Yvonne V, JB, Theresa L, Adalyn B, Jami, Christy S, Jennifer J, Susan L, Megan L, Jasmine B, Lolly G, Theresa L, Bonnie M, Maria V, Monica, Kristian B, Michael E, Ashley S, Megan B, Misty P, Yulya Z, Cat M, Lauren A, and Ella H.

To Paul at Trif Book Design, who took my ideas for this cover and knocked it out of the park! Thank you for creating this stunning cover. For the special edition hardcover, thank you to Yosbe Design for the jaw-dropping foil design and sprayed edges. I can't stop looking at it. To Lulybot for the stunning artwork. I'm in awe of your talent. I'm so excited about the edge printing that Painted Wings Publishing created for the paperback version of this book. It's absolutely perfect!

Thank you to my copyeditor, Sarah Ward, for jumping in at the last minute to copyedit this book and for all your editorial notes. You are a dream.

To Amy Parker and Vivi Barnes. You're probably sick of being in every acknowledgement, but you totally deserve it for all of your support.

A massive thank you to my MiG Writer group: Andrea Mack, Debbie Ridpath Ohi, and Carmella van Vleet for your critiques and feedback. I'm so glad we have our Cabin Slack group where we get to "write together" every day!

To Julianne for reading a very old and rough version of this book. Your advice was so helpful!

I'm also so grateful to Amy Parker for reading a painful first draft. I can't believe you actually made it to the end. Your feedback and insights were so valuable.

To Janice Hardy and Sarah McGuire for workshopping those difficult scenes with me. I would still be stuck without your help!

To my sons for great feedback and advice on the fighting scenes, cover, and artwork!

Thank you to the love of my life, Doug, for giving me the wings to fly. Being with you is a fairy tale.